WORK SHY

WORK SHY

JAMES DOUGLAS ROSENTHAL

(a novel)

WORK SHY
a novel

iUniverse books may be ordered through booksellers or by contacting:

iUniverse
1663 Liberty Drive
Bloomington, IN 47403
www.iuniverse.com
844-349-9409

ISBN: 978-1-6632-0720-3 (sc)
ISBN: 978-1-6632-0719-7 (e)

Library of Congress Control Number: 2021902954

Print information available on the last page.

iUniverse rev. date: 06/18/2021

DEDICATION

I've heard you should never let a brother edit your book but thanks to THR for his literary chops and proofing! Thanks also to those at the Mermaid Inn who listened intently to my sporadic readings on Poetry Night and laughed at all the right moments. See you soon I hope! And thanks to Edith for reading the whole manuscript in its early stages.

"Work is a Four-Letter Word"
The Smiths

1
CHAPTER

Edgar Bloom was a buddy from art school who'd recently overdosed on prescription drugs. The cops called it an accidental death, whatever that means. I *call* it a party. Pursuing art can make for a tough life but I never figured he was the type to commit suicide even if his career stalled. This made me curious. I'd given up making art to write advertising copy and wasn't sure why I was invited to the funeral. Edgar's wife Sherrie must have found some remnant of my whereabouts in one of his address books. She called me out of the blue and asked if I wouldn't mind writing an obit for the Philadelphia Inquirer. What could I do? It went like this:

> Artist, Edgar Bloom, (44) died Wednesday, February 3, 2006, after a short illness and a mixed career. He had a Bachelor of Fine Arts from the Rhode Island School of Design and a Masters of Fine Arts from Northland University. Although he never became an art star, Bloom was a lively character in the Philadelphia scene and was vocal in his opinions. His provocative work never appealed to the general public but is in many local collections. He leaves behind his beloved wife, Sherrie, (37); son, Kurtz (10); and brother, Victor Bloom (46); of New York. Donations should be sent to The Bloom Foundation, P.O. Box 247, Philadelphia, PA, 19116.

On occasion, Edgar and I ran into each other in Center City and promised to call. We never did. This pissed me off. In spite of his obvious ability, I believed he had been wasting his efforts trying to get attention that would never come. It never did. A long time ago, we were both aspiring artists and thought creativity was worth dying for, literally I guess. Several of our college chums went out the same way, reaching for a distant brass ring. We figured anyone could join the corporate mass in order to keep the world from falling apart but very few had the gift to make real, honest-to-goodness art that made a dent in history. We aimed high, but if you were going to do something as antiquated as painting then you had better be damned good.

I arrived late to the cemetery when my car scraped an angled cement slab in the parking lot. The damage to my bumper was minor but the dust caught the attention of a large man in a grimy cabbie's cap. The undertaker's chauffeur was smoking a guilty cigarette outside the gates. He leaned against an immaculate black Jag and looked me over as I approached. He was tough and his worn suit shone uncomfortably in the winter sunlight. I surmised from the blood splatter on his collar that he had shaved that morning and was left-handed. Did I not have enough to occupy my mind? He could have been a minor character in one of my "bestselling" crime thrillers. Let's call him Joe. Now, don't get me wrong. Writing is a creative and competitive field but I would never compare it to the difficulty achieving notoriety in the Art World. Writers still ply a qualitative, lyrical craft (for the most part) while contemporary artists use a shiny wall of smoke and mirrors to make what is considered admirable. If the art they make is acknowledged by key curators, galleries and museums, there are wonderful, lucrative careers available. You jet around the world making elaborate site-specific installations for Art Fairs that make the Cannes Film Festival look like summer camp.

My writing career had been rewarding financially but not critically among reviewers at the New York Times. Fuck them. I never wanted to be a household name or kowtow to some asshole in a suit. That *is not* success

2

in my book. No pun intended. In fact, only one of my books ever made it to film, *Blood Sandwich*. The Hollywood people didn't let me write the screenplay. The executive producer hired his son-in-law to make a lousy movie. Luckily, it went straight to DVD. You may have seen it. I've collected a few at garage sales to keep them out of circulation. It starred some of the worst actors in the history of cinema. I will name only the lead, Vince Weavel. We are not friends. Still, Hollywood bought the option and I got writer's residuals. Maybe one day I'll return.

Joe was heavy and I wondered if he really was a hard guy or merely a throwback to when men had menial jobs and were glad of it. "Nice car," I said, not expecting a response. He nodded and closed his eyes halfway in acknowledgment. Walking on through the tall iron fence, an elaborate Victorian sign announced Suburban Lawns, 1886. In the distance were a few solemn Civil War veterans with stone beards who oversaw the proceedings. Lincoln's soldiers didn't move. On the other side of Bloom's grave was Samantha Currin. I remembered her from Northland where our group received Masters Degrees in Fine Art. She was still cute. The coveted MFA prepared us for a world of disappointment. Sam was dressed like 1956, complete with pearls and a black veil. Her vintage melodrama included rugged boyfriend Nick English who was holding her closer than necessary. I had known him briefly years before when we were all struggling for recognition in New York. He was now a marginally well-known art star. This meant he no longer required a day job. He got by with gallery sales, residencies, grants and teaching gigs. They'd been a couple for years but the news was that they were breaking up. Shame. He was going back to New York to join the big fry. Unlike Philadelphia, I'd heard that there were people in New York who are both intelligent and rich. They also bought art. Samantha was glued to gainful employment. She worked for Zachary Quinn who stood behind her checking text messages on his Smartphone. Two steps behind Quinn was attractive flunky Charisma looking vacant, her cleavage in mourning. In front of them was Victor Bloom. A little on the wide side, Victor was a shy man. His behavior made me think he was in a witness protection program. Sherrie and their boy Kurtz stood next to him looking down at the coffin, shattered and pale.

After the service, I lingered a bit and looked down at the hole in the ground. I pictured Edgar's gaunt features inside the mahogany box, "Told you so, pal." There was no reply. On the way out I looked for my friend Joe the driver but he was busy loading the limo. Driving to the reception, I tuned in shock jock Griff Malton. He gave me a lewd civics lecture about how liberals were infringing on his right to carry a concealed firearm in a sock. I shot the radio with an index finger and switched it off. The day turned cloudy. I wondered why friends lost track. One has so few real keepers to show for a lifetime of graft and corruption. Upon Edgar's demise, Sherrie became a widow. There was going to be no windfall, only a few proceeds from a crusty life insurance policy. Edgar died an impoverished outcast in desperate circumstances.

The Bloom house was a wreck of a 1930's job constructed before house-husbands existed. It was painted a cool retro-blue, a color that would appeal to Edgar's sense of irony. There was a yellow sign on the lawn picturing an idiotic woman in shoulder pads sporting a pitch smile. The realtor's name was fitting: Vicky Tripe. I sat and looked at the house. Victor was taking off in a rush in a large German-made sedan. Was this how life ended? A cold wave suddenly blew over me. I got out of the car and vomited on a special all-weather tire. It took a minute to steady myself then I joined the other mourners feeling right as rain.

Edgar and I had shared a peculiar respect for the past. For us, art was always best when silent and only attainable to a few brilliant folks. We encouraged each other to strive. *RISE ABOVE,* he'd say. When we were on better terms, we used to drive out to country flea markets and collect all sorts of ancient ephemera. He stuck this junk in his work expressing his own version of the shattered American Dream. From the beginning art was an obsession but he began to grumble when no one ever seemed duly impressed. It was to remain misunderstood. As a student of photography, I picked up historic old photos that would end up on my piano. They pretended to be images of dead relatives. Perhaps they were.

It was an odd gathering full of relatives, friends and Edgar's former bosses. Formally dressed men at the center of the reception brought with them suffocating platitudes. To take the emotional load, Sherrie's girlfriends played hostess. I was introduced as an "old friend" of the deceased and sensed some unease amongst the ex-employers. I was used to it. Overweight, Tom Blanket worked in non-profit development. He eyed up my black *Dolce & Gabbana* but looked straight through the guy inside. "Nice Mustache," I said. He chuckled, awkwardly. The name stuck. He had gone to Penn and wanted me to know he went to Penn. "The armpit of the Ivy League." I said hoping to get his goat. He stood there open mouthed for a second like my prisoner in a shitty blue blazer. "How did you know Edgar, Mr. Blanket?" I ventured.

He managed a few words. "He worked with us at the Philadelphia Consortium. I was his supervisor." I let his remark hang in the air as I weighed each word.

"The Consortium, eh? Were you fond of him?" I said this like Michael Caine for some unknown reason. He looked nonplussed then managed to say that they all liked him very much. His puffy eyes looked sharply to the right and he tried an archaic smile. I didn't have to see many cop shows to know he was lying.

"Who exactly are you again?" he asked. I told him I was a writer, someone who went to Art School with the dead man. This impressed the hell out of him.

"What do you write?"

"Detective stories of a low quality."

"I don't read that sort of thing. I stick to my Horticulture Gazette."

"You studied at Penn, didn't you?"

Mustache Man was to prove crucial in Edgar's decline. The Consortium was as close as he got to regular employment that might have led somewhere. It lasted two years and he was let go after 9/11. Something about a shrinking endowment from Penn. Edgar never forgave Blanket or the Saudis. His job history was, at best, sketchy. Before the Consortium was Art Bank, Zachary Quinn's altruistic non-profit where Edgar worked as a free-lance designer. It went well at first and was to be his high-water mark. He thought his training would finally come in handy but he was fired after three years. Last and least was Mrs. Stark, a Martha Stewart look-a-like. She owned Quik-Fix Home Services. This was part-time drudgework for my old friend. *Any port in a storm,* said Edgar. Stark stood in a corner taking notes and drinking wine. She was wondering how to catch some work off the grief stricken next of kin. Vulnerable families often needed help sprucing up their digs to sell for profit. It's the American way. I thought: with bosses like these maybe Edgar did have a legitimate reason to despair.

I was about to finish off my first drink when a fat bloke approached and inquired if I was who I was. I nodded. Tommy Graves was a journalist and sometime friend of the artist, Edgar. He claimed he had read my latest thriller and was wondering if he might get a few quotes for a review in his weekly paper. "I want to cover some of our home grown detective fiction practitioners." He told me that he'd written a short obit for Edgar that would appear in the next edition. "Thanks, Tommy. But I'm not in need of a review. My PR people do that. I'm here to grieve my friend."

"I respect that, Mr. Frank. If you change your mind, I'm in the book."

"No offense, Tommy."

He smiled. "None taken, Mr. Frank. It's a real drag about Edgar isn't it." I nodded. We shook hands slowly and I watched him waddle away.

After re-filling my G & T, I looked for Samantha and Nick. They were hiding in the TV room looking at art books. Sam looked a little surprised to see me. "Is that really you, Mr. Frank? I thought that I saw you at the graveside. You look smart." It was a swell reunion. Hugs all around.

"You clean up very well yourselves."

"Were you chatting with Tommy Graves?" asked Nick.

"I guess I was."

"He thinks he's Hemingway or somebody."

"We're all sick about Edgar," said Sam, in mock confidence.

Still queasy, I agreed, "Me too."

There was a wee pause as we sensed the lost connections between us. Nick was cheerful. "We've been enjoying your books."

This admission surprised me so I played at modesty. "It's easier than painting," I said.

We all laughed, not sure if I was serious.

"You got that right, brother," said Nick. "Writing's fun. I've been working on some reviews lately for The New York Arts Journal." Was the guy serious?

"Writing can be time consuming, though, Nick."

"I read one of yours on the beach in France last summer. What a riot." Nick confided.

"Which one?"

"I really don't remember. There were several killings."

"What did the cover look like?"

"There was a dead person on a beach, I think."

"Right. Was there a spear in the neck?"

"Yeah, I think so."

"That one's called *Permanent Siesta*."

"Great title," said Sam. "What are you working on these days?"

"There's a new one I'm kicking around. The working title thus far is *Good Day to Die*. I've finished the rough draft."

"Sounds a bit like a Bond film," Nick responded.

"Yeah, it does." I laughed a bit and silence ensued. Sam and Nick were clearly occupied with personal negotiations so I made a move to mingle.

Sam urged me to stay in touch. "We should get together and talk about old times." There was a scent of guilt in the air and perhaps a hint of my breakfast.

Like Edgar, Sam was a classic Never-Gonna-Be-Art-Star and proud of it. Some called it denial. Nick, already successful, was hard to read. He spoke intelligently but there was a cold, confident glint in the eye I didn't like. I knew that gleam well. It was a dull sparkle that said he was not as smart as he pretended. I would learn a lot more about him. For instance, Edgar and Nick English enjoyed arguing about art and had lengthy bitch sessions at Dirty Bob's. This was an old Philly establishment that sold cheap beer. I remember visiting their Men's Room once to urinate and visit the ironic dirty pictures used as wallpaper.

Zachary Quinn sat in a corner glowering out the window. I gave him a wide berth. His dark-rimmed eyes had the look of spending too much time online. I disliked him immediately. I wanted to ask him, "How did you know the dead guy and why did you fire him?" Should I crush his pricey phone under my heel violently just to see the look on his face? Charisma was returning with his drink and suffering alluring stares. She was used to it. Her painted fingernails were so long I wondered how she held on to the glass. I moved on and suppressed a lascivious growl.

Sherrie was busy with social tasks so I ambled over to the record player and was startled to see Edgar's vinyl collection stacked neatly on the floor. I sat on the edge of the sofa in order to peruse the records better and immediately recognized a few bands. I pulled one out for inspection. Joy Division's *Closer* was perfect for a funeral. On the album cover is a Victorian photo-work by Bernard Pierre Wolfe aptly depicting a tomb! Looked great in the 12-inch square format framed in white. Painter Julian Schnabel appropriated this later. Or was it vice versa? Remember him of the broken crockery? He was sort of like Jackson Pollock except he used dishes instead of tasteful paint splatter. Schnabel was the ultimate star painter of the 80's before confidently moving on to Hollywood movies and cooking programs. Nothing is harder than painting. Ask anyone. It is an act of defiance in these days of widescreen and chat rooms.

Closer was Joy Division's last album. Their lead singer, baritone Ian Curtis, killed himself the night before their first U. S. tour. Odd timing.

It is now the stuff of legend. From my hunched position, I looked up and saw Sherrie offering me a coffee in a vintage fiestaware cup. "Can we talk, Mr. Frank?"

She was a vision in grief. I kept that to myself, thinking, "Edgar, you fool, letting all this domestic bliss go." She sat next to me and we sipped awkwardly on the couch. "Where is Kurtz?"

"He's upstairs playing with friends. The neighbors have been wonderful."

"They seem nice," I said softly. She turned finally, and thanked me for being a loyal friend and writing the obituary notice. The tears were hard to take. "It was the least I could do, Sherrie. I'm sorry I had to write it." We stared ahead quietly and drank more of our coffee. It seemed she wanted to tell me something. This was not the time. I imagined Edgar must have told her about the early days. *History can wait,* said the newly buried man. I suspected she had been somewhat prepared for what happened to her husband – it took years after all. Perhaps now she was resigned to moving on. Did she wonder why things went from bad to worse? We agreed to meet later on.

An hour later, I snuck out the back porch and stood on the lawn for a moment. It took no time to finish my third gin and tonic. I was trying to give up quinine without much success. Across the street, kids were playing on a tire swing. The drive home was uneventful; the working class edge of the city gave way to urban decay that abruptly became sought after downtown high rises. Odd, how Edgar and I ended up living so near after having given up on each other. I reached my apartment after parking directly outside the Dominion. Home sweet home. I stood at the door with my key and watched a big garbage truck appear from around a corner. It sported a colorful, flowery mural. The trash men were embarrassed so they adorned the grill with a gigantic, waterlogged Snoopy. That's how Snoop Dogg got his name. Don't spread that around or he will kill you.

2
CHAPTER

Sherrie and I met the following week at Café Mystique. She took my hand formally at the entrance and thanked me for helping. We joined the line of coffee drinkers. It consisted mostly of well-to-do Chestnut Hill types, one housewife novelist and a few college kids. Sherrie was taller than I remembered but it might have been the heels. I ordered a tall decaf in a ceramic mug with plans to spike it but I never got the chance. She had a bastardized Double-Macchiato withholding all fats and sugars. This required a severely pierced barista named Lupo and lots of hissing noises. He was good at his job and we waited patiently. I repeated to myself her question from the week before, *Can We Talk, Mr. Frank?*

We carried our hot drinks to a free table and sat down in a corner far from myriad lap toppers. I read her soft face and tried not to drool in my emasculated coffee. She looked younger all of a sudden. After a short preamble about Edgar's dissolute career, she explained how difficult his working life had become and how personally he took the rejection. "Kurtz and I couldn't take it anymore. Edgar moved out to the Bungalow temporarily."

"I wish I'd known."

"At least he had his work to keep him occupied."

"Look where that got him."

"Yes, well here we are."

"Yes. Here we are."

She then leaned forward and said quietly, "I need you for something."

My blood pressure dropped. "What is it, Sherrie?"

She jumped to the point. "I want you to dig up Edgar's writings."

This surprised me completely. She waited for my response that I fancy was a curious expression some men make when they don't know what expression is expected. I decided to ask her a question. "Edgar's writings about what?"

"The journals. His journals that spanned nearly his entire life. They're in his studio. You must have seen him writing in the old days."

"Yes, I guess so. Most art students keep journals."

She persevered. "They are kept in boxes at the bungalow, I think." They'd bought the little house when his estranged father Oscar Bloom died in 1996. I'd imagined Edgar's dad as old-school Philadelphia, an alcoholic who worked at the Navy Yard and carried a baseball bat. "Edgar walked mostly. He drove when the VW was working, which wasn't much. I am planning to sell both buildings and the car." I asker her why she wanted his diaries so badly and she replied, "They might shed some light on his motivations or secrets."

I nodded slowly, thinking, "What's her game? Was she was after the family jewels?" "He was perhaps overcommitted to making art?" I ventured.

"But was art worth complete derailment?"

"I don't know, Sherrie. It didn't work out for him. Me either. It's always a crapshoot. Creative people have no choice sometimes." I told her I would have a look into what happened but made no promises. Of course, if she asked me to stand on the table and recite the Gettysburg address in falsetto, I may have done that too. Maybe, I could buy her some relief. To fill a gap, I asked about how Kurtz was coping.

Sherrie replied, "Remarkably well, considering. He worshipped his Dad."

"It must be devastating."

"We have been ready to move on whatever happened to Edgar. Now, we have no choice." Sherrie switched gears and asked me if I wanted to split a muffin. I did as I was told. I bought two in fact. I stood in line behind a man with a blinking blue light behind his right ear. He was having an earnest conversation with some important person far away. The cashier glared at him. While paying and being wished again to have a great day, I

11

pictured Kurtz in later life. He was going all Rambo, exercising his tattooed deltoids and loading assault weapons. Cue cheesy voiceover: "It's Payback Time For The Art Mob." We cut the muffins down the middle and waited for the tabs of butter to melt. Sherrie settled into her seat now more at ease. How novel; have I met a woman who likes to eat?

She explained, "Something happened towards the end, Mr. Frank. I don't know what. Edgar got quiet. I thought it was a bad sign. His brother Victor came down from New York to help. It was apparent his life was going to end in a mess. Even Kurtz knew his Dad was going off the rails."

She finished her first half of muffin. "Yummy." They were melt-in-your-mouth muffins.

"I wish I'd known, Sherrie. Maybe I could have helped."

She shrugged weakly. "There was nothing anyone could have done, Mr. Frank." The more she told me about Edgar's grim story, the worse I began to feel. Was I partially responsible for my old friend's demise?

Sherrie paused, sipping her coffee and holding back tears. I was helpless in my suit of armor, all shiny. "He had a break down and was seeing a doctor." I stopped buttering. All this was news to me.

"He hadn't had a grant in years. Then his boss let him go after 9/11."

"The Mr. Mustache job?"

"The what? Oh, you mean Tom Blanket. The Consortium"

"Yeah, him. I met him last week." She agreed he was a pompous jerk.

"I noticed other arrogant Penn grads. Why were all those bosses at the reception? I found that strange."

"I don't know. I invited them and they showed up. Maybe they felt guilty?" She paused, slowly refocusing. "After the dismissal from the Consortium, Edgar's optimism and ego both disappeared. The unemployment payments eventually dried up and he ended up working for that crazy Stark woman."

"Martha Stewart?"

"Yes. She paid cash." I sat back and mused. Doesn't this go with the artistic territory? That was why I gave it up and never regretted the decision. There were supposed to be up-sides sure; rare ego-boosting moments where whiffs of praise were squeezed from elite quarters. Sherrie and I managed to complete buttering then ate the remains of our respective muffins. "You look like a muffin man," she said. This made me laugh. "And you look less tough when you laugh." I continued laughing, my mouth full of bran. Funny how intimate we are with total strangers. We agreed to meet once a week. Sherrie exited gracefully and I floated out the door behind her. We were followed by the smell of rich coffee all the way from Nicaragua. Back at the Dominion, I poured a short rye with a sniff of ginger ale. I turned on the radio and tuned in a jazz station. Was I nuts? I'm a writer not a detective. I took a mini-swig on the drink and looked at an old pre-digital black and white photo I had taken years before. It was a candid shot of a desolate building on Broad Street. I'd laboriously developed the 35mm film and painstakingly printed the photo by hand in a very dark room. On the back was the title: *Divine Lorraine, 1994 by Douglas Frank.* There was a label on the back. The price was three hundred dollars. It never sold. I walked into the bedroom and tried to locate my old address book – the one held together with a double size rubber band. It was in a bureau drawer under a box of old wristwatches. There was also a silver pocket watch that had stopped in 1908. I found both Sam and Nick's out-of-date addresses. Curious, I kept digging. At the very bottom was an ancient journal of my own from art school. It made me uneasy and gave me the creeps so I left it where it was.

3
CHAPTER

The next week we sat at the same table with coffee made by Lupo and friends. I told Sherrie I could spare a few days to check out the Bungalow and look for Edgar's journals. She grabbed my arm and used that magical whisper of hers, "Thank you, oh thank you, Mr. Frank." My heart expanded uncomfortably and a ray of sunshine danced across the room. We started buttering the muffins and ate them like we hadn't eaten in days. I asked again about Kurtz and she said he was busy drawing robots. I asked about the studio. "It's close to Germantown Avenue. Two blocks east. The address is 120 Russo Street. It's looking a little worse for wear these days. Edgar liked chaos." She plucked up courage to execute her plan and held up the studio keys. They were attached to a Metallica keychain. "These are for you, Mr. Frank. I knew you would say yes." When she handed them to me I got a tingle. We were making a pact. "I hope you find out something positive, Mr. Frank."

I laughed a wee uncomfortable laugh. "That's possible but it may lead nowhere."

"I know but it might make me feel better."

What did she want me to do exactly, something forensic? Visit the scene of a real crime? The sun played on her face. "Sherrie, you aren't suggesting something hinky with Edgar's overdose are you?"

"Oh no, Mr. Frank. I don't think that. I honestly think he was self-medicating, messing with alcohol and drugs. It got out of control or he got carried away. I guess I want to know why he couldn't pull out of the

14

nosedive; something like that. And I need someone trustworthy to oversee the removal of anything important like art as well as the notebooks."

"It sounds like he failed you, not the other way around."

"It's not guilt, Mr. Frank, it is just that I need to know. It needs doing." There was the soft, sultry tone again. "Do you want to use Edgar's old VW at the blue house? It's in the garage."

"That sounds crazy, Sherrie, but sure, why not?" She must have envisioned quite a project. I drove a '98 Miata and could always retreat to The Dominion. It had a new roof and AC. More comfortable especially in the heat of summer, in winter temperatures and when it rained.

She added quickly, "It's got antique plates and spends a lot of time with Incognito at the garage."

"Incognito? That must be hard to find in the Yellow Pages?"

"That's his name. He's the mechanic."

We were standing outside the bistro. "Ok, but I'm trading up when we make a lot of money." This comment landed badly. And her face dropped.

I hugged her shoulder lightly and said, "Sherrie, I'm kidding. I could use the car to bring in some materials and it would fit into the hood better."

She smiled, relieved. "That makes sense. Thanks." We boarded our respective vehicles. Sherrie returned to the Blue House in her car. I followed and continued past towards the bungalow. She waved and smiled sweetly. I gave her a dumb grin and an idiotic thumbs-up.

It is amazing how down-market you can go in a mere four blocks. There were empty houses and unkempt lots full of plastic bags. Everyone owned a pitbull. I parked outside the house and approached carefully. The key worked. I creaked open the door and was greeted by a small cockroach that fell on my head. Sweet! A buzz bomb had hit the place. Next was the smell of mold, stale beer and oil paint, not necessarily in that order. I ventured in slowly as if there was a ghost waiting. There was something else, urine, faint yet unmistakable, Ground Zero; the pantry. I looked for the landline. Edgar never used a cell phone. I found it under piles of books and magazines on the floor. Guess what color? Avocado. Not surprising. The line was cut off.

I imagined my first port of call, an old-fashioned telephone connection. An outmoded request these days. My cell was not to be involved in my Edgar research on principle. That would complicate my life. Plus, if I ever needed to sort out expenses properly with an accountant. You never know. I was already out the cost of two muffins. In the main storage closet on the second floor, I found many boxes covered in rags and clothing. In the basement there wooden stretchers and more artwork in folios, canvas and panels. Some of the boxes were conveniently marked with contents and date. "Nineteen Eighty-Eight: Diatribes." Fairly tidy for an imbibing painter. The dust was making me sneeze so I made an attempt to open a few windows. Hay fever has plagued me since childhood. I popped an antihistamine and downed it with bottled water from my knapsack. This is when I noticed the iron bars. Were they to keep Edgar in? Others in the neighborhood used glass bricks on basement windows. Front doors had extravagant and tasteless wrought ironwork. Inconspicuous security cams dotted the places. Only thing missing was sandbags and gun emplacements. After an hour or two of aimless sorting, I decided to re-deploy the whole she-bang to the living space where there was better light and a wide floor. This took nearly two hours and looked like a mountain in the middle of the room. I sat down in a worn sofa chair and unplugged a can of beer. I had found one in the fridge with some rather green looking foodstuffs. Men are such bad housekeepers. I held it up to toast Edgar's *Legacy of Scrawl* and smiled.

4

CHAPTER

The next day I found myself in the same chair sitting amid piles of Edgar's life drinking a latte. Where did he go wrong? The studio was as he left it, stuck in time. It was a makeshift lean-to, hanging on a half-collapsed bungalow (with serious subsidence) on the wrong side of the tracks in Germantown. Overgrown weeds, broken windows and a saggy roof. Most artists of note tend to work in big ex-industrial spaces well away from their living rooms and domestic situations; hiding far from suburban anodyne. Edgar couldn't afford the luxury. I'd found a few small paintings and stacked them near the door. They might have passed for early Fauvist works by Matisse or Vlaminck, heavy outlines and distorted, bright color. In Edgar's case the subjects were different: Eighties Nightclub scenes. By the workbench there was a record gathering dust on his turntable: Shostakovich, Symphony No. 5 in D minor, Opus 47. Odd choice for Edgar. I removed a big clod of dirt off the ancient needle and set the machine going. Walls of dissonant violins rose and fell together filling the dysfunctional world. It was amazing to listen to the crackle of a *diamond* on wax. Was this his last LP, spinning over and over as he lay dormant and dying full of diazepam and vodka? Not exactly a Celebrity Speedball. It was an accidental overdose or possible suicide, they said. Cops had no reason to think otherwise. *Just look at the state of the fucking room. An unstable person lives here.* Of course, cops didn't know art from a bag of fleas. That doesn't make them stupid; most people don't know anything about art. It's odd, but that may have been part of Edgar's problem. With no popular exchange between the elite and those watching Fox News, there is

17

no place for it anymore. I had no notion I would ever see the police – I was mistaken. According to Sherrie, there was no forensic evidence collected so I began the inquiry into what I started to call "death by neglect." I was more concerned with the circumstances that led to Edgar's 'misadventure.' Whether it was accidental or not was immaterial.

The journals were hard to read at first, full of half-scripty print. Edgar documented the world he inhabited with great detail; the oddballs, minor talents and some snobby painters who were entirely behind the times. In the UK, they are called 'Stuckists' with some affection. They believed the best has gone from society and art. I see where they are coming from – Edgar was a bit Stuckist himself. He also documented some keen opportunists whose sole attribute was ambition. Nick English was on that list. They had talent but that wasn't what drove them. The ones I've met had soul-less eyes. *Creepy*, Edgar called them. I cracked one of the later journals four years before his untimely death: *May, 4, 2002: We are the unsung heroes! Someday a reckoning will come. Mark my words! It'll be served cold baby!* Did I mention he was a painter? His voice came back clearly, reading aloud from disjointed writings sometimes in the shape of a celebrity impression like Joe Pesci. Soon, he was speaking to me as if he was in the room, fiddling with some sculptural piece, aiming a glue gun. I'd be sitting in the comfy chair with my Doc Martin brogues on a hippyish ottoman.

"How's this, Frank?" he'd ask, "Fucked up, right?"

"You bet, Edgar," I'd reply to myself. He'd make a shit-eating grin. I didn't speak to him aloud but I started to wonder which one of us was actually crazy. This was pro bono, after all. The payoff was of a different sort. I sank deeper into the chair and he filled us in copiously from beyond the grave:

May 3, 2004. The Art Mafia controls everything. They run the important galleries and sit on the boards of all the Museums and non-profits. They view everyone else as if they have two heads. When it comes to contemporary art, these experts are train-spotters. Their standards are high which makes competition exclusive; only a certain caliber – world class — is preferred. For them, there's only one sort of art considered worthy, of worth aesthetically; it's called Neo-Conceptual. There are lots of Arts Stars — raised with the paradigm — who easily fit the bill. Everything else is filler.

Good news for them but not for Edgar Bloom or other artists outside the pale of cultural significance. No wonder he had a beef. Art World success stories were everywhere, full of achievement, while his life read like a singular progression of neglect, lacking in opportunity. More precisely, chock full of missed opportunity. The art booms excluded him and his 'dated work.' God forbid you fall behind the times. We'd lost touch over the years — our affinity through art had disappeared — but after my contact with the journals, I was sold. Maybe I was thinking this new investigation into the past could be profitable? It might be a great way to shelve writing all the crap forensics stuff and hit the big time, literally speaking. Edgar's story could be just the ticket; an historic memoir or non-fiction or something inbetween. The denizens of the Creative Class would eat it up! These ideas lit a fire under me. I began to sort a few notebooks by date and made notes as to what period they came from. Sherrie wanted to know what happened more recently so I made a special spot for anything after 2005. They were not hard to find. Edgar had categorized those. His art school period and trip to Italy were already boxed. As I shifted them around, the mountain of boxes and pads now looked more like gentle hills.

I gave Sherrie's proposition some more thought. Could I take a little time off from my next book? Maybe it would lead to something, a twist in my career. Too soon to tell. Albatross Books (my publisher) might understand but they were expecting another Freddie French thriller soon. It was half finished without a title. I was calling it *Death on the Delaware*. No, I'm not Dashiell Hammett. But maybe they might warm to the idea of a collection of artist's writings? They were always complaining that my books were somewhat pedestrian. They were supposed to be. Pedestrians bought them to read.

5
CHAPTER

Bloom's diaries became addictive and I was content to be immersed. Each day I would crank up the VW in the garage and toodle up Lincoln Drive full of beans. I told Sherrie I wouldn't accept a dime but she thought some work was the least I should get out of our deal. We sat in our usual spot for our third meeting over coffee and muffins. I was hungry and had a few more questions.

"You should accept whatever renumeration shows up within reason, Frank."

"Fair enough, Sherrie," I agreed.

"That is great news, Mr. Frank."

"You said Edgar was seeing a psychiatrist?"

"Oh. Yes, he did for a while. I forget the name. I'll find out for you. We didn't have much money for that."

"I have to say I am enjoying the diversion."

She eyed me up suspiciously, "What do you mean?"

"The diaries are proving interesting. It might take a while."

"I'm glad it seems to be working out so far."

"And I'm helping you with some loose ends. And Edgar and I weren't on great terms."

"I don't know about all that."

"Let me know the name of the shrink when you can."

"OK. He will probably have some details." She drank her coffee and looked out the window. A few attorneys were rushing to the R8. "Life goes on."

"Did you ever read one of my books?"

She wondered for a moment. "I don't think so. Eddie might have."

"Edgar liked my Freddie French thrillers? That's funny. I guess it was me he didn't care for."

"I wouldn't say that. He had trouble with his past and everybody in it."

"I can relate. I keep my friends close and my enemies closer."

"You are so strange. You're quoting somebody."

"I must be but I can't remember who."

"Sounds like your Freddie French guy."

"No, but close."

"Eat your muffin."

After the coffee date, I spent the afternoon at the Bungalow reading a few of Edgar's 'primary texts.' He eschewed some comforting theories about art that were not the least contemporary and struggled as he made an attempt to leave behind academic painting. But some of these elements he treasured. He loved the mark of the brush and the contradiction of looking at a flat plane and seeing projected space. He would start with an outline then block in temporary color, fuss with the edges of the shapes as they found their way into place. Edgar would then pull forms forward or push them back. A lot of this was done with black shading leaving final dashes of brighter color for later. Then he played with the edges again. Make the perspective a tad askew. Lots of tricks in a paint box! Of course this is what cubism dispensed with historically, the window. At least, theoretically. It changed everything and left "representation" and the public behind. Thus began their jokes about "pictures" painted by six-year-olds. "My kid could do that," says the public moron. This goes on to this day. "Does your child's handiwork fetch millions at auction?" I counter. This usually shuts them up.

People also complain about high-minded or Literary Writing aversed to Popular Fiction. They can't seem to get past the worst of the low-grade thrillers. Many citizens don't read at all. WTF! I'm not sure how they get through the day. Speaking of that, I shouldn't complain about Freddie French; he pays the bills and the unwashed need something to read on the beach. Personally, I love Dan Brown and his tales of duplicitous Knights Templar. No kidding. These 'historic' puzzles are easy to read. I also like so-called literary books, critically acclaimed novels with lots of punctuation and five dollar words. (Raymond Chandler hated punctuation.) My latest release published by Albatross is called *Seventeen Stiffs*. I put the royalties in a piggy bank. My protagonist, Freddie French is an aging hipster with a penchant for the ladies. He drives a vintage '82 El Camino that needs paint. In his latest incarnation, he stumbles over a complicated murder. Parts of seventeen people – all different races, genders and eras are discovered, sewn together in one "body." It was found at the Franklin Institute right under Benjamin's nose. I borrowed the premise whole-hog from a popular HBO series. The local cops are mystified and summon my shamus. He's a suave sucker and quite inconsiderate when you get down to it. His ego is the size of a mock-Tudor with Corinthian columns. Here's a snippet of the book my agent insisted be included here free of charge. All rights reserved:

French eyed up the girl from behind the desk, every sinew under close scrutiny. She was lighting up a cigarette when the door swung open wildly and a barrage of gunfire tore up the room. The drop ceiling dropped and a thick dust cloud descended. French found himself under the desk with his hands grasping the shotgun in the waste bin. As the echoing blasts died down, a man said, "Veronica's dead. So's French." There was a pause and the other man said, "Let's make sure, Enzio." The Italians walked over the rubble, slowly crunching around the desk. In one beat, they would fire again. Simultaneously, French kicked both their weapons toward the ceiling and found the trigger. The men were knocked backwards by the shredded bucket. Gino tried to stand, turn and fire, eyes wide. He didn't have time.

The second barrel ripped into the man's chest and out the other side. He ended up lying on top of Enzio face to face like a human hoagie. Freddie stood up and surveyed the scene.

"That's the last time you call me a dick, Enzio."

6

CHAPTER

Three weeks after the funeral, I was reading in my usual spot when the new landline rang. I took in some extra oxygen audibly not knowing what to expect. It was the City Art Museum.

"Mr. Frank, are you there? Mr. Frank, the author?"

I was especially cordial. "That's me, sir. How can I help?" You never know.

"This is Richard Forrest-Green, Executive Director of The City Art Museum on the Parkway. Do you have a moment?

"Yes, Mr. Forrest-Green. What can I do for you?"

"Have you heard of the new exhibition planned for next year at the museum featuring local artists?"

"No. Why don't you fill me in."

"I was wondering if you would be interested in this project. We require your services in your capacity as a writer."

"Can you be more specific? My agent usually sets up my work for me."

There was a squeak and echo on the line. He persevered. "It has to do with Edgar Bloom."

"The late Edgar Bloom?"

"Yes, the painter who recently passed."

"Yes, exactly." They were thinking about including Edgar's work in an exhibition? Why would they call me? Was I Edgar's biographer now? These were the same folks that went out of their way to ignore this guy when he was going downhill.

The Director continued, "We were saddened by his passing but would like to honor him with a retrospective of sorts."

"Well, that's interesting, Forrest. I didn't know you were on speaking terms. Tell me more."

This went on for a while but I put him off saying I was too busy with a new novel. None of that mattered now. It was too late for Edgar. Too late for his family. After hanging up I required a drink or two. Was I somehow an agent for protecting Edgar's profile? I looked at some paintings and wondered. After an hour, I changed my mind. Maybe this could benefit little Kurtz somehow. I called Tree-Forrest back and agreed to discuss the project. He was gleeful, as much as a Director can be. He set up a meeting with Martha Trout, Head Curator of Modern Art for Tuesday morning the next week at eleven sharp. I would be met at the West Entrance at the back of the museum. It seems my original premise was accurate: an artist had to be dead before being accepted into the canon. It doesn't make sense. After death the art ceases to be made. Maybe it has to do with the rarity of the product when the artist is no more. Prices rise; supply and demand.

There was a small office in the bowels of the Art Museum. It was not large and had no paintings save an early modernist work on the wall beside the desk, a sweet little Pissarro. It was bathed in soft daylight and made me happy. It was the only warm thing in the room. I sat across from Martha Trout, the Curator of Modern Art. Her transparent eyes looked elsewhere while talking. I didn't want to know where. Looking attentive, I shifted in my chair. My credentials were good enough to warrant this meeting but she seemed to need some reassurances. I reached inside for strength to withstand an Art World Inquisition. It helps when you don't give a shit. Her assistant, a shameless sycophant, wore an expensive Italian suit. His shiny, designer shirt was buttoned to the top. Deiter looked like he might choke any second. He resembled a skeleton with skin and looked at me with such a deep, searching expression, I had to hold back from asking him what the fuck he was looking at. Eventually he settled after I made a few resentful jokes about the art public. "Ah, the masses," he said, or something to that effect, "all those baseball caps." Martha was another sort. *We are not amused.* I had known her briefly many years before when I was a student and had worked at the museum as an intern. She scared me then. Now, I felt like the scientist who gets the credit for discovering a new species of praying mantis. Cool, as long as I'm not the intended mate. Trout asked me about Edgar's pedigree as I got up to inspect the painting.

When she took a breath, I injected my own thought. "Edgar *had* no pedigree, Martha, not when he was alive anyway." This stopped her dead. Deiter stared. As I turned around, she looked me straight in the eye for the first time. I froze, thinking of Medusa.

"What does that mean, Mr. Frank?" asked Trout.

"Well," I stalled, returning awkwardly to the desk. "You know what I mean. He had no career, no life, never the slightest break." I didn't say this maliciously but for some reason this brought a half-smile to her face. She was relieved. The penny dropped, as the Brits say. They *wanted* a broken man. From then on I kept my cool.

She continued describing her master plan, "The rubric of poetic-justice is a post-millennial enterprise designed to re-contextualize generational movements. This involves pinning down all parties including our Mr. Bloom. We begin in 1980. From this point hence, we unpeel the onion…" This went on. Sure, I was being played but now I knew why I was there. This was my element after all; bullshitting with experts. Trout paused and realizing this was not going to be straightforward, or expedient, ordered us some coffee. Deiter removed himself without a sound. I waited out the silence as she looked intently at my right cufflink, which took the form of a small skull. Martha was about to switch sleeves and ask me if I was a Satanist but Deiter came in. I felt braver now and suppressed the urge to pinch his tight behind as he passed by. He was armed with a tray, cups and a French press machine. He pressed, waited then poured.

I consumed mine quickly and said, "Thanks, Deiter. Delicious."

Deiter responded in a flirtatious tone, "You're most welcome, Mr. Frank. Good to the last drop, as they say." Trout gingerly spooned in three sugars after some clinkage. It was not surprising to see her sweetening her coffee; her teeth could have passed for British. She was purebred WASP and an original member of Daughters of the American Revolution.

The conversation resumed. "Now, Mr. Frank. As you may know, we are thinking Mr. Bloom's work would be the centerpiece of a major touring exhibition of minor or emerging artists, some regional, that en masse form a new collective statement. Luckily, the CHIP Foundation is sponsoring the exhibition. We think this transformative moment is well overdue, curatorially." She stopped and listened. When applause didn't come she went on to list a few big names I was supposed to know but didn't. "We have most of the other participants like Vanessa Vestiale in LA and Snowy White, of course, from New York, but Bloom seems to fit the local East Coast publicity plan." I pictured the punny headline in the Alternative Weeklies: *Homeboy Makes Good Art!* "We thought you could produce the main catalogue essay, given that you are compiling his writings and given your present relationship with his former wife." This bulldozing I took in stride.

"We saw a few of them posted on your local art blog, Mr. Frank." added Deiter.

Martha gestured vaguely towards a discreet laptop in front of her. "What is its name again? I forgot." Yeah, I'd posted some of my notions, but my bits about Edgar were purely incidental.

"Genius Convention. That's the title of the blog. The term describes our RISD fraternity. We were Masonic smart-asses."

There was a small delay before Trout pushed forward, "I see, interesting. The writing seems to be of the same tenor as our presently proposed interpretation." She had me nailed. Edgar, she also had nailed. He always said: *One day they will cash in on my desperate state.*

I took the initiative and said genuinely, "I would be happy to help in any way I can. My old friend Edgar was a talented man and deserves the recognition." There was long, suspicious pause as she scanned me, terminator-like, tilting her head slightly, listening for doubt. That was that. No blood sample was required. Trout's face moved on to business. The next twenty minutes were spent filling in more details and signing a contract of some sort. After shaking their cold hands, I told Deiter that I thought his English was excellent.

He asked, "Why shouldn't it be?"

"Aren't you German?"

"*Whatever* gave you that idea?" he winked. Somewhat confused, I walked around the galleries and a better mood began to descend. Standing in front of Cezanne's Bathers, the one in the shape of a big triangle, I mused calmly. A fountain burbled. The guard looked straight ahead through dark, gold sided shades. He was the spitting image of Bo Diddley. As I walked out through the revolving doors, I thought I heard what might have been the last gasp of escaping air.

7

CHAPTER

The next week I took a break from the archeology of script and made time to talk to some people who might be able to shed light on Edgar's last few years. My list of contacts wasn't long. I started with folks I already knew like Samantha Currin. She was happy to talk. We planned to meet in an unpopular pub called Crusties in Old City. On the scenic route south the VW managed 35 MPH downhill, passing houses George Washington must have known. "Clivden" is on the left, a beautiful Georgian mansion with several musketball holes in it from the Battle of Germantown. Musketballs (having little velocity) make a round dent. I'm no expert. Eighteenth century mansions are sitting ducks.

The bar was tucked away between an antique lighting shop and a thrift store. It was dark inside. Sam greeted me at the door with a big platonic embrace. She was shorter than I remembered but maybe I'd grown an inch or two. Yoga does that. We ordered draft beer and I paid upfront. She protested and I held up my hand. "I have an expense account, sweetheart." She giggled at my alpha man routine. "Let's sit by the window so I can see what I'm drinking." Samantha agreed. As Edgar's former confidant in crime, she had much to say about his rise and fall. She bubbled with stories about the man particularly his trouble getting his work shown in Philadelphia.

"He could get a show in London but not here, too conservative. He was so talented, poor thing. It doesn't make sense. His pictures were scary perhaps. Scared galleries away."

I nodded, "So, what exactly happened to him, Sam?"

29

First, she had to unload about her breakup with Nick English, "It's been awful. We are all caught up in keeping up. Selfish, I suppose. Contacts are more important than friends. Edgar spiraled down without a safety net."

I sat a moment and said without thinking, "I think there is more to it, Sam."

"More to what?" She looked a little confused and I ordered another round. Sam could drink.

"Don't you think there was someone fishy hanging around the funeral? It was a curious collection of mourners."

She laughed. "Funerals are weird. I really didn't notice. Let me think. I saw you arrive. That was a surprise. There were some old bosses like Quinn." Sam began a long story starting when she heard the news of Edgar's OD: she was sitting at her desk at ART BANK. It was 11 am. Zachary Quinn was hovering over her waiting for her to complete some pointy-headed web task. When she told him Edgar was dead his face remained unchanged. "That's terrible news," he said.

"He tried to concoct some sadness but only managed concern for his own condition, bordering on self-pity; another blow for him. Charisma kept filing her nails." Edgar hated Zachary. He called him Quinn the Eskimo. Zach had let Edgar go for some sham reason."

"Edgar really had some bad luck with bosses," I said.

"Edgar showed him up to be the inept asshole he is. Zachary retreated to his office, closed the blinds and hid behind his Mac. Charisma joined him. What a slut."

"I'm sure she could input data if required."

"Not with those fingernails!" Samantha ignored her boss and called boyfriend, Nick. He was still in town packing up his studio. They decided to meet for lunch at Green on Red in spite of Zachary's warning, "No more long lunches people." He repeated this ad infinitum every morning to little affect.

The rundown continued: Nick was stunned when she embraced him and cried openly into his shoulder. He led her to a booth while Mickey, the owner, looked on concerned. Nick held up two fingers for coffee. Green on Red was run by Mickey Mauser, an ex-coke-freak who loved baking and his wife June. It was an up-and-coming establishment but still attracted all sorts of down-and-outs. Several Basquiat posters decorated the restaurant. Pockmarked and van Dyke-bearded, Mickey's rugged face showed a long road.

His raspy voice said it all, "That was in the 80's when there was even less going on in Philly. There wasn't even a fucking Rocky statue then! I love that Balboa guy. Punk Rocky, I call him." Mickey wasn't aware that the museum hated everything Rocky: the steps, the statue, the actor, his movies and all the rubes photographing the damn thing. Mickey now stood over the couple and asked pleadingly what was wrong. When they told him who had died, Mickey's body sagged and his jaw went slack. He was speechless, nearly. Nick asked him for some water for Sam. June handed it to him over the counter. "Crazy Eddie, he was a wild talented guy. Crazy Eddie, shit. Man. I saw him two weeks ago! He seemed OK. This is really bad news. I have to tell June." He was up and running again. Nick asked Sam to tell him what happened that morning in detail like a fictive detective milking a snitch.

Sam spelled it out, "Sherrie called me at work. I told Zach. He crawled to his office moping like a jerk. I called you." Nick imagined Charisma licking his wounds.

"Zach is a shit; we know that. He had his own issues with Bloom. These things happen, Sam." He looked at a Basquiat poster on the wall, a black face scratched out with the word "Malthusian" scrawled over the image. The poster was surrounded by an over-wide frame with blinking Xmas lights. Remember what we said about art after the artist is no more? Poor Jean-Michel. He would have had a daytime talk show by now. *Fame kills*, said Edgar.

Sam lost her rag. "For god's sake! Quinn fired him. That didn't help much."

"I know you liked Edgar," said Nick. "Before me, I mean. You know what I'm saying." She looked into her cup, tears splashing. "But really, it doesn't bode well for our treatment of artists in this city. That's why I'm going back to New York. Maybe Berlin, then LA after that. Sick of winter, period." He took a moment, "Did the divorce ever go through? I mean, Sherrie and Edgar?"

Sam shook her head and sniffed her coffee thinking her ex-lover doesn't understand. "No. They were going to patch it up."

Subtle indifference was etched in Nick's face. He put in the other back handed foot, "He was one of our own whether he was talented or not."

Sam's eyes popped. She stopped crying and countered, "What does that mean, Nick? He was a committed artist with tons of talent. Very brittle. He deserved our respect."

Nick drank coffee tilting his head back dramatically. "You need more than talent, Sam. You need nerves of steel, patience and determination. You need to connect to what is happening in the present day."

She had heard the speech before. "Isn't that code for asshole?" A rhythmic Talking Heads song in the background chanted a catchy *"still waiting"* over and over.

Behind the bar, June entered with Mickey in tow. "Stop bullshitting me man!" This was the Mausers' favorite phrase.

"I'm not bullshitting you, June. We get a lot of them around here." He'd lost a lot of friends over the years. Many thought he'd be next but June insisted he clean up his act. Howie was in the picture now, a six-year-old with a small head and enormous, pale eyes. "I swear, I'm not bullshitting you, poodle."

"Don't *poodle* me."

Mickey sat down again and shrugged. A flask appeared from out of his sportscoat. "We need some brandy, people."

He poured while June made herself busy behind the counter mumbling loudly about burning cupcakes. "It's like chaos in here. Fucking Valentine's Day."

Nick had to grin. Sam smiled weakly. She touched Mickey's hand, "You're sweet." She then turned back to Nick with new energy, "It could have been a conspiracy." Mickey took the hint and headed back to the burning batter.

"The reporter, Tommy Graves or whoever was at the funeral, remember? Somebody is keeping the lid on something."

Nick stumbled, "You mean the suicide?"

"He's working for someone. Do you get it? And nobody said it was a suicide."

"Who?" Nick took a slow sip of the brandied coffee and pulled himself together. He tried patronization, "Why so angry, Sam?"

"Because you haven't been much help. Jerk!" His mouth sat open with nothing exiting. It was a rare moment for Nick.

Mystery Man, eh? I hope you appreciate how I am piecing this together for you before I even know the outcome. It's a crapshoot, as they say. Last thing I need is another snoop cramping my style.

Sam and I discussed this matter before parting. "What did this guy look like? An artist? A dealer? A police?"

"I'm not sure, Frank. I wasn't paying attention."

"But you think something weird is going on?"

"Don't you agree?"

"The jury is still out for me, Sam."

I called Sherrie to see if she had any dope on this. She did. The man who was in charge of Edgar's case was a large man by the name of Detective Finch. He wasn't at the funeral but his underling was there in a suit.

I asked her, "Why would a cop go to the funeral if it was a simple overdose?"

She said she didn't have any idea. "The cops didn't show much interest, Mr. Frank."

I asked her for the name of the first officer who'd spoken to her. "I think she said his name was Packard. He asked a few questions about preliminaries to rule out funny business. There was no struggle or anything. Just the usual mess. You know, pictures and books everywhere. Edgar was a slob. The cop did ask about Edgar's medications, you know, for depression. They found all the prescriptions and empty bottles. It was cut and dry."

"Packard, huh? Like the car? So the case is done?"

"Yeah. Packard is a car?" then Sherrie added, "Oh, and there was another woman."

I was dumbstruck. "What?"

"I think she was an artist. Sanchez was her name. She wasn't at the house."

I had heard the name. "Sherrie. I am so sorry. Emma Sanchez and Edgar?"

"I don't really know. It's a mess. Don't be too tough on him."

"Don't be too tough? You're being too kind. He needs a punch in the nose." Maybe it was time to check what happened with the police.

8

CHAPTER

Sergeant Pecker sat at his desk impatiently twiddling his Chase Utley bobble head. Utley's oversized head nodded a few times then said no. Pecker was waiting for Detective Finch to arrive with coffee. They did not drink office Java. "It sucks," they would announce to their inferiors, "but help yourselves. It's free." Uniformed patrolmen mumbled FU at low volume. "There's donuts too guys; yesterday's from Wawa." Louder FU-ing followed the announcement. "Imagine calling a store Wawa?" thought Pecker, why not "Pee Pee?" Those happened to be his initials, P. P. for Peter Picard. He had long since given up trying to get fellow work mates to forgo use of his disparaging nickname. It haunted him since grade school. "It's French, he used to say, Picard. Like 'discard' but with a P. You've seen Star Trek, haven't you? The Next Generation?" As he saw the boss's bulk coming through the glass door he retreated to the seclusion of Finch's enclave behind blinds, the scent of Star Buzz everywhere. They sat calmly among the potted palms. Un-cop-like, Finch loved greenery. He was from Newark, New Jersey.

"How is Mommy's babies today?" he asked the plants as he watered them carefully.

Pecker devoured his croissant and gulped the steaming brew after removing the top and flicking it into a bin, "Nicaraguan?"

"What?"

"The coffee?"

"No, it's Ghanaian today, I believe. I put half and half in yours, the way you like it."

35

"You are sweet to me, my Captain." Finch smiled at the endearment. "How did we ever drink that shit before boss?"

"I honestly don't know, Pecker. It was from the bad old days."

They began discussing the inquiry that was Edgar Bloom. Finch wanted to know why a hack writer was looking into a case for nobody. Pecker related the particulars of my phone call.

"This Mr. Frank guy is weird. We played tag for a while. He's not a journalist. He writes thrillers or so he says. What is that about? He won't be straight up about what he wants. He already visited the Pathologist; Wong in her puny office at Drexel."

Finch thought for a second, "Dr. Wong? What did Wong tell our Mr. Frank? Do you know? She use her fake Oriental accent?"

"Yes, boss. 'Wong number! You need autopsy, Jack!'" They laughed in unison and only stopped giggling when they heard some FU-ing outside. Finch asked if Bloom had a record.

Pecker looked through the file, "His sheet has one DUI and a possible disturbance of the peace, hi-jinx of some sort. Not criminal. Reported by a Howard Rochelle, a big wig on the citizens committees, you know, moneybags. Bloom worked for him sometimes. Rochelle is an art collector."

"That could be coincidental, Pecker."

"Yes sir. It could. We found a diary underneath the body. It is in evidence. Not exactly a suicide note like we were hoping to find but I have copies."

Finch said, "This is a tornado in a teacup. Read me a bit of the journal, will ya?" Pecker read Edgar's words as if at an audition:

> *"Tuesday, March 19, 2005: Feeling like hot stuff tonight. I know it is brew talking or the phenylalanine, drank several rum and cokes as well. In reality, I don't really exist. I am one of many schlubs without quantifiable merit. According to that bitch Sanchez and all the others. C'est fini mon ami."*

Finch rubbed his chin. "Quite mindful, if you think about it."

"Yes, but also clinically depressed, eh? I guess we are forced to have another look."

"Bloom's therapist looked at it and agreed, right? What's his name, this psychiatrist?"

"Dr. Klingon."

Finch looked shocked. "Are you kidding me? Star Trek? That's totally bizarre."

"Truly."

"Do we have a line on the girlfriend?"

"Yeah. Not sure about the relationship. Sanchez. Shall we bring her in?"

"Not yet. Sanchez is a woman?"

"Yeah, pretty Latina." Pecker looked serious, "The trouble is that her profile makes it an issue. There is a story already in one of the Weeklies. All the 'creatives' want to know if we were negligent."

"What? How could we have been? It was routine. It says here that Patrolman Abhoud called it in and her partner, that moron, McGee. They made a casual sweep for narcotics and firearms. There was nothing illegal, no hydrocodone, oxy or cocaine, only prescriptions made out to Bloom and suspect housekeeping. It was deemed a non-specific death, nothing special. No decomp. No disturbance or defensive wounds. They informed the wife. He and she were separated and he was unemployed. They found those crazy words in the notebook. It's not nice but nothing criminal." The discussion ended here and the cops looked out the window at the USS New Jersey across the river.

9
CHAPTER

After a month I had shelved the novel and was digging into Edgar full time. I still hadn't told Sherrie about the developments at the museum. Not sure why. Maybe she wasn't going to like it. My systematic directory of the journals was hitting a snag. I needed to digitize everything and that wasn't my cup of tea. All attempts at setting up cloudy things ended when I forgot my passwords. This is the most aggravating part of modern life. Even though I kept a notebook with all passwords in it, they never seemed to be updated accurately. I began researching the territory. Television's *Cold Case* was based on the Vidocq Society, a real group of semi-retired sleuths and Crime Scene Investigators who looked into unsolved cases. Eugene Francois Vidocq (1775-1857) was French, the real-life model for Sherlock Holmes, so they say. I always thought Sir Arthur Conan Doyle invented the Sherlock character because he was upset about the Jack the Ripper murder spree at the end of 1888. Let's not quibble. The first Holmes story was published in *The Strand* in the fall of 1887. Edgar was always a conspiracy nut. Particularly grisly murders:

May 1998: We can get Jack the Ripper's DNA now? Fantastic! Maybe we can match it to Prince Charles? I am dying to know the answer to that question. I'll swab his cheek myself! Open up, Charlie. And who killed Princess Diana, by the way?

In 1888, Scotland Yard was mystified. They didn't have a clue and didn't much care. Now, Ripper Conspiracists blame the Royal Family. Can you imagine Queen Victoria murdering prostitutes? More likely it was her nephew, Prince Willy or somebody who had impregnated a whore named Mary Kelly. It was all an elaborate cover-up. Two victims had that name. Coincidental? I think not. *Cold Case* is set in Philly because the Vidocq Society began life here in 1990. Yet another non-profit, go figure. Overweight, Gerard Depardieu played the criminal turned crime solver on screen in 2001. I don't recommend it. Victor Hugo also based characters on Vidocq. Remember Jean Valjean in Les Miserable? Dickens's, Great Expectations? Speaking of books, Cranston was in close touch so that *Work Shy* began along the lines he imagined. He'd run it by some publishers. Devil Books were looking for something with a racier story, a thinly veiled novel that lambasted Philly. I had no problem with that as long as it had some extra literary weight and a whopping great advance. A bargain with Devil Books? Could publishing do any harm to Edgar's unknown legend? Could it do any harm to Philadelphia known for nothing but a two-hundred-year-old bell with a crack? Sherrie wouldn't be too keen but she didn't have the full story. Edgar "warts and all" wasn't going to hurt anybody. My agent invited me up for dinner on the upper West Side. I had kept the would-be project close to my chest but Ronald B. Cranston soon got wind of it. The walls have eyes these days. He was pissed off for a week or so. His boyfriend, E. Cornelius Biggs, who edited Catalogue, a cool, art-style magazine, thought it very exciting and a good move for me. There was something creepy about that but he was convinced I was on to something.

"Try and avoid literary homicide, Mr. Frank," Biggs advised me over the phone.

"Trouble ain't my business," I told him. I decided to splurge on the Acela from 30th Street Station so I could continue making notes on my laptop. It was fully charged. Not far in miles, the distance between Philly and New York is metaphorically vast. New Jersey has its own Mason-Dixon line. Above Trenton they read the New York Times and the New Yorker. Below Trenton they are confined to the dull-brained Inquirer. This difference in news intake created a wall of perceived snobbery. On the outskirts of Philadelphia, we were pelted with stones. Upon arrival, I navigated my way out of Penn Station. A short subway ride left room for a pleasant walk up Broadway. It smelled as I remembered before gentrification, but the place had changed. New York City had become a dull global village. A legless musician from southern Timbuktu was strumming a cheap guitar. There were some single bills in a guitar case. There was also a pile of CDs for sale next to him. Inside was the secret number for a free download. I gave him two dollars. His look said, thanks a whole shitload dude. This made me blush slightly. Ron and Biggs met me at the door of their brownstone on 88ᵗʰ Street. Gay people love me! Maybe because I'm tall, dark and strange. Biggs was as wide as Ron was tall. I won't mention Laurel and Hardy. They stood over me for a minute with their cropped heads shining. They lived in a stunning example of New York mansion architecture, a four-story treasure trove of art publishing and vernacular design. I was envious on both counts. In the living room there was a medium-size painting by Alex Katz over the fireplace. It was a picture of a woman on a sandy beach throwing a ball, an homage to his own collectors perhaps. It was titled *Woman on a Sandy Beach Throwing a Ball*.

"Make yourself at home, Dougie. Drink this," Cranston demanded.

I obliged and sat beneath the painting, "Love that Katz." They beamed with pride.

"It was a gift from the man himself." They immediately launched into the Edgar story. Eventually they sat close together on a modern love seat shaped like a kidney. It fit into the baroque overkill.

"Go ahead, Frank. Where are we at? Do you have the premise for the book? Is it a memoir of the artist or an expose?" It was at this point I realized that they thought a book was possible. Up to then, it had only been a wee notion. I needed a pretty good reason to leave my Nordic noir comfort zone. Freddie French was secretly Danish.

I replied with a timeless notion I thought they'd like, "Does an artist have to be dead in order to get any attention?"

"No, Dougie. That is the plot, the story. What is the premise beneath?"

"Oh, you mean like, ruthless ambition leads to destruction?"

"Yes, Shakespeare, as in the Scottish Play. Yes. That is exactly it."

40

"Well, gentlemen, this is a little different. The twist might be that *Ruthless Ambition Leads To Success.*" They both laughed.

"We like that idea, young man. It's so un-romantic," Biggs said for both of them. I loved it when they called me young man. I was neither of those things.

Cranston showed concern, "You aren't planning to have a go at the establishment are you? I'm not sure I approve. Not sure if it would sell either. Let's not be negative." I told them I wasn't the whistleblower type and they bought it.

"And what is the nature of the book? Is it True Crime? Do you think someone killed your friend?"

I responded with my best straight face, "Yeah, I think someone did."

"I want to meet Trout soon," said Biggs. "She sounds interesting."

"You have no idea."

"You don't think she killed him do you?"

This caught me off guard, "Well, I'd be surprised but that is where the research comes in. She's at the helm. The cops are still investigating a suspicious death." I imagined Philly's finest hard on the trail in an Art Museum looking at all the naked ladies made out of marble.

Cranston chipped in, "The museum always gains when an artist kicks the bucket, don't they?" I tried to contemplate the consequences of my exaggerations. Biggs tried to convince me the project was a gift. I must have looked cautious, downing my drink.

"Why the qualms, Frank? Don't trust authority? You're the perfect man for the job."

"Look, Biggs," I said, "this is like a vulture picking his brother's flesh."

"Roadkill, eh? The guy is gone, Frank," he said. "Break a leg."

"I have no bone to pick with that, Biggs." Cranston was getting bored.

Biggs continued on skeletons, "Stop ribbing me, Mr. Frank."

Ron stared at his mate and said, "Biggie, if you say, 'boner' I'll crane you. I swear, I will." They exchanged looks.

"In the cranium, hubby, I hope, my least vulnerable spot. Let's not quarrel in front of our guest."

It went on like that for a while until I refereed, "Gentlemen, will you please stop fucking around."

They stared at me in disbelief then broke into hysterics. "We are not gentlemen, sir." More laughing. Dinner was scrummy, something pan-Asian with a fish in it. Mozart in the background. "Keep us posted as the thing develops. We suggest you carry on with the museum and let us know how the research proceeds."

"Anything before you go, Mr. Frank? More wine or chicken?" asked Biggs.

"It's not fish? I thought it was fish. It wasn't fish?"

They chuckled at my Philly ignorance. "Mr. Frank. You can be a dope," said my agent. After a perfect decaf espresso, we parted with smiles and hugs. Cranston suggested that I keep him in the loop this time.

Biggs was especially cheerful, "Go, go," he said, "before you become dessert. You are on to a winner here, Frank, don't forget it. An art world murder! Right up your alley!" In mid-bye-bye, without further ceremony, Cranston slammed the door in my face with a disconcerting New York bang. I guess we'd made a deal.

10
CHAPTER

New characters began showing up at every turn and the Bungalow became less quiet, always a bad sign. I began making a proper study of the volumes so there would be enough bio for a decent monograph (a book of pictures with an esoteric essay attached) in addition to the catalogue. Any extra material was channeled into side-research for the would-be book. There was also plenty of art turning up.

"From where?" I asked myself. Was someone collecting the work before Edgar's death? How did Martha get a lead on Edgar in the first place? Martha insisted she'd heard of him from an earlier show at a gallery called the Poor Haus. I'd never heard of it but she made me point man for the whole operation. The more reading and writing I did the more assistance was needed for fact-checking. Trout got in touch with Cranston for advice. He sent an editor, Sally Brick, a studious librarian with a feisty attitude. She set up a little cubby outside mine in the Bungalow to protect me and screened incoming calls. A little tyrant on the phone, she didn't mind the receptionist bit. My willing minion began scanning key diaries instantly and we gravitated to the Italian years.

Our Ivy League Art School was down the hill from Brown University in Providence. When I first met Edgar, we didn't hit it off. He was affable with long frizzy hair and I was up my own ass. Most Genius Convention people are. Our relationship was later cemented by intense experiences senior year traveling around Europe. There were lots of drunken exploits in the cause of bettering American Foreign relations destroyed by Vietnam. They called it "European Honors!" How we survived the Culture Shock, I'll never know. We were supposed to become infused with culture, the Italian language and Renaissance Art. All that. Edgar had it worse; he was sensitive, writing long love letters home. I enjoyed the veneration of this poor, shaken slob. We shared every waking idea for months and a lot of technical aspects of painting. It was unavoidable. Everyone called us the Arbus Twins. Look up photographer Diane Arbus, 1936-1968. Creepy yeah, but we were like cellmates not soul mates. Certainly not Siamese Twins joined at the elbow. That's gross. We had no mentors, no place in history and little guidance. My father – who killed Germans in WW2 – was pissed off he had to fork out for it. Only in retrospect did I see that I was being slowly weaned off incredible hubris; an entitlement that was a severe handicap. Poor me, eh? Letters from Mr. Frank Senior were full of stripping down. "I lost my wife, legally speaking and you don't see me whining and moaning. Buck up. I got shot several times by the best snipers around. Hans and Fritz. Real Nazis in trees. Builds character." Edgar's letters he clung to, re-reading them over and over. He had left a sweetheart behind so he was in constant need of assurance. I obliged. It wasn't my first bromance. He served as a precise moral compass for me. I could use him now. Have I mentioned the Italian Leftists who hung on to the 60's like grim death? Edgar wrote about these irritating guys.

Italy, 1983: Jesus, so outmoded. Europe underlines the fact that we have nothing to offer. Excepting Italians themselves, who live in a time warp. In front of the Pantheon, the piazza is spoiled by strains of Pink Floyd wafting over the tile roofs. It's fucking 1983, for god's sake! Our view: trying to become an artist is an impossibility but what else is there?

There was Cassandra Giovanni. She was the only one in the group who knew what she was doing. Her parents were known artists so it came naturally. She knew the lingo. A few years later she showed up prominently in art magazines, post mortem. Another creative suicide? Why? Can you

44

see this 'dying young' thing cropping up often in *Work Shy?* It reminds me of forensics stories. Nothing as interesting as a case gone cold like the Zodiac Killer. Gives me chills to this day. We agreed art school was a con-job. It finalized the last remnants of counter-culture in our minds, i.e. that both Left and Right were a joke. Rather prescient for young men turning twenty, don't you think? We managed to absorb the foreign culture in spite of ourselves but made a point of dismissing the waffle of professors. They discussed art as if it was a fragile, sanctimonious state of enlightenment that few understand.

"That is all bullshit," Edgar would say.

I agreed, "Bullshit, man."

"Our art – if we get that far – is not going to have a thing to do with art history or ancient Rome."

"Total bullshit, man."

"You got that right, Frank." Edgar wasn't much of a travel writer:

Roma, Jan. 14, 1984: It rains a lot in Italy. We would be much happier at The Roxy watching the Talking Heads. Instead, we endure this ancient city. We pick up reality. "Ho fatto gia" as the locals say.

I translate that as: Been there. Done that. We perfected ordering Cafe Latte with panache while standing at glass espresso bars. Happy Days. Continental breakfast included a delicious sweet pastry with a funny name. Our own personal barista Massimo lorded over Bar Arugula on a small cobbled alleyway. It was a dark hole in the wall with two tables lit by a broken florescent bulb. Massimo thought grandiose mustaches were still cool. We tried to dissuade him but we didn't know the word for mustache. Cappelli means hair, I think. He may have thought we were suggesting he get a hair cut which was totally *Serpico.* His Pacino impression was impressive. "Patzo" he said, pointing at us. Means "crazy" if I'm not mistaken.

Italia, Feb. 3 1984: Most Romans are all taciturn, in fact. Massimo is a grouch but begins to see some humor in our situation. He probably thinks us homos but it is hard to tell with Italian men; they pal around embracing each other and kissing. Those are the straight guys. Massimo is happy as long as his pants are too tight. I prefer Mino, his son. He has a sense of humor and shows respect to women.

There were advantages: Pretty Ladies on the street called us "ponks" as we ran by to escape riot cops' tear gas. The Carabiniere didn't fuck around. Can't go into that 60's hangover now. Well, perhaps a bit. We worshiped the beautiful women on the street and graded them with a numerical precision, the top being Venus (or Aphrodite, if you are Ancient Greek) or Hedy Lamarr (one of Edgar's favorites) from the silver screen. There were more of them than you would think, strutting around in leather trousers or with the layered, late seventies look. It continued well into the next decade. These pretty women would not give us the time of day, much less evening. One drunken night, I think Arnold Crane was with us, an awkward New Englander with an oversized Adam's apple – we wandered into a red light district and were nearly raped by creatures out of the Hobbit. We were stoned, OK? On the ground was a trail of lascivious postcards advertising the wares within. We thought they were women but were not positive. I'd already had the clap and didn't fancy a re-do as tempting as that sounds. After our escape from the Fellini movie, we retreated to Café Arugula. Mino made our Latte Caldo happily and suggested we sit in the booth, no extra charge. Coffee bars charged an extra fee for sitting down. Very un-American. We poured ourselves into the chairs and noticed Crane was no longer with us. Mino carefully delivered our drinks in tall glasses on saucers. He surprised us and sat down and lit a Marlboro with a wooden match. He looked tired as he offered us two filtered death sticks. We smiled at each other huddled silently in the match-light. It was like a Baroque painting. Mino said, "American friends. I love you."

Our professors didn't seem to notice Crane's departure. "Tuesday we leave at 6 am for Firenze. We will be back in five days." So we gladly accepted his per Deum in case he turned up. The Grand Tour paradigm was oddly conservative for art schools where the "happening" edge was stressed. The college should have supplied therapists instead of language coaches. Old hippies! Edgar was convinced we were on the cutting edge even considering our ineptitude. Rome underscored the fact. We pursued the present day, looked to London (not far away) and defiantly cut our hair short.

11

CHAPTER

My dad's sister greeted me in her South Kensington house a couple of days before my short hop to Rome. I was over-dressed for her benefit and had had no sleep. She led me up to a deserted attic, maid's room. "Have a long nap nephew. You look like shit." She wasn't kidding.

"Bless you, Aunt Judith."

"How's your mother."

"Dad refers to her as the dead woman. She's dating again."

"That was a nasty divorce."

"Don't remind me."

"Get some sleep and we'll catch up later." She exited and I heard footsteps echo down the stairs. My mind was fuzzy. I don't recall dropping off but it was soon after staring at a photo of the Queen riding a horse in a long parade. There was a clop-clop sound coming from the closet.

Auntie's house had some Georgian remnants but was mostly re-jigged in the early Victorian era. I soaked it up willingly. I know London well now but at this point, I'd only been once when I was nine. God, it was dreary and didn't live up to all the swash-buckley movies I'd seen on a small screen. Moriarty lurking in the shadows. Top hats in pubs. Those were the days.

When I woke up not knowing where I was she greeted me with a mug of tea. "Hot, sweet tea, Dougie," she said, "cures a body of most upsets." Who was I to argue with the British Empire?

"Thanks, I need full restoration." Judith was a first class snob; what a surprise. Maybe that is where I get my pretentious attitude? She had a dark complexion probably owing to some ancient link to the Middle East. Her long chaotic hair was worn up elegantly though outdated to my eyes. Like many "seventies" people, she wore huge designer shades constantly even when it rained. The London Franks were highly regarded, apparently, which meant they were in the fraternity of well-attired, wealthy Jews. How did they skirt rampant, inbred anti-Semitism? Not sure. Within days I was accused of killing Jesus personally and invading Granada. This bias didn't exist in the States with the same ferocity. I made it through high school with out any major slurs coming my way. "Hey Big-Nose or Afro-Boy." But Europe? While bartering down Brick Lane Market for records, I was accused of 'Jewing-Down' the seller. I thought I was shopping. The bigot, in my case, was a fat skinhead with a tight "Crass" Tee shirt. The punk band, Crass were complete anarchists who now work in finance. He wasn't hostile but I was amazed by his use of the word "Jew" as a verb. Brick Lane is also a Jack the Ripper murder site known for Indian Restaurants. There's a brewery there now where the disemboweling took place. A small plaque indicates the spot.

When I told Auntie about the exchange later, she smiled and mumbled something about Fascists, don't let them get you down. "I never understood Punk's working-class revolt thing, Doug. Nazi sympathizers are another thing. We're conservatives."

Judith is the smartest member of the family by far. "I get that, Auntie, but how can revolutionaries be anti-Semitic at the same time?" When Edgar faced similar lightly veiled derogatory comments, he paraphrased Jello Biafra, singer in the Dead Kennedys: *Nazi Punk's Fuck Off!* Mr. Biafra was gifted with a song title: *Holiday in Cambodia,* for instance. That's witty enough to give Oscar Wilde a stiffy. Though Oscar would probably be more of a Smith's fan.

April, 5, 1984: The Revenge Languages. What are you gonna do? Fascist assholes will always be with us. They have constitutional rights to express themselves. And the trains run on time. Before Mussolini Italian trains never ran on time.

"The UK has no Constitution." she said. Judith finally admitted there had been goose-stepping Englishmen but I was too young to know about it.

"What about Wallace Simpson and the abdication of the would-be Edward the Eighth? They cozied up to Germany in the 30's." She was amazed an American had this knowledge. From the mantelpiece, she handed me a cream colored Coronation Mug from 1939 with 'King' Edward VIII's profile. He was the brother of the stuttering man who would be King of England, George. I stated that the coronation never took place.

"Dougie, I'm truly impressed." She warmed a tad and this made my day. My performance inspired her to give me the tour. We started with the wall of family mementos. There was a photo of my father looking handsome atop a Sherman Tank holding a Christmas tree. She pointed proudly. "If you look closely, you'll see he placed a Star of David on top. He was with Patton for a while so always dressed well, even in foxholes."

"I've heard that story. They stood out like hedgehogs on a wedding cake."

"I've heard the stories too."

"That worked until he was shot in the Ardennes in December '44."

"Let's not go into the details." She laughed mirthlessly. "Do you want to see the art collection?" We passed through the stainless steel kitchen – expensive appliances but still no mixer tap – into the older part of the house. The library was well appointed. Full was cozy chairs and the smell of leather. We sat down with our mugs of tea so I could have a good long look. Jet lag created a small haze and figures in the scenes vibrated slowly. I admired Auntie's paintings, several spinning Hogarth prints, common enough. Her pride and joy was her sketch by English painter, George Stubbs. It was brilliant, a small drawing of horse's entrails from 1767. It seemed alive, as if crawling away. I asked her if she would mind leaving it to me in her will.

She looked un-shocked by the request, "Not a chance, young man." She gave me a mock slap on the shoulder.

Back in the parlor, we drank our tea and watched England unravel on tellie. Everyone was buying safety pins and pirate shirts! When I left for Heathrow the next Wednesday, I promised to send her a postcard of my own "entrails" soon from the Vatican. She gave me an evil grin. They run in the family.

12
CHAPTER

Edgar's Italian journals obsessed me. I read the whole batch over several weeks as I was hearing about the future exhibition at the museum. I finally had to let Sherrie know. I told her over the phone and she wanted to meet at once. This is not what she had in mind when she first sent me over to the bungalow. I tried to explain how my life was sloppily entwined with my old friend.

Edgar had not been ready for the Roman experience but former classmate, Cassandra Giovanni was. She made herself at home in her own apartment owned by her parents and vacationed in Tuscany with them. Her journals were scribbled in Italian! Unfortunately, these advantages lead to tragedy. She took her own life in New York at the age of 27, an overlooked genius. "If she'd only waited a few years. After her death, her notoriety expanded. Now, she's almost famous."

My assistant, Sally was intrigued. "Why is there such a trail of suicides in the art world, Mr. Frank?"

I shook my head sadly. "My group was on the cusp, Sally."

"What cusp?"

"We were the first batch to realize that art history is what you make of it. This means you tell everyone else to go to hell."

She nodded, "There is a literary equivalent, Mr. Frank."

I nodded, "*Tell* me about it. Our formative years co-incided with the end of the American Century and Modernism. I'm still working on what that means."

Sally lightly touched my arm, "Poor, Mr. Frank. That sucks. I had no idea. I was raised with Pong." I asked her if she could drive a stick shift. She said, yes.

Sally began to learn Edgar's back-story outside in the journals as I filled her in. "Italy challenged us on a gut level. In Rome, we had to pretend we knew what we were doing. We knew nothing about bartering for vegetables at stalls full of grumpy old Italians from the Nineteenth Century. We didn't know how to cook a fucking vegetable." Swooning over art history wasn't our cup of tea either. We were missing out on too much current stuff. *Anarchy in the UK,* for instance. "All the abstract-conceptual shit was out. New Image and Neo-Expressionism was what was going on. It was real sea change."

"I *have* heard of Post Modernism."

"Our professors never once alluded to it."

"Were they completely oblivious?"

"They were stuck in the post war era. Hippies and Minimalism."

"You can't blame your teachers can you?"

"Why not?"

Our studios were in Palazzo Vecchio, a great place to hang yourself. Several had. Poison was more popular though for dispatching competitive siblings. It was near the 400 year old Jewish Ghetto next to Teatro di Marcello but we weren't aware of it at the time. We could've used a comforting bagel or Italian Lox! Edgar and I were both suppressing our multicultural backgrounds. Which tribe's allegiance did we relate to? We were there to study Pagan and Christian Art from the Millenium on. Edgar told me to *Forget Chanuka. Madonnas ad nauseum. Gawdy stuff.*

"My consciousness had been raised but had nowhere to go." I continued lecturing Sally, "All this was pretty cool, but we didn't have our real muse:

American Culture. It was like living in a decaying mansion. Full of long dead ghosts after a period of slow decline watching real life cover them up. As General Sherman said, 'Other people are hell,' especially Americans. Sherman knew how to burn a place down."

"I get that," said Sally, "but you have the quote wrong."

"What do you mean?"

"The line is *War is hell.*"

"Who said that?"

"Sherman!"

I was confused. "Who said the other thing?" Edgar continued summary:

Nov. 15, 1984: Precious Dystopia. The gap – hard to describe – dividing spoiled 'Suburban' Roots and this dense Ancient Urban place is vast. American students! The crumbling Forum a block away. Who cares? Yankee Doodle-Dumb Asses.

There were no hamburgers or IHOPS. The beer sucked. Our art was abysmal. For comfort, we bought a shitty turntable to play my copy of the Sex Pistols' *God Save the Queen* over and over. I'd bought it budget priced at a Woolworth's on Oxford Street for 35 Pence. Can you imagine that? It is now fetching eight thousand pounds in mint condition on Ebay. It saved our lives. Didn't matter that we were late to the party. The rest of the students were immersed in a hippie paradigm, well rehearsed. We blasted the Pistols' power chords 8 or 10 times a day in sixteenth century common room with a Ramones record for good measure; *gabba gabba hey*. The other American students didn't get it. They'd leave the room, disturbed, practicing past tense Italian, "Fatto niente, fatto niente." These cultural tourist types often appeared idiotic to Italians. We pretended to be Italian without speaking. Clever, eh? Don't wear a fucking camera around your neck! In retrospect, I wonder if an American can be a foreigner? Everyone else is the foreigner. After long boring days of enforced cultural tourism, our feet ached. For a nightcap, Edgar and I frequented Bar Arugula on the side street near our lodgings. We enjoyed a Latte Caldo, steamed milk with sugar in it. It was comfort food. Massimo's son Mino was there. He was more polite but had the same unfortunate facial hair. His cousin Mia sometimes helped out at night. She was frail, beautiful and off limits. No mustache. Her suitors lined up at night for coffee, strange looking men. Today, Mia has four kids and weighs three hundred pounds.

I didn't realize that Edgar was suffering from depression. It was way beyond usual teen torpor, which can be bad enough. Comfort can be rare when you are in a strange environment. Classmate Cassandra had similar symptoms. More than enough for a clear diagnosis. Aren't all young people depressed? They see life as a sad, complicated mess where they have no place. *Sheer Terror* as Edgar described it. Are they wrong?

The part of a dream you wake from when it can't get any worse? Yes, but here I am awake. In pain, confused. Don't go down to the basement! Tortured and alone. No one gets it. No TV for comfort. Can't talk to anyone except these selfish Americans. The only joy is the realization that I am suffering like the rest of the world. It ain't safe out there.

We might have learned loads from Cassandra. She 'documented' her art performances photographically before this sort of documenting was vogue. Her art was Eva Hesse-like stuff. What they call scatter-pieces now, any old metaphoric rubbish installed on a studio floor. The more slap-dash, the better. She was good at it, sort of channeling a visual equivalent of Sylvia Plath. Her proto-installation work about female anatomy was ahead of the curve, you might say. Ovaries and ovens. Cassandra was genuinely fragile: part kook, part insider.

Compared to Cassandra, we are so stupid. I don't mean because of our broken-Italian. Because we are uninitiated. There was a critique Friday. It was held at her flat in a fascinating maze of cobbled streets somewhere behind the Vatican. Her apartment has amenities, all mod cons as Brits say. Not like the crap Pensione Morte, where we got ripped off daily. She has her own fucking bathroom! Jealous, Me?

I always wanted to live in a hotel. Let me explain to Americans. As the first modernized nation on earth, you understand bathrooms are very important to us. If you leave the country, you may be shocked. We are used to hot water and soap even in a Biker Bar on Route 66. A penzione is a small hotel with high ceilings, a bit like a British bed-sit minus the small cooker – so you can have ubiquitous beans on toast before you hit the pub. For some reason, Penziones include a bidet, which isn't much good for a "fry up" but works OK if you have to pee in the middle of the night. So, both are grim by standards of the USA. It's a hard choice. What you gain in decrepit grandness in Italy you lose in modernity. Bedsits in the UK at least have a sink and a tellie. Often, they have a heater coil in the fireplace that accepts an eight-sided 50 pence piece for a few minutes of warmth until you venture out to the local boozer. That is what they call pubs. Our professors in Rome lived in proper modernized apartments with indoor toilets owned by the school, nicely set up in a non-tourist area. Sounds like a tough job, eh? Some female students, they became particularly close to if you get my meaning. I'd sell my body just for access to a clean shower stall.

We gathered to discuss Cassandra's work, soaking up cheap red wine, a singular and significant rite of passage for students in Europe. Her furniture was covered in tapestries and it looked well lived in. We chatted in English before regarding the semester's work. Edgar was late as usual. The place was not easy to locate. It was proto "shabby chic" in the extreme. On the black and white marble floor she placed pebbles from famous churches in Rome in the form of a Madonna/Prostitute. We stood round bemused. She presented some earlier photographs behind glass. They were finely grained with rough black edges. These were full of naked women staring at the camera.

"It is anti-pornographic, theoretically," she assured us.

The professor praised her, "I love these, Cassandra. I am moved, truly." She blushed and there was a long silence punctuated by Fiat engines and horns.

Palazzo: I may vomit. Frank tells me Cassandra has been seeing Richard, a seemingly, cerebral hippy painter in our group with a beard and wire-rims. He was grateful for the sex, which he brags about in detail like it is a menu at a tavola caldo. He explained he is sharing Cassandra with some Italian guy, a communist. Eduardo. Kinky Roma! Manage a Twerp? In Eddie's mustache you could hide a vole. He is an old school who deals a bit of dope on the side. Thanks, but no thanks, Eduardo. Don't want to end up in a cell with a Turkish toilet and fifteen gay shoplifters, recently incarcerated. I'm not kidding.

Our one Italian Professor looked a bit like writer Umberto Eco, but wasn't. This was before I knew who Umberto Eco was. Come to think of it, lots of Italian men looked like Eco. It was a good look for portly Italian men with beards. I can't remember a thing about him, except frumpy jackets with elbow patches, maybe a pipe, signor Marco. Cassandra was patient with everyone, explaining mostly in English – she spoke fluent Italian and German – that she was trapped within flesh.

"My body circles the sun," she stated affirmatively. We grinned uncomfortable-like. It was cosmic stuff and made us look like anachronisms – didn't take much.

"Woman birthed the world." We knew that already, of course.

Palazzo Vecchio: Is Cassandra psychotic? Met some English Students last week at the British Academy, upper crusties. I didn't realize how anti-American they could be. They kept talking about Foucault and Marx. I thought they meant the toy company. A scuffle occurred. A Cambridge bloke was picking on Cassandra so Frank smacked him right in his snobby chin. Decked the sucker. The British intellectuals weren't expecting a frontal assault from Yank hippies. Fun evening and our reputation is secure.

Later that week, much like the Victorian gentleman that I am, I walked Cassandra home through the Fiore section of town. Yes, they sell flowers. I was hoping she might jump me but I was mistaken. We bought some gelati and chatted about home. Her "limone" breath followed us over the cobbles as she spoke. It took nearly two hours. She was nice and I got a cold peck on the cheek for my efforts. A full moon was reflected in myriad tiny puddles, hundreds of years old. I walked home on a cloud, re-tracing my steps through the Sixteenth Century hoping not to end up the victim of a Vespa hit squad.

The next day we were to leave on a five-day excursion to Ravenna on the Adriatic Coast to see what happened directly after the Empire fell. Then, further North to Venezia, a very damp city. Wake up call: 7 am. I was a zombie until I consumed a Cafe Latte from Bar Arugula. The trip went badly for Edgar.

North Italia: Something disagrees with me. Mio Christo. Perhaps it is the whole of Europe. Caught short on the fucking bus. Dove il gabinetto? Today, che bella citta – while my guts burn? Freaking Venezia? Another bowl of indifferent pasta? Romeo, oh Rome. Romance disagrees too. The language of Romance? Run out of Love Letters. Something wrong there. Cassandra got me some Pellagrino. Or was it Orangina? Bless her, my Madonna. What would I do without bottled sparkling water? Belching helps somewhat but when nature calls, it is a mudslide.

Thanks for the image, pal. Venice was dreary with canals, as you'd expect, not romantic in the least. From church to museum. Museum to church. I gave my buddy a sleeping pill I procured from my divorced Mom, the alpha doctor. Edgar slept the whole trip back. Cassandra kept an eye on him. She asked about Edgar's girlfriend. They were friends back in Providence. It seemed ages before. The next day Edgar decided that was enough so we went out to celebrate. He left in early May on a big Alitalia jet, rather hung-over. He wanted to salvage the relationship stateside but it was already severed. He'd been replaced. He said goodbye to Europe: *May 7, 1984: Arrividerci Roma and I ain't kidding.*

After returning to the States from the land of the Caesars, Edgar and I didn't need each other anymore. However, the fates intervened and we ended up at the same graduate school in upstate New York the following autumn; Northlands University. In the Arctic, we were surrounded by cheerleaders and snow. There were also more Brits. I was right at home and for once, Edgar landed on his feet.

13

CHAPTER

My next port of call (research-wise) was Judy Cheap. She hadn't been at the funeral but I figured she might have some "down and dirty" from the 90's. She had mentioned some lost tapes when I called her. Considering her lifestyle, she looked pretty good when we met up at the London Grill, heavy with black eyeliner, thrift store skirt and massive Doc Martins. She kept using the phrase, "Back in the day, Mr. Frank." She'd hit me on the arm as she said this and it was starting to get painful.

I tried to distract her, "How's the guys in the band?"

"We're good. A new EP out soon, *Shitstorm*. We're hoping they'll play it on WPRB. The line-up has changed a lot. Bing has a kid now. So does Mickey. You know Mickey from *Green on Red*? We kicked him out a long time ago for the drug use. He took Edgar's place. Riff is now guitarist. Used to play with Post Mortem. He's fantastic."

"I'm glad the Trauma Queens still live."

"Well, barely. I'm still waiting tables. Riff works at the Museum doing exhibitions. He told me about *Forlorn Poets*."

"Shame about Edgar." I said, trying to keep up.

"Yeah. Another casuality." She took another swig of IPA. "Sorry I missed the funeral. We had a gig in New York."

"No worries. Plenty of ghouls came out of the woodwork."

"Really? Sounds ominous."

"I learned a lot."

"I heard there were a lot of previous employers in attendance."

"Yeah. That's right. I can't figure it out. You were one of those, no? Employers, I mean."

She laughed, "Yeah, but we didn't fire him. Or give him a regular paycheck! Do you remember the time Edgar was thrown out of the Khyber? It takes a lot to be thrown out of the Khyber. Man, he was shit-faced!"

"I wasn't there that night. Must've been fun!"

The Khyber Pass was Philly's premiere Punk venue "back in the day." It was a mosh-pit with a shitty bar attached, barely room to skin a cat. "It has lost its luster over the years and we are quite ancient now." She walloped me again. "I miss those days."

I rubbed my shoulder and we smiled at each other over the pint glasses. "But music is still worth doing."

"We make new memories now."

Our drinks were draining quickly. "Let's have another and toast our fallen comrade."

She raised her glass, "To Bloom!" The beer was soaking my wrist.

Together we chimed, "To the Khyber!"

From behind the bar, the waitress raised her sponge, "To the Khyber!"

Afterwards, I drove back up the hills of NW Philly. Sherrie visited me at the Bungalow and I gave her an update. She sounded jealous. "Who's Judy Cheap?"

"I must have mentioned her, Sherrie. She was the singer in Edgar's band." Sherrie wasn't buying it. She now knew about the exhibition but I certainly wasn't ready to tell her I about my book project until it was off the ground. We sat in the den. She looked the room over as if not recognizing it. "What do you think?" I asked, handing her one of my special espressos in a little cup. Sally and I had painted the room a dull possum grey and added two yellow sofa chairs.

"Thanks." She nodded approval, "It almost looks business-like in here." I beamed. She noticed the décor. "Very tidy. I don't know these pieces. They're weird." We sat under the painting that was hung snuggly over the fireplace. "Is that one of the 'Punk Pictures'?" The picture called

The Duchess of Anarchy depicted a spiky-haired singer who resembled Cheap. The scene had an overly ornate frame. Judy Cheap was central to Bloom's anarchy paintings. Imagine what Goya would have done during the Reagan Administration. I kept smiling. "What are you so pleased about, Mr. Frank?" Luckily, Sally hadn't arrived yet. She had helped me fix up the Bungalow including redecorating with new bookshelves and a comfortable couch for me to ruminate on. Our 'Cold-Case' board was locked in my office away from prying eyes.

According to Trout's timeline, the 'punk pictures' were Edgar's first real achievement after Art School. They featured all sorts of anglophilic emblems and coats of arms saying things like *In Vino Veritas. Bugger the Queen* was another title. You get the idea. They were to be analysed in the monograph that I hadn't written yet. Edgar's next achievement was merely surviving. Unfortunately, this exciting period of New Image faded abruptly with an unfortunate sharp economic downturn. Edgar escaped barely with a signature style and neurosis. Flashy Baroque canvases gave way to installation work that would be sanctified by the art world for the next fifteen years. Little guys couldn't compete. Many young artists stalled and gave up. Warhol died. Basquiat died. Suddenly, angst didn't appeal anymore. This was a shock to priestly Edgar who'd just found himself. He wanted the luxury of producing something of value, something wholly original as opposed to wholly derivative like my books.

It was apparent that Sherrie would be a problem. How was I to spin the diaries while they were fueling a new Edgar Bloom? The exhibition, "Forlorn Poets" was gaining momentum. It had started to inform the novel already in an unusual way. The book *Work Shy,* though hardly begun, linked up nicely. It was designed to be an intellectual postulation posing as a goofy page-turner. The more it formed, the more I had to include arcane references: Benjamin, Foucault, Levi-Strauss, Eco and Baudrillard. Edgar did this himself conflating art theory with musical subcultures. In fact, it was reciprocal. The thinkers wanted to explain the street, the queer, the

60

uncanny, the dystopian present and the misread past, all through the lens of Karl Marx. You'd think they would have known better.

In New York, Edgar sucked up some street style and learned a lot. On a good day, he had the constitution for it. His friend Cassandra never did, unfortunately. He wrote songs about her – one was called *Gone Again Goodbye*. I wrote one too fancying myself a vocalist, Cassandra, Cassandra. Sounded French. My early songs were poems that lead me to non-fiction and then fiction. What's the difference? Memoir, Fiction? Who cares? Hold that prose. Edgar's tune had a second life with an arrangement by the Trauma Queens. Judy sang, "Come back, Cassandra. Cassandra, come back. All is forgiven," pleadingly. There was a b-side as well, *My Dead Sweetheart*. This was made into a rare recording produced on seven inch red vinyl. Was it too late to mention in the book?

Again, there was the problem of funds. Trout's payments were OK but not enough considering my totalistic investment of time and effort. We discussed this.

"Try not to get overly involved, Mr. Frank."

"You know me, Martha. In for a penny, in for a pound."

"What does that mean, Mr. Frank? We're all invested in Bloommania, no?"

"We are manufacturing a saint, Martha. That was not our intention." I stepped closer to the sink.

"Is that martyr or saint, Frank?"

"I don't care. Does it matter?"

"Perhaps not."

"We have the title for the show: *Forgotten Poets*. Richard came up with it."

The walls shrank a little. "I know. Word is out." I leaned backwards. "Sally?"

She appeared silently, "Yes. Mr. Frank."

Martha needs a little more coffee."

Sally chirped, "Yes, sir. Right away, sir."

"Your assistant is a little peculiar."

"Sally's omniscient, Martha. That's a wicked title." I conceded.

"He was thinking Poe, Keats and dying young."

"Yeah. I get it. Poe lived in Philly."

Trout's blank eyes stared me down. "Speaking of titles, I know about *Work Shy*. Word is out. Is there anything you want to tell me?"

"Yes. I figured you knew. I hope you don't mind." Sally rushed back in with cups and retreated again.

"On the contrary. I trust you completely." Sally returned with the French press. Trout heavily sugared her drink and raised it to her lips. "All for the greater good." This felt like a ghost walking over my grave and peeking in my medicine cabinet.

14

CHAPTER

Bloom's diaries remained addictive. Sherrie wanted to read The Grad School ones personally. This distracted her from some of my other activities with the Fuzz and the Doctors. Mostly schtum. Drugs were another story. I discovered what was left of Edgar's pills in a coffee can in the toilet tank of the bungalow and in a *Kung Fu* lunch box in the attic. They still come in handy for back pain.

The cops were on a roll and had just finished their mid-morning second breakfast. "What else we got, Pecker?" inquired Finch of his second in command.

"There is some guy messing with the Mayor's computers."

"Like to get my hands on him, Pecker."

"Must be some Otaku dude."

"A what?"

"Otaku. That's Japanese for geek, a computer loser, mother's boy. Oriental nerds in dark basements. Some people think it's cute."

Finch winced at the word, 'Oriental.' Didn't sound right, "Really, never heard the term before. Otaki? How do you pick up on this shit, Pecker?"

"Otaku. I see it as my job, Captain."

"Well, thanks, anything to keep us in the eye of Mayor Nutt. The Commish will be pleased too," said the Captain thoughtfully, "Don't want to piss off Jackie Straw either. The DA is a firebrand. She wants our plates on the fire."

"You mean our butts on a fry pan."

"Something like that."

Captain Finch sat back and started a short soliloquy: "Mayor's hard to crack sometimes. He's a bean counter. I like that. Unemotional. I like that. Ordered, I like that. He's got balls too! You like that, Pecker!?" Both policemen started giggling. After the laugh attack subsided Finch and Pecker sat quietly and ignored the FU-ing from the squad room as obtrusively as possible. After a spell, they became maudlin again and stood looking out at the cars below. "We are the pride of the precinct, Pecker."

Pecker responded, "And we have the dubious distinction of being the armpit of the East Coast."

But thank goodness we ain't Camden, Sergeant." A few moments passed. The Sergeant pointed to the massive grey shape moored across the river. "They at least have the New Jersey Battleship. It's a thing of beauty."

"Indeed it is Pecker but it was made at the Philadelphia Navy Yard; 16 inch guns. Boom. That would certainly stop a perp in his tracks. You'd find bits of him in Ohio or maybe just his wristwatch. Used to shell Pacific Islands.

"The guns are now aimed at Fishtown, Captain."

In the squad room, Officer Kathy Abhoud received my fax inquiring about an autopsy. She crossed the room and knocked. "Fax for Pecker," she yelled through the door. The squad room let out a singular, muffled laugh; the joke was never old.

Pecker opened the door and grabbed it saying, "Just the fax, Ma'am." He laughed ignoring the patrolmen.

Abhoud scowled and rolled her eyes. "Shitheads," she whispered as the door clicked shut.

The men looked up. "She called us shitheads again, Captain."

"We are shitheads, Pecker." Finch reached out over the desk. "Gimme that."

Pecker laughed, "I love that joke. *Just the fax, Ma'am.*"

Finch grinned anxiously for a different reason. He had a secret crush on the lady and knew damn well she'd never seen an episode of *Dragnet*. "Pecker, the patrolwoman doesn't like your jokes."

"She has no sense of humor. She's Muslim."

"That is rich coming from a gay man. Aren't you supposed to be all one world village or something?"

"No really, Arabs have no sense of humor. It is a fact."

"Were you born in Mississippi, Pecker?"

"What does Mississippi gotta do with it, boss?"

"You sound like a redneck."

"You saying that people of the South are inflexible bigots?"

"No, I'm saying you don't know anything about Muslims.

"I know patrolwoman Abhoud."

"She is from Baltimore, you idiot."

"Ah, I see what you mean. Thanks." A few moments passed as Finch read the fax. Eventually, they got back to my dead buddy, Bloom.

"Also, get in touch with those Vidocq people. They might be able to clear this mess up." Pecker was confused. It wasn't the first time. The members of the Philly-Forensics club had a lot to answer for: every CSI show on TV for the last twenty years and (not least) for the non-metaphorical use of the word seminal in each episode six or seven times. The group wasn't pretty but Vidocq had succeeded in solving several long-dead cases.

My cold case was doing me a world of good. It was fun hanging out with Edgar's widow and I wondered if it would be nice to settle down and become surrogate dad. We watched TV with Kurtz. He enjoyed black and white oldies with Basil Rathbone and Nigel Bruce on the trail of the devious Moriarty. Amazing Holmes! One day we caught *The Portrait of Dorian Gray*. All about vanity vs. death. Wild about Wilde. Sounds Steam Punky.

The Art Mafiosi claimed not to watch TV. They missed definitive cultural moments. Pity. Everyone knows TV drama is several cuts above the film arts now and borrows whole hog from art theory. I am not referring to Reality TV but shows like *Homicide* and *the Wire*. At the end of every episode on NBC's, *Cold Case,* the pale female detective stared wistfully through a linked fence, catching a brief glimpse of the now redeemed spirit, wandering the streets of Philadelphia for justice and a final water ice. Sometimes the murderer is a sicko now in custody or serial killer still on the loose. *Cold Case* was cancelled in 2010 after a good run. In Edgar's episode, I'd be sitting in the Volkswagen parked out front of the Bungalow. He'd wave, brush in hand as he steps inside to listen to Joy Division one last time before dissolving. *She's Lost Control* is a song Ian Curtis wrote about a mental patient.

15
CHAPTER

After two months, *Work Shy* was going great guns. It took shape behind the scenes with Sally's help and Edgar Bloom was beginning to look like an honest-to-god historical figure. Could he become accustomed to the notoriety, albeit late? I hadn't quite decided if *Work Shy* should be a send up but it was going in that direction. Otherwise no one would believe it. I sketched out the book broadly and slowly filled inner parts. All I had to do was create linking passages within the time frame. From behind the din I heard Edgar faintly: *I need a Valium and a scotch.* Or was this my own wishful thinking? I concentrated on the book in earnest while Martha's people fretted over exhibition details. For the catalog, we collected a few photos from Sherrie. This was all part of the intrusive service and an excuse for me to see her again. This may have been disconcerting for her but Kurtz bounced on the couch and yelled, "Uncle Frank is here in Daddy's Car!" That's me. Sherrie's grieving continued through the usual difficult stages – she lost a little weight – but she was already building a new life. There was another guy in the picture, a doctor fellow. I pictured a paunchy surgeon with fusty mustache and thick, frameless spectacles.

I tried to find some pictures from my own collection. They were at my Dad's house outside Washington. I'd have to make another visit over a weekend and fill him in on all the Edgar activities. Frank Senior paused the war movie he was watching. There was a Vietnamese village going up in smoke. "How's that book going, son? Looks like that buddy of yours is going to eclipse you soon." He was catching the *Work Shy* bug.

I groaned, audibly, "Edgar is dead, Dad."

"Quite a ladies man, I hear."

"What are you getting at, Pop?"

"He's an interesting guy. That's all."

"I'd rather be less interesting and alive."

"Can I borrow some of those diaries?"

"No. You cannot. You can wait till they're published like everybody else.

"That's no fun, son."

"You hardly knew him, Dad."

"Yeah, but he left a pretty corpse."

"Can we have a little decorum, Dad?"

"Decorum? That's my word. You must be getting old son."

The seasons changed. After two months of little income and many outgoing expenses my pockets were empty. I reached down for my alpha-man but he was out. While on the phone to Biggs, I nursed a little fire in the fireplace burning some of Edgar's hoarded furniture. There was loads of it. I guess it was not going to get into a sculpture piece. Was this wrong? Biggs said he'd pave the way with Mister Cranston.

My voice rose, "I'm a little over extended and sticking my neck out here, Biggs."

"I'll work my magic, Frank. *Devil Books* is talking about a sizable advance." So was *Deadbeat,* but all were thrown by the impending eBook dilemma. I fancied a bidding war.

"Bookstores are no more!" What to do? Will books survive without Bricks and Mortar? How will publishers get paid? How do you download an eReader?" I don't know. I hate that shit.

Edgar's view: *Digital Fucking Books?*

"*Work Shy* is a complete gamble at this stage. Understand, Mr. Frank? They want your literary pedigree."

My voice rose even more, "I am the creator of fucking, Freddie French for Christ's Sake!"

Biggs put his lover on the phone. Cranston explained some of it, "Don't worry, Mr. Frank. There is a transition taking place. Many of the publishers have cut and run already. You can't argue with progress. They have meetings with lawyers while putting the wagons in a circle. Consult media-gurus. Vacillate." I heard the distant sound of bickering.

Biggs came back on the line, "I figure it'll calm down one way or another. One more tech advance will set the stage. It happens all the time. So hang in there, Mr. Frank."

Edgar's view: *Steve Jobs fucks us up even more. Endless enhancement. Not everyone can write a book. Not everyone can read a book!*

I finished a pretty good timeline by this point. We set up large calendars – 1980 to 1990s – like a 'police procedural' going both ways in time. The two projects paralleled, informing each other. I didn't care so much as long as there was a cold six-pack and some chocolate cake in the fridge. Sally purchased new cartridges from Staples regularly and the printer never stopped churning. The Bloom Archives were in good hands.

16

CHAPTER

The "Bloom" team came together and the Bungalow was headquarters. Martha added a contemporary art specialist to ensure accuracy in that department. "Fewer retractions, that way," she said. Troy Manchild arrived bearing gifts, so nonchalant he seemed to float. He began by handing out over-sized exhibition cards for the newly organized *Post-Historical* show at the museum. Troy was, after all, Assistant Curator of Contemporary Art. He showed up on a skateboard and rode it a block from his car. He was clean-shaven when he shaved. Downright, button-down with slacker hair, longish in front, I had an instant distrust of the endless pop-cultural references related bi-laterally from Anthropology to Art. Luckily, Troy worked out of the museum and would spend little time in the Bungalow. He referred to me as the "Old Hipster." Coming from him, I figured it was a compliment.

Trout also sent in packs of docents (widows of stockbrokers) to keep tabs on Mr. Frank, the writer fellow. These were older, well-spoken women in white turtlenecks and pearls. They loved me and were thrilled to talk about Edgar and myself as a package deal, linked at the navel. Not the Diane Arbus thing again? The Bungalow improvements continued. I hung a few of Edgar's pieces that I came across; my rendition of the infamous Barnes Collection with its erratic mix of fine modern painting, African masks and kitchen tins. They were intriguing to see everyday. Sherrie showed up with a few paintings from early Edgar too. I took a look and suggested she not sell them in a yard sale.

The crew was completed when a tall, handsome young lady called Dion Milroy arrived at the Bungalow. To say she dressed provocatively was missing the point. "Quite a heap, Mr. Frank," she boomed as if we were recently divorced, "Martha said you were a handful." She sat down making sure to show me her legs then proceeded in downing vast amounts of espresso. Dion was the chief designer of exhibitions. The legs were not bad. She brought with her 3D versions of the exhibition space. The interpretative panels we worked on together. Dion streamlined the internet service so she could fend off Trout's micro-management and keep my editor amused. "Email-crazy people."

Forgotten Poets on Facebook?" I asked.

"You bet!"

I frowned. "Geesh."

"Digital Blooming," said Sally shyly and without irony from across the room.

Dion continued, "No social network will be missed for maximum outreach and positive outcome." I stared at her blankly. "You're sincerely behind the times, Mr. Frank."

They both stared at me for a moment and I found a puppy dog voice. "Proud of it."

Big eye-rolls from Dion. "Don't you want to see exhibition highlights on your iPhone?"

"Why, for god's sake? It might cause me to spill my drink." She threw up her hands in defeat. I let the twits tweet, not understanding how the micro-blogging had any affect on anyone. Before the day was out, the Bungalow was teeming with productivity.

My meetings with Trout became numerous but I kept her in the dark about my dealings with Pecker and Finch. I was losing control but when she learned about the real nature of the book, she was thrilled. "This is another aspect to my creation. It will add cachet to the exhibition." I still wasn't sure that the book itself was feasible.

"You don't miss a trick, Martha." After several months she lightened up. She may have realized I was not quite the fool she had thought and Edgar not the convenient lightweight she had imagined. He was her dark horse, a gift from curatorial heaven. She was slumming, literally – not her thing – but this was her baby. It reminded me of the praying mantis problem so several cans of Raid were kept hiding under the sink. She had staked a claim to sole ownership of a new historical moment. Trout was the legitimizing link to the artist's posterity, at least stage one. Back in the 'Museum Squad Room' it was easy to picture Chief Inspector, Martha Trout as my senior officer. She was tough but fair and kept close tabs on me, the department's loose cannon.

"Is this Bloom Case warm or cold, Detective Frank? Is it a case at all?"

I looked at her with all the charm I could muster at 8 A. M. "Very warm indeed, Chief."

"How warm, exactly, Detective?

"Quite warm, you know, warmish, Martha."

She held up her Mona Lisa mug, "As warm as this coffee?"

"I have no idea chief. Who made your coffee?"

"The place around the corner, Java the Hut."

"Well, then it'll be quite warm indeed if not scalding."

"It keeps me awake so I can stay on top of your bullshit."

"I'm glad you have such confidence in me. I won't let you down, Chief."

In real life, I knew she and Cranston were maneuvering behind my back. You see how this is developing? No wriggle room for me. She was determined to ensure ownership of Edgar's story and claim his art resurrection. At this point, I decided I needed an insurance policy. I rang up my old friend, ex-boxer, Jimmy Dee at the Art Museum. He was now head of security. His husky recorded voice said he would get back to me. Not sure if I believed him. I'd been out of touch for a while which was a long time and I needed some info about Trout's set up. Would he be my museum mole? First, I needed to finish up with the cops and the medical professionals.

17

CHAPTER

My phone interviews with doctors confused me. They weren't reticent to divulge sensitive information to a strange voice over the phone. This brought me back to the Police where the Chase Utley bobble head greeted me. He was humming his awesome Led Zeppelin theme song, *Kashmir*. It played when Utley approached home plate at Citizens' Bank Park, a sublime moment when anthemic music overlapped gleefully with sport. I showed up unannounced at the Quadrangle. Pecker was not busy. "You are like a bad penny, Mr. Frank."

"Meaning?"

"Meaning, you are a pain in my ass."

"I know that Pecker."

"Sergeant Pecker, to you."

"What should I do about this dead guy I'm looking into? I need your help."

"You're yanking my chain aren't you?"

"Gosh. I wouldn't wanna do that, Pecker. I'm stuck."

"I suggested you contact Dr. Susan Wong. Have you done that yet?"

"Yeah. I found voice ghettos and emergency numbers."

"So you didn't get through at all?"

"I guess so. Not exactly."

"What are you looking for, exactly?"

"I just want to know if Edgar was as fucked up as you seem to think."

"You would know better than me. Bloom didn't even have any cough syrup in his cabinet. If that is what you mean? Not even a poppy seed bagel."

"You mean like *Robitussin?*"

"Yeah, you know, like the drug used to make worse drugs. *Nyquil* and whatever. Knocks me out when I have a cold. I like the purple one best."

"And what about bagels?"

"Poppies. You have heard of that. It's an opiate. C'mon, Mr. Frank. What century do you live in? I think it's the way Jews medicate."

"Edgar was an artist not a drug addict."

"Can't he be both?"

"Not in this case."

"And why not exactly?"

"I just don't buy it."

"Then you're a sucker, Mr. Frank."

"Thanks, That helps a lot, man." I gritted my teeth and turned to go. "You should study up on Judaism, Pecker."

He watched my retreating glutimus. "Sergeant Picard to you." He then went back to his paperwork deep in thought. "Not a bad behind for an asshole." Chase nodded over and over.

The Pathology Department was in the Whitmore Building, a non-descript stump of twelve floors named after Sidney Whitmore, physicist and funder. Dr. Susan Wong was a sympathetic Pathologist with the bedside humor of an undertaker not unknown amongst Medical Examiners. Her office was downstairs and had a strange smell of spirits. There was a calendar of cats wearing doctor clothes on the back of her door. She was about as tall as my armpits and got right down to business. "We may have to dig up your friend."

I looked at her impassive face and dropped my pencil. "You gotta be kidding! You want to dig up Edgar to rule out funny business? It's a bit late."

Still impassive, "It's never too late."

"How do we do that?"

"With a shovel, I suspect." She was expecting me to laugh. "Not funny? We need just cause, Mr. Frank."

"Such as what?" I asked.

"An anomaly. Something not adding up. Ask Finch. It was his case. And Dr. Klingon was not convinced."

"Not much of a case, they told me. I just came from there. Routine stuff, according to Pecker."

"His real name is Peter Picard. It's French. We seem to have a *Star Trek Next Generation* thing going here."

"Interesting, Susan. You mean Klingon and Picard? I think of him as Pecker." I said. "He did all the ground work."

Wong told me to go back to the shrink and take yes for an answer. "Ask Klingon about the antics of ADHD folks. Manic behavior caused not by meds or chemical imbalance but by social factors. Edgar may have been reacting to outside pressures, drugs or no drugs. It's complicated. Call me when you find out."

"Thanks, Susan." I said, shaking my head. Her laugh trailed off as I scooted through the green halls to the push sign on the door. Sunshine greeted my face and a cold breeze. "Wong number!" I giggled. It never gets old.

I walked down a few blocks of University City to Edgar's psychiatrist – all doctors are clustered in West Philly. Not as heavy as Susan Wong, Dr. Klingon looked a bit like Leonard Nimoy tucked away on the sixteenth floor. He sat Buddha-like at his desk at Drexel surrounded by books on sexual deviancy and African masks. I admired the scene as I entered. "Thanks for seeing me Doctor."

"Please take a seat, Mr. Frank."

I sat like a neurotic patient across the coffee table from the shrink, "You have quite a collection here. I feel like I'm in the Congo."

"I'm a big auction goer."

"Klingon? Is that Jewish? Spock is Jewish."

He rubbed his beard. "I get that a lot. He's Vulcan, actually." he said. "I find it amusing."

"Shatner was Jewish too, for that matter."

"Of course. Everyone knows that. You're Jewish too, I take it?"

"Only on my Mother's side."

"The only side that counts."

I told him I knew a woman in college named Klingon.

"That is fascinating, Mr. Frank."

"She was in textiles. She told me that's where the Star Trek alien name came from. Her father was a scriptwriter in LA."

"Interesting factoid. I can't confirm or deny. My background is European. Our name family was Americanized from something difficult to pronounce."

I returned to business. "So about my friend Edgar."

"I'm not sure I can help you. Edgar Bloom's case, all the files are confidential."

My lie expanded, "I respect that fact but this isn't going into a book or anything Doctor Klingon. It is a family matter."

Dr. Klingon gave me a shrinky look, "I really couldn't care if it was but I'll give you a brief run down. Mr. Bloom was creative and clearly suicidal. That doesn't mean anything. A lot of people walk around thinking about ending it. Diazepam was a good try. It's trendy but not effective without other help. According to the notes I have here, he was self-medicating and drinking a lot. His death might be called suspicious. At least unusual, I'd say."

"That's nothing I didn't know. The cops are unconvinced."

Klingon sat back in his seat, "That's not surprising."

I leaned forward and tried another line of questioning. "Politics aside, what did you think of him, Doctor?"

He wasn't listening. "There was an autopsy performed, it says here."

I dropped my pencil and leaned in further towards his papers, "You're kidding me?"

He leaned back further. "No. I'm not. May 12, 2006 at Chestnut Hill Hospital"

Still surprised, I asked, "Did his wife know?"

"Could be. Go ask Detective Finch if he authorized it or if the State wanted one."

"I thought you did that. He didn't mention it when I spoke to him. Neither did Wong."

"It would normally be up to Wong and the investigators. They had no reason to inform you. You're just a family friend."

"Well, I'm more than that, in fact. I'm a pain in the ass."

"I can see that, Mr. Frank." He continued. "Edgar was thwarted on all fronts. Psychic episodes. Not surprising. Creative right-brainers are often ADHD and a little spaced out.

"Spaced Out? That sounds highly technical, Doctor."

The doctor laughed. "You got me, Mr. Frank. Space cadets who are always flitting from one topic to the next. Edgar was paranoid about some things. There is a lot of that going around too. Mild delusions in a digital world. Heads in clouds."

"Interesting. 'Spaced out, space cadets.' Sounds like Timothy Leary."

The doctor reminded me. "Timothy Leary's dead."

I smiled. "Just because Edgar was paranoid, doesn't mean he wasn't being followed. Can you tell me what medication you prescribed specifically?"

"Of course. Diazepam and Prozac. Routine low doses. Ritalin for ADHD didn't work for him. He was on the spectrum, I figure. Edgar was hearing voices or as he told me, 'seeing ghosts.'"

"Seeing ghosts? That's common too, is it?

"No, certainly not. That is delusionary. Seeing things. You don't see things do you?"

"Ask Gladys."

"Who?"

"Long story. I see ghosts all the time. Artistic license for writers."

Klingon eyed me. "Are you serious? Ghosts of whom?" He leaned in, unsmiling. "You should make an appointment for yourself on the way out."

I stood up. "I'll think about it. Thank you, Doctor.

"Mr. Frank?"

I looked back from the door. "You don't look like a newspaperman."

"Thanks. You've made my day."

"And you weren't kidding were you?"

"About what?"

"You really are a pain in the ass." I smiled my best 'pain in the ass' smile and shut the door.

As I left I scanned the waiting room and checked my cell. Nothing new from the Bungalow. Several patients were pacing. A short young man with a shaved head was counting backwards from ten down over and over. There was a fine art print on the wall that was nicely framed but badly cropped. I pegged it as the American painter Marsden Hartley due to the signature Iron Cross. It was painted for a lost lover in the Great War, a German fighter pilot. Strange choice for a psychiatric waiting room.

I called Wong back. No answer. I tried Detective Finch from the car. He was not waiting for my call but he picked up. "Detective Jack Finch. Talk to me."

"Not, Arnold? Detective Jack *Arnold* Finch?

"No, Arnold Fitzgerald Finch, Mr. Frank. I dropped the Jack. There was a pause. "Who gave you this number?"

"You did. I have been to see the doctors."

"Look, I'm busy, pal. This was an overdose. Simple. You're friend was a junkie, a near homeless guy. No Brainer."

"You think so, don't you?"

"Stop busting my ball guy. You've seen Wong?"

"Yeah, briefly but Klingon says there was an autopsy."

"This is none of your business. Look, there was no evidence of a crime so why an autopsy? Probable suicide."

"Detective, why would you order an autopsy normally?"

"Because cause of death needs to be determined. Normal procedure. Is it drugs, gunshot, heart attack, stroke, something else? We didn't ask for it."

"You didn't?"

He paused. "Could have been the wife."

"Sherrie Bloom?"

"That's her. Pretty lady."

"Yes, she is. You've seen her? When was that?"

"That's all I got, Mr. Frank. Get on with your life."

He disconnected and I looked out the window onto Market. "Thanks, Kojak."

I called Sally next before setting off and asked her to set up cocktail hour. "Our favorite time of day, Mr. Frank."

"Is Gladys around?"

"No. Who's Gladys?"

"Gladys is the ghost of a previous owner of the bungalow and I was keeping that fact to myself mostly." "Haven't seen her. How was Wong? A character, eh?" That summed it up. I told her I'd be back soon.

I took the fast way home on 76. It was a beautiful day and I felt the need to smell the roses. Down on the Schuylkill there was one solitary rower. It could have been Tom Eakins but it was too far away to tell. I got off at Manayunk and headed up a steep hill. My mind didn't stop churning the whole way back to the bungalow.

Sally met me at the door. "Drinks are ready."

"God bless you."

"You must be enjoying this Mr. Frank?"

"Enjoying what?"

"This is 'Marlowe' territory."

"Oh, yeah. Did you know there was an autopsy?"

"God, no! That's terrible. Is it terrible? You're pulling my leg. What does it mean?"

"I'm not pulling your leg. Klingon told me. I guess it means Edgar wasn't merely partying or checking out of his own accord. It wasn't done at Wong's facility."

"So what does that add up to?"

"I figure somebody out there is looking for the truth or trying to cover it up." We sipped our drinks both deep in thought.

18
CHAPTER

Sometime afterward in the Blue House, Sherrie sat reading aloud from an Edgar journal dated November 1998. She looked up and faced me at her kitchen table looking concerned. "You're sweating, Frank"

"Yes I am, Sherrie. Women overheat their houses."

"Are you nervous?"

"Not particularly."

"Are you sick?"

"Don't think so."

Sherrie put her index finger up to pursed lips. Her brain was beginning to stir. "I have a few questions for you." I stared back calmly waiting. "This is interesting stuff and I don't get it. *The Outsider and The Spectacle?*"

"How can I help?" Sherrie had studied Illustration. Illustrators don't need theory. That was before she became a nurse. Nurses don't need it either. We continued, "Yeah, crucial ideas, Sherrie."

"I missed the Eighties, Frank. I was a child. Tell me why do artists need to read all this bewildering philosophical material?"

I shrugged. "So we can feel superior."

"This stuff about *The Other* is disquieting." Sherrie's mother was a DAR and always prided themselves in their divine privilege.

"We all aspire to be *The Outsider* in some way, but we are the opposite. Artists pretend and still feel superior. It's a conundrum."

"You are smothered by *The Other*."

I blushed, a little offended. "That's a good one, Sherrie."

Sherrie read some more: *My lovely, wife. Where would I be without her? Born in 1975!* She paused and choked up then burst into tears. (I was not catching her on the rebound was I?) I may be thick, but you'd think Edgar's death would have brought an end to the relationship? I hugged her shoulders lightly and she looked up at me. "He really cared about you no matter how it ended." Tears fell on the notebook. Aw, heck! Bloom's shadow was growing. Could I keep her out of this mess?

Sherrie cheered up quickly and opened some wine. "Tell me more about this Silvio." Kurtz was asleep and we sat on opposite ends of the sofa.

"I steered him through many a cold night. He was trouble but he added comic relief to seminars."

"Go on."

"Silvio was Glaswegian of Italian ancestry and wore a trilby with a thrift shop suit several sizes too small."

"I know the type," she said. "Seen them in movies."

"I'm not sure you have." I gave her an example of symposium banter using a smattering of poor British accents: "Students would complain, whining, 'I don't get it. What do you mean Professor Mito?' He would respond with illuminating silence. Walter, the art nerd, replied, frustrated, 'What does Wittgenstein have to do with it?' Mito would not connect the dots – perhaps he couldn't – only ask more questions."

"What an asshole."

Silvio picked on Walter continually. "What is it that makes you love Sir Claude Levi-Strauss so much?"

Walter couldn't defend himself, "He's pivotal. Levi Strauss's theory on social, I mean his view. Tribalism and societal structure…"

"Yeah, sure. I get it now," mocked the Glaswegian. Poor Walter. He meant well. "Levi-Strauss? What do blue jeans have to do with it?"

Levi-Strauss got that a lot. Sherrie laughed, "I get the joke, Mr. Frank. I'm not stupid."

I was interested to read Edgar's personal perspective on the MFA at Northwoods. Here, I could fill in gaps and Sam could verify. He wrote a little about me. Now, I was returning the favor! My subject and I both wondered why grad school was such a defining moment. There were lots of Brits at Northlands – ahead of the curve – all smoking thin, tobacco roll-ups – on generous freebie scholarships. I found out why they were so snobby; they were way more tuned in. This bunch of Anglo-Saxons and Celts were not the privileged class like the sort we'd run into at the British Academy in Rome. Quite the opposite. We partied with them and exchanged records. Edgar dug the whole thing. He dyed his hair black.

Northwoods: I'm the Jewish Sid Vicious. Snarky. That's the British word for the day. Snarky. I'm snarky. It's like chutzpah but snarkier.

Despite the accent barrier, Silvio was Mito's favorite son. He sat next to him so they could spar verbally and create solidarity and discord. *They are both after our womenfolk.* Silvio does all right there, to our chagrin. They hung out together in college bars with their respective, underclass flames.

"Mito was divorced."

Sherrie wanted more. "This is getting juicy, Frank."

I obliged. "Silvio's main squeeze was Karina, sexy New Yorker into punk. They were attached at the hip but had an open relationship which meant they were free to attach themselves to other people's hips."

"Mr. Frank. You have such a way with words." We left it there for the evening. As I drove off, I thought maybe this history stuff should be kept schtum for Edgar's sake.

19

CHAPTER

Abhoud and Pecker stopped at StarBuzz before returning to base. Their conversation continued. "You like *Pulp Fiction*?"

"Yeah, I guess."

"The "Burger" scene."

"Which one, the Royale?"

"That's a euphemism."

"For what?"

"Just a euphemism." They sat silently after she came back with the Captain's brew. "Abhoud, you're a lesbian right?" Abhoud felt like she's been slapped in the face and sat with clenched fists, shocked. Her stomach lurched. Pecker continued, "Well, you know I'm gay. I was just thinking we could patrol together and you know. We'd make a great team. Great partners."

Abhoud stared straight out the windshield gritting her teeth. It took a moment to form words that she delivered in a monotone holding back rage. "You're fucked up, Pecker!"

"People say that. Let's get this back to the Captain. He hates cold coffee." As Picard drove, Abhoud fingered her Glock wondering how far she'd get if she popped him there and then. One carefully placed round. Boof. No one would notice. They returned to the Quad without further conversation.

The next day, Abhoud sat angrily at her desk. Pecker joined the Captain for tea at four for an update on me. "Frank's been busy, Captain."

"You and Ahboud have a fight, Pecker?"

"A disagreement, Captain"

"She says you came on to her. She texied me from her phone."

"Oh no, I merely suggested we become the Gay Squad of the Police Department."

"Wow. What a great notion, a gay-Arab initiative. Does she speak Muslim?"

"You mean Arabic, Cap. All Muslims aren't Arabs."

"Oh, you sure? That confuses me. Anyway, you are such a great cop Pecker, very modern, very PC. Gay Arab Investigating Team! G-A-I-T. That'll be popular. Don't ask me to tell."

"Don't ask, don't tell. What did she text?"

"Something short. She used textie letters WTF. What does that mean? Wed, Thurs, Friday?"

"It is profanity, Captain." The dialogue at the Quad continued all day sometimes without much work going on.

"How many homosexuals out there you figure, Pecker?"

"Thousands. Some still in a closet. Ten percent of the population. Got a problem with that Captain? Twenty percent are sociopaths."

"I dunno. No, no. I find it curious. We used to crucify them for some reason."

"Using 'faggots' or bundled sticks. You do know I'm gay, Captain?"

"Of course, Pecker. So was Sulu on Star Trek, but we are friends. He has a great voice. That's different. I'm not a bigot."

"I see your point. You are being frank with a friend."

"Ha ha, yes, frank." They laughed at the word.

"Oh yeah, Mr. Frank, our present nemesis."

A moment passed. Pecker broke the silence. "Are you implying you are jealous of gay men?"

"Absolutely. Nobody told me life would be like this. It came as a shock. But I figure most of them don't take to crime. Besides where would I be without your sartorial advice? You offer me some great fashion ideas. Before you, I was a fat ugly bigot. Now, I got style. Not ghetto style either. Real style."

"Johnny Carson style."

"Johnny Carson style? I like it!"

"I feel outnumbered sometimes. Emasculated."

"If you ever become surface to requirements, I will miss you."

"I'm at your service boss, day or night. If I ever become 'suffice' to requirements you mean."

"What? You said surface."

"Yeah, Surface to requirements. That is wrong; it should be suffice to requirements. You're a misanthrope."

"What did you call me, gay boy?"

"A misanthrope. That is somebody who uses words wrong."

"I thought a misanthrope was some rich guy who gave to charities."

"No captain that is Philanthropy, like Andrew Carnegie."

"I've heard of him, Rubber Baron. He was also a philanderer."

"You got that right, Captain Finch. A philanderer from Philadelphia. Everyone lived in Philadelphia; John Coltrane and Billie Holiday."

Finch sat back, smiled and cleverly changed the subject. "Oh and thanks for the suspenders you gave me last week for *Love My Boss Day*. They are fab."

"You look great in those. It's true, if I don't say so myself."

"Next advice from you involves my man cave. My daughters have insisted. I need a new soap dish."

"You're kidding, Captain. A grown man looking for a soap dish?"

"Yeah. Sounds ridiculous. Philip Marlowe never shopped for a soap dish. But these are different days. Everything has to say style, manly style. I don't mind telling you I have been having a hell of a time finding the right one."

"Try *Bread, Bath and Beyond*."

"Is that a store?"

"On the force we call it *Bloodbath and Beyond*!"

"That's a good one, Pecker. I'll have to remember that."

"I hope you do."

The policemen looked out the window. "So tell me Sergeant, what's our Mr. Frank up to this week?"

20

CHAPTER

Sherrie eyed me suspiciously as if I were pulling her leg. "Semiotics, eh?" I wish I had been pulling her leg. "I don't get it at all. How does the science of signs relate to the arts?"

"Yeah?" Our discussions continued. "How much time do you have, Sherrie?

"Who are these Semioticians?"

"They have an answer for everything."

"Who put them in charge?"

"Not sure. French intellectuals I think and Communists."

"And then there are tropes? Like tight ropes?"

"I agree. It rhymes with grope."

"It's cumbersome word, Mr. Frank."

"I told you this might take some time." She didn't mind. "Let's try again. It started with architecture and the Bauhaus in Europe. Modern architecture led to Post-Modern turning over the former. Now, it's a free for all. There is nowhere else to go. This led to McMansions and really crappy skyscrapers everywhere. Third hand Brutalist architecture."

"I'm not sure I'm taking all this in. Though, McMansions are ugly."

"My method is to just let it drift by and hope some of it sticks."

"That sounds like a plan."

Academic critics started with literary tropes. Then theorists and artists caught on. Tropes about art categories: German Expressionism, Color Field.

It expanded to include any sphere of similar attributes. Fighter pilots or breakfast food. Filmic tropes: Cowboys or Boxing. Genres, basically; as in Science Fiction. *Ever noticed how many movies start with a jet landing at an airport? Sets the scene. Stranger in town. Fish out of water.* Nowadays, we mix and match, overlapping them. "How many tropes can fit in any given paradigm? Get it?"

Sherrie sipped her wine almost listening. "Give them enough trope."

"Ha ha. Are you referencing the Clash album?"

"What? I never liked the Clash."

"You know what I'm referring to though?"

"You bet I do."

The seminar readings came from one insular book, Lucy Lippard's *Changing, Essays in Art Criticism.* This was 1983 and these earlier texts (copyright 1971) were read by post-grads in MFA programs. It later clicked in college development offices that MFA courses could be big money spinners. Every college now has one. *Ripper offers.* No way around it. The next compendium, *Art After Modernism* came in 1984. The first one of its type is still well-known, Hal Foster's *Anti-Aesthetic* from 1983. I now use *The Visual Culture Reader* from 1999. It includes many of the same seminal essays. My favorite remains the one by Walter Benjamin. All contained the building blocks of contemporary thought. This was before all this morphed inexplicably into the generalized and bogus "Critical Thinking" and students ended up with mountains of debt.

Don't leave the house without it!. Develop your work. Get your MFA. After lack of success, work your way back into teaching, something you decry. Is that a loop? Tautologically Speaking?? MFA from the University of Detroit? It's a contradiction, art as a moneyspinner, isn't it? Evade the pitfalls of the Working World. Motor City kills itself, news at eleven. Some places hold more weight, like Yale, same as in the real world where back room deals are made.

Ever since *Blade Runner,* (SF-slash-Detective story), cinema-wise, there has been a specificity about pigeonholing genres, crossed genres, multiple genres and brand new genres never conceived before. Of course, all this theoretical discourse goes deep but never achieves any purchase on the "Big Plateau." That is what Edgar called Debord's *"Spectacle."* Full title: *Society of the Spectacle.* The surface reflects image upon image racing to the horizon. *A carnival flat earth mirror.* There is no original.

"We stupidly call this media."

She looked at me. "That makes sense in a crazy way. It is on the Left and Right."

"Wow. Yes, you got it, Sherrie! This is quickly diluted as it leaves the academy and is subsumed by the mainstream. Made tidy and digestible into binaric political opposition. Coded language and signs." My mind rushed ahead and sensed the end was near.

"Binary?"

"Yeah. Left vs. Right. Black and White. Up and Down. It's simplistic. After twenty years, it finds itself discoursed away. A several headed monster swallowing itself without ever peeking over the parapet. Joseph K. Truck Driver doesn't care about Umberto Eco or Roland Barthes just as Edgar Bloom didn't give a shit about NFL quarterbacks."

"Or contemporary Pop."

Yeah, Sherrie. He hated new crappy music."

Post critique: Walter is an idiot and makes frustratingly anal art with no punch or reason to exist. Are these things mutually exclusive? What's your best bet? Northlands University? Give me process baby, but make it mean something! Old Hippy doesn't know what he is talking about! "Levi-Strauss said this…. So, I do it this way." I can see clearly now. Greek Myth is nothing. Freud, nothing. Fuck Oedipus!

Edgar anchored himself in one art period after another. He'd always liked neo-expressionist stuff depicting biplanes, iron crosses and machine guns. World War One was cool. Afterwards, it was World War Two. Is he ten years old? That's why he loved talking to my Dad. Dad would get out the purple hearts and his service revolver. "I'd just taken out Hans and Fritz with my mortar crew, right through a barn door. Good aim, if I don't say so myself." Yes, he knew the names of the Germans he killed. "Then some shrapnel from a Tiger Tank caught me in the shin. I was jumping for cover under a tree. Nice Shot by Maxwell the Hun. Killed all my buddies. The tank swivels on its treads to aim rather than turning the turret. It was a lot faster. Clever Nazi Bastards"

"Then what happened, Mr. Frank?" asked my friend.

"Two P-48's appeared outta nowhere and blew them to hell. Turret blasted into the air. They should have spent more money on those Nazi jets they were experimenting with. Doug, have you seen my dog-tags?" They were in the kitchen drawer. "They have a Star of David on them, a guaranteed firing squad for us. I gotta tinkle, anyway." I suggested he spare Edgar the details about the last part of the Battle of the Bulge.

"Check my website for more, Eddie, BattleoftheBulge.com," My old man ambled out of the room. We heard utensils being chucked about.

On the drive home, I pictured winter-camouflaged Tiger Tanks attacking the Maryland highway system. "The Germans wore white and you wore grey, Edgar"

"I see what you're doing there, *Casablanca*." Edgar discussed his new work: *tank tracks in snow, beautiful use of whites.* These musings show up in MFA journal, *Das ist mein Panzervankampfwagen! Dynamic visuals.* I visualized a big bloody, snow-scene like out of *Patton*. A great role for George C. Scott, damn it. My dad interpreted for us, paraphrasing, "Nobody wins a war by getting killed for his country, Frank. You win a war by killing the other dumb bastard."

"I hear you, Dad."

"Yes. Mr. Frank senior." I needed to leave.

We drove north and Edgar described the pictures. "Whites, shiny black metal, greys and pinks and just a tiny smear of crimson."

"Sounds lovely. Didn't he get an Oscar for the role?"

"Mr. Scott? Yes. He killed Germans, won the war and got an Oscar for the effort." Edgar blabbed and fiddled with radio knobs. "Can't get the New York stations yet. Strangely enough, after all that, he died in a car crash."

"Who? Patton or George C. Scott?"

"Patton, you idiot."

I nodded looking for the on-ramp.

CHAPTER

It was a steam room on the top floor of Speck Hall's pointed tower. Harry Potter was not yet born. After removal of clothing, down to paint-splattered tee-shirts, we gathered round the table and read our clumsy responses to *Changing's* insistent text. The essay was called *Perverse Perspectives*. It was art-specific and fuck you if you didn't get it.

"Are you ready Sherrie?"

"There's more?"

"I shall paraphrase so as not to be sued."

"That's a relief."

"Basically these artist dudes in the Sixties and Seventies reject all painterly and post-painterly tenets."

Sherrie's eyes had glazed over, "Yeah, tell me about it."

Was she mocking me? I continued to man-explain, "If you painted, you needed a good reason and a solid concept."

"Like Anarchy?" Sherrie chuckled.

"You're cute when you're stupid!"

Sherrie fluttered her eyelashes my way. "Damn straight."

Edgar mused from a book: *Art boils down to a Minimalist Ghetto with no real relevance! What's the point?*

Other essays introduced me to a whole category of the esoteric for the sake of it. *Let the namedropping begin.* Lippard's essay went on to mention McLuhan,

Robbe-Grillet, Wittgenstein and Beckett to name a few. McCluhan wrote *The Medium is the Massage*. The book is not called, *The Medium is the Message* like most people think. It is misquoted perpetually out of sheer laziness or to avoid the crappy pun. Other cognoscenti were mentioned as an aside as if it was all common knowledge. It's a step up from standard undergrad use of *Ways of Seeing,* John Berger's book on contemporary culture. This was Media 101. *Ways of Seeing* got used as a primer to introduce some basic ideas about technology and art. This was ripped off from Walter Benjamin's *Art in the Age of Mechanical Reproduction.* Nothing is original anymore thanks to mass production. Media studies about TV and Newspapers were now entirely old hat. Art and its theoretical base expanded dynamically to attempt to replace philosophy itself.

Tuesday: The White Box! Donald Judd is god! Hyperbolic Nonsense. Nothing visual about it.

Edgar's animosity took several forms. He threw snide barbs the professor's way (and a few cigarette butts) and made up inane and illogical narratives to confuse the issue.

Silvio defended the teacher. "Edgar is a silly boy."

"Go back to Glasgow."

"Lend us a fag, will ya?"

"They're Marlboro's."

"That'll do me fine."

"Gentlemen, please!" Mito absorbed any criticism without emotion saving up ammunition for a final scathing word. Not so the MFA students:

"Shut the fuck up guys. We want to hear about *Perverse Perspectives.*"

"And please stop coming to class drunk!" All were vigorously trying to discover their path and make it relevant to their personal stories. Not pretty. This was the purpose of a graduate degree. Find your niche.

Dec. 14, '84: My barracks studio: I am Native American. My parents are divorced. I am a Black Vietnam Vet from Detroit. I am a Lesbian from Lisbon. Armenian is family. Walter Chekov, an Intellectual!? Not really. Mito is half Japanese. That's a cool band's name. My legacy? Banal Whitebread.

Is anyone outside the art and academic scenarios aware of this? No. This is where the responsibility of privilege comes in although it doesn't really look like privilege. Growing up in the suburbs is equivalent to growing up in a small town without any of the good things. Edgar grew up a mere 30 miles from New York City and had no idea! Minimal art happened when he was ten; the Empire State Building visible only at night. The very top was green for St Paddy's Day, red for Christmas and blue for July 4th. Even higher, seen from New Jersey, the tops of the Trade Center Towers sent messages to space. After watching the city's glow, Edgar spent hours looking at a super thick book on Van Gogh. He figured he could do that – Van Gogh – minus the insanity part. Minimal art? That made no sense.

NJ, 1982: There is no emotive traction. I've always admired the ear lobe given to a pretty prostitute story. There is a theory that Gauguin cut the ear off with his saber. Drunken Bastard. What does a post-impressionist need with a saber?

After this section, I went back to the prologue for the exhibition. Looking for that right quote from the artist. I figured it might come from the Northwood's episode, but no. It needed a later period.

I feel like Syphilis pushing that damned rock up a mountain. Yeah, I may have the name wrong but I know who Camus is. He wrote The Stranger. It inspired Killing an Arab, a song by the Cure. Not my favorite, but not bad. An unhappy bloke, Camus was no phoney, as Salinger would say. Camus makes Holden Caufield look downright cheery.

The evening wore on. Sherrie stirred, "He didn't have syphilis, did he?"

"Of course not."

"That's comforting. He *was* my husband."

"The questions raised by the theory made us mad for work. We did not want to think after the saturation point. Shoot from the hip sorta."

Sherrie made a gun out of her hand and blew sexy smoke at my forehead. "Gotcha."

I forged ahead, "Ha ha," and I tried to explain the massive task presented to us. "Superiority was not merely an intellectual battle though it started to be at that point. Rosalyn Krauss and *October Magazine* were a must read." I glanced at the clock. It was 2 am. Sherrie had nodded off. Unable to drive a mile, I stretched out on the couch and dozed with a notebook on my chest. Sometime after that I was trying to piss in a whisky bottle. There was a crucifix attached on the bottom inside. My dream thoughts must have been an attempt to criticize organized religion.

Kurtz was on me first thing in the morning. "Did you sleep with Mommy last night?" I began coughing and could not stop. Sherrie was brewing coffee and making eggs.

She yelled from the kitchen, "I want to hear more about Silvio."

"Who's Silvero?" asked Kurtz. I was still coughing. Kurtz ran to the kitchen then came in slowly with a brimming mug. "Did he have Siffilus?" I drank and spat it up, still coughing. The mug came from the Rodin Museum and had an image of *The Thinker* thinking on it.

"Come eat some scrambled eggs, Frank." I sat at the table with Kurtz.

"I like scrabbled eggs!" said the boy. "He was Skottish!"

"Was who Scottish, Kurtz?"

"You know who!" he said through food.

He was then gone. "Do you like the scrabbled eggs, Frank?"

"I like them very much scrambled."

I had to resist putting my hand on Sherrie's across the table. For ten seconds we enjoyed the coffee. Kurtz appeared in little boy clothes and Sherrie brought an end to our domestic morning, "Time for school, you little monster." We put Kurtz on the bus and I heard violins as I walked over to the Bungalow. Wage slaves were revving their engines and heading off to WaWa for watery coffee. A couple of stray pit pulls inspected the trash. One of them had four legs.

At the bungalow, Sally was waiting out front with arms folded. She looked me over suspiciously, "Where's the bug?"

"Right here. Out front."

"But you aren't in it."

"The battery was flat."

The judgmental moment passed. "Back to work, Mr. Frank?"

"Yes, boss," I said. "Have you seen any mention of VD in the journals, Sally?"

"No. But I'll cross reference the data base if you like. Tell me what year and I'll check."

"Who's next on my visitation list, Sally?"

"Martha Stewart."

22

CHAPTER

My visit with Terry Stark was short. To get to the front door, I drove through the fanciful Medieval arch of her stone mansion beyond Chestnut Hill and maneuvered around two brand new Land Rovers. Despite her Martha Stewart looks she made no offer of refreshments or fresh flowers. We sat in her living room that was decorated in Hi-Tech Bourgeois, huge flat-screen and a large, modular sectional sofa in a tasteful dark beige. The side of the room by the bay window held a desk with a very streamlined computer set up and outmoded fax. An ergonomic chair protruding. Conventional art was here and there with a nod to the Hudson River School (repros) and the more affordable New Hope, PA impressionists. Yuk. She shook her head, "We'll have to make this brief, Mr. Frank. I have an appointment with Lord Williams in Chestnut Hill. He is putting up the rates on his properties again and stores are folding. I'm going to stage several of them."

She sat in the sofa chair and motioned me to the couch. "That sucks, Terry. I heard he owns half the Hill."

"Ha ha. That's the truth."

"I can only afford Mt. Airy. Lower Chestnut Hill, I call it."

She faked a laugh. "That's a good one, Mr. Frank. How nice for you."

"I think I saw you at the funeral."

"Yes, I felt obligated. He was an employee. Very sad."

"What was your relationship with Mr. Bloom?

"Relationship with Edgar? Well, he was on my staff for a short while if that's what you mean." She paused uncomfortably, "Excuse me, but this is odd. I thought you said you were writing a book."

"Yes, I am. About Edgar's life. This is called research."

"Research into his previous employers?"

"That's right. In order to understand him more fully. I want to create a picture of the man and his art."

"Can't you do that online like everybody else?"

"Yeah, sure, Terry. But I like meeting people."

She stood up. "Well, you sound like a cop."

I stayed seated. "Some people say that. It must be my personality. I'm trying to decipher the social nature of Edgar's demise. Police are positive it was self-induced because of his mental state."

"And you don't abide by this theory?"

"No. Not really."

Both her eyes bulged beyond comfortable size. "Well, this is highly awkward, whoever you think you are. I think you should take this to my lawyer and not waste my time.

I stood and looked at her pretending I was a little afraid. "Your lawyer? Is that necessary?"

"I'm thinking, yes. I have a brand to protect."

"You didn't know Edgar would end up dead shortly after his stint with you."

"Of course not. Are you crazy? What difference does it make?"

"Why was he fired, if you don't mind me asking?"

"I do mind. We let him go because he could be infuriating and anal-retentive. Some of the clients complained." She ventured out of her comfort zone. "He was a peach compared to you if you don't mind me saying."

"No leeway given for artistic license?"

She laughed a confident laugh and started to lead me to the door. "I'm a Business Woman, Mr. Frank, not a charity."

I pretended to laugh. "That's a good one. But you have to admit it didn't end well."

"Not my business. Not my problem. Are we done here?"

"Yes, we are definitely finished."

She opened the door. "You will no doubt find my Lawyer's name online. Good Luck." As I exited I noticed a small, framed painting in the foyer that looked like late-Bloom.

As usual, I went back to the diaries to check what was really going on. Quik-Fix started out well making maximum use of the latest trends in house ownership. House-staging was born because people didn't stay put very long. If they did, their home needed a complete makeover. Sometimes full gutting. This became lucrative. The first decade of the Third Millennium was high times for building companies and people in the housing trade not to mention Silicon Valley. The world produced shoddy materials for our consumption at a vigorous rate. Outside Philadelphia all the way to Lancaster, Pa. McMansions scattered themselves over the once rolling farmland like Monopoly Hotels. Amish Country was sucked into Edge City. According to *Edge City*, a trendy book, the metropolis declined and the suburbs transformed into office blocks. Commuting was lateral, not in and out of cities, so public transport was useless. 4 x 4's everywhere. Unsustainability. Oddly enough, the Amish (stuck in a 19th century time warp) didn't mind living in split-levels after turning off the mains. You call that progress? I don't. Amish Slums? They should live in very old houses without electricity or toilets. A house should reflect the neurotic lives of the owner. Quik-Fix would sometimes make their own bids on homes, approaching the owners discreetly. Oddly, Terry Stark would send Edgar in undercover to try and make an early assessment. This suited him because he loved old buildings and arcane stuff. Of course, Edgar's many jobs seemed to fit at first only to sour later. That was a cycle he could not avoid. His therapist (prior to Klingon) finally decided it was ADHD. This didn't surprise Edgar but answered many questions about his attention span. He was assured it was an artist's "thing."

The sum of my interviews was starting to cause anxiety. One disastrous narrative. Quik-Fix became another. Although it paid for alcohol and rent, it was no fun for Edgar. Imagine being depressed, divorced and downwardly mobile while clearing filthy basements with no air circulation. Though, sometimes he'd discover something rare in the rubbish. It might take the form of an archaic bottle opener. Edgar had a collection of many featuring logos of local sports teams. They are on the "Bloom Shelf" at the Dominion with other memorabilia awaiting a visit to Antiques Roadshow. For nasty grunt work, cleaning greasy kitchen and bathrooms, Terry hired Latinos. When they were sick, she gave the job to Edgar. Small fix-it jobs he loved: painting trim, glazing windows or plastering small holes in hundred-year old walls but a cleaning assignment was not his thing. "Down on my knees in the muck." The Peruvians took care of cleaning the grimy kitchens and terrifying bathrooms. Vile Work. They did a great job sometimes using vinegar and toothbrushes. Spotlessness! If Edgar was lucky, he'd get the opportunity to collate family heirlooms he'd find in the trash. Other items were destined for the dumpster. Some days he'd be left to clear out an attic on his own. Edgar would dig into a trunk and pull out an old man's hat. It was fated to fit him perfectly. Sure enough, he would soon be hearing the compliment, "Nice hat," from the natives of Germantown. It became an unfinished song, "Dead Man's Hat." I found the lyrics in a box. *Gladys loves the hat. Says I look like Malcolm X.* Malcolm X? If he'd thought about it, Edgar might have gone into the vintage clothing business, seriously. He had a sense of style and color. Or was he was better off without work?

If unemployment is the natural state of the artist philosophically, then what is all the stress put on secure jobs that really are never secure? Jobs that you hate from the get-go. Now, casually referred as the gig-economy, it suggests that everyone is becoming an outsider or an artist in some sense. "Ne Travaillez Jamais," as revolting students said in 1968. Ask a visual pundit for a comment about the shambolic, cyber-punk mess around them. Ask Edgar. There isn't enough time in the day to pin down all the strategies making it possible to work in parallel with society or outside it. My mind swirls as I try to glean the essence from Edgar's point of view – mine is jaded – and make some sense of their meaning. Endless streams of dialogue; leaps of logic and imagination. For the sake of clarity? My editors use that word a lot. Am I being clear? Can't my editor add clarity?

America gave up on style around 1973 when the car companies got hit by the oil embargo. When I was a kid, Dad was given a new company car each year, mostly Chevy sedans. But he dressed like a man. Never without tie or suit. At home they listened to classical music all day long. They held fancy dinner parties and played bridge with like-minded GI Bill characters.

Dad continued to buy American cars like the Crown Victoria (or the Mercury Marquis, similar chassis) even though he was not a Police. He'd say, "Fuck the Japanese!" Ever since then, for some reason, grown men have aspired to be children and dressed accordingly. Take from that observation what you will. I'd sometimes discuss this with my own father.

"Don't you have anything more pressing to think about, Doug?"

"You're right. It's pathetic."

"You dress like a Salvation Army. I guess your artist friend Edgar did the same. He looked like a kook most of the time."

"You got me there, Dad."

"What a crap job that Quik-Fix must have been for a man of his talents. He should have called me for help."

"Bit late for that, dad. Nobody really knew about all this."

"Damn shame. I could have housed him in the garage and he could have sold pictures at the town market. Like you selling remaindered books at Walmart."

"You are making me ill, dad."

"Can you get me one of his pictures? I have space over this couch. I like war stuff." He pointed.

"I'll try Dad. But they are going up in value and I thought you hated modern art."

"No, just abstraction."

"I get it. That's different."

"Hitler hated modern art."

"Thanks for the history lesson."

"One Man's Junk is Another Man's Treasure." Who says that besides my dad?

CHAPTER

Grad School was fun and so were Edgar's diaries about the experience. Sherrie and I worked through these MFA years together and Sally fed us newly printed excerpts complete with page numbers. They were hard to digest in places being so top heavy with theoretical jargon. This included all sorts of offbeat, pop psychology from Bloom. There were bits that Sherrie understood and parts that were over her head. Luckily I was there to help. In Grad School, the theories of Post-Modernism ruled. Fortunately, there was anecdote to all the reading and discussion: Art-Making. Famous contemporary artists showed up regularly and smoked huge cigars and sometimes gave individual critiques in studios. Scary shit. They gave pompous slide talks and we realized it might be possible to have a career after all. We became self-important and dug into the studios where we re-tooled our work dramatically. Even Walter. Many of us started copying the art stars. It wasn't that hard to do via photography or aerosol spray. The "end of history" as we knew it! We were presented with the latest theoretical readings that were crucial in updating yourself. In retrospect, those two years went by fast and Edgar Bloom took advantage of the situation:

1985: The program is academically cool if not cutting edge. We do not share studios. We teach figure drawing in our inept way. Compared to fucked up Rome, this is deluxe. There are actually teachers, critiques and a proper thesis to write, not to mention American beer if you don't mind boozing with Jocks. Don't miss Peroni!

There was connection in Edgar's mind between what 20-year-old musicians did and what the cutting edge of art was addressing. He took up his new place in the scheme of things and regarded the past with malevolence, music being the ever-important backdrop that underlined our unique historical place. The diet of post-punk from the Clash to the Police – for the uninitiated, it was hard to tell the difference – was crucial. Here the bifurcation was clear, something happened that ended the era of the Beatles and Stones. We ditched it whole hog. If an artist's studio resounded with the sounds of the Grateful Dead and *Penny Lane* in 1985, the artist was out of step, poor devil. Myriad bands showed up to work in tandem with the POMO zeitgeist. The Cure, I always enjoyed. These early purveyors of post-punk and Goth must be pleased at their longevity and wider influence. They later vied for top mopey-band with the Smiths a few years hence. Both were in the UK charts Top-40 next to a number one by Joy Division, *Love Will Tear Us Apart!* "Mope" became a record store sub-title along with Kraut Rock, House, Hip-Hop, Rap and Dub and thousands of other rarified categories. We poured over copies of the New Musical Express for clues to the next musical messiah. It was a long wait but there were lots of contenders like the Gang of Four who brought Marxist views to the forefront of punk with some funk thrown in. Well-read, smart musicians. Much later, Nirvana finally hit the scene (1991) making punk respectable for mass consumption minus the socialist politics. Cobain's music was important to us too – a culmination of rock's progress – but we were too old for long hair again. Plus, we'd given up lumberjack shirts. It hurt when he left, abandoned, sacrificed to mammon or so the story goes at 27. There's a theory about that. Basquiat left at 28, a few years before.

The blossoming at the beginning of the Eighties was inspired. Out of the punk ashes… Basquiat and Haring were carrying ghetto boxes blasting out Blondie and early Hip-Hop. Distinctions were everything. Today, trivialities and anecdotes are all we have left. More recently, somebody coined the term, Steam Punk, an over-arching category now applied in retrospect to an aesthetic that melded science fiction with the clunky past. Throw an old typewriter or an archaic turntable into a movie! I remember *Brazil* that way and the classic *Blade Runner*, (1982) a milestone in the pantheon of Visual Culture. A rogue bounty hunter is hired by an evil corporation to dispatch punky-looking Androids. The 'private dick' in this case was the spiky haired and fully-chinned Harrison Ford! This movie's art-direction alone spawned thousands of other copies, not to mention music videos so representative of the era.

Later, 2 AM: The face of a generation of future geeks along with Princess Leia. But it is Decker of Blade Runner that was the seminal part. He is in both movies for god's sake. I've read the piece in OCTOBER about it. This post-modern landscape is shaped by music's fervor and a generational shift. Mohicans of the future unite! Anyone who noticed things can see it clearly. Look, a blimp with a video display like a flying billboard!

Not bad, Edgar! That is a pretty close observation of the future as it turns out. Now it's digital of course. I see this vision borrowed on a daily basis in films these days. It's common. The dystopian paradigm hasn't changed much since *Alien* and *Terminator*. We're still waiting for the end.

Cozy in Winterland. Glaswegian Shinto Silvio? See how all this fits together? Thousands of categories! Don't play with guns! Geniuses with guns? Punk retribution? We'd rather be a subculture please.

Back in the day, subcultures were all scrambling like insects to hide from the media light! Gotta stay pure and uninfluenced. Opposite of today. Everyone wants a bull-horn to the world. What a disappointment. This culture kills. Success kills. Edgar had the opposite problem. No spotlight.

Back to the castle starring Peter Lorre as Mito. Lorre's not Japanese, is he? He's German.

How politically incorrect! The journals capture the period. Reading words paraphrased from discussions that I took part in a long time ago was strange. I am recorded as saying in a diary, "I agree with Edgar, how can we make this judgment?"

"Gosh, that does sound like you, Mr. Frank."

"Thanks Sherrie. Let's move on."

Mr. Mito frowned and asked another open-ended question about the essays. This is before MFA students seek out only what is pertinent to their studio practice in their second crucial year. They boil down all the esoteric shit and synthesize it down in a personal stew. Where does the impetus of their creative desires come from? Edgar took this opportunity to devise and develop a character (that he possessed) that is taken from the mediated world and a suburban (unreal) upbringing as opposed to Armageddon approaching. This connected deeply with his earlier mystical phase as a teen in the Late 70's.

Walter's ponytail is repugnant. Mystic Man on a journey for truth and money. Is that mutually exclusive? You're stuck in your Canadian Tuxedo. The nuances lost. Typical among young artists trying to gain a foothold on the ideal. Delusions from day one.

The discussion ground away amid the smoke, Silvio's arena. Tempers frayed. Only the extroverted among us responded. Mito (reigning mentor) listened with a faint patronizing smile. What is the name of that stupid Star Wars character that speaks backwards? Always frustrating for Edgar. He felt it was all meant to undermine him personally.

He's actually getting paid for this? Snack Room later: Berry inter-esting. Outside class, over pints Silvio lectures us about the Sex Pistols. Silvio lectures us about Minimalism. Silvio lectures us about "The Bricks in the Tate." The Bricks in the Tate is the ultimate minimalist piece. The British tabloids hate it, but it is a house-hold word – the fucking bricks in the fucking Tate. That's how it was expressed in Merry England. They point to it as a waste of time and all artists are overeducated conmen. Tis' true. But at least these plebs have heard of it. "Less is More," says Silvio! He's so pleased with himself. I see that it completes a modernist progression stated a long time ago. Detached, yeah? Big

Boots and Elite at the same time. Doesn't connect at all to now. Sculptors cast molten metal while chugging beer.

"That sounds dangerous."

"Not very smart."

"But Edgar paints."

"Painting goes cerebral because it has to."

"Wasn't it already?"

"Yeah, I guess but not like this." Or does it? Big Boots meant "Alpha" artist tough guys. Big sign on the door: Outsiders welcome. It is confusing. Disconcerting in one way, reassuring in another. It had done all it could do progressively or with chemicals. With the swell of new thinking comes a prospect of career, a glimmer of a chance to succeed at a creative life. Impossible before. These ideas surpassed the "learned" part of the craft by all previous margins.

"Total eclipse of the paradigm, Sherrie."

"What does that mean, Mr. Frank?"

"Everything underpinning everything changed."

"Still don't get it. Isn't that a song?"

"Let's continue."

London '87. Patriarchy is gone and all that, potentially anyway. British Punk fades in to the Eighties mega-dance-mix. Nothing wrong with that; an excellent pastime. The new hardcore punk is cool but will have a short shelf life. It is a little narrow.

Edgar's dead wrong; no pun. Might as well have said Hip Hop was a fad and will never catch on. They both still go, 30 years and counting! Serious moshing. Surely this qualifies as proof positive of the Decline of Western Civilization?

Cultural Brain Death? Best example of the fusion is the Beastie Boys. Hip Hop is metalized. Punked up. It catches on in LA. Damn Californians. I resent the fact that these vicissitudes make me old at 25. Can't find my inner 15 year old. Don't want to. Shock of the News. Alvin Teflon was right. The face of success. Art whores rule. Ask B.B. He is an expert. No less, no more, shot by a 44. See Shootout at OK Corral.

Edgar is referring to Johnny Blueblood – I'd rather not mention him – a self-important arts-hole. Born rich. Born privileged. He steals my best girl then impregnates her dearest lady friend, all in a day's work. I went to see him about that, a male duty. Fisticuffs ensued. He was pretty good at that too so after getting a bloody nose, I called it a draw. I was without a girlfriend and now my face looked like an eggplant. B.B. and I had a short bromance before that but left me at the altar. Sounds queer, doesn't it? So steer clear my dears, unless you need a sperm donor. Sometimes they come in handy. That didn't quite sound right. B.B. uses his little brain below the belt but I guess he is honest about it. Good Ole Blue Balls! He was clever but no help to me professionally at all. He and Silvio formed a trio for a while but broke up after feuding over many of the same women. *Two asses of a similar stripe?* What an operator! He had art star written all over him or perhaps, murderer. It's as if they both had large testicles, I mean literally. These loom large in their art and on photocopies. Enough said.

Let's keep the ball rolling! Some stories are better off not told. Like mine.

"That guy is a real asshole, Frank. I hope you washed your hands after hitting him."

"I took a cold shower, for sure."

"I'm not sure how you men survive with each other."

"It's written in our DNA somewhere."

"You poor thing."

As for painting, Edgar started to get it. He had switched from a dated figuration (trees and shit) to a more obvious Post Modern look where he appropriated styles he came across in art history. In fact, he started literally in 1905 and worked his way forward from Matisse to Picassoid emulation. By graduation, Edgar was somewhere between the wars in the 1930's, healthy place to be in 1986. After the Max Beckmann phase, he quickly discovered

Philip Guston, grand-daddy of what was then called New Image painting. Guston was formerly an Abstract Expressionist who'd gone 'rogue' the critics said. Clement Greenberg was shocked and said it was 'bad' art. Good for us. Guston bridged the gap across generations. He was our missing link. How many painters can do that? He painted big cartoon-like figures full of subjective content often commenting on the nature of being a painter. Guys in Klan robes with hoods. Big-eyed painters sleeping or sporting cartoon cigarettes. Wow. It turned abstraction on its head. Edgar adapted his own creatures into Punk Rock characters that were both timely and timeless.

24

CHAPTER

Philadelphia warmed up as news spread about *Forgotten Poets*. I was getting calls from all sorts and began to sense a gleam in the darkest shadows of the scene. Was it murmurs of an Art Messiah? At the top of the food chain, there were exclamations from the mob. Dion had assured Martha that the show would be a "People-Puller" with national attention. She gave me the schedule for the show in the upcoming year with all the events attached. They planned to fit the opening of the show between the summer and winter mega-busters, Cezanne's Favorite Fruit or Glorious Spanish Forgeries. *Forgotten Poets* had gained a new place in fund-raising activities. This included me and I began wondering if the pay was adequate. I was driving Edgar's 1972 Volkswagen for goodness sake. Martha helped but was extra-high maintenance so I disconnected my cell every night. She had warmed to me slowly and I could not stop visualizing bugs eating their mates. Edgar remained ambiguous. He could not see these mechanizations from heaven.

May 5, 2004: Work Shy and Proud! I call their bluff. It is not timeless perhaps but predators such as these are always there taking advantage of the repeated pattern set by reckless young people. Lazy Bastards. It is too much work for them to do otherwise. Work is my escape; it makes you. It's not really work. It's life.

One day while admiring vernacular architecture of a massive Banker's Tudor with a dramatic sloping roof, Edgar was spotted by a squeaky clean man in a bathrobe. Edgar was not a pervert, but this habit invading peoples gardens often lead to that conclusion. He would wave cordially and mouth "good morning" to Yuppies as if to prove he was not a peeping Tom but a legitimate contractor. He could have been a curious neighbor out for a stroll in someone's hedge. Edgar stayed put in the Oak Leaf Hydrangea pretending to admire the foliage. *Too late to run.*

In crowded urban areas, this behavior was not considered in any way remarkable – but, when this happened in quiet Suburban neighborhoods, where the rights of the individual house owner were somehow magnified and human interaction limited – it could lead to an angry call to the cops. Edgar had a police record, just so you know. All artists worth their metal should have one. Mostly small stuff, a DUI and some druggy misdemeanors, all medicinal of course. This is how he met Harvey Rochelle, well-heeled stock options trader and part-time art collector. The police quickly showed up. They found Harvey (with his shotgun under his arm) and Edgar calmly discussing the plantings around the south side of the house. After a tense moment, the homeowner casually gave up the weapon. "All a big misunderstanding, officers. Mr. Bloom here is helping my Realtor, Stanley Chase. I've just hired him." The officers were worried about the gun. Edgar had somehow managed to neutralize Harvey but the law needed real pacification and shoved them both in the squad car. Harvey was pleased to help our hero and Quik-Fix if it was going to help him unload the house. It had become a crippling financial burden after the dot-com bubble burst.

May, 6, 2004: I was spotted! The boss will not be pleased. Luckily, Harvey is not so bad for a Yuppy.

No, Terry Stark was not pleased but she sucked up to high profile Harvey who seemed happy to adopt her arty workman. Terry liked antiquated stuff and thought Edgar's profile as an artist added an air of quality to her start-up. She was right; her clients liked him. He in turn, imagined that she appreciated the fact that he could glaze a window if needed or paint a room quickly. She wasn't going to connect with the fact that he was an anarchist – she didn't know about that – but the notion of contemporary artists on her payroll was tempting. He could also make a rough space presentable with paint and plaster, something none of her "ladies" could do, particularly Martha's new site manager, Astoria. The ladies were compelled to buy stuff at Target or Marshalls to solve decorative problems. Edgar disliked Astoria, a failed predatorial Lawyer that enjoyed bossing our hero around.

Sept, 2, 2004: Terry is my best boss to date which is perhaps not saying much. The Frou-Frou Ladies? Neo-Narcissism or whatever. Lonely souls out there, I can relate. Wow, collecting mania. I thought yours truly had a problem. The Place is stuffed top to bottom. Several days to clear that out. A Big Dumpster was needed and the Salvation Army. This won't look good on my resume. Starvation Wages.

Inspecting decrepit homes and assessing the aesthetic and historic worth were right up Edgar's street. So what led to his dismissal? One reason was his inability to bend or focus fully. He kept the paint cans in the Volkswagen where the Blackberry addicts could not access them. This gave Edgar responsibility and some room to move. Unlike Astoria, he had reasonable experience ordering people around. Astoria (who was hired several weeks after he was) thought this was her job and made his goal impossible.

I angered Terry, again. How unusual! Our creative royal family is inbred. Chairmen of Full-Frontity Nerdists. My mouth opens and the foot goes in, sometimes two. Smoothed it over this time I think, but I am besmirched. Next is the chop. So, I must be on best behavior. Clean up my act, start shaving and develop my clothing. Can't afford another chop.

Is this an eccentric perspective? Other psychological clues about this creative theosophy were found in the diaries. He admitted he shared much with the Quik-Fix clients: major hoarding, for one thing. In their houses, he found large shrines to out-of-date periodicals. This was not interesting ephemera you find in thrift stores but real junk, old newspapers from the 80's, piles of *Gourmet Magazine* and *Better Homes & Gardens*! So much fat.

More: We have found giant mildew archive, a Tower of Babel made out of vintage National Geographics. It spirals towards heaven. Dismantling it took all day. It is impossible to throw one out without checking the contents for more news of King Tut's demise or a story on Vulcanology. Re-configuring the up-datedness of the present? All of this is time consuming.

Are kids' Transformers of any historic value? I mean, come on? Compared to a capital object? Like an airplane, a house or phone? Real artifacts? Having said that, this is being typed on an outmoded scallop-shaped Apple iBook. Pixelated novels on a half-shell?

Security by ADHD Security Company? I can relate. Some stuff is still alive. The past is never past. It connects you to your grandfather's era, somewhere in 1940 or before. The art comes from this place marking the lost and the obsolescence. Why do we dismiss this as gone? It makes today. But we continue with that mis-conceit. Building McMansions, which if deconstructed semiotically, are some sort of Oedipus thing. Size Matters. You will have bigger success than your father, Luke, (heavy breathing here) especially after you kill him. Architect builder whores! Make a lot of money selling to people with no taste or a manufactured rather than learned taste. The worst part of Post Modernism is that it is true. Home building is one thing buy don't get me started on the state of the auto. Cars haven't had aesthetics since around 1939. Think about it. I have theories about that.

Of course, the clients were aging and had assorted collector manias. But this tacky junk? It serves no purpose other than to clutter. Another symptom of societal ADHD? On the other hand, artists need starting points, objects to inspire them. Art is constructive, additive. It takes stuff to make stuff. Found objects, trash, paint, old signs. Non-sequitors. Tangible things represent ideas, right? This makes every consumer an artist of a sort. Every decision involves individual minds to the clan, the collective whole. The peak was sometime in the 70's. We just don't see it. The Seventies was actually the end of the Sixties. I was there as a kid. It was fucked up.

25
CHAPTER

Edgar got his degree eventually but by this time MFA's had become inflationary. Thousands of dim painters had the same idea. *Get a Post-Grad degree then teach.* A flood of newcomers had the same idea and it didn't work for everybody. Unfortunately, Edgar was starting to get stuck between the Art Mafia – a group he was only beginning to recognize – and being a populist. This put him in a double bind. Me, they liked. I was an asshole who could teach basic photography.

However, before graduating, a thesis had to be written. Edgar's was titled *Who's Your Fatherland?* His attempt at academic writing dealt with class, art and subculture and caused unrest. He also targeted reverse discrimination in gender issues and pulled no punches. What is does it mean to be a man? Edgar's paper blasted Art School Graduate Degree conceit. His professors hated *Fatherland*. Mito took offense because he was a main target. *Hippies on a Stick.* Other advisors were pissed off too especially Chisel Face. Her real name was Cheryl Fey and she was a lifer. An academic after her own Masters degree, she lived in a college bubble. Edgar labeled them behind the times, a serious slap in the face for artist/educators. The paper was incoherent but oddly on target:

Stupid Debates. Post War? Cold War? Police Action. Hot and Cold Running War. What can possibly follow that ultimate melt down? Joy Division I guess, named after the Nazi Pleasure Palace. Bad taste in the extreme but a fabulous name for a band.

Music saved my life. It replaced the church. Post-Church, post-Temple. Amen to that. We are only shadows in a Science Fiction now and cannot be held responsible. We are not who we are anymore.

We never were, pal. These are vague distinctions that may not matter any more but his punkish rants were heartfelt. Generally speaking, Edgar was more punk than myself. This means his attitudes tarnished quickly. Such is vanguardiness. I was post-punk, more hesitant. Now, I'm a bloke pining for simpler times. We were supposedly anti-mainstream. Hugging the outskirts of it, in any case. Otherwise, how can you be against it? We now all live in a mental "Edge City." The term was over-used in the Nineties as pop-intellectual short hand. From Bloom, 1984:

What would Joey Ramone do? He'd say, I'm against it! Gabba Gabba Hey! So many Waves. New and Old. Working on my thesis. It's about subculture mostly. Relying heavily on a book by a guy called Dick Hebdige. Me and my generation of post-Hendrix people are a large subculture! I wish I was a minority. Spanish, Greek, anything. Newsflash from Britain via Meta-Music! Joy Divison re-forms to become New Order. This causes much debate. They've gone all disco-dance beat or something; a punk taboo. This is confusing. I guess it's about being egalitarian again.

Edgar's advisers took Edgar aside. "Your thesis has no basis in fact!" The running monologue was proto-ADHD. Most aggravating. Yeah, things changed fast. Too fast for most to see. It was not just another youth movement in a long line of youth movements. Mito had him make corrections, frowning. "What is your beef, Mr. Bloom?"

"My beef? My beef is bullshit. You know, it's all bullshit. Quoting Sontag, so what. Who is Sontag? I was raised watching TV not reading Ancient Greek."

Mito: "I see your point, but what is it you want from us?"

"I want you to wake up and swallow some humble pie."

114

"Humble Pie? For why? For what, I mean?" Mito should have gone to Yale obviously. I admit, I am making most of this up, but some similar conversation took place.

Chisel Face told Edgar he had some nerve passing out such blanket shit. "Who do think you are? A genius?"

Edgar nearly exploded, "How would you know if I was a genius or not, Professor Fey?"

"How dare you. You little schmuck!" Cheryl's face turned a purple not in a Crayola box and left as gracefully as a newborn giraffe.

Mito rolled his eyes and conceded. "See Mrs. Raunch in the Library before next week. She can help you back up your statements with some proper citing."

Bitch. What does a genius look like? Bugger the Library. I believe there is no such thing. It is a myth. Punk is on the dance floors with all the other Madonna-shit. It has a groove too. That is what counts. The Higsons also got a spikey groove! Saw them with my brother, Victor in New York. We made a crowd of two, spastically dancing in a big ballroom. They must have thought those two weird New Yorkers bought their record? Victor Lazlo Bloom bought the one copy for one ninety-nine!

Winter from Hell: Subliminal Seduction. I knew it! Sex and Death sells products. Fucking Freezing Weather. Saw Warhol's, "Empire State" last night with Frank and Silvio. Or most of it. I love the Empire State Building. We snuck out half way through for a few beers and came back. It was still going – not surprising really – and we caught the famous changing film reel bit reflected in the building's windows. Everyone else in the room was asleep! Losers. Grad school is the height of many of their short-lived careers. Many discover they have not what it takes. You read myriad essays, succeed in achieving a signature style in the studio (of sorts) and think you are hot shit – or as Silvio would say, "shit-hot."

Not keen on that expression. The Empire State features in Edgar's life as much as it does for any New Yorker. When it was finished in the height of the Great Depression, it was called the Empty State Building. Many newcomers to New York find it of some comfort. It's been there a long time. Post 9/11, it remains a symbol of our greatest century so far. An MFA? Two short years and you're done. You join the Association of College Professors (ACP) and look for jobs with your best exposures of new slides.

Sherrie could see this was a critical point in her husband's life. "Why was this so important, Mr. Frank?"

"Many had to choose a real job at this juncture, the one to support their creative habit. We had to choose."

"Or to support a wife and kids."

"Yeah, that too. We put it off."

"I get the job thing is a problem. And the ego."

"Were we more important than regular people? Hell yeah, we said. We certainly pegged ourselves a step above our teachers who were mired in the Seventies."

"What happened to Silvio?"

"Where is he now? I don't know. He may have turned. I mean he became what he hated."

"Is that so bad?"

"I think it's a waste of talent and meanness."

"Yeah, but look where it got Edgar."

Maybe there is a career out there. Basquiat aka SAMO, used to spray paint subway cars, now he hangs out with Warhol. Saw combined show at Tony Shafrazi in SoHo. In the poster, they are both pictured as boxers with scarred abdomens. The scars are real in Warhol's case, bullet wounds. Basquiat's is from an appendectomy. Ideal isn't it? Maybe I will hang out too when we get out of this frozen shit-hole.

Edgar was doing his best and making great leaps forward; in two years he was almost contemporary in a pre-post modern sort of way. The RISD 'Genius Convention' disappeared, absorbed into the world. I was glad to see the back of them.

CHAPTER

"What is this 'Male Gaze' thing, Mr. Frank?" I had been reading aloud to Sherrie at the Blue House on a rainy afternoon, our relationship in check.

"It's all around us, Sherrie. Invisible. Left over from the teetering Patriarchy. But ours is new and improved. Lewdity is everywhere today not discreetly hidden in the drawing room behind shuttered maroon curtains shared only with the Dukes and Squires holding brandy and cigars. Anything less would be deemed prohibition. Life's a big bachelor party. Call me prudish."

Sherrie's brain was satisfied for the moment. "You aren't prudish at all, Frank."

"Would you like me to be?" We studied sexuality in painting carefully like art historians. These guys were very anal, studying every wrinkle in pictures since the Greeks. "Are you there, Sherrie?"

She goaded me on. "I'm still listening, Mr. Frank."

"Prefiguring of Freudian stuff was evident to us everywhere even in religious works of the Fourteenth Century. It wasn't new. Painters are not Saints. Roget Albert Smutt of Antwerp was a great nudist. Where did he find such voluptuous creatures? Baroque Venuses raping armies. Today we call them obese."

The next evening, Sherrie came over unwillingly to have another look at the Bungalow. She sanctioned my plan for completion in about nine months since the show would require that much time, like birthing a child.

A book however, was going to be more involved than an exhibition with many details to be worked out. Cranston thought maybe the release could coincide with the opening of the show as it toured American cities. That depended on the deals he was brokering, of course. I had serious doubts.

Sherrie was overwhelmed as I leaked these details. "So we have a big exhibition planned plus a book about Edgar?"

"Well, I guess that's the way it is going. I seem to have little control over the Museum's activities."

We sat with two glasses of lousy Merlot that tasted better than it sounded. "But what about our agreement?"

"You mean setting this to rest?"

"Yeah. It looks like you've brought him back to life so everyone can have another go at him."

"That's a bit harsh. I've discovered that he was off track but not by far. He had trouble fulfilling everybody else's expectations. Everything will work out, Sherrie. Believe me. Edgar will get what he always wanted."

"But what about me, Mr. Frank?" Her eyes were now sad and disappointed. "It seems you have discovered what I wanted more or less. Edgar was a lost cause and I can now move on knowing none of this was my doing. I played the part I was given."

Yours Truly was starting to feel like a heel. "No. It wasn't. I was hoping you would be happy about it all, Sherrie."

She took a long sip of Merlot and frowned. "I don't believe that for a minute and neither do you."

"I'm sorry. I guess I got carried away. I should've told you all this before."

"Damn straight." I drove home later through the hood to allow more time at stoplights so I could nurse my ego and alter my mood. How had I screwed this up so badly? The honeymoon was over.

27
CHAPTER

My imaginary conversation with Kurtz begins here. I had to fill in things his father had no time or inclination for. "Your father lived long before our age of Pharmaceutical Takeover, Kurtz. He did see some commercial advertisements before TV disappeared."

"What are talking about Uncle Frank?"

Edgar sums it up the year before he dies: *Being an artist is much too much like theatre. Each show is an audition. It's not fair. Like doing an audition in front of no one. You can do this for years, like actors and singers, except they get a definitive no. Artists keep thinking they are about to turn a corner. Working at a low level until disasters happen. A life spent looking for the right part? Wasting all that time.*

Post Nasal Dysfunction. A running stream of disclaimatories at the end by fast-talkers. If you are having palpitations go to the nearest hospital. If an erection lasts 4 days or more see your doctor especially if you are a woman. Ask your Doctor before trying Zoflux. I'm telling you now. They clarify the risks of medicines and the fact that some users died of cardiac related issues and bulging eyeball.

Ah, the drawbacks of being a man. We're an endangered species. "What's an erection, Dad?" asked Kurtz. The artist jumped out of his chair as if hit by lightning and pulled out a monograph on Mapplethorpe from the nearby bookshelf. He opened the book.

"Don't you dare!" yelled Sherrie. "You have to have a chat with your son now. Just tell him the truth for god's sake." This is what he says to his boy. "It's like shooting at squirrels, Kurtz. Take aim and pow."

Again, this is post-Moi. Edgar fell in with some hard-core remnants of the Genius Convention, New York types wearing tight black jeans – very specific cut bought on Eighth Ave – they were called drainpipes because of the shape. Oddly enough, they are back in fashion a couple of decades later. Who's counting? Jeans manufacturers picked up on a new demarcation: only thin young people preferred these pants. They could fit into them. Put on a small ill-fitting Trilby and you're done. Dapper as hell. This lead to a new way to verify X-Gen from post whatever. Who cares? However we may refer to them is splintered, confused and over. Aging destroyed them. Now they are unbelievably old at 40. Sadder than old Grateful Dead fans all of whom are now Great Grand Dads.

Ha ha. The reaper gets us all in the end, Pavement fans. Watching the young firebrands all go through what I did already several times. That is depressing. Longevity is a thing of the past. Few trendy bands that are real big at first make the correct adjustment for maturity. Stupidly you aren't meant to give them much of a chance. Thanks, fan-base alpha.

Now, they can't fit into super skinny jeans which guarantee your inability to have kids – too bad – if you happen to be male. I tried the regular skinny type on recently in Wanamakers (aka Macys) and nearly caught my thingy in the zip. Nothing to brag about. It was nothing to do with my natural endowment but simply the ridiculous urge for self-preservation of the species. Also, an effort to stay fashionable and attractive for TV spots. Yes, I get asked sometimes. Lots of reading in Liberal Art Departments too as well as the Art Schools. Professors ask me barbed questions like I am a Nazi sympathizer. The jeans were a little stretchy, but I got them over my butt eventually.

Famous Roman General: Glutimus Maximus. Looks like chicken in new wardrobe! News of the World Headline: Dick catches Dick in Zip. Other rules. Never wear shorts on stage. Rule number two: if you have lost your hair, wear a hat or have enough tattoos to make up for it. Baldness is caused by testosterone friends, nothing to be ashamed of. I've lost my edge, as the song goes. Fuck you anyway young people. I never had an edge.

A nice profile though, Edgar. Anyway, some particuarly slim Genius-Conventionaires end up mainlining. Times up in Time's Square. They imagined themselves to be Lou Reed. Am I still talking about them? When do we get to the good part? The come-uppance part?

If art schools had reunions, they'd be thinly attended. It is uncool. Can Lou Read? Ha ha. How did he make it through? Keith Richards, I understand. He has a strong constitution. He's rich enough so he doesn't have to speak in coherent sentences. But Sid Vintage? We salute you. He went down in flames, living and dying with convictions intact. Vintage Vicious. He didn't mean to knife his girlfriend.

Did it ever occur to Kurt Cobain? Il Cottone de Proust? Walter Benjamin translated Proust. Did you know that? I imagine that is difficult, French to German. Both writers analyzed what we call the past. Edgar is also forever explaining his view of memory from "back in the day." That phrase again. This preoccupation is Proustian and implies we are washed up at thirty. Temps passe. Perdu? Dernier, n'est ce pas? How absurd to envy numbskulls who can't yet shave or prepare a sophisticated dinner party. They used to call them punks in the 30's and 40's; the original use of the word: a nobody. Nobody-ization. This was well before the term "emerging artist" was coined. It was all about being hip. Your work and you. It's now or nothing.

The past eats itself. I'm about making new memories. Gets tough as you age. At 21, it's a given. Facial hair is a historical marker. Look at Lincoln or Marcus Aureleus, the one in Gladiator who got suffocated by his son. He was Dumbledore, previously. A great British actor underplaying it well behind a Second Century Beard of his own making. Dumbledore's was fake, I have been assured. My stubble? Makes me look like I'm a dosser. I like looking like a dosser. See my Dosser's Dossier for more information.

"Dosser" is English for derelict. Sounds tasteful. A Dossier is a personnel file. I am working on Edgar's. He was nearly homeless once or twice. That coincided with his bearded phase a nod to Vincent, I suppose. Corny, isn't it? Clean-shavenly presidents rarely look like they haven't a big fancy home and hearth. Who started this trend? McKinley? Wilson? The look of the Capitalist Twentieth Century meant no whiskers. Kennedy, a clean shaven playboy if there ever was one, had no beard. Nixon not so much. He had a five o'clock shadow at noon. He's not a crook like Al Capone, just resembles one on TV. Edgar didn't live to see the return of the beard to America's Favorite pastime. One-hundred year retro, though no one cares but re-enactors like at Gettysburg. Strange. Next, the Phillies will be carrying muskets. Turn-of-the-Century all over again.

Jesus, look how the plot thickens and goes off course? Take stock statistic fans. Who was the first bearded pitcher with an ERA below 300 in two consecutive seasons? I dunno. Edgar missed the play between the bearded San Franscico Giants in 2010. Alpha Beards and the Philly beards. Quite a battle of pitchers. Freud might say "uncanny" in German. Sometimes a beard is simply a beard.

CHAPTER

Sally sat typing. It was a Friday in January. My brogues were relaxing on the ottoman while I was attempting to decipher a tough section of Edgar's punkish musings. Most of the crew hadn't yet arrived. The phone rang. We looked up at each other and wondered who would want to destroy our domestic bliss. Still holding the journal, I cradled the green receiver to my closest ear hole, "Filbert's Rare Books."

"This is Mr. Saki Mito. I am trying to reach Mr. Frank concerning the late Edgar Bloom."

I stood up in fright. "Mito Bloom, who?"

There was a pause and a garble. "Is this Mr. Douglas Frank?"

"There must be some mistake. Rare books." I hung up. I thought I'd heard the last of Mito. Edgar's past was catching up with me.

"Who was that, Mr. Frank?" asked Sally from behind her desk.

"Wong Number, Sally." I said.

"That is racist, bub," Sally replied. "You should get that seen to."

I made a puppy face. "It was an unwelcome blast from the past. Am I bad?"

She corrected me "The phrase is, "My bad?"

"Well, am I?"

"Yes."

"Well, you answer it next time it rings."

"Why should I? You're a grown man."

"I don't feel like one."

"So it is the Mito character."

"He doesn't like me."

"You haven't seen him in fifteen years!"

"That is true but will you pick up the phone?"

"I will if you stop being a baby and get me a glass of wine."

"Very well, madam." I walked stiffly into the kitchen and returned with a bottle holding it down waiter-like for her to read. "May I interest you in one of our California Reds?"

One morning, Mito sat in an old stuffed chair with a freshly squeezed espresso, perusing the latest copy of Visual Culture Magazine. He had turned to the reviews at the back to see if any old British mates had turned up, when he noticed a small article with a photo. When not teaching, Mr. Mito puttered about his studio, polished his ego and milked contacts that wanted milking. He was preparing for a show nine months away in Cincinatti, another place he taught. His work looked the same as it always had but he rarely showed in New York anymore. It was always cast white plaster blobs made into minimalist vagina-like shapes. Isn't everything shaped like one genital or another? Today he recognized someone in a post-dated obituary. He stood up slowly as recognition formed fully in his brain. His eyes moved from text to picture, picture to text. What followed was an investigation that took up Mito's whole weekend. Luckily, he wasn't much of a detective. Surprised to find an old student turn up dead after fifteen years in the wilderness, he wasn't sure what to do first. That upstart from upstate, what was his name? He turned to the front of VCM feeling as if he had missed out on something significant. He found the full-page ad for a group show at the Art Museum in Philadelphia called *Forgotten Poets of a New Age*. The curator was a woman named Martha Trout. Full-page ad – this was serious money. He made a sweep of other art publications and a few on-line sites. Mito hated the internet. It was not tactile like his sculptural instincts. There it was again just on the periphery. Ads and reviews a plenty! Shit. Underneath the title was a short list of names including Edgar

Bloom who appeared to have top billing. Was he the leader of this band of miscreants, unknown artists?

"Let's cross reference," said Mito calmly. He located a full-page review in the New Yorker and was dismayed. It was a rave. New York critic, Richard Mayer – a man Mito had met personally – did not bullshit around. Mito's jaw dropped and his John Lennon glasses fell on the coffee table:

These tortured contemporary of misfits play at referencing themselves with ancient poets in ruffled shirts who delved into drugs for mystique before it was fashionable. In between eras, these vagabonds also link themselves to grander poets with Greek names. If they were musicians, they'd be the Sex Pistols.

"Son of a bitch!" Mito picked the shades carefully, swearing, one arm stuck in a leftover prune Danish. To top this off, he noticed an essay in the exhibition catalog. *Double-Whammy*. It had my name on it. "Two ex-students in one week? This is unprecedented. What are the odds?" He sat down, finished the coffee and lit a cigarette. He'd tried to quit eight times, but never succeeded. It was part of him, his work and a ploy to meet smoking women. Mito was a Seventies guy. He called Cheryl Fey at Academy of Arts and Science to see if she'd seen the news.

Cheryl Fey was sitting at her desk, fidgeting when she picked up the phone. She had quit smoking because drunken critic, Barney Scribner, told her she looked like an Egyptian Mummy. He was not referring to Liz Taylor. CF quit cold turkey. Though she was swamped with running her department, she made room for her buddy Mito. They'd both outgrown Northwoods at the same time. New York life was good and they did pretty well at first. But things change and recessions occur. One ages and loses track. I am losing my edge and I don't care. By noon, they had met up in the faculty lounge – near her college studio full of dated conceptual work – and she confirmed that this was indeed legit. She thought back to college. Same Bloom, same Mr. Frank? "They are just having a bit of luck. It happens."

"I wouldn't say dying is a bit of luck, Cheryl."

She made light of it, admitting the art world was always looking for new crap by youngsters. Mito registered a sense of caution in her voice. "A show is a show." She'd been burned by her gallery recently and was petrified of becoming a has-been. There was a limit to her sucking up, apparently. Are there limits to sucking up? Edgar wondered. She'd lived long enough to see some of her die-hard students go on to surpass her achievements. Bloom was certainly never going to be one of these.

"This is impossible, Mito. They were both shitheads. You either have it or you don't."

"But it's happening, Cheryl."

"Let me do some research, Mito. You go home." He went home and tried to relax. Mito could not wait for Cheryl. He checked some old alumni mags. He began looking for Mr. Frank. This led straight to the Bourbon. He got the number in the old fashioned way, the phone book. This led to ginger ale. Specifics eluded him. Then some Googling. No Edgar online but *Forgotten Poets* was everywhere.

I blanked the call and worked up a quality fabrication – my speciality. I called Mito back the next day when I had my story straight. He was keen, almost friendly. Edgar was barely Google-able yet and the publicity wasn't going to include details. Dion and the publicity people knew what they were doing. Causing Unrest. Laying it on bit thick if you ask me. I fed the museums PR people soundbites as best I could. I loved getting my name in the paper: Douglas Howard Frank, 29 Hotel Dominion, Philadelphia, PA 19167. Occupation: Hack.

CHAPTER

Edgar's story now begs the telling of his disastrous 'solo' exhibition of 2003; a culmination of years of networking. Like the man himself, it was late in developing. Unlike like a maiden outing in New York, which supposedly began a career, a solo show in Philly was no big deal. DAS POOR HAUS GALLERY was small potatoes and ensured anonymity. The irony of the name made me pause. I read it again. You can have too much irony. His journals report:

The Nineties are over and I complain about juggling shit jobs while working towards the rare solo show involving a small time art bigot who thinks he's a gallerist.

Here we meet Colin First, Goldsmith and Yale educated, but a burnout nonetheless. Colin was not fully convinced about Edgar's work – nobody was. A sincere crusty with dirty dreads who smoked a lot, Colin was beautifully twisted. This is why a real and influential director, Richard Kray of Kray Brothers Gallery, let him go. Nobody messed with Kray. When I met him for an interview, his appearance made me shiver. He had mid-length grey hair, a distinct shade of silver, that was combed straight back. This offset the frosty, British made, blue chip suit. There was only one Kray brother – not sure why – but he had clout. Kray Gallery was the best private contemporary venue in town and only showed Art Stars or emerging locals who'd been vaccinated. Kray knew the rules of the Art Mafia well – he helped invent some of them. He took his artists to big time Art Fairs dotting the world.

Basel, Miami, New York, London, Delhi and talked them up. Nick English was one of them. Once branded properly, they'd sell like hotcakes, join the mob and talk the talk. Mr. Kray hired sharp suits as curators. They all spoke a smattering of German, Italian and Japanese. Were they snobs? I don't know but they all did a good imitation. Kray went through staff quickly, though, not as fast as Art Bank's Quinn. Philadelphia was now littered with Kray's ex-employees and they eagerly talked to me if I asked nicely. Most of them knew about Colin and his dope problem.

Mr. Kray described it as "washing down powder with spirits; sometimes, he sniffed Elmer's glue, Mr. Frank." He smiled, searching my face for intelligence with opaque eyes. "No, really." I wrote down his comment, stifling a grin. Eventually, I laughed. Kray joined me, "Colin was fucked up." I also wrote this down. Edgar knew Colin well:

Dec. 8 2003: Poor huffing Colin never learned the art of exhaling. He is certainly on the down-a-lator, as an artist, gallerist and human being. First is Last, like Jesus said.

Best news I've heard today. For some reason, Kray made sure critics steered clear of DAS POOR HAUS. He wanted to crush Mr. First without mercy. Maybe Colin was blackmailing him? I have found no indication of this. Kray held grudges, sure. Plant a seed in a few ears and word spread fast.

"Sink, little shit," he admitted. Kray had never heard of Edgar Bloom. I was charmed by this asshole. "Did my friend get caught in a crossfire?"

"Who knows? Who cares? Why are you looking into all this shit about First?"

"I'm writing my PhD at Penn."

Kray laughed. "A thesis about total losers?"

I laughed through my teeth at his dismissive comment. "You'll be in there too, buddy."

Kray stopped laughing. "You are a brave man, Mr. Frank." He sneered.

"What's brave about asking a question or two?"

He gave me a deep and ominous look that said nothing. "You have no idea, do you?" I left thinking the guy was imagining himself a Bond Villain of some sort.

Kray didn't mind competition. There was none in Philadelphia. He had to work connections outside the city to keep alive. Getting reviews in International art magazines was the key goal towards prosperity, all gained through channels or word of mouth. This confirmed you were a player. Colin was riding high for a while, then went from art circles to crack-wagon in one strategic motion. There was a positive side. He could get his stash quicker. Similarly, Colin First was convinced he could set provincial Philly on fire with contemporary art fervor. The gallerist was unaware that Edgar was one step ahead. His show was a conscious negation of the whole scene, a final statement titled: MELTDOWN. No networking needed.

Jan 5, 2003: Blind Leaders of the Blind. Aristocratic Refugees? It is about society sitting on its ass, consumerizing, not philosophizing: Destroying the Earth by default. At least, we will all go up together. Instead of the nuclear blast over Manhattan that I was wishing for and always half expecting, it will be death by climate. Hot and cold storms, disappearing coastline, populations sinking. Isn't there a Science Fiction Novel where London is underwater?

That's J. G. Ballard's, *The Drowned City*, I believe; not Philip K. Dick, like you were thinking. There is certainly a little Science Fiction in Edgar's themes. It grew as his life unfolded, starting with Toffler's, *Future Shock* in High School. Later it was Australian Art Critic, Robert Hughes', *The Shock of the New*. Two best sellers that explained both art and SF to normal people. Hugh's easy prose was supposed to explain all the artfulness to idiots, or at least Australians. Dave Hickey – the *Air Guitar* man – was the latest culprit who tried to explain art in real terms. In an unconventional essay on the art world, he blamed Morley Safer and the ancient news program, 60 Minutes. Safer marked the art world as a sham. Easy to do. Pick a jaded gallerista and ask them questions on camera. Listen to the bombastic and unearthly replies. Edit it. It is also easy to call 60 Minutes a joke. Pot Calling the Kettle Black? News at Eleven. Ballard's book, published in 1968, was way ahead of global warming. London is lost when the lions drink. How Philip K. Dickensian! I imagined my Aunt Judith in a rowboat and wellies paddling up to the corner shop for a Twix or a Chicken Tikka from the top of the Marble Arch curry house. The post office tower is the Queen's new residence! Edgar's riffs took even Ballard to new heights.

30

CHAPTER

Colin's trademark was his jean jacket. It was an ordinary coat but he wore it buttoned to the top and strangely, without a shirt underneath much unlike Marlboro Man. For Kray Brothers, this made Colin an anomaly, just weird enough to be viable, until he crossed the line. Several lines on a mirror, actually. His sartorial problem barely topped his serious halitosis. I first met him in New York and thought he had a dead raccoon in his knapsack. My reaction, a mini-gag, prompted him to pop a Mentos breath mint. He did not blanch. How does a person navigate society this way? Edgar also wondered: Do all curators have awful breath? Sorry, Frank. Working with Colin is a morgue. They both struggled with mental issues. Colin's real story was unknown. He was sort of a genius. Not an undiscovered outsider type or Nobel Prize winner, but different from the rest of us, more like a sociopath. He was, however, no Malcolm McLaren – the Thomas Jefferson of the punk explosion. God rest his soul. McLaren could make revolution out of a paper bag. Edgar first met Colin in London on a teaching scheme in a disused mental ward named after Prince Charles. It was re-training scheme for returning Yobbos to society after breakdowns and extreme doldrums. In the Edward P. Nutter Wing, they had desks lined up like beds. Colin put yellow sticky notes on Edgar's desk two places away.

"See me immediately!"

Edgar walked 12 feet and asked him about the notes. "What does this mean, Colin?"

Colin explained there was a meeting in an hour in the cafeteria. "Don't be late." Years later, they re-met in New York Art Mecca, SOHO and resumed their acquaintance. Again further south in Philadelphia, Edgar waited two years for the right moment. *How about a show in your new space for Old Time's Sake?* I won't let you down, mate. Not entirely. After waiting a week, Colin said OK. Before assenting, Colin questioned Edgar about his intentions, the purpose behind the show. Colin called about endless details, dropped by the Bungalow unannounced to see if things were going well and was a general pain. Did such a small exhibition warrant such Big Brother-ish surveillance? It involved a lot of work and no money for the artist. Das Poor Haus was that kind of space. Down and Out in Philadelphia and New York.

2004, May 12: Stop pestering me, Colin. This reminds me of an incident that happened yesterday. I was picking up Kurtz from school and while waiting I was reading Orwell's Down and Out in Paris and London, a book I really relate to. My kid crossed the street. He was carrying a book with a similar cover. It was Animal Farm, the kid's version. I held up my book and he chuckled, "same author, Dad." I excitedly, suggested we high-five. Kurtz shook his head emphatically and said no. Back to Colin. He's dead.

Three years before Edgar's untimely exit, Colin got his own personal call from the reaper. He was sweating a lot and his stomach hurt. It might have been the beta-blockers or something else, but his doctor sent him for a colonoscopy. The upshot was a cancer the size of a small melon, or a large orange; depending on what kind of fruit you prefer. It was wedged up against his liver. Six months to live. Colin didn't seem perturbed. "Life is inconvenient," he was quoted as saying in his only obit, a small piece in a weekly by cultural observer, Marge deStephano. He did not like hospitals and could barely opt for the colonoscopy in the first place. Get it, Colin-oscopy? So he decided not to have the life-saving operation. It would have likely left him with a colostomy bag. Always awkward on first dates. I mean, in addition to the halitosis. Colin was not going to have patronizing doctors opening him up with their exacto knives! They might see his chest. In typical Philly fashion, it was time to pass the hat and set up a public charity:

BURY COLIN FIRST FUND. Another board was hurriedly formed. All proceeds went to a ghetto garden for poor kids to be covered in awful, hippie mosaics. I thought they needed to pay the casket makers and morticians! There would be no post-mortem, natural causes, so to speak. Zachary took the reins of a fundraiser for the funeral arrangements before Colin actually died. Many people sent crappy artwork to Art Bank. This seemed to thrill Quinn. Charisma sat at her desk and put a massive lipstick stain on a white coffee cup. Propped up in front of her on a Mac was a fashion magazine, three inches thick. Sam and Mike (new intern) opened the packages like it was the Berlin Airlift. There were twelve mis-matched envelopes each with a five spot. There was a check from an unknown gallery dealer for one thousand dollars. "Look at this," yelled Sam, "from you know who, I think. This means Colin is going out in a nice cedar box."

She mouthed the letters K-R-A-Y to Mike and he nodded without the slightest idea what she was saying.

Quinn was watching, "From Kray, I imagine."

Mike said, "Cool" and wondered if the guy was dead yet.

"Have you seen the obit in the City Weekly?" asked Sam. Edgar had the last word:

Feb 14, 2004: Terrific week. Start the Parade of Lows. Gravediggers of 2003 for refugee aristocrats! The funeral for Colin was Tuesday. Tommy Graves did not write the obituary himself Dope. His students will miss him, I guess. Several wore jean jackets without shirts and buttoned all the way up. At least, this saves me the awkwardness of pleading for another unsuccessful solo outing from the idiot.

31

CHAPTER

I wasn't at the opening but I'd seen the space. DAS POOR HAUS was a small shop-front off the trendy drag called the Front. Edgar picked up the commentary: "DAS POOR HAUS has changed hands and quickly becomes nothing. FLOP HOUSE, ROUND HOUSE, CRACK HOUSE, CAT HOUSE, BRICK HOUSE. No use to me at all. Thanks so much Colin."

Mr. First had set out some pretzels and gummy bears! Cheese squares are passé and I miss them. Merlot in boxes, I don't miss. The building had been a shoe store when Larry Fine lived in town. In the recent past, it had been a thrift shop, not big enough to swing a rat. Small installations worked well there. Colin's artists were receiving review after review from the alt-weeklies. Where are they now? Gen-X pains in the ass. I care not.

Feb. 14, 2004: Post Show: Miserable and pissed off. Samantha is encouraging but Nick is a drag. He said Colin is a con merchant. He's right of course but Colin is a lot of things. Nick is Jealous more like. Colin's nasty habits, calling artists, checking on some pointless detail of the opening, installation time. Yet, Colin never said anything about the strength of the exhibition or directed efforts towards actual publicity or collectors.

Back in the early 90's, some genius decided that earmarking every 'First Friday' of the month would spark up the nearly comatose scene. It worked but did little for real contemporary galleries or contemporary artists. "Well, why?" you asks? Because it was merely a social event. It was a must to hang out on First Fridays and the artists' community made it a tradition that never went away. Too bad; it was tedious. Many were mistaken in thinking the activity was leading to high times, a breakthrough. Local groups planned special events and pitched stuff to the Sunday Papers. Editor, Tommy Graves put artists on the front of his weekly. Spreads ran inside on the new local scene and Edgar collected the clippings. They make for interesting reading 15 years later. Little progress was made apart from improvements of internet speed. The names changed, that's all. The press was spoon-fed by pathetic local business organizations. Of course, this is not the same as a consortium of galleries that keep standards a tad above a flea market. Groups of organizations don't make up for real galleries and serious collectors.

Jan 4, 2004: This is my last Rinky-Dink outing. Colin is used to dealing in work of trendy skateboarders. Big on West Coast! Graffiti. Vans footwear? How does he make these connections. Over a bong? I thought that era was over. Who was that Hispanic Chick? She looked familiar.

Who indeed? Emma Sanchez was there with her compatriots taking in the scene cautiously. The place was full. Luckily for me, Edgar documented most of the night. He got pissed off. Some hanger-on rested his plastic glass of Merlot on one of Edgar's paper floor pieces. These Warhol-ish boxes were delicate. Edgar picked up the glass instinctively, danced around for a minute and threw it out the door. The perpetrator was speechless. Edgar did not recognize the collector from New York who was invited by Colin First. Edgar menaced him, "Have you lost something?"

"Excuse me?"

Edgar pointed at the artwork. "See that, shit-head?"

"Help!" cried the New Yorker.

"You damaged my piece." Sam and Nick looked on aghast. Even more so when Edgar grabbed the man by the lapels and ejected him from the gallery. The man's friends interceded quickly and an animated fistfight ensued on the sidewalk. Mr. Snout defended himself well and his fist connected with Edgar's left eye. Edgar was tanked and swung wildly. One punch hit the mark and the collector went down like a sack of soggy mulch on a wet day in April. Edgar was restrained by friends and foes alike, still cursing the Philly-steins and out-of-towners. In the gallery, some of the crowd applauded. Most were offended at the mere sign of any emotional intensity, much less from the artist himself. Nick English, who was chatting with Emma Sanchez, laughed loudly.

Realizing no sales were coming his way that night, Colin skulked off in a huff. "Right," he thought, "beat up the fucking clientele, Edgar." Snout eventually caught a cab back to his hotel with a hanky held up to his nose.

Terry Stark, Edgar's boss of the moment was there. She and her Quik-Fix girls enjoyed themselves but the imbroglio was a little more than they expected. They expressed concern and made farewell air kisses. "Great show, Edgar." He wasn't sure if they meant the scuffle or the art.

Edgar rejoined his friends in the half-filled gallery and took a bow to scattered applause, the Scarlet Pimpernel. "They seek him here, they seek him there." Some artists commiserated with a comrade in distress and some had some sincere praise for Edgar's "social statement." But it was clear no real art world peeps of note were there apart from the damaged collector. Critics had better places to be. *Bugger Critics. I am officially washed up.* The evening went downhill after this point. Edgar grumbled to himself as he sat in a corner behind Colin's curatorial desk and drank. He found a second to relax in a post-virile, show-is-up moment.

Samantha sat next to him. "Why isn't Sherrie here?"

"She'd have been mortified! She hates these events anyway."

Sam felt a tingling from the work and could not explain it. She never could. It went into the eye and straight to the brain via the gut, a curve ball. Beautifully inked washes with odd statements. The exhibition screamed, "Is this art and if so, why?" Edgar sensed Sam's response and bewilderment. Appreciation from a fellow traveler. "This is very impressive, all new stuff?"

"Oh, yeah. I worked my ass off."

They linked eyes and clinked plastic cups. "It's a strong show, you know. Openings are tough."

He smiled, "I fucked that guy up good."

"Not one of your better moments."

"Something to tell the grandkids."

"I can tell mine too!"

Edgar saw the humor and laughed, "Collectors. I hope he doesn't sue me, the asshole." He'd been there many times before. It's all a waste of time even if you pull it off. Nick hovered and made himself scarce.

Later, Nick escorted the drunken artist home to his dingy bungalow after cheese-steaks. "Let's go, Mr. Warhol." On the way, he couldn't resist offering advice on dealers. "I think it went well, considering."

"You must be kidding."

"At least he didn't need a hospital."

Edgar laughed meanly, "Colin may need one."

"You have to romance these people Edgar, not punch them."

"Romance Colin and Mr. Stout? They can go to hell."

"Edgar, you can't make art without those folks, you know that."

"Why not? Those folks can't dictate what art is supposed to be. Colin dictates. The industry dictates."

"Industry? The art world is not an industry."

They pulled up with a jerk barely missing the curb. Edgar countered showing real anger. "Of course it is, you fool, all self-flattery."

"A Country Club maybe. Don't take it out on me."

"Thanks for the lift and fuck everybody."

"Jesus, Edgar! Never mind."

Nick shouted out the car's window. "The show looks good. That's what counts."

Edgar may not have heard the remark as the BMW's engine drowned Nick's voice.

"See you Sunday. Chill a bit for god's sake."

Late Evening, Sept 24, 2003: "Yeah, I'll fucking chill, Nick." This New Millennium Sucks. Our whole system will collapse! Nothing went wrong with the computers. Osama happened.

For Edgar, the years 2001-2006 were blank, a bleak desert the result of a plateaued culture. The beginning of a decade void of substance – even without a decent moniker – I call them the Bush Years – full of empty, pointless words and IEDs, the ones that explode. Edgar called them IUDs, mistakenly. Luckily, the 90's continued (in spirit) half-way through these Zero Hours, giving them some flavor. Fallout from the Poor Haus continued into 2004. Turn's out, Terry Stark didn't appreciate some of the not so coded messages that were secreted in Edgar's pictures like "Alpha-Whore, Chronic Nerd and Bitches Strike Gold." Neither did she appreciate the farrago with Mr. Snout – he went back to safely buying art from Gallery Brut in New York. "This could tarnish my company image," she thought. As 2004 began, she got snippy with Edgar. By mid-winter, as if on schedule, he was targeted for dismissal after several sticky emails. This was doubly upsetting because of the sinking of his exhibition, without so much as a mention from Tommy Graves and his local press. "Now, I am really fucking depressed. No, really. It's true!" Doctors doubled Edgar's medication. He obliged and doubled the alcohol.

32
CHAPTER

Six months after the failed show at The Poor Haus, there was some construction two blocks from Edgar's bungalow. A flagman yelled, "Get off the phone, ghetto-ass!" He waved his red flag violently urging drivers to detour to the right but the line of morning rush-hour traffic continued straight for him. He rolled his eyes, "Jesus Christ!" He took a deep breath and repeated loudly, "Get off the phone ghetto-ass." By this time, he had his sweaty gloved hand on the hood of the first vehicle and stood glaring, steam and dust everywhere. The over-dressed woman behind the wheel had stopped but was trying to conduct a conversation. She didn't seem the least bit perturbed that there was a large man in a day-glo orange vest dead ahead. The 2003 BMW had a personalized license plate reading LUCYLAW.

Lucy the Lawyer complained into her cell, "There is a flagman in front of me and he is yelling. Damn, my beamer is covered in muck." She was late for a foreclosure.

The flagman continued, "People from Philly have no sense of law and order. If they did this in Jersey they'd be in court in two minutes. One hundred dollar fine. Damn!" LUCYLAW finally got the message and turned right. The next auto came straight for the flagman tentatively. Others followed. "Do you know what Detour means? Get off the phone, ghetto-ass!" Emma Sanchez turned right at the light when directed. Edgar watched her brown GM car, smoking slightly as it passed in front of his. Did she see him? He forgot to move and the driver behind honked. This activated road rage and interrupted a few endorphins. He recorded his reaction:

Sept., 4:35 PM: Shut Up, Asshole. I am looking at a woman, you fool. Wasn't that Kurtz' art teacher? Yes, I believe it is. I spotted her in a 1980 Chevy Malibu, brown. There was Indian Red, primer on one fender and blue door. She was going south and I was going north. Maybe I can start over. Every great artist has a partner who lives in shadow. I don't mind the shadows. This is awkward. Maybe she can be shadow woman. Jungian Shadows, Shrinks might say.

Edgar recognized the art teacher from his art opening but did not know that Emma Sanchez was soon to be a recipient of a Goldwater Prize. Winners received a grant of fifty grand, more than any self-respectable artist knew what to do with. Some quit the day job the next day. Most focused on the art solely; buying materials and video cameras etc to make themselves more viable. Push my envelope! For a few years they are all very much in the public eye. The public eye relishes this. Poor things. The public eye ain't what it used to be. Sanchez made the leap from struggling (emerging) artist to sanctioned practitioner, a 'made-man,' in Soprano parlance. They are invited to join the Philly art mob and given the key to the city. Edgar was too late and knew it. He was lost to the system, a complete unknown. How does it feel to be on your own, no direction home, like a rolling stone? He assumed incorrectly that since she taught art in public school, she must be a naive and full of hope. It paid well and she was glad she had gotten her teaching certificate while working towards her Masters in Sculpture at City College of Art.

Emma and Edgar had met at Kurtz's school functions. As an opportunist, she noticed the guy from the Art World. Wedding rings weren't obstacles and she warmed further. At one student art show she made hints about visiting his studio. In an unmarried world, that is code for hooking up. Have you seen the etchings in my bathroom, my dear? He thought he might give the dating world a go and she seemed game. Sally and I reviewed this period closely as you might imagine. She suggested we include this in the book, "You need more sex, Mr. Frank." She meant the book, I think. Sadly, the opportunity for one liner passed by.

"Edgar was lonely and on edge, wasn't he?"

I replied he didn't know how lucky he was. Sally mused, "Sanchez was a full-fledged fantasy in Edgar's mind. He was approaching middle age and that was possibly worse for an artist than a Joe Public. They are desperate to keep up with the speed of creative developments. Edgar and Sherrie were separated so a young female was a red flag to a bull."

"I guess you are right." This was much as I'd ever heard Sally utter at one time. I suggested to her that he felt moral qualms but they were lost in other confusions including lust. Here follows a diary excerpt from the Sanchez period:

May 12, 2006: Let's face it Edgar, you are an asshole imagining the perfect Alpha Man and Omega Girl. Kurtz, my little friend, beware the fatal femmes. The world spins too fast pour moi this afternoon. Maybe these terms should be reversed.

May 14, 2006: We have so much in common. She has a unique role; her specific talents are utilized for a greater good. That is admirable; a day job relates to her real calling. Edgar offers Emma advice: Later: I should fill her in. Warn her. It is a crushing life here. You should split quick. Maybe we could disappear together! Gauguin and the Dark Venus. Now, I'm a Creepy Frenchman. She could save me too! Mutual saving. That sounds like a plan. Is that a yes, Emma Sanchez?

I must interject; I've aspired to be a creepy Frenchman all my life. Can you blame me? Europeans have few ethics. Maybe it was Sanchez's status a rising star. Maybe it was that curious curl of her upper lip? After the grant her priorities changed. So did her status. She knew she'd mistaken Edgar for a mentor or at least an artist of some standing. He'd mistaken her for a deep soul. Mutual Stupidity makes a great relationship. Suddenly, he looked old hat and network-less. Didn't matter if his work was exciting or not. As my deadline approached, I called her for a view on Edgar's last days. I found the former art teacher's number in the Smithfield School Directory online. As I dialed from the bungalow, it occurred to me she was noticeably missing from the funeral.

Sanchez picked up, nonchalant as a mackerel on a plate, "I'm kinda busy now, Mr. Frank…"

"Only take a second"

"You mentioned a book. What's that all about?"

"A mutual friend of ours, Edgar Bloom. His rise and fall."

"Why on earth would you do that? Who is your publisher?"

"Albatross."

"I think my boyfriend knows someone there, one of the editors, Sandra Axe."

"Great! Can you comment on a few things? I need a few quotes, if you don't mind."

"OK, go ahead."

"Thanks, Emma. How did you feel when you heard about Edgar's death?"

She exhaled cutting me off at the pass. "We weren't close." Her fib hung there on landline copper wires. Translation: She didn't require the association anymore. This breakup was easily accomplished after the awards were given.

"But he mentions you many times in his diary. Quite a big crush he had, I think."

She was remarkably forthright, if not rude. "Not at all."

"Not what I heard."

"That's weird. Barely knew him really. We hooked up once or twice. I don't remember exactly. He was crazy and drunk and married. Or divorced."

"You've heard about his exhibition at the museum?"

"Yeah. I have been asked to put a piece in. Martha Trout called me herself."

"Oh. I've been working closely with Martha."

"Anything else?"

"No. I guess not Emma. You have been most helpful." The copper wires burned. Sally looked up from the digital archive and seemed to be mouthing a word.

33
CHAPTER

Dion kept a careful lid on publicity during the winter. When she was ready and all the text was perfected, she let out short scripted press releases so as to muster up interest slowly like the early stages of a plague. She made strategic leaks through specialized social media. *Forgotten Poets* was unlike the usual Museum Blockbusters that had huge PR budgets from the get go. Dali was the one I worked on. It was for the plebs. *Forgotten Poets* was for the elites.

"How big is it going to be? How fast to gel? That's how I roll, Mr. Frank." Dion winked. "Trout asked me for a decade definer and I'm not going to disappoint." The crew was watching.

"Are you winking at me, Dion? It looks like you are winking at me?"

"It looks like she is winking at you." Sally added.

"She's winking," Troy said. "Not at me."

"Please stop, Dion. I may blush."

Troy tried to help. "Leave him alone, Dion. He can't focus with you around."

I went to gather myself in the foyer and Sally followed me. "Don't fret, Frank. I think that woman is in heat." We returned to the workspace and all was quiet. Sally suggested we head up the hill for lunch. My savior. The Chestnut Hill Pub makes a mean roast beef sandwich!

As the show's profile increased, I thought Sanchez might be able to add further comments. She'd already left her teaching job. I left a message on her home contact number in Fishtown and waited a few days. A PR guy named Matt Sullivan from her gallery in New York intervened.

"Who are you and what is this about?" From the sound of his voice, he didn't have two minutes to spare. "I'm sorry, Mr. Frank. We don't give out that sort of information, only press releases. Besides, Emma Sanchez does not give interviews."

"Poor thing. How do I talk to her then?"

"You don't."

"It might be in her best interest and yours."

"I can't imagine how. Look, I really have to go."

In the media light for less than a year and she forgets how to use a phone. I knew this Sullivan-type (Deiter-ish, but worse) and figured he might be busy and frustrated, so I kept him on the line as long as possible. "Is there no other way I can contact the artist? It is really quite important I get in touch with her." He put me off again so I pushed it. "Are you Irish?

"Of course. Sullivan is an Irish name."

"There was a WW2 ship called *the Sullivans* named after four brothers who were killed in a battle. Ever heard of it?" Sullivan replied informing me there had been five brothers killed and he was not related. He then hung up.

In June, *Forgotten Poets* went above ground as Dion opened the floodgates. It popped up everywhere, next to the best holiday suggestions and best Margaritas. *Forgotten Poets* was the IT show for the coming season. As far as Sanchez was concerned, this put Edgar Bloom back in the pecking order. She was asked to be more prominent in the exhibition and her tune changed. All sweetness and light. *Forgotten Poets* legitimized Edgar and they were purportedly 'a thing.' Sanchez admitted this later when called me out of the blue while I was shaving.

"Where have you been, Emma?"

"Sorry. Several shows going on at once. You know. I heard you were trying to reach me."

Foam crept into my mouth. 'That's right. I was. Your gallery was most unhelpful."

"Sorry about that. They can be assholes and I have a new phone."

I spat some foam out. "That explains everything."

"Are you OK?"

"Don't worry about me. I'll be fine."

She finally agreed to meet. I suggested Café Mystique the next day. I showed up at 11 and she showed at 11:45 looking a little like Frida Kahlo except with two eyebrows. She seemed to be favoring her left forearm that was black and red. I waved stupidly from my usual perch as she approached. I noticed Lupo had made her coffee with some flirt-ish behavior. He grinned but kept his Spanish to himself. No muffins.

She sat down and asked, "How is the prep for the show going?"

"Well. Trout has been very kind so far. Not what I expected."

"She's my favorite curator of art but that's not saying much."

"So you wanted to tell me something about Edgar."

"You seem to be in the loop already. I'm not sure why you're so interested."

"I was given a job to do. That's it."

"Well, that's awkward. It was convenient, Mr. Frank. You know, time to cuddle up. He's not bad looking, Edgar. I mean, he was good looking and talented."

"And physically unavailable." I said.

"So what? Business is business in the art world, Mr. Frank. It's no pity party."

"Dog eat dog, eh?"

"Yeah, you could say that if you want to. We can now share the spotlight."

What a cold piece of work! "You have to keep your brand untainted, I guess."

"Brand? That's not it at all. I am not a brand."

"What do you call it when you reach a certain level where everyone pays attention?"

Blood rose in her cheeks. "I don't know what you're after, a confession? I just produce work. It's not my fault that it warrants attention."

"I'm not sure how to characterize your art and his."

"So don't."

"I like your new tattoo."

"Thanks. It's Johnny Cash."

"I can see that." Suddenly Sanchez was on the phone and disappearing. Lupo gave her a big dirty smile as she left. On the way out, he gave me a long wink. I stuck a dollar in the tip jar and flipped him the bird in one easy motion.

By July, it was unruly hot. I let a week breeze by before installing an old AC unit downstairs so we could breathe again. That helped. The Phillies were doing OK. Shortstop Utley broke a dry spell with a double, highlight of my day. Sally cheered. A few years hence, after the city's World Series win in 2008, I lost interest. And again when Jayson Werth went to join the Nats.

Watching the game on the box, I shook my toes. Sally looked in on me like a mom and asked if there was anything I needed.

"How about a cold lager?"

"Sure thing, sailor. I'm out here if you want to supervise my work." Sally knew serious writing was often done in front of a TV. She returned forthwith.

"Get a beer for yourself"

"Your such a dinosaur." I thought about my friend. It wasn't so easy for Edgar. He'd been smitten. For Sanchez, it was simply another date gone awry to be forgotten chop-chop.

"Chalk it up to ambition," Sally said as she departed toward the fridge, "Sheeza bitch."

"I won't disagree with you, Sally." Fair enough. Sanchez was another generation. Of course, Edgar idolized her. He didn't care about any of that. He sulked for weeks and went to his crazy jobs. At night he drank a lot of beer. To this his diaries attest:

Night time, Feb, 2004: Fucked up now and then some. I will be revenged, god almighty I will. I will take the wrath and stick it somewhere into the sun, the moon and into the earth. Bloody Hell, this hurts. Shadowy figures. Very well hidden. Pry open box at your peril. She is an artist but no depth is involved. It is a conundrum akin to show business. Bitch Goddesses have ruled since time and memoriam. Ask Plato.

Like most artists in Philadelphia, Edgar had craved the Goldwater Prize. The odds were low and he had given up after several applications. Look at all the ass-kissing channels artists go through. Shining their pedigrees. It was true. Kray was lobbying for Sanchez behind the scenes. String pulling is a very subtle process. Perhaps, they met on park benches on the Washington Mall? I imagined they used hand signals in a sort of code rather than meet in dark alleys to exchange manila envelopes or bodily fluids. The prize was cake-topper for the already celebrated artists who were slowly sanctioned and heading towards real accomplishments on the Philadelphia Cultural Conveyer Belt. PCCB. In this way, they could be quantified, beefed up and made less goofy; more substantial. Their updated CV's included the critical solo shows and scads of palfrey reviews from sub-par critics. *DeStephano and her friends suck.* Antics for the press. Favoritism in my city? I don't believe it. How can art be judged by a panel of suits? Edgar's assessment was spot on. It didn't matter if the work was banal or in fact, derivative and owing its soul to another better practitioner. What mattered was that it was bolstered by the system of entrenched government funding. Pure name recognition. After a beer or two Edgar rose up declaring it was all a fix. Many artists voiced similar opinions until their turn came; fingers crossed. *I was this close. Son of a Bitch!* If they managed to get the money, they were welcomed into an exclusive fold.

April, 2005: I'm in a minority here. Drop that name now. It's a trickle-down effect, except it doesn't trickle down. The artists go towards the light and try not to be seen with unpopular denizens of the underclass. I drink with this tribe who've been passed by. We like each other. Our gatherings smell of failure.

The incident with Sanchez was bad for my friend. Disillusion set in. He hated the fact that he (in some way) was ambitious in a way similar to her. He did not regard himself a mercenary. One day, modest artists were living difficult lives, complaining about being downtrodden. They then dropped their low status and stabbed each other squarely in the back. It was easy to ignore the ones left behind. Some took note, become normal citizens and put feet on terra firma. They preferred security and a boss. A wife and perhaps a kid. As Emma's star rose, all Edgar could do was watch. After 15 years of disappointment, this really was the last straw.

Thursday: I don't get it. How can these people get away with this? It is so transparent. Yes, I knew her when... They seem to have radar for each other and a shield that keeps out intruders and lesser beings like myself. Maybe it was the Chevy Malibu. Maybe it was the tattoo of the battleship on her calf. The Belgrano, I think. Odd Choice for a young Hispanic. That should have tipped me off. I screw it up over and over and insult the wrong folks. Tepid individuals who are not experts at all. They run the country club.

Emma Sanchez was Argentinian. So was the *General Belgrano*. It was also an ex-WW2 cruiser – the *U.S.S. Phoenix* – sunk by a British Nuclear Sub in a silly dispute called the Falklands War in 1982. Not an equal match. This inspired a new character in my Freddie French sketches, the sly killer, Helena Fernandez. These were used in books when needed:

> French stood menacingly over the femme fatale seated in her leather sofa chair. She goaded him, "Is that a machete in your pocket or are you just in a good mood?" Normally this would have been an unmistakable invitation but that wasn't what was on French's mind. He'd discovered that Fernandez was his partner's murderer. End of story, literally. Before she could continue teasing the macho man, a small red hole appeared in her forehead. She raised a palm and tried to speak, surprised. Anger appeared around her mouth as a tiny trickle of crimson ran down the side of her elegant nose. Her eyes faded like drying flowers in slow motion. French was in no hurry. He replaced his weapon expertly then stared at his work and said, "Right on both

counts, sweetheart. I'm glad to see you go." He watched a dark pool form beneath her. Before he left he checked the time and lifted her pants leg a few inches. The Belgrano continued to sink.

Very Mike Hammer if I don't say so myself! After a few weeks, Sanchez realized that Edgar was excess baggage and a persona non grata, a career mistake. This she would rectify. She had decided Edgar was a good artist and began mulling over some of his awesomely dark themes. "These all deal with death, Edgar. And gender, like my own work."

"I deal with gender too, Emma. Male gender. It's decline. Death is always there, isn't it?"

Edgar was blinded for the most part: Out of the mouths of babes. And I mean babes. Imitation is flattery, I guess. Great artists never steal. They borrow. No, it is the other away around. These notions, she updated using the appropriated ideas within her usual shtick, the perspective of a young, non-white urban female. Theoretically sound if mundane. How many women have used this trick? How many outsiders?

My reading paused. "Burned again, Edgar?" I asked out loud to my old friend.

Sally joined in, "What a tragic figure. So unlucky. Are you reading the Sanchez bit?"

"Yeah. What finishes a guy off better than a love triangle? It's like a sit-com."

Sally looked at me sadly. "It must have been a mess."

"Maybe he figured he and his wife had split up for good. Does that make him a creep?"

"Men are men, Mr. Frank. Mostly creeps."

"What is that supposed to mean, Ms. Brick?"

"You oughta know." With that she disappeared into her cubby and left me with several slow realizations none of which I could readily fathom.

Tuesday, 12 May: I am high and dry with out a puddle. The young can be so mercenary these days. Lost my glasses again. Left them somewhere in my travels. Fuddled brain. Oh well. What do I need eyes for? Crashed the car last week. Broke sunglasses. It is some sort of comedy. Fancy car smashes cheap car. Write off cheap car. Save on insurance but can't be anywhere on time. Unfortunately, my uninsured self-walks away unscathed. Luckily, the guitar is not damaged. It wasn't insured either. Small Favors. Thank you, Lord.

I was out of town a lot and had never heard of Elizabeth Sanchez. Beth was young and full of the sort of hubris we despised having once possessed it in spades. Edgar should have read the writing on the wall from miles away. "Idiot! You'll end up like Pollock, sans the notoriety, wrapped in a steel coffin." I guess I said this out loud.

Sally showed concern, "Time for a break, Mr. Frank?" I learned about the boy's brief romance through other channels as well as my primary source, the diaries. Nick knew Sanchez; possibly another hook up; can't prove this right now. He would deny it if asked, certainly. Back to research: Edgar was in tirade-mode so most of the content wasn't perfectly factual. Sanchez had him pegged as someone worth networking. This included sex for a short period. Very short. You shouldn't do alcohol on top of Prozac. Emma was not bothered. The affair did not last long. It started as a fun night drinking and dancing. Edgar could dance and also make women laugh; two points in his favor. Sanchez was well practiced with morning after rituals. They spoke about theoretical readings, comparing notes. Edgar caught a glimmer of her ambitious phrasing. Inter-contextualized? What does that really mean? I kept these facts from Sherrie. She had been worried about Edgar's close calls on Lincoln Drive. His drinking didn't help his erratic driving. Sherrie alerted Victor. Victor told Sherrie he would help out financially in an emergency, thinking he would become the health care provider. They were convinced a fatal car crash was imminent. Victor Bloom was a nice man who lived a private life in Manhattan. Sounded ominous. I had his cell number but he never answered. I hate that. Where are you Victor? Leave a message after my tone. What if I don't like your tone? If time permitted,

I'd leave a tactless message. "Victor. This is Mr. Frank. About your dead brother… Please call me back when you get home from wherever you are right now if it is not too much trouble." Meanwhile our hero continued to descend into his own words: I'm broke and dejected and can't think straight. This aggravated me, "Snap out of it, man! Look where you are heading. Your ex-wife (widow or whatever) is very pretty and your son is a godsend. He has grit and wisdom. If I was in your shoes, I would have gotten a decent job to make it all work." Head to the gravestone. Maybe I should settle down? But, with whom? So many fish in the sea: Dion, Sally, Sherrie, Trout or Deiter. What about Sanchez? Was she out of my league? I mulled this around in my own journal. Don't worry, I am not publishing it.

34

CHAPTER

Near the end of the project I was expecting Martha Trout and company for a meeting to discuss final preparations. The publicity people were also after me. What a couple Cranston and Trout made! Deiter was in my corner and I wasn't sure if I had room. First, I had to finalize the details of my last period of occupation. This involved fending off Sherrie who had her own timetable. We'd discussed this several times. I was nowhere near finished with the cataloguing, much less the reading. I now had a major exhibition on my plate, Edgar's rehabilitation attached and an unfinished book contingent upon that. The publishing date moved around but the show was lined up to make bang for the buck. All was in flux and I was facing eviction. How did you get into this, Mr. Frank? I made the mistake of mentioning the Quik-Fix people to Sherrie. She was having trouble selling the houses after a month or so of trying and had never heard of staging a property for sale. A specific sort of spruce up. We agreed both places could use the makeover. Edgar's studio needed more than that; an exterminator to start and a really good plumber. Possibly a Priest to exorcise the place.

"Sherrie, what if I bought the bungalow as a summer place?"

"Mr. Frank! You would do that? That would speed things up for me. Why would you do that?"

"I'm getting sort of attached to it." I fluttered my eyelashes and she gave me a big kiss on the left cheek. Eyelashes are key. "Let me mull that one over. But I sort of like the idea."

I figured since I was already ensconced and part caretaker myself then Sherrie would have one less headache. Who knows, maybe the city would get around to sticking up a historical plaque to Bloom:

Original member of the
Philadelphia Artist Group Forgotten Poets
artist EDGAR BLOOM lived here
1994-2006

When I called her the next week, she confirmed our real estate plans. She said she'd sell one place at a time. Phew! I went to sleep with milk and vodka thinking I'd sorted out a problem. Quik-Fix was starting Thursday at the Blue House and things were falling into place. When I awoke that morning, all was calm and I began grinding beans. Then the penny dropped. It suddenly came into my mind – knowing their ways from Edgar's journals – the first day was when Quik-Fix trashed everything deemed unworthy! My goof-up rushed down a track towards me like a choo-choo as I relaxed on the rails reading a newspaper. I jumped in Edgar's bug and tore across the hood at 60 mph. It was foggy and there may now be one or two less bag ladies in Germantown. I think they were bag ladies. When I arrived at the Blue House, there were some trash pickers hovering in beat-up cars. I became assertive and made a special show of my entrance utilizing screechy brakes and burning rubber. A massive pile was already growing on the sidewalk and a dumpster was being delivered.

I saved several old paintings by Bloom. Two were from the Trauma Queens period, pictures of punk bands. There was some mold on them. These would go for three figures at auction before this story ends aka Antiques Road Show on PBS. Several sketchbooks from the same era I also snagged before pausing, out of breath. The pile grew as a gaggle of illegal aliens continued to bring out tons from the house. Some of it was truly rubbish and some of it just looked like rubbish. I sifted through and pulled out some nifty antique frames and old kitchenware as well. After a time, I stood back and watched what they removed from the house. My god, Edgar lived on in me these days – Douglas Frank, disciple of Bloom. I sought the goblet and the true cross. Twenty minutes later, I was found on top of the precarious mound in the dumpster sifting.

Terry came out frowning, "Is there a problem?"

A new hire was with her, Taffy, "Can we help you, sir?"

Sherrie hurried out after them in a fluff and introduced me, "Terry and Taffy. This is Mr. Frank. He's Edgar's friend." I was sweating like a pig. Steam pouring from my nostrils. Terry finally recognized me.

Taffy lightened, smiling at the recognition. "You are the man writing the book about Edgar!"

"Nice to meet you. You have me at a distinct disadvantage."

Terry was thinking, "What a nightmare but the book is a godsend for my small business and Frank brings unpaid advertising to support my new mini-brand. Optimum outcomes." After some awkward chit-chat, Sherrie invited me in. We headed straight for the kitchen. Off limits to QF staff for the moment. We shut the doors of her sanctuary and brewed some coffee for tall mugs. Before I knew it, she was in my arms, crying. I handled this with aplomb. I hadn't realize how attached she was to the house and her possessions. Time stopped. Or seemed to until Terry came in silently with packing tape and looked at us. I signaled her out with a rude pinky. She obliged, head down. Sherrie admitted that she wasn't as prepared as she'd thought. Kurtz didn't want to leave his school.

I gave her an earnestly felt platitude. "You'll do fine, kid. Kurtz will be OK."

Taffy poked her head in with scissors and duct tape and quickly un-poked herself. Sherrie let me go and smiled. "That sounds like dialogue in a crappy movie or a book of yours."

"Real life is not fiction."

"I know you mean well."

Well, I hope you don't mind if I try and recover some 'maybe' masterpieces from this steamroller."

She smiled. "Go ahead. I should have looked through the stuff more carefully before today."

"Not your fault. I should have warned you about the Quik-Fix methodology."

She looked around the kitchen avoiding my eyes. My endorphins were on full alert. "I'm going to miss you and our meetings."

"Me too," I said as I moved for the door. "I have to save a few more things. And yes, we'll always have Paris."

She giggled as I headed back out front, "I've never been to Paris."

March 4, 2004: Stand up for the little man and Fuck this weather. It's damp and cold in vacant house. The Day Job persists and I have a hard time keeping my cool when the show disappears into oblivion before it even starts. Here comes the cow. I call her Queen Astoria. Get it? Astoria, Queens? Shouldabeena artist; she is snotty enough. She has aspirations and no talent. She will marry well next time and dabble.

I am no therapist but many Quik-Fix clients clearly had a collecting disorder. They were in one of life's major markers, a tight squeeze between retirement and the grave. Many had alpha-boomer kids and ancient parents of a previous generation. They had shaken off their radical roots to take on a more pro-401K perspective, though they still listened to appallingly redundant music from the Counter-Culture era. Edgar didn't like their hippie records, but their parents? That was a different story. There was plenty of Easy Listening and old Jazz, even some Yiddish folk songs on 78 RPM. This wasn't stealing. Terry had sanctioned him to help clear out the place fast. Boxes of records were cumbersome and heavy. After nearly two years of this, his Bungalow was overflowing. Edgar illustrated this well with gleeful descriptions of domestic treasures in detail.

Feb; 2, 2006: QUIK-FIX houses are full of decades of accumulated rubbish and it was often difficult to persuade clients to part with their collections of golf balls, magazines or ancient newspapers. I do all the shit labor and don't get credit! These people don't know they are sick! They may be wealthy but they are not well organized. Terry considers most people's furniture too hideous for display. She is right!

Clients had piles of newspapers and periodicals intermixed with boxes of office supplies, mingled indiscriminately with antiques, family photos and dirty socks. Some people were so out of touch, they weren't aware there was a problem. Always the clincher! When Terry suggested that things be simplified – meaning 'everything removed' permanently to sell a house – they sometimes took offense. Some put up a fight. No one at the company had any training in proclivities of this sort. That was a stretch of job skills. Who was best versed in dealing with sad people's problems? Edgar Bloom, of course. Subtle persuasion was needed at every stage; a delicate personal touch and a sleight of hand. What should be discarded, or at least stored? Much got thrown out by Astoria on the sly. She was merciless and preferred to chuck out valuables like family heirlooms and collectible antique children's toys.

"Disgusting old trash," she'd say, offended. Clients assumed their own abodes looked fine cluttered with debris, a lived in look they were comfortable with. Terry was paid to take charge and help them decide what to throw away and what furniture to keep. It was down to the crew to make it happen. Hopefully the client would be out. Edgar loved the rummage sale atmosphere and the perks. He'd laugh as he rummaged through the lifetime's accumulation of collected consumer good. Astoria thought this was low class. "These people live like pigs," she said, grimacing. After her last trip to the dumpster, she took off her blue, rubber gloves and washed her hands twice. She lived up to Edgar's description as a shrill hag. Seeing Edgar's ex-work mates in person was weird. The next day, I was looking for Sherrie when I sensed the Amazon's approach. She had noticed the ancient green bug, (brought back to life) and suspected trouble. Yes, I have inherited Edgar's car, girl, get used to it! She loomed up and I offered to help her lift a large trunk. "Why don't you leave us work?"

"You have his job, aren't you happy now?

She sneered, "We're on a deadline."

"So am I, sister."

She scowled, "What are you doing here, writer man?"

"Damage control."

"You are very funny man, yes?"

"Hilarious, I'm told."

"Not from where I have been sitting."

I stared at her, squinting me eyes. "Why don't you go back to Siberia?"

She starred back, squinting her eyes. "I am from Ukraine."

July, 12, 2003: Houses are vernacular museums. Does this make us voyeurs? People have the strangest record collections. Got this great hat, I am wearing as we speak. Dolls and old baseball mitts. Fantastic cultural objects, if not antiques per se. My orders are to downsize it and chuck the junk in the dumpster. Terry views it as crap. A lot of responsibility for me, I think. The next family moving in will have no awareness of the previous suffering or lives lead here. Who died? Who moved? Everyone starts to forget them at this stage. Who cares? Domestic Regime Change?

A day or two later I got in the last word, snuck up behind her and whispered darkly in her ear. "Don't think it hasn't been fun, because it hasn't." On my way out, I spotted Miguel holding a milk crate of Edgar's LPs, heading for the dumpster. I had really screwed up. He handed me the crate and I chucked it into the front seat of the Beetle and tore back to the Bungalow, both relieved and upset. I must learn to be more diligent in the future. I bought some Jim Beam and a bottle of ginger ale for my insomnia. Joy Division cheered me up and the first drink felt fine. For side two, I made another drinkie and sat down with a calendar. I began thinking the house would make an excellent investment and fixer upper. The place made the project possible. Who knows, the impossible might happen and the neighborhood might return from the dead.

35

CHAPTER

Nick English was on a roll. He had moved to New York where he met friends in the Art World and was milking it. Youthful Brooklyn "creatives" were doing the reverse, all keen and hungry. The New York Times Magazine inferred in 2006 that Philadelphia was now the "Sixth Borough." Did that mean Brooklyn was the new Manhattan? Nick still turned up in Fishtown to visit Sam for comfort and gloating. They'd visit their old haunts that had turned the corner from hip-dive to hipster-dive, if you get the difference. He'd invested years with her, a hard habit to break. They'd talked about making it a permanent arrangement but the idea didn't take. "You can't network with a baby in tow, Sam." he stated. "All these people settling down. It's the end of their careers." Sam was hurt but pretended to understand. Presently, Nick was working furiously towards his first one-person show at a Chelsea gallery called Dead Seventeen. There was light at the end of his tunnel (the one named after Lincoln) and he left no stone unturned in order to create sensation. He was good at it. The Gallery had discovered him by chance in Miami where his work was set up in Motel Esquire, a satellite of the Miami Art Fair. The artists had promo folders on beds in hotel rooms and the dealers were as happy as sharks in a Bond Movie. Botoxed people with expensive jewelry poured in trawling for hidden or undiscovered wrecks. They zoned in on uniquely driven talent. Nick fit the bill. Dealers hoped to scoop up bargain artists from known and unknown sources. Edgar was jealous.

Dec. 22, 2004: If Nick can do it, so can I! Put your best resume forward. Look at these bogus bios with bibliographies listing the hundreds of poxy reviews mentioning their name! Future Art Stars? My ass! Beware. If you get sucked in, you are labeled. Nothing unusual pour moi. Sounds nasty, but there were times when I thought I almost made it. I will live to tell the tale.

Or not, dear boy! I met Nick at Green on Red the next week. Mickey was delighted to meet another friend of Edgar. "I've read one of your books, Mr. Frank!"

"Which one?"

"Can't remember the name. Lots of wise-cracking and gunplay. Cool stuff."

"That could be any one of them."

"Are they all the same?"

"You might say that, Mickey." I liked MM immediately and decided I would take a bullet or two for him. The former grease monkey turned crack addict then baker was charming.

"This is on the house. guys. Your money is no good until I say different or June says. She wears the pants. You and Mr. Frank sit in the best booth where you can watch the hipsters walk by. I think they are hipsters. They have stretchy tight jeans. Velcro-ed or something. They look fucking cool to me." He joined us and I realized was sitting with a Mick and a Nick. Me, the private dick? Get it? I began to identify with my character French. Even to the point of flirting with June, who was no calendar girl. She took our orders with a business like unfriendliness. I was composing in my head:

Her face was heavy and worn, the result of a thousand late nights dishing goulash. Her demeanor said no but her tight buttoned blouse was saying, please do. She stood in front of him and leered, "Anything for dessert, buddy?" French could think of one thing and it wasn't cherry pie.

A mental email note arrived from Sally Brick to Mr. D. Frank: Mr. Frank, please keep French character in check! Back to reality: Nick started a new rant. He derisedly mentioned Zach. "I think Art Bank damages Sam's career and sucks energy out of the city." I let him go on while keeping an eye on Millennials and bag ladies. "At functions, Sam is conscripted to talk up new artists. This isn't unpleasant really." He sounded a bit jealous.

I interrupted, "But aren't you an insider now, Nick, my friend?"

He made a face as if choking on a plum, "No, no, Mr. F. That ain't the case at all. I have to put up with them. It's a fine line. We infiltrate the conglomerates."

"Oh, I see," I said, unconvinced.

"At Zach's events, Sam is on display. There is plenty of booze and glamorous, influential folks to ogle. She likes that but it gets her nowhere."

"I'd like it too." Mickey added, feeling a little left out. He looked towards the kitchen. "But I have my Junie." Edgar joined the discussion from inside my head:

April 6, 2000: Sam is overly charming. We made a good team but she abides by the rules. I hate being polite. She is quick to learn new behaviors. Not me. I'm old school. Fucking Websites and storage devices. It Bytes. Sam has an amazing fortitude in regards demeaning work. I respect that but she deserves better than Eskimo Quinn and all his shyte.

Who was I to disagree? Art Bank was a good place for BFA's to start the day job routine and stay connected to a youthful cutting edge. All this, before deciding an MFA was crucial. Five years later you realize that it was all for naught in economic terms. Don't believe it, an MFA was never the new MBA. The models for art "careers" had changed fast in the Late Twentieth Century. "Sam is a good kid," Nick went on. "She has plans to visit the Armory Show in New York with me." I let that sink in then asked, when? Nick said, "Friday. It opens tomorrow. The Spring Art Fairs are the high point of the Contemporary Art calendar."

With untypical enthusiasm I said, "I must go Nick, part of the Edgar research! Can I accompany you guys?"

"Of course you can, Mr. Frank. You'll be inspired. It's at the pier on the Hudson River."

Mickey pouted. He had to stay home and mind the store. "International Cupcake Day is tomorrow and we are going to sell a billion heart-shaped cupcakes! Maybe you should buy one for Sherrie?" He shot his wife a quick glance, busily baking. They had a special bond.

36
CHAPTER

The New Jersey Turnpike opened up in front of us full of promise. I had picked my art friends up in Old City and we drove over the Ben Franklin Bridge. Nick was navigator and Sam was in the back. They carried coffee thermoses and were already caffeinated. The jabber about exhibitions began: "This year looks to be particularly interesting."

"There is lots of installation and a special video by Wilfred Banks."

"I've read all about that," said Sam. "He's a genius."

My eyes were on the road. "Hang on. Are we going to bandy that term around?"

"Well, he is. The critics agree."

"Who are the critics you keep mentioning?"

"Art Forum, New York Times, Art Review. Everybody."

"What do they know?"

"Frank. You are such a doubting Thomas," said Nick. "You need to lighten up, dude."

"I want to see the wounds in the side. Yes."

"He wants to see the wounds, Nick," said Sam. She continued from the back seat, "We'll show you what's what and you'll be converted. Too bad Edgar can't be with us!" We all nodded as the Philly skyline receded in the rearview.

The cars sped up and the traffic thickened. Downshifting began. Before we knew it, the first toll needed paying. Unfortunately, there was no EZ-Pass in Edgar's car. "God damned, EZ-Pass!" I said vehemently as we paid. "It was a mistake to take the bug. My Toyota has EZ Pass."

"Don't worry, Mr. Frank. We have plenty of time."

"I hate slowing down every twenty minutes to chat with these boring people."

"It's all part of the process," said Nick. "The Zen of the Turnpike." As we settled in, I got more dope on the art aristocracy from my friends. They were warming up to ask me about Edgar's departure and the museum. I played dumb. Didn't take much effort.

"So how is Trout treating you? Is she behaving herself?" asked Nick finally.

"She's a real crone," I replied, keeping my true thoughts hidden in my head.

Sam inquired, "Do you have the advance, Mr. Frank?"

"I can't say yet."

The day clouded as we passed New Brunswick and I felt a déjà vu coming on. Nick turned to me, "Aw, come on, Frank. You must have a sense of what is happening."

"Soon, I think. It's bad luck to discuss it like a premature baby shower."

I was driving like Tommy Lee Jones on his way to church. Nick wasn't bothered but Sam sucked air through her teeth in the back seat, "This old car moves pretty good. If only Edgar were here."

"Think this is fast? Watch me pass this asshole."

The engine flexed. Sam began to read license plates to relax. "Here's a good one. 'AHE, Adam Hates Eve.'"

"I like it," I yelled back over the engine.

Sam screamed like a ten year old in my right ear, "GBH!"

"What's that stand for?" asked Nick, "Good Body Honey?"

"No, you fool. 'God's Big Head.'"

"No, 'Grievous Bodily Harm?' It's British." My friends laughed loudly over the motor.

The traffic thickened again around New Brunswick. We passed several minivans that were hogging the middle lane. They slowed up the entire Eastern Seaboard. There were several Town and Countrys all in good condition like bloated, champagne colored whales. They struggled along in clutches or should that be schools? New Jersey was only moving at 54 MPH. A Black Chevy Suburban was in a particular hurry, weaving outside the obstacles. Nick pointed. "Look at that skinny bitch go."

"Perhaps she works for the government," said Yours Truly.

Sam hopped on board, optimistically, "Homeland Security! No, she's late for Lipo Suction." We all had to chuckle.

"Or breast implants. skinny bitch." Nick added. We edged dangerously into the woman's wake to pick up time but were jostled aside by a Jeep Laredo with a cloaking device. This hopped-up asshole blew by at 85 MPH and his airflow buffeted our vehicle. Nick reacted dramatically, "Did you see his bumper sticker? 'I'm a Dickhead!'"

Sam laughed, astonished. "You're kidding, right?"

"No. Look, Sam," he pointed vigorously. But she couldn't make verification; the bumper was out of range. I smiled. She fell for it. His sticker actually read: GUNS&GOD and there was a Jesus fish next to that.

"I hope the cops get him."

"It takes all kinds. Maybe he's late for the Art Fair," I said.

They found this remark hysterically funny.

"What's funny?" I asked, baffled.

"Not the type, though collectors come in all sizes," said Sam. "All it takes is money and attitude." Maybe it was true. He could have been a serious art buyer also into god, guns and lousy grammar.

The traffic got thicker and I spied a new maroon Honda Odyssey shaped like a suppository. 2006 was a good year for suppositories. Nick the navigator became angry, "This always happens." He stretched his palms on the dash. "Another one. Who wants a car up their ass?" Nick muttered obscenities about the lack of aesthetics in the commercial sector and smacked his fists into the shredded dash. We were all thrown sideways when a Toyota Freeloader lumbered by emitting a huge sonic wave of rap music. The car seemed to inflate and deflate rhythmically. Luckily, it was muffled by closed windows. There was a bass speaker in the vehicle that shook your solar plexus and sphincter. I rubbed my eyes and slowed down. Next obstacle was a bashed-up Nissan Sienna with several seniors trying to read the GPS device.

"Here's some old coots," I said, "I can smell the Ben Gay from here."

"Sounds like a porn star, doesn't it?" added Nick.

"Ben Gay," repeated Sam. "That's so funny, boys."

A few more Windstars glided along, grumpily. One elegant, dented Nissan Quest from before the last war; I mean, Desert Storm. A rare Pontiac Montana snuck by. It was silver and had been rear ended by a high-riding Dodge Ram from the look of it. The copper color had burnt off the hood in 1999. It was heading back to the inner city to hide among multicolored doors and fenders, vehicle transplants from body shops. Nick suddenly commanded. "Time for coffee and a bathroom."

Rest stops on The NJ Turnpike offer massive walls of urinals to service forty caffeinated male travelers at once. There is a certain gag factor in the summer.

Sam concurred, "I gotta go too." We pulled off at the Joyce Kilmer rest stop and parked in between two massive trucks. A large family of large people was disembarking from one. I couldn't help but make a cultural assessment. Large blue-collar dad in construction whose wife was over-tanned and ran a nail salon. Two obnoxious kids, one into 21st century hip-hop, the other sporting an odd third generation Emo attire. The *My Chemical Romance* Tee shirt was a giveaway. Neither kid had a cell phone. Now, that was odd.

After Sam's pit stop, our group headed straight to the Starbucks. Sam needed a sandwich at 11 am. Nick and I ordered twin Lattes. We sat far away from the madding crowd near the McDonald's and the pizza joints. Sipping coffee, Nick and I watched Sam closely. She tore open the package and began devouring it. My thought, same as Edgar's: Hungry women are always pregnant and vice versa! Furthest thing from Nick's mind, I could tell. Must have been my feminist side. I held up my Latte, "I need this caffeine, Sam. I was up late doing Edgar's work."

Sam didn't look up but Nick's comment caught me off guard, "Ah, Lord Edgar. How unusual, Frank. Was your secretary there?"

"Huh?" I looked up, menacingly.

"Your secretary, Sally. What's her name?"

"Brick, Sally Brick. None of your business, chum. Editor."

Nick continued missing all signs of my umbrage. "She's a peach, I guess. And that Trout? She's a piece of work. She is honoring Edgar as well as using him. Creepy. What's their deal?"

"You know as well as I, don't you, Nick?"

"Do I? How do you figure?"

"You're on the inside of this art thing. It pans out well for you."

"Not sure I get you. I work hard. And you're wrong. Do you mean museum as graveyard of culture and that old hat stuff?"

"No, I mean that artists are treated like commodities once they succeed. If they don't, no one gives a damn."

"It's much more complicated than that, buddy."

"So says you."

Sam may have overheard as she greedily washed down the Toasted Turkey Sandwich with her 16-ounce Grande. I let pass the urge to give Nick a knuckle sandwich with extra mayo. His day might yet come. "What about the book?" Sam asked, mouth full. "Does Edgar talk much about me?"

I nodded, still angry, "No spoilers. But yes, you make an appearance, Sam. Of course, you do, more than a cameo."

Nick wanted to know too. "Do you mention me in the book, Frank. Does Edgar in the diaries"

I looked at him and he waited for my answer. "Edgar certainly does but the book isn't written yet so I don't know."

He looked back at me. "I'll be in suspense now."

"I guess you will, Nick. Cross your fingers."

"We were good friends."

"Don't worry. You'll do fine."

Back in Edgar's Bug, it took a moment to regain optimum Turnpike speed. Nick fiddled with the cassette player then gave up and tuned in a radio station manually. A white Dodge Caravan careened past on the inside. "Not so fast, creep," I said, as we sped up slowly, bug style. We forgot about art. A blue Chevy Venture boxed me in. "Minivan Hell!" I shouted, downshifting. I dropped back and changed lanes. "These guys are working in cahoots."

My passengers yelled, "Get them, Mr. Frank!" We could no longer hear the radio. I eased by the road whales at maximum RPM.

"Hurrah!" We shrieked.

"It's all about competition, isn't it?" Nick yelled over the din, "Life, that is. Can't let them win." We managed to squeeze past. "Way to go, Frank!"

"This is a fun video game, isn't it?" yelled Sam, "Or it could be."

I filled my lungs and yelled leaning backwards. "We must use extreme tactics to kick their butts. Is there room for a right turn, navigator?"

"Go for it," Nick urged. "We are on course, Captain."

Seeing Newark Airport on the left side ahead, we exited right towards the city. Satisfied that German Engineering had gotten us to New York, I began discussing the project again. "It is rewarding, guys, helping artists who need help. Did you know Joyce Kilmer was a poet and a man?" They assumed I was being funny, but it was true. "He was a poet and a man; wrote a poem about a tree." A few miles after exiting the Turnpike, New York loomed up. I couldn't see where the Trade Center used to be. My landmarks were gone. It was disorienting and sad. The area was now camouflaged by other structures; surgery where a band-aid would've done. We approached the Holland Tunnel and I imagined swimming to the surface in an emergency.

"Let me off in Hoboken," quipped Sam, as if reading my mind. We crawled through a long cash-only line and forfeited six bucks. No smiles were required.

I clicked on the lights. "Going to be eight bucks soon. Damn tolls." As we sank under the river and into the tunnel, the radio turned to static. My ears popped and I tried to stay in my lane. No one turned the static off. We emerged on the other side in a different world as the college radio came back in range. The sky looked different. The air smelled different. Everyone was late for an appointment. The street people had Blackberries. After ditching the car in a lot, we hijacked a Pelham 123 uptown. Hurtling through the underworld across town with madmen was always a thrill. The whole of humanity was present, good, bad and ugly as well as a few guys who thought they could sing Doo-Wop for change. They sang well, but New Yorkers are tight. We rolled upstairs out of the bewildering cave and into the blinding light of day. We were then jostled by quick-moving crowds of monstrously-sized human beings in heavy coats.

Nick led the way without looking up to get his bearings. "Every MFA should know the subways of New York by heart."

I whispered in Sam's ear, "What an ass."

"You ain't wrong." I reached for my scarf and wondered: how come in New York, the wind only blows from the direction in which you are traveling? I also asked myself when had Nick become such a fuck-head? The two piers stuck out into the icy river like massive fingers, pointing ominously at New Jersey. We forked out twenty smackers each and entered the gates of the Ivory Tower.

37

CHAPTER

The first New York Armory Show was held in an Armory. It was 1918 and 'Modern Art' was about to break. This was different. Like most outside the biz, I'd not been keeping up. Shame, but every time a civilian picks up an art magazine they feel total loss. It's a foreign language. This trade fair had smarts, echoing the working week and referencing the entire twentieth century full of blanched cubicles, large and small. They were filled with expensive oddities and some art historical standards for the Demi-Monde. A few Warhols, a real Leger canvas or two and many Damien Hirst butterfly prints started the ball rolling. *Drop a few more names!* I noticed several stalwart Alex Katz paintings.

"Lots of Katz." I said to Nick. They were easy on the eye even in a shitty setting.

Nick pronounced, "He's prolific and hasn't changed his methods in 50 years, a quality Blue-Chip Jew." We stared at him and he regretted the remark immediately. "That came out wrong, sorry." We gave him more looks and let it slide. A crowd was gathered around a white '67 Oldsmobile. The rust bucket was covered with dead leaves while a video chirped from within. A disembodied Valley Girl voice was whining, "Buy me, buy me. I'm for sale. Totally." She must have been painting her nails, buried within. Typical work from well-known artist Perry Greed of San Diego, whose art museum, incidentally, already owned the piece.

Our leader, Nick proffered an opinion. "Very insightful, supposedly. A droll enterprise. I give it the benefit of the doubt because I like vintage cars and Perry is a woman. Look over there, a whole assortment of new abstraction. It looks like a trendy recombination of established vocabularies."

Sam cut him off, "We don't need a complete commentary, Nick." She had an excited look on her face, eyes darting wildly. "I prefer her cousin's work, Mr. Frank, Chelsea Wormwood. They were both foster kids."

"Never heard of either of them, Sam. Sorry."

She leaned in touching my arm, "Can't you smell the money?"

"No, but I think I'm allergic to the carpet. I should have taken an anti-histamine."

"These dealers are from all over the world, Mr. Frank." I nodded, stupidly. They looked it, clearly exhausted and hung over. The gallerists from the Big Apple were well attired and appeared genuinely pissed off. Nothing new. Why should they learn Chinese? They groaned: It's a Trade Show. But it is worth it. In most cases, their art survived only in a controlled gallery environment. Kudos to them for trying to make it happen in a hideously decorated convention center. Best to stick work in vitrines and be done with it.

I felt ill and thrashed around holding my throat. "This is suffocating. I am suffocating."

Sam grabbed my arm. "Cheer up, Mr. Frank. Take it all in, good and bad; commerce and art battling it out."

We turned a corner and I stopped short. I grabbed them both by the elbows. "Holy shit. Look. Cassandra Giovanni!" They became silent and followed me into the booth. I approached the white walls slowly.

"She is their old friend from Rome."

Nick said to Sam, "I thought she was dead."

It was an elegant display of grainy photographs. Enigmatic shadows of footprints in dust, long gone. No salesperson encroached. Cassandra never faced the camera, but her body was seen in ghostly, unlived-in rooms with broken plaster. An uncertain breast was visible here and there, mildly erotic. Blurry whiffs of an outmoded chemical process, pre-digital. In a corner, was a lo-tech SONY video of her looking out a barren window, face half hidden. A breeze blew the curtains and her hair. It was bleak, projected on a mute cubicle wall. Beneath the frames were little red dots indicating the work was selling fast.

"Jumping off the walls. Gone before the show is even fully underway," whispered Nick. I'm not using the word schadenfreud again, OK, because we are beyond that sort of thing. No mockery here. I would call it abuse. There was no evidence of any dealers. They weren't needed. We hovered alone with Cassandra. She never lived to see herself 'Googled.' My friends were impressed. For twenty minutes we are transported from our loud, shitty world to a strange inner landscape. Even English was moved and he hadn't come to an Art Fair to have emotional responses. He wanted to see the market parsing intricate theoretical positions. "Does the Museum murder Art?" It started to get crowded so we went for expensive coffees served in ceramic cups. We sat tightly together around a shiny, stainless steel table the size of a cake, our elbows anchored on our knees. I filled them in about Cassandra and Edgar in Rome; first hand poop. Neither Nick or Sam knew her work well but they knew the legend.

I spoke emphatically without thought. "She was a mystery and inspired everyone she met."

"Too much earnestness makes me ill," uttered Nick.

"What about genuinely 'earnest,' Nick? I don't know much about art my friends but this is the real deal. She was doing this without the art market in mind, before the art star thing existed, with a 35 mm Nikon." Nick said the pictures reminded him of a few artists. They hung on my next words. "Sure. A lot. But those are all copycats, dude. You can see that. They are cashing in on her life." Nick knew when to stay quiet, stirring the hot drink with a thin piece of wood.

"When did she die, Mr. Frank?" asked Sam.

"Let's save that story for the trip home, Sam." Nick looked relieved. I imagined hundreds of stationary taillights on 95. Thankfully, Nick was going back to his place. I'd have Sam to myself.

I remembered Giovanni. "Poor Cassandra. Now, digitally distributed, libraried on YouTube with random trash. The medium reduces the message, reproduced ad infinitum."

"That sounds like Walter Benjamin talking, Mr. Frank."

"No, it's me. Nick. I'm considering Cassandra. Had she made it through to this phase, she'd be a fixture in the 6-figure range, a transcendent global franchise, dark horse rather than a sacrifice. Now, every inch of her life is scrutinized, every laundry list. Nick was working out the relative auction prices with a pencil.

I went on uneasily. "She needed more than cigarettes and a drink, not just to be included into the canon of photography, no pun intended. She needed some TLC. She was in a depressed, friendless place." They hadn't known I knew her so well. For them she was a distant figure in the Who's Who of Contemporary Art. I probed Nick. "Who do you think has the copyright to make these prints, Nick? They are priced at five thousand a pop"

"Not sure. Maybe the Giovanni Foundation, in her name and some lawyers. Are her folks alive?"

"Yeah, I think so."

He caught my eye seeking approval. "I'll look into that for you if you like, Doug."

"As time went by, Cassandra Giovanni became Edgar's flagship or was it Titanic? After her death, her star rose steadily."

"Edgar certainly needed a peer model," said Sally.

I mused aloud. "It's eerie how the news leaked out over time when it appeared to be advantageous to someone. Her parents and galleristas were in cahoots. They keep the full story in shadow."

"It's the way of the world." Nick mumbled. "Artists need a template to go by."

"Maybe by the end of *Work Shy*, we'll have a working model that doesn't combust; one that functions practically."

Sam agreed wearily, "That would be a good thing Frank, for all us Edgars of the world."

Edgar disagreed of course, bloody contrarian: I want to end up like Sid Vicious. (I call him Sid Vintage!) Ignominious and gone, baby. Once you are digitized you are finished. Unreality sets in and you don't exist. It's belittling. Your aura is gone if you ever had one. The sharks then tear what is left of you apart. *The jaws, the jaws...* Edgar left this mortal coil before High Definition and possibly re-united with Cassandra. Dead Poets Society, Ha ha. Everybody, especially collectors, love a crash and burn. Marilyn and James Dean. Pollock and Van Gogh. Jim Morrison and Hendrix. Basquiat and Rothko. For punkers, it is Ian Curtis. A later generation had Kurt Cobain. Post war, it is Kennedy, Kennedy and Kennedy.

After caffeine, we skirted Kray Brothers' exhibit space carefully. It was busy. We saw the top of Richard's head, an iceberg in a sea of yuppies. We exited to the extreme West Side where we found a small Cuban bistro run by Koreans on Eighth Avenue. Just the ticket. Art talk continued. "Modernist royalty distracts me," confessed our tour guide.

"Why can't they leave it in the museum?" asked Sam.

"Good point. Modern and Contemporary don't mix well these days. In fact, contemporary no longer means 'today' or 'modern'." Nick agreed. "I hear the Modern age now starts with daVinci. Does that make any sense?" I listened and ate my dinner.

Sam and I were finally alone in the green beetle buzzing back to PA. We had plenty of time to chat loudly over the high-pitched wall of engine noise at full tilt. We listened to indie music on late night college stations, an endless somber drone and squeal followed by a ten minute dissertation on the bands we just heard. "Sam, that was wild but the space was too restrictive."

"There's not much you can do with that kind of building, Frank. Doesn't matter a fig." Sam continued, "I could stare at a Morandi all day. Perks of the job."

"Yeah, Morandi is undervalued."

"I'm glad we discovered Cassandra. They seem somehow joined."

"You mean Edgar and Cassandra?" We started discussing Edgar's atypical views.

"Yeah. They are now both gone."

"There is a difference. Edgar was a flaming moderate."

"How so?"

"He distrusted all the clubs people join and positions they take. Artists side with subversiveness, at least on the surface. Sometimes it's a sham. Edgar had no invitation to the dance."

This lost Sam, "I thought artists dedicated themselves to cosmic truths, ultimately."

"Which one, Sam?" She went quiet, thinking I'd insulted her. Hadn't meant to. The little German motor chugged efficiently towards Independence Hall in sync with the ambient music. She nodded off and fell silent. Pregnant women need to sleep a lot. As we pulled down the ramp at speed, I woke her gently and hoped she wasn't angry. "Sam, I think I had too much to drink last night."

"You say that every day, Frank. Thanks for driving. This is one noisy car." I got an impersonal hug when I dropped her off in Fishtown. I instinctively turned south and headed to the Dominion. Trust my luck. There was a spot right next door between two mini-vans.

38
CHAPTER

I slept late and had a coffee around the corner at noon. I arrived back at the Bungalow at around two. My crew was already planning an attack and had put wagons in a circle. The critics were due the next day. By the end of the day, we had a plan to deal with the journalists and my crew disappeared. Sally remained as usual.

There were also loose ends of the exhibition and *Work Shy* to deal with. We decided to focus intently on the combustible MFA period as well as the last final moments. Sally fired up the trivia search engine posthaste. My uber-English major suggested we go back to find the first diaries for comparison. We could show the critics some of the actual "evidence." This wasn't easy. Boxes had to be found and better organized. We sifted through what we thought were the earliest notebooks – covered in Star Trek stickers. A small pile formed on the floor. We sat around on the floor and worked it out. I found myself oddly relaxed watching my assistant dedicate herself to Bloom. Sally cataloged by magic! We sorted through shoeboxes full of family snaps, iconic archives of a personal nature. I put on an obscure record by Cabaret Voltaire and opened an Australian Cabernet with a convenient screw can and a woody finish. Everyone else had gone home. *Date Night, Mr. Frank?*

Sally held up an artful Polaroid, "Who's this?"

The years dropped away disconcertingly, "Ah, Grad School picture Professor Mito, our post modern guru. File it under shitheads and never look at it again."

"Is this the first selfie?"

In the second year, Edgar went further. He ditched canvas completely and experimented on walls like Keith Haring or A. R. Penck, anything with a German-Expressionist bent – very happening; Neo-German-Expressionist, to be precise. Of course, the new German Invasionists were old school conceptualists in disguise, like Immendorf. How underhanded! At the big critique before Thanksgiving Break, Edgar showed a painting to the assembled multitude, including Mito. Everyone stood around seriously smoking and squinting. They sipped coffee from their respective studio mugs mostly ugly ceramic things. "Turning a Corner" was 3 by 4 feet and depicted a killing. It might have been made by Otto Dix, the German Expressionist (1891-1969) if he'd gone punk – Dix had enough things to worry about. Mito hated this. It was too felt, simple to read and didn't illustrate any of Michel Foucault's theories in any way one could easily pontificate upon. Opinions flew and Edgar got burned. There was a fat old man there too with a very high opinion of himself. Clement Greenberg calmly discussed the formal qualities of the beautifully painted picture. "The marks are aimless. The color fails to alight in any way. It's muddy." Walter's work was next. Greenberg approved. "This is economical and flat." He liked it a lot since it was all blobs and meaningless colored triangles. Walter's explanation of his own practice was incomprehensible but didn't seem to matter to the great critic. He'd heard it all. My work he seemed to think passable. "Is this man a pervert?" Mito laughed. Sam wasn't there. She'd chickened out.

Nov. 20: The illustrious Clement Greenberg shows up! I am over the moon. I have tricked the most famous Twentieth Century Art Critic in the history of the world. According to him, my work is muddy. He is, of course, right, but still contends formalism is everything. Silly Bugger. Content is not his bag. He didn't seem to notice that the subject of the work was taken from old illustrations in a kid's book, Jack the Ripper and the Whitechapel Murders. "Evisceration just Around the Corner." The deed was done by a trained surgeon in a top hat, someone who worked for Queen Victoria. We all got pissed afterwards. Silvio got too pissed. Blue Blood vomited on exiting a bar. Everybody cheered. Loser.

Sally and I started to re-organize the shelf beginning with Diary Number One. That honorable volume's designation kept changing. As far as we could ascertain, it was a spiral notebook from Woolworths. A little pink price tag said 39 cents. "Remember the five and dime? Prior to the decorated shed?" I asked my assistant. She shook her head, no. Inside, there were no dates, only adolescent scribbles. Lots of them, close to illegible. This young Edgar I'd forgotten; he was a romantic constantly thinking he was in love and going on about spiritual matters. We would discuss how art and love were the only things worth living for. Aren't they? Having a job wasn't on the list. Here's a snippet: The moon was so full my heart burst. There is nothing left of me.

"Damn, a painter and a poet," said Sally, "these genius convention guys! He is so sad, like a puppy. I want to cuddle him"

I skimmed the books once and was fairly certain they were close to being in order. Several phases of life clearly demarked. The mood of the diaries changed. Eventually, Edgar began to look to the past, rather than his current misery. Nearer the end, it was all backward looking, analyzing his life, revising theories and mulling over mistakes. Stoking grudges. The wrongs done towards him were quantifiable but not exactly Dickensian in nature. I concentrated on the later version of the man since I didn't know him so well then. Sally worked on the younger man suited to her own age. It didn't take much imagination; Edgar had a superb memory.

The wine took hold. We danced a little romantic box step. We lost our shoes. No pressure. She let her hair down and shook it out like in the movies. An appalling dancer she was. Didn't matter. "Let us listen to this depressing Joy Division people all night. She's lost control again." I turned up the stereo and it sounded even better. My Girl Friday soon passed out without a peep on the sofa. I covered her up like a loving father. Sleep tight, little girl. I read a diary till I fell asleep with it on my chest after looking up a poem by Baudelaire from Fleur de Mal. Still trying to improve the French. Sally woke me the next day with coffee and said, "Let's work, boss. I have a few ideas for the interviews." We began moving furniture. I put tacks on the seats to keep bumbling critics from getting too comfortable. This is odd behavior, I know. I am a fellow writer who sometimes reviews books. What's my beef? The rest of the crew arrived slowly, infectiously grinning to one another.

"Sally slept over," I announced, "We worked late and danced till dawn. We are hoping to produce a child. Any questions?"

Sally winked violently. "Do you have something in your eye, doll?"

39

CHAPTER

Dion waited with glee for her victims and flashed her gams in celebration. *Little Big City* editor Tommy Graves sent his best art correspondents, Schwartz and DeStephano, the notorious local press. We were all seriously caffeinated and began to gnash our teeth. They turned up around 11 without fanfare at the Bungalow; two dumpy Boomers of a certain ilk. I called them the Bobbsey Twins. Who are the Bobbsey Twins, anyway? The journalists were not impressive in person. I could see they bought their clothes at discount store, Marshalls. When the "bag lady" look was still in. Contemporary Art People have a certain way about them. They are sharp. Holier Than Thee. The Twins had none of it. Docents offered espresso from all sides but nothing to eat.

"Do you have any green tea?" Hippies. I knew it.

Sally looked at the ceiling. "Sorry, ladies," she said. "We have beer."

They scowled asked a few impersonal questions to start. I accommodated them. They'd done some homework on me and started fishing. "Mr. Frank, how well did you know Edgar?"

"We were schoolmates. How well did you know him is a better question. I understand you never actually reviewed any of his shows." I let that barb sink in. The two chortled at each other as if passing a code.

"You're wrong, Mr. Frank. He was difficult but we love his work. The whole city is shocked by his passing." My stomach churned but I held back; the city hadn't noticed at all. The twins sat together both with notebooks ready and press releases for *Forgotten Poets* in their cold hands. Dion and I had stressed standard items: Edgar's antecedents, accomplishments and high points. Hint to reviewers: compare him with renowned artists like Rauschenberg, Koons or Richard Slack who made huge, gothic collages on the West Coast.

"What makes Edgar important, in a nutshell?" they asked.

"That's easy, ladies. His constancy and aversion to being a phony." According to the Weeklies' critics, we were all in the same boat in our rough-scrabbly little town. Edgar agreed: *Crappy little neighborhoods!* I'm quoting.

"Edgar was clearly misunderstood and we have always tried to be ardent supporters," DiStephano offered. Edgar, (metaphorically on my shoulder) added simply: Bullshit. Schwartz picked it up there, sing-song platitudes, whining, "Philadelphia has so few venues." This was a standard fall-back. Blame the city, blame the scene. I was inaudibly groaning and looking thoughtfully to see if the ceiling needed dusting. It did. I forced myself to look back at the two cabbage women. They were a lost cause. "We understand that you are also working on a book about art in the city. Can you tell us about that."

"Nothing to do with the exhibition I'm afraid. Sorry." They looked stern. Try again, Knuckleheads.

"It's all in the press release. Everything you need."

The critics were burned but too embarrassed to show it. After they left, I pictured "stooge," Larry Fine of Philadelphia, plumbing himself into a maze of pipes in a tub. He's Philly born and bred! Nice, Jewish Boy. It is a very funny scene, especially if you are stoned in a dorm room – unless you are a woman, of course, or not in a dorm room. Stoned women hate the Three Stooges. All women do, actually. The would-be critics left with even less pomp but armed with a CD of images from *Forgotten Poets*. For some reason, they mentioned that they'd be seeing Emma Sanchez next.

"Good Luck with that," I said as they departed.

"Namedroppers," said Dion after the door shut.

We stood around for a moment not sure what to do next. "Paul McCartney told me never to namedrop." I replied.

"I'll get you some real press, Mr. Frank." Dion grumbled. "If we're lucky, they'll drive off a bridge." The journalists took all our good humor with them when they embarked and I pictured the tragedy, smiling: fire and flames, crumpled Honda Civic. "There's no point writing about art in a casual way. Art ain't never casual. I mean that in a double negative sort of way. They keep the status quo low by moving between the high-end shows and low-end shit making no distinction between the two. Like art is some sort of social protest."

My protégé, Sally was listening to Dion, "These variations need to be studied carefully and we have to compare them with primary texts."

Dion and I looked at each other surprised. Dion concluded, "Let's make their life a misery!"

I imagined the dimwits' conversation on their way to Emma's studio: "Mr. Frank is a strange sort of fellow, don't you think, Binky?"

"Oh yeah, Steff. Mr. Frank was being evasive, don't you think?"

"Oh yes, I think you're right, Binky. He is taking advantage of the whole situation. They want us to make Bloom a martyr."

"Shall we, Steff?"

"Of course not! We have bigger fish to fry! Like that woman, Trout."

"Who is Trout?"

"You know, the Museum's head curator. Let's interview her."

"Our editor will tell us how to present it cleverly with a punny title like, Blooming Ridiculous or Curator in Frying Pan!"

"Ooh, I love that," said Binky. "How about Curator Swims Upstream?"

"Also good."

"We have our reputation to think of, Steff."

Schwartz got thoughtful for a second. "Bloom's work is riffing on Rosenberg."

"You mean Rauschenberg don't you. Rosenberg was a critic, like Greenberg."

"Oh right. I always confuse them. They're all Jews. Isn't that interesting?"
They both laughed a nervous old lady laugh.

"We are busy art bees, Steff." These dopes colluded on a local blog in 2006 that took off like a rocket. It exists today and has outlived the unfortunate Weeklies killed to death by the internet. Another story. What did they call their blog? Philly-Art News! It was not demanding art to review, mostly cobbled together co-op gallery artists. All-hands-on-deck. The parties were great, lots of locally brewed beer. Self-congratulatory forums with lots of locally brewed bands.

The critics arrived at the large industrial Hart building that housed art studios and Emma Sanchez. They were armed with their own green tea this time and trail mix. Sanchez buzzed them in and they puffed all the way up to the fifth floor. Sanchez was waiting impatiently at the top of the stairs in her paint splattered overalls. Behind her was a large poster of Che Guevara. He was surrounded by hundreds of exhibition and business cards all attached to the wall with masking tape and push-pins. Beside this was a motor from an old GM car and several garbage cans full of engine parts.

A sub-sect of the contemporary cabinet, Emma's work was typical Identity-Agitprop, proto intersectional. Years before the Woke-water broke. She played the Latino feminist with bells on, using the natural materials of her native land – she was born in Hoboken. There were piles of objects lying on the floor that resembled big tacos. The objects were covered with what looked like synthetic Spicy Salsa. Sprinkled on top were hundreds of pairs of dice. "These works represent a cultural meme of day to day oppression. A fable of paralleled reality." The twins were in heaven discussing tired feminist tropes, long withered. The artist explained, "These are constructed of blankets, towels and flags wrapped up, like artifacts." Standard, vaginal references courtesy of Georgia O'Keefe. The Art Ladies ate this up. Emma Sanchez was no Cassandra Giovanni, but she was alive.

CHAPTER

My adoring confidant Sally had a crush on me but I knew she needed a real man with a paycheck. She was checking the email. "Keep your friends and enemies close," she said,

"Clever ruse, Sally. Evasion, so we can do important work."

She nodded in approval. "Stick it to the Man like Lou Reed said."

"That's 'Waiting For My Man.'"

"Let's unleash hell, Mr. Frank," she whispered. Librarians can be that way.

"Sally, you are my Watson."

She blushed, "Evidently, Holmes."

I banged my chest with a fist, "Strength and honor!"

She spat at her screen and I wiped my brow. "This... is... Sparta!"

New York critics caught wind of the show quickly thanks to Dion and Ron. The "Bobsey Twins" followed suit. They disregarded Edgar until he was placed in the pecking order. As the project grew, I didn't think I'd catch up with Trout's timetable, but we did. Many brands of coffee were tried but we ended up with el Castillo, a classic, or whatever was on sale at Pathmark. While I worked on interpretative text with Dion, I set aside time each day for the catalogue piece. Trout's assistants were crawling all over the Bungalow searching for more artwork. Curators showed up with plastic gloves like it was a crime scene. Wasn't it? *My life is a crime scene!* Edgar admitted, *For fomenting deceit. Guilty as charged.* They found some interesting things and (other clues) under the floorboards all destined for the Bloom Archive Museum. No skeletons, unfortunately. All this was transported with great ceremony by hairy, tattooed men to the museum for cataloguing and verification. Edgar put drawings everywhere. In phone books, on table-clothes, drug packaging; whatever. The ladies were also helping me with the odd decoration so as to meet Trout's approval of decency. Photographers from glossy magazines began shooting pics of the Bungalow inside and out. *Hood Envy, says Freud. American Classics made easy.* Deiter suggested art deco drapes to match the Mission style architecture. This décor, I called Boho, whatever that is. It was sparse and deliberately worn like pre-shredded jeans. Johnny Deep would have been right at home. Sorta Steam Punk but more tidy; stovepipe hats and gold pocket watches. The docents weren't so sure about Dion, who was expanding her kingdom. These complicated females were everywhere. I discreetly placed one can of Raid on the counter and offered them beer at 11 am.

They chimed in unison, "You go right ahead, Mr. Frank."

"Cheers, Ladies." I said, chugging my can of PBR.

Big laughs again, high pitched. They were working with a professional. I caught a look of disapproval from alpha-female, Dion and tried to wink. She frowned and went back to fiddling with knobs and scanners under a desk. I watched her lustfully with a corner of my left eye. Later, when we were alone, she cornered me and went out of her way to infer she was not one of Trout's minions. I agreed, she wasn't. I wasn't either.

"I can see that," she said. Her smile betrayed an array of layered female emotions I could only guess at. I edged back slowly to the counter and reached behind for Raid. She stood her ground until we were interrupted by Sally.

I held up the empty PBR. "A beer, my dear?"

She looked at me intently and said scoldingly, "It's 11:26 in the a.m., Mr. Frank. And you should remember Jane Austen's motto, 'Never edit when smashed.'"

Dion sighed, "whatever," and returned to techie-wonderland. With all the help, sartorial and otherwise, the book developed quickly. The research blossomed and paved the way for the show in an unprecedented manner.

Dion got us big-time press. Glamorous interviewers from Catalogue Thirteen and Vanity Fair who'd never been in a WaWa or Seven-Eleven, even for milk. The International press corps began to arrive like I was Princess Diana. They were dolled up; pre Botox. Not my type. Dion looked plainish in comparison and was hurt deeply. These media creatures certainly knew their artists and clothing designers. I wore my flashiest Italian tie with a wicked contrasting shirt, tucked in for the occasion. The cravat got mentioned immediamento. *High Fives for our side.* Edgar and I breached the wall at the same moment. *Molto Grazie, Pretty Ladies.* I answered questions about Edgar like some self-appointed art czar. Talk about embellishing. Still, no one saw the reality, the awful truth. It stood out too much. I put my hand briefly on Dion's left wrist for solidarity. She feigned fainting and slapped me away. I wasn't feigning. I was taking her pulse. Edgar had never seen attention like this himself. I put on my best Libertine hat, the clean one, and pretended to own the state of Maine.

41

CHAPTER

Editor Tommy Graves was just shy of fat. He sat at his shabby desk at the shabby weekly, *Little Big City* on the shabby end of Chestnut Street, famous for flash mobs. He was reading a shabby book by Noam Chomsky, *Beyond Military Industrial Complexity*. Edgar agreed: *Pre-digested marginal propaganda.* Take my word for it; Chomsky is not the most important intellectual in America today like his Philadelphia mural claims. A morbid socialist, Graves was thinking he wanted to change the city but he didn't see how art could help. "Except murals. Murals are for the people." His bosses: a conglomerate of media companies without identity that he railed against impotently. "Nobody cares about art. Art is for suits." Green imagined his publication was the Village Voice at the height of New York hippie-dom. This meant never wearing a tie. What a rebel. Said Edgar: *Never trust Hippies. They have no taste.* Especially Journalists who think they can change the system. On what basis, bitches? The Arts Section in the Weekly took up less space than the burgeoning adult classifieds. Tommy's art critics, Steph and Bink kept it alive with bits of rehashed press releases and pandering to whomever. They mentored aspiring ditzes like themselves who chipped in. Most of the paper covered local politics, exposing mini-despots in City Hall, Tommy's favorite ploy. "Man the barricades!"

Unfortunately, neither Steff nor Binky had a clue about what it meant to be contemporary in the first few years of the Twenty-First Century. The pack suffered from the common illusions many in the arts hold dear. "I am

creative and thoughtful. What's more, I'm liberal and politically correct."
You paddle through the flood of bullshit. Don't offend Quakers or Poor People on Drugs!
Raging Libertines. Edgar means Liberals, perhaps. "Good Will" does not
make art.

Let's distinguish: Art is not the same as "the Arts." Art is more important
than the Arts. This big misconception becomes more ominous as Fine Art
becomes less and less vital in the course of mainsteam culture. Dentistry
mimics society not art or Brew Pubs. Look how much sophisticated high-
tech goes into a simple crown mold. Fuck Michelangelo. Pharmaceuticals
mimic society. *Art is for a dying breed of tortured intellectual.*

The city suffered from massive denial. An endless stream of lame
artists formed cozy clicks, all buddy-buddy, in opposition to selling out
at a truly professional level that would mean they'd have to be critically
aware enough to criticize and improve each other's work. I mean, really
aware. Clearly, nobody was up to it. The co-ops supported their efforts and
connected with the town's vast, inept funding sources. *Collusion, Collision.*
What a conundrum. There was a lot of money there theoretically, though you
wouldn't notice when looking at an artist's tax returns. Many artists lived
below the poverty level, had breakdowns, failing health and went down the
plughole. Go Philly. Mural making builds character. Sorry, Mexican-style
Social Realism wasn't any good to anybody. *Leftover of Hippie Days.* What a
sop; the city government banned black graffiti artists in the Eighties. Truly
brave souls. That was the folk art of the time! Where has JINGO gone?
Long ago my family saw some graffiti being produced on a trip when Dad
made a wrong turn off 95 into the Bronx. We were petrified. "Look at
those young Negroes spray painting that bus. Simply phenomenal! Looks
like downtown Beirut. Luckily, I've got a 38 in the glove compartment."
Mother screamed that he was scaring us kids and he was.

The Art Blog became a fixture along with trendy First Fridays. Public
Radio didn't help. They didn't know anything about contemporary art
either. *Fresh Air* please, I'm suffocating!!! Commentators constantly dated
themselves. *Keep it to yourself old-timers!* The Art Blog was so feeble-brained

that downtrodden artist, Peter Stoke (who was learned in HTML) launched a spoof called Art-Blag. It was inspired satire and did manage to pillory the doltish critics good and proper. Unfortunately, it led to more enmity between factions. I went out of my way to talk to him about it.

His view on the phone: "Inky and Blinky are enthusiastic amateurs." Yes, they still exist. "They heap praise on the undeserving so I shove some criticism back their way. The term "Blag" is British for blowing smoke up someone's ass in order to make their accomplishments more than they are."

"I know the term, Peter. Thanks. It seems you have a lot in common with my friend, Edgar Boom."

"Well, yeah. We knew each other. He was cool. A little distracted perhaps. We both hated critics and curators, the city snobs."

"I see where you're coming from."

"I had an ally in Edgar. Now, I'm on my own." He offered to help in any way he could. I told him I'd be in touch. Stoke was accused of aggression and not niceness. He saw the art scene as a social club. Make your own words count for much more than they are worth in real time. It works. Local stars rise above their station. *Sick of this. Fuck the Net. It makes fools of us all.* The scene did look lively to newcomers. Many artists were in bands – always a bad sign – so there was mucho live music and a co-operative budget for a keg. Ah, youth! Edgar tried to get in on it especially when he first arrived in Philly but he hadn't gone to school with any of them so there was no real connection. Stoke ran out of steam and gave up the Blag after six months of abuse.

As if the plot wasn't thick enough, I decided to up the ante and hire my own PI. More of a henchman. Marshall Gibson, I knew from my Freddie French research. His architecture of personality was best left alone, thousands of inconspicuous tats on dark skin, meticulously shaved head. He was short with wide asymmetrical lips but all muscle. Marshall ate nails for breakfast. "Kill-adelphia is Chocolate City, Mr. Frank." Citing its high murder rate. "We proud of it." Was he joking on ebonics? I didn't care to inquire.

"We certainly are, Gibbs," I agreed, "We are tough cats. And we have hoagies."

"Ha ha, Hoagies from WaWa." He smiled his gold teeth and gave me a hug that nearly dislocated my jaw. "Love ya, man." I tried never to disagree with Mr. Gibson. We discussed Bloom briefly and I set him up to watch Schwartz and DiStephano. "Just a hunch," as Richard the Third might say and overkill possibly. Gibson tailed them for a week in an oversize sedan from the Nineties. It didn't stand out in Philly neighborhoods.

The critics might have noticed. "Are we being followed?"

"I don't know Steff. I have a weird feeling."

"Could be menopause, Binky."

"I did that last week, Steff."

Marshall was cynical too. He told me that they attended every fucking art event in the whole fucking city. "I'm exhausted. People suck up to reviewers, Mista Doug. They at Sanchez place now, boss. She's a hot lady and shit. Like to hook up with that. They moving. Gotta go." I started to think I was living in one of my crime books. What would Freddy French do in this situation? Contact Mr. Strange? French's snitch was called Leo Strange and he was. Trout had her secret agenda but I'm not sure what she would make of me spending Museum dough on ex-cons like Marshall.

Life in Bloom's Shrine continued. Sally was out. Dion was there, not at the Museum as usual. I was doing some light housekeeping with a scrubby sponge when Peter Stoke called me out of the blue to interview me. "I heard my nemesis was there, Mr. Frank."

"You mean Steff and Binky? That is correct but what is plural of nemesis?"

"Yeah, those critics. Can I get equal time?" He pleaded with me and I told him it was up to the Museum. I lied.

Dion looked at me, listening carefully, mouthing, "Peter Stoke?" She moved her index finger in circles over her broad temple, whispering, "He's a nut ball."

Troy agreed, "He's nothing but trouble and he's old."

Peter was going to write about it anyway: Bloom Death goes viral in Shanty Town. "You are barnstorming me, Mr. Frank." Stoke spoke curtly through a scratchy cell connection. He hung up after accusing me of taking sides. At least, that's what I heard. *Fucking Cell Phones.*

"I told him, I'd mull it over."

Dion nodded firmly as if she was making a decision. I went to visit Stoke in South Philly. He was a miserable guy stuck in a time warp with a big studio in what would have been a living room. Nice and sparse. The work was abstract and small. Little marks, scrawl, barely visible. Stoke had rubbed shoulders with the art mafia but they passed him by after a time. There was a moment when abstract was back then gone. He still exhibited and was represented by a die-hard minimalist gallery. He was intelligent but a Stuckist who rallied round the cries of "we must have meaning." As opposed to blatant irony or spectacle? The front door opened and we looked up. Me, Dion and Troy. Sally came in and headed straight to her desk without looking at either of us. She was clutching a book. "What is that, young lady?"

"Nothing. It's one of your books, Mr. Frank."

"Which one, darling? There are thirteen."

"It is called, *Kill Me, Twice Again.*"

Everyone laughed. Troy confirmed it was an "excellent" title. Dion rolled her eyes. I told them it was one of my best where the main character is killed off. Sally was brave enough to give us a short reading in her best mock masculine voice:

> French was blotto. This made him mean. He had been
> stood up by a contact and considered that a fair reason to
> have twelve cocktails. One of each type, all with little paper
> umbrellas stuck in pieces of pineapple and other fruit. He
> had hit on each woman standing at the bar and was about
> to start his rounds of the tables. This was just before his
> arrest by Captain Morgan and his heavily mustached cops.
> Disturbance at the Bermuda came the call. FF is lying on

the floor of the cell face down listening to Captain Morgan who told Freddie what he had done.

"Not a thing, flatfoot."

"That's not what I hear, Mr. French. You went on quite a bender last evening. I have here a quote from Stinky, the barmaid via patrolman, Harry Pistiola.

"Let's have it," mumbles French barely audible through the tiles.

"Individual states he is from the US Board of Health. Announces an immediate breast implant recall from Silicon Valley. He was the local inspector, apparently. Tells ladies in the crowd to come with him to his Federal Building on Broad Street. Several burly boyfriends approach menacingly. Suspect brings out weapon. He is overcome and taken into custody. There were several other injured parties. Lucky punch, eh? Blah, blah, blah. You're lucky no one wants to press charges."

French slowly flipped over onto his back and sighed. "Thanks for keeping me abreast of the situation."

"Thank you so much, Sally. You may get back to work now." I imagined my fictional hipster's Borsalino flying slo-mo through the air before he was immobilized with an empty bottle of Sam Adams over the head. Dion was looking at the ceiling. "OK, I am a misogynist or my alter-ego is. Did you know people look sexier when ovulating, especially women? Guilty as charged."

Everyone got back to work as the interns arrived and Troy skated out the door. "Awesome day out there. The press is buzzing. All good. Mr. Frank has been doing his Michael Caine impression."

I needed to hide and watch TV. No interns allowed, no cells, laptops either said my hand-painted sign. They all agreed. "Yes sir, Mr. Frank."

On occasion, Dion would knock if she needed something and park her silky knees next to my right ear. I did my best to ignore the knees. "May

I?" When she needed to go to the bathroom on the next floor, she made a real event out of it.

"The toilet is free. And no one is allowed to say 'awesome' either, Dion." She claimed she never used the word. She preferred "fantastic." The bathroom had been spruced up by the docents and was now downright spotless, even the hundred-year-old railroad ties in the wall and rusty roll top bath. One of Edgar's plywood signs, opposite my couch, adorned the wall. A graffito arrow pointed up the stairs. It contained cartoon letters reading, "Piss Relief." I figured the British Museum would be taking it for their collection and put it next to the Rosetta Stone. *Awesome. No translation necessary.* The white-collar ladies with pearls had made sure there was aromatic hand soap in a dispenser. It was chamomile and lavender scented, with added vitamin E. There was also hand moisturizer. A small relief sculpture made of wood hung over the toilet. 'Waste Not, Want Not' was painted in Old English type borrowed from Shakespeare. Tasteful towels were folded ever so neatly, finishing the look. It was a pleasure to have clean well-oiled hands. More interns showed. I bought some stronger deodorant and more coffee. We moved the chairs around and put a futon on the second floor. Some were fresh-faced kids who didn't shave. The boys looked a bit like Bob Dylan circa 1966. "Awesome," they all said. Troy was their mentor.

Philly continued to simmer, hot and humid. Schwartz and DiStephano were hanging around like ravenous wolves over fresh meat. Leading up to the opening of *Forgotten Poets* in late September, these two would-be critics wrote short pieces about the upcoming exhibition. One was titled "Edgar Allen's Poets." Not astute, Schwartz and DiStephano knew only when something was up but didn't catch the big picture. Not that a mediocre review in the Philly Press meant anything at all to any one in the real food chain. *Small fish praising small fish. This town sucks.* It satisfied tin-pot editors like Tommy Graves. His hands were full of petty crooks in City Hall. "Stress Bloom's OD, guys. Drugs is sexy. Let's expose the elitism. What the artist suffered at the hands of the establishment!"

The nitwits concurred, "Yeah, sexy." Edgar had them figured out:

Jan, 12, 2003: How annoying. We live in a huge art ghetto. Who cares if the city government is corrupt. Could have told you that. Heard some curator, Martha Trout on PBS discussing how vibrant Philly's art scene is. Parochial assholes. I hate these people with power and no brains. Cynical Wisdom Prevails! No, make that wisdom-less cynicism. Windowless Cynicism? All monies are spoken for. Write about that for a change reporters. Three elite women run the whole scene. Everything passes through them. It is cleverly hidden this Proverbial Monopoly. Kiss my boney asses.

As Dion lit more press candles, other local blogs and what was left of hard copy press started to feature multiple posts about *Poets*. Everyone got on board. They needed to vent. A new volume of correspondence was reached. *Pointless Tipping Points?* It was causing a breach in the status quo. Peter Stoke was quite vocal, representing (to a degree) the old guard of emerged artists with one grant and a tired gallery. *Culture war like the one I remain submerged in. Where were you in 82? Folk Art, Let's Dance.* He did not get along with the weeklies and did everything he could to get up their noses. That was about the only thing he achieved.

He railed about the old days when rents were cheap and when he wrote for an art magazine back in the 70's. Who cares? As far as I can make out, that must have been a dull, hellish time. There was even less exposure for new art and that was run by the mafia squibbs. The scene was full of hippies or punk rockers, neither of whom seemed to get the point. This narked Stoke who never let up the tirade. *Forgotten Poets* gave both camps the opportunity to have a fresh go at the opposition. This was exactly what Dion was hoping to ignite. She lined up release dates, the exhibitions and press, both local and national. She made great use of the Bungalow research we supplied. PR with a vengeance.

Forgotten Poets was doing me good on all fronts. Sales of my crime books rose as my star became visible from behind literary dust storms. This pleased my keepers at Albatross. This was good because they realized I wasn't all that ambitious. The notion of myself as semi-retired "Genius Convention," two-bit writer was disappearing.

"What does it take, Mr. Frank? Opportunity? Seredipity? Luck?" Sally wondered aloud.

None of these Edgar had seen. "I don't know Sally, a lot of sucking up?"

"I prefer books to people," she replied, "Don't have to suck up to a book."

"I love you, honestly, I do."

"I know that."

I took Biggs's advice to stay involved to the hilt. "What is the worse that can happen, Frank?" he said, "Apart from you becoming a nasty sort of prostitute selling your values? This is your window of opportunity." Was he trying to cheer me up? Edgar was almost enthusiastic: *Step up to the plate Frank. You can do it. Don't screw it up like me.* This I'd imagined would happen, a perfect storm for him, albeit man-made. The more ruckus the better, the whole point of reading *Work Shy*, in fact. Or the imaginary sequel, Viva Unemployment. I was spending most of my time immersed with the book's final completion and charting the due date. The plans for the marketing got big.

"Thing's going viral," Troy enthused, "spreading like Ebola." Everyone was shoveling it on with a shovel so I steered clear for a while.

CHAPTER

By the first week of September the show was half up and due to open in a week. I had succeeded keeping Dion at bay. She was old enough to be my daughter and she knew it. I referred to her as the Protocols of Dion. Funny, eh? She wasn't Jewish so she didn't get the joke. Not that there is anything wrong with that. I respected the job she did and her obsession with interpretative writing.

"Let's make this accessible," she would say.

"Accessible?" I asked.

"A tip, Mr. Frank. Don't use the same word twice in a paragraph."

"Good advice. What about the word, t-h-e." Coffee took hold she chuckled much too loudly. She then confided in me about her inglorious past. She had wanted to study Classical literature in college but was too social. Extrovert, be careful! Cards on the table? I never appreciated candor but I needed her feedback. She advised me on how to wrap up Edgar's story neatly. Biggs and Cranston had a bias toward conventional (bog-ordinary) writing for high school juniors. *What did structure ever do for me? I'm used to non-fiction or strong ambition. Just my own problems.* Roger that, Edgar.

The Bungalow was now habitable thanks to many style tips from Quik-Fix! Terry knew her shelving, downsizing and storage techniques. Just in time! Biggs and Cranston were visiting the Bungalow tomorrow! They never left New York if they could help it. *New York Bubble Boys.* "Surprise, Mr. Frank." They finally met Dion and Trout. *Bull's Eye.* There was a bubble to break, a point to tip, fur to ruffle. *Money followed buzz. Buzz followed money.* Now, I was nervous. We started awkwardly, Biggs in my chair with a cigar. It cleared the yuckier smells from the room and most of the human beings. Cranston next to him. We discussed the "branding" of *Poet's* as opposed to *Work Shy.* This was dodgy territory. Books and galleries; natural bedfellows? We tried getting all cozy with cups of tea. Deiter couldn't sit still. Biggs was eyeing him up. Not helping., dude! Shall I add levity here, editor?

Trout ordered Deiter to stop pacing. He went to the kitchen and put on an apron. "I'd rather have an espresso, Deiter," asked Dion, sweetly. He blew her a kiss and held up the package of coffee. Dion relaxed and exposed her legs not that anyone cared except me. "So where are we in the process, Mr. Frank?"

Troy held up his Red Bull. "Let's go. We all have our respective drinks." Everyone chuckled mildly and held up their beverages. I stood up and began to outline things. Some applause was heard. My agent smiled. Had I finally gotten ahead of the game?

"Everything has lined up well, folks. Much thanks to Dion." More applause.

Martha mentioned finances. "I've tapped Barbara Schwenk, the Head of Development at the Museum to help." Schwenk had a genius for sucking funds out of culture pools and Governments of the People. Schwenk was in the Bahamas spending some of her own cash.

Troy added, "She's a genius when it comes to money!"

Forgotten Poets paved the way perfectly for the book. I sent the manuscript in before the end of March. *Work Shy* was published in the summer, six weeks before the opening, with hopes it might get onto art school students Autumn playlist. My due diligence? I had checked out carefully the competition in Google-market for books about contemporary artists. A high-end journalist had already written, *14 Days in the Art World.* It was pitched as an outsider's view. Scoff. Journalists are not outsiders. Sylvia Sheldon had written several expose books. The subtext is that art subculture is a fraudulent, self-perpetuating art college system. Let's not talk about the CTA – the College

Teacher's Association is a meat market. Arcane and archaic. Sheldon was simply too attractive to be serious. The pitch is perfect? Anyone can write these books. My problem with *Work Shy* was broader. I wanted to explain (to the masses) about art and artists, dispelling myths about splattering of paint and how it helps to be crazy. My first choice was *The Horse's Mouth*. It was a book in 1944 about a fictitious English painter before actor Alec Guinness took on the film role. The other popular book was key: *Lust for Life* was written in 1934 and was adapted with Kirk Douglas playing the disturbed Dutchman Van Gogh. Coincidently, both books were made into movies in the year 1956. More to the point and time period was a little graphic novel from the early 90's called *Art School Confidential.* It had some accurate and hilarious portrayals of art education but the subsequent movie (2006) drifted into a pointless murder plot. A missed opportunity.

Other critics and intellectuals chose to write about the end of criticism or the end of history, period. Odd that, like shooting yourself in the foot. There were all sorts of theories. Like an Umberto Eco character once said in one of his books, "Take the cork out." A busy summer passed by quickly. Two weeks after the publishing, I heard back from Pecker. He had read *Work Shy* and had a new perspective on Bloom. "Finch asked me to buy him a ticket to *Forgotten Poets*. There is something curious about that?"

Yeah, I agreed. "Is it in his professional capacity"

"Yeah, he thinks Edgar had some sort of pact with Cassandra. A farewell gesture."

"What? That is magical thinking and doesn't make sense. And it isn't in the book. Where did he get that idea?"

"Dr. Klingon, I think. My fault. Finch has been reading Freddie French too. It's addictive."

"That ain't right." I thought. "Klingon has a lot to answer for."

"Could Cassandra really read the future?"

"That's a stretch, Pecker."

"We heard from the Vidocq people too. They're a little late to the party."

"Wow." I sucked air in through my teeth. "That's interesting. Wonder why they're sniffing around?"

"Not sure I know that. Maybe their staging a comeback. They're getting on in years.

"Thanks for reading the book, Pecker. My bank account appreciates it."

I found out the next day when I had a call from Sergeant Sweeney (retired) of the Vidocq Society. The group had heard about Edgar and had read *Work Shy*. Sweeney was one of their original Police Detectives and had misgivings about the result of the case. "What case?" I asked him.

"Your pal, Bloom, Mr. Frank." He mentioned something about the gas oven in the Bungalow being on. It was not in any police report. "It couldn't have been on without manipulation. I mean Edgar might've had it on previous but he meant to turn it off. Or he didn't. There's still the suicide angle, of course."

"You think it was beyond Edgar's abilities when drugged up? Nobody mentioned the oven to me."

"We think someone maybe mitigated this fact to cloudy the waters. If you could auger enough energy to take a re-look we'd appreciate it."

"I'm not sure what I can do now. It's getting cold, as you say."

"You should do it as soon as possible, Mr. Frank."

"Let me get back to you guys. I do appreciate your interest, Sergeant Sweeney." Now, we had another mystery and possibly an honest-to-goodness cold case. I mean murder. But who would have done that to Edgar? And why? Did Sweeney suspect someone in particular? Many gained indirectly from Edgar's death. I went back to my notes and thought about calling the cops again. "What do you think, Sally?"

"I think it's a little late in the game. Isn't that why they work on cases that are cold?"

"You have a point."

"Why don't you wait until the show is up and dusted?"

"You are wise for your age, Sally Brick."

Renaissance Man, Me? A rank dabbler, sir. Those left behind? If raptured, I have to leave my vinyl behind. Bummer.

I imagined I'd have to contact those crazy guys at Vidocq the next month after the opening and parties. What were they thinking? Did they have something the police had missed? From where? Had they made a clay likeness of the would-be bad guy? Were they offering to make my life easier? Unlikely.

43

CHAPTER

Walking into the museum one week before for the gala, I felt the grip of cold elitism. This was my first look at the hanging. Everything out of the box. Not sparsely hung like most exhibits where the amount of white walls indicated import, it was difficult to gauge which artist was which. *Forgotten Poets* was like an explosion in an art history book mixed with a tornado in Silicon Valley. Edgar's images were clustered inside a busy barrage. More is better. Less is a bore, said one of his signature wooden panels. Standing in front of the work, I felt a sadness I'd never experienced in a museum. Life's residue? Art was "detached" these days and not meant to be gut wrenching. This was shockingly felt. Other sections were collaborations by different artists blurring things even more, an IQ test. I heard later that Sanchez wasn't thrilled by being the token woman – there were two, actually – and sharing so little space with artists of less stature. The museum knew what it wanted. All or Nothing. Take no prisoners. People were excited. This wasn't theatre but real artifice, as oxymoronic as that sounds like the term for ersatz antiques: "Authentic Replicas."

I strolled along the kiosk slowly looking for Dion. She was out front. A massive yellow banner was going up outside to be seen from miles away. Dion joined me on the Rocky Steps for a good look and familiarized me with final prep and signage.

"Did you choose the typeface, Dion?"

"Sure did. You like?

"Is it Baskerville Italic?"

"You're good, Mr. Frank. I distressed it a bit." We continued looking up and she continued talking. "There is much anxiety in town, Frankie. The status quo is being threatened. Are you prepared? The public art people are worried how it will affect their paychecks."

I was getting nervous. "I didn't know you cared but you are right, kid. People sense something going on."

She drank and nodded. "I blame you." Was Dion was blushing!"

It was a juggle to think about my next project as a "French" novelist, a sort of forensic thriller in a museum. Made sense. Plus, some dude in Hollywood had contacted Cranston. Biggs gave it away. A film company was out to buy the rights to *Work Shy.* Epic Productions. Oh shit. I didn't know what that meant, but the book was growing legs before the ink was dry. Was I pleased or mortified? We discussed the impending activities based around the show. *Forgotten Poets* seemed well researched and the museum was prepared, but installations always caused great stress. It can be a nightmare behind the scenes. There was usually one moment where everything seemed to avoid completion. There was adrenalined panic. The technicians sped about hoping they were part of something transformative. Dion called about delays with printers and some last minute corrections to my text. Caffeinated assistants kept bothering Trout with minor details. Nor was I thrilled by my upcoming PowerPoint slide presentation about painter Bloom. The blurb read:

Foremost expert on Bloom's work, writer Douglas Frank, will discuss the late development of the artist. Author of many novels, Frank knew Bloom in his difficult formative years. Talk begins at 8 p.m., Venturi Auditorium.

Now I was an expert? The Late Bloom it should've said. At least my job – the paid part – was almost done. The upcoming book tour, half paid, had nothing to do with the museum. Though the connection started at birth, they both began taking up separate lives. Are artists the only people who know what makes up the stuff of the world? It certainly isn't information technology, every idea reduced to some processing chip or nanobyte. Edgar broke my stream:

Crap. Rubbing shoulders is painful! Modernism probably ended in 1962. We didn't know this of course until around 1990. It was the Brillo Boxes that ended the timeless search for purity in high art since Da Vinci. Makes sense to me. The world is too weird. Future Shock of the New!

There was talk that the book might go straight to digital publishing. Oh no! Kinder Digitalis. Biggs was appalled. Headline read: Cultural Dumbing Down Permanent. In New York, Professor Mito booked two tickets on the direct train to The City of Brotherly Love for the weekend. He and Chisel Face had little time to prepare. In the meantime, they could polish their own stories and status as the *Poet's* mentor. *Money follows buzz. Buzz follows money.* Mito had called me the day before out of the blue. This was a bad sign. They represented everything elitist, fatuous and ingenuous about art and artists. Edgar referred to them in his college diaries as King and Queen. Mito helped spread the word in New York and Dion's wicked press releases had done their job locally. Philadelphia's *Daily Dispatch* finally called. Their so-called arts reviewer was not a fan of the contemporary. Critic Richard Worth was a dunderhead and not aware of any painter after 1910. His readership (not to mention his editors) were clods and weren't even aware they were unaware.

Two days before the show opened, I entered the building and showed my temporary ID. Johnny Bee stood like a bouncer on duty at the main door. He made a thin version of George Frazier but twice as tough. He shook my hand violently. "Nice straw, brother! This is cool stuff, huh?" I loved it when people of color called me brother. It almost makes up for hundreds of years of racial injustice. Johnny had worked at the museum since he was 23. He always looked good in the dark blue guards uniform and didn't seem to mind the Ante-Bellum Spirit of the place. "Down deep we all know this is Chocolate Town!" he said.

I reprimanded him quietly, "Johnny, that's not PC and you know it!"

"Fuck that, Frank!" We giggled and grabbed each other's shoulders. After feeling up each other's biceps, he led me personally to the exhibition area like a proud parent. Trout was there in command of her troops. She was ordering minions around, mostly recent MFA grads who had learned to genuflect sufficiently. She waved, too busy to talk. Chaos was evident. We watched the young preservationists and technicians doing their thing. Some youthful curators pointed at images being moved by installers up ladders. They were mostly failed artists but got to be in a museum one-way or the other.

May, 2004: My natural state, promoting what is looked upon as stupid, groomed on classic rock for god's sake. It was preposterously romantic and unreal – irreproducible on my amp and guitar – and in opposition to Suburban Stasis all around me, parents accommodating lifestyle, their half-fulfilled American Dream. That half-life drags me down like cement. For the Convention it is an illusion. They may not have had a solution but we had seen the best on offer, and it simply isn't good enough.

Trout spurred Dion on like a stage parent. Had she got carried away with the momentum of the show?

I'd given her an outline of key points in *Work Shy*. Good advice from Dion, "Most people aren't going to get it but it'll help elucidate the arts situation." Spell out the hidden things and dispel the crap myths that abound. The interpretation panels were still not back from the fabricators, so I went up to Dion's office to review the copy and design for the tenth time

"What do you think of the show, Mr. Frank?"

I was unsure what response would be the best received. "It's impressive," I said staying reserved amid the sexual tension. "I'm a little surprised at the obsessiveness."

She was showing signs of stress and her knees. "This is going to be special, Mr. Frank. I don't know why everyone gets so worked up about this cultural stuff like it was life and death."

"Maybe, in this case, it is."

"You could be right." She sat behind papers and rough designs all over the desk with a wine bottle on top. She was wearing glasses I'd never seen before. She removed them and shook her head in order to fluff her hair. This accentuated a dangerous widow's peak. "Care to join me," she asked in a mock sultry purr.

"I only drink on duty," I replied, stepping back an inch. Her legs were aimed in my direction. She then began a narrative about her numerous lesbian affairs. I drank quickly and tried to compose my face into a version of ironic shock. I then mentioned a few of my own erotic adventures hinting they weren't all straight.

She punched me in the chest. "Oh Frank, you are a card." Dion had already been crossed off my list and I was thinking about Sherrie Bloom. "You aren't gay!" Dion laughed manically as I stood corrected. She kept laughing and for the first time, I joined her.

44
CHAPTER

Next day I tried to relax. This was impossible. Dad was visiting. He simply stopped by. This overlapped with Biggs and Cranston who wanted to see the installation first hand. We went out for dinner at the Rib Crib. I'm kidding, of course. Can't give New Yorkers gooey ribs, something they'd have to eat with their New York fingers. We ended up at up at a fancy wine bar, Che Cubana. In Mt. Airy the wait staff were acquainted with fussy customers with beards. It was lower Chestnut Hill, actually. Mt Airy is different. It resisted being enveloped by the hood but embraced difference. Thoroughly unique, crack dealers living amidst yuppies, deadheads, Jewish refugees from the Golan and almost completely normal people. It was not quite Brooklyn. Another story. Before dinner we rendezvoused at the Bungalow. Dad had never seen it. He needed a scotch so I obliged. He sat there for a moment looking stern and prepared to address the society around him.

Biggs began, "This is queer."

"You tellin' me?" Dad answered politely. I clutched my drink and nearly broke the glass; a thick crystal job with knobs on.

Cranston added to the assembled, "So that's the way it is, is it?"

"Yes, I guess so." Off and running.

"You are from the greatest generation, I assume?"

"Fuck all that shit."

I interjected. "Dad was a marine and they used colorful language."

"We do too, Frankie." A moment passed and the male couple in the room exchanged glances and re-approached the entanglement. "Mr. Frank, tell us how many Germans you killed, exactly. What was it like?" I continued to quaff strong gin and tonics with only a whiff of Schweppes.

My Dad got serious and completely straight for a moment, "I enjoyed it. There was a job to do."

"Most people would say that taking a human life is painful and will be regretted for the rest of their lives. It haunts them."

"Well, I ain't everybody."

Feeling left out of this exchange, I slipped in a comment. "Thank god."

"I think we were being shelled and I found myself behind German lines. I instinctively lined our Sherman behind an 88 installation. Blew it to hell. We then got hit and scampered. Panzers galore. Not sure how we made it back. We were pleased as punch to stop some of the devastating rain of destruction on our guys." The New Yorkers were all ears. "Schwartz was a fairy from Brooklyn but he died with his boots on in Luxembourg saving his friends." I gave up and went to the can.

An hour passed. "So how do feel about Edgar's resurrection?"

"Well, I think your art world killed the fucker off, if you'll pardon my French. Pardonez moi. My French, c'est poof. I don't give a shit about art frankly but I know when someone's getting the shaft."

Again Biggs and Ron exchanged meaningful looks. "Speaking truth to power, eh?" Were they bonding with my old man? Christ. This is one for the books.

"Whatever you say, guys."

Dad looked around the room and made a clever segue. "Frank, did you buy this dump?" I nodded, smiling, watching my biased and dated father continue. "It's a black area, isn't it?

"Not totally. We are actually in the middle of the Gayborhood," I said.

"The what?"

"Courageous couples of a non-heterosexual nature fix up old Painted Ladies in ghettos down on their luck," stated Ron proudly.

"Painted Ladies? You mean prostitutes?"

"No, Dad, they mean fancy old houses from the Victorian period."

He nodded, "Gay Men refurbishing houses?

"Yes, Mr. Frank."

I persevered, "There's a couple of nice Queen Annes."

"Picking purple color schemes and hanging tasteful curtains, doilies and such?"

"Yes, Mr. Frank."

"Have you ever rehabbed a house, Mr. Frank senior?"

"Can't say I have. I was busy saving the world from Nazis and Communists. Have you ever rehabbed a house, Biggsy?"

"Not personally. It involves a lot of heavy lifting," replied Biggs.

"And the love of a good man," added Cranston. I almost blushed. Then the room broke into whole-hearted laughter. Phew.

On a roll, Dad continued, "All Gays look alike to me." We all laughed loudly for different reasons.

Next day on my own at the Bungalow, work eased my self-doubt. I started some meandering tasks and was feeling rather mellow. Let the chips fall, like Edgar says. It was Saturday and I drove around the hood for a while and caught a few yard sales. There were some interesting books in one of the 25-cent boxes. Medical books with weird lithographs. Another box was chock-full of old family photos, Black and White from the early 1920's it looked like. How much for the whole box? Not a beat went by and it was mine. "5 bucks." Art and Text. There are some great bargains in the hood these days because of the Great Recession. Some yard sales are held at night like parties. Surreal. By the afternoon, I was well into a six-pack from a Great Lake State and listened to Closer again, second time in a week. I'd erased several messages from Mito. 'Time to chill' Frank, I thought. Time to plan. I had started buying records to fill out Edgar's collection. Apparently there was a whole new category of pop punk that followed the legacy of Joy Division. The likes of Interpol and Editors, a stylish band from England. Wonderful baritone singers; Echo and the Bunnymen-ish. Not surprising, I guess. Makes me and many others happy.

My list demanded some attention. Still hadn't finished following up with doctors and cops. I had a few days to dwell on the big day and work on other things and buy a new suit for Weddings, Funerals and Private Views. This I bought at Boyd's on Chestnut because they overcharged. I wanted something that said, up and coming writer; watch out or I'll eat you for breakfast. Sue me if you want, I dare you. Playing the successful suit card. Sweet!

Forlorn Poets was reviewed favorably everywhere in the Universe except Philly. It was bringing in a new era of truth at a great juncture in Man's development or so I mused. I called it the third millennium after Jesus H. Christ. Edgar was finally being taken seriously. About time! So was I. The reviews even crossed over into Academic Journals and the international art mob. Schmitter-Fob!

Biggs and company told me to behave on NPR's wildly popular radio call-in program. My interview on "Top of the Morning" was Tuesday and it went swimmingly. I dressed writer-ish for the microphone, a Steve Jobs turtleneck seemed appropriate with an academic blazer with elbow patches. I was pushing it. "What do you think Sally?

"Is that what you are going to wear?"

I held out my arms for all to see. "What's wrong?"

"It's a bit much, isn't it?"

Dion approved. "He looks fine. Almost sexy."

I admitted as much. "Thanks."

Troy made it unanimous. "He looks great. It's only a radio interview!"

Dion gave me an affirming stare. "Go get them, Mr. Frank."

Troy added, "Mr. Frank has got a face for radio."

"Thanks, Troy. I guess I'm all set."

I was preparing to whine about the art scene for a whole twenty minutes with Edgar on my shoulder reminding me not to overdo it. *Let them praise you, Frank! Don't be modest.* The interviewer Jeanette Cochran, knew she had a controversial guest. "Potential talk show gold," said her producer at WHYY. The book was being spun to death as the first anti-literary, non-fiction of the Twenty First century. Either way, it was press and I was floating in sweet circles. Jeanette took the offensive and began by questioning Edgar's authority and mine. I shot back and never let go. "In America, you are supposed to doggedly pursue your livelihood like a wolverine to gain success, money, power. Even a wife or husband. Security most of all. It's BS, if you'll pardon my French, Jeanette. An artist needs these too, even more so. That crappy myth about creative obsession and suffering for your art, it is bullshit – sorry, bleep that, sorry – giving to a community, BS. Sorry."

"That's a little harsh isn't it, Mr. Frank and tough on our city?"

"It is what it is, Jeanette." Maybe I'd had a little too much caffeine but the phones lit up. "Swift and Daniel Defoe wrote novels because there was a new industry in the Eighteenth-century that required them! Simple Market Forces, Jeanette. It defines progress both technical and creative. The publishing industry needs books. Art proprietors need wares." Jeanette took a call and introduced me to "Jack" from South Street. He asked me about the relationship of the exhibition with the book. "Good Question. It's complicated, Jack. You can't have one without the other in this case. The art work in *Forlorn Poets* speaks for itself and *Work Shy* goes deeper to establish a narrative." The caller accused me of selling out. "Bloom worked this out accurately and look what happened to him. Notoriety? No. It's a crime." Jack hung up with a loud crackle.

It took a lot to un-nerve a pro like Jeanette. "Another call from Asha in Kensington."

Asha swore at me on the radio. "You suck. Philly-basher. You're nothing but a carpet bagger!"

"Asha seems upset," said Jeanette.

"She should chill out. Read a book for a change."

"Another call for Mr. Frank from Abdul in Kensington.

"Hi Jeanette. Long-time listener, first-time caller. Your book reads like fiction to me, Mr. Frank. Did you make up the life of Edgar Bloom?"

"Thanks for the call. What a great question! No, Abdul. It's all true. I'm afraid people do evil things in the art world."

209

Jeanette read from her notes: "Aren't we discussing the wider cultural fabric of the city?"

"Yes, of course, but who controls it?"

The host, still addressing me, began to frown. "The arts community? Creatives and their process?"

She shot a glance towards her producer and signaled with her pinky.

I laughed half-heartedly. "You believe that, Jeanette? You are a journalist, right? But you don't make the news. You're a conduit." Lots of angry Philadelphia art lovers began to ring in for some reason and told me I was dissing their city and I should shut the fuck up. More gesticulating with the producer, a dumpy woman with headphones and awful specs. She was making an Italian gesture for cutting a throat.

Jeanette began shutting me down by re-introducing me. "Our guest has been writer Douglas Frank discussing his book *Work Shy* about the life of his friend Edgar Bloom, the late Philadelphia artist. Bloom is featured in an exhibition called *Forgotten Poets* currently at the PMA. You can see an online review on our website." Blah blah blah.

I kept right on. "They are cousins born of the same mother. Sent for revenge, serving it cold." The theme song for the 'break" came up in my cans and I noticed two large men in ill-fitting jackets appear outside the recording booth. In my left ear, I heard Edgar say, "All right, dude. They called in the muscle!"

Jeanette thanked me for visiting and I was escorted politely out of the building by the security men as the next guest – an indicted member of City Council in dark glasses – was escorted in.

This talk show farrago was only a warm up for the next day. It started with seminars, talks and gallery walk-abouts for big wigs. I was startled by how well attended the first talk was: New Philadelphia Art: *Forlorn Poets*. Martha Trout and I sat side by side at the table with two microphones. Peter Stoke was there with those critics I'd rather not mention, Topsy and Turvy.

I fielded their inappropriate questions about the hype around Edgar's out of the blue discovery. "Let me say first that Bloom has been working in anonymity for twenty years. His diaries revealed a great deal about his inner turmoil and frustration. The disregard directed at Edgar's work says something perhaps about the creative climate in the city. There are many quasi-opportunities but this is outweighed by a ghetto-ized mentality. Fear of the unfamiliar. This is not a forum on that issue." I heard a few groans and stifled shock.

Trout, sounding false, pleaded, "The museum has rescued Bloom from obscurity for eternity. It needed doing and will benefit us all."

I continued. "In fact, this situation itself had something to do with the incubation period for work of this type. Not only for Edgar but many others. He simply happens to represent the idea best, I believe."

Howard Rochelle raised his hand. "Mr. Frank, I can hear you channeling Edgar's disappointments but he wasn't a burn out. He was happy go lucky. Really funny art, he made. Some of it."

There was a murmur of laughter then I answered. "This is all true, Howard. Can I call you Howard? All of those are issues Bloom raises in spite of himself, perhaps."

Trout thanked Howard for the comments. I was not there to sell books but as Dion put it to "create buzz." She was lobbying for a job in New York through Biggs and company. *Fag Hag!* My talk included considerable deconstructing but was also used as a plug platform for the upcoming book. Cranston had insisted. "*Work Shy* will be an indespensible companion while you travel down the road to your own MFA." Off shelves and on Blackberrypods. "A challenge to latent provincial thinking everywhere. Beware of *Work Shy*, the narrow minded."

They finally got the message. Praise Be. I was then responsible for a few informal tours avec Martha. By 4 pm, I was shattered. Trout disappeared and I headed for McNabb's Pub on a backstreet around the corner. It was like the mournful hours before a wedding and the place was packed.

I needed to brace myself and segue into wider gratuitous sociality. "Where are my colleagues?" Samantha stood out, her red hair draped over a Vodka and Tonic. She was alone and almost tearful. "You look awful," I suggested helpfully.

She looked up and smiled. "Where've you been? At the seminar?"

"Yeah. It went well."

"You look exhausted."

I shrugged. "Are we still in mourning, Sam?"

"I guess. I feel strange, torn. Lots of things." I leaned in and gave her a consoling hug.

"This shouldn't be happening. It's a cliché," she said. "Famous Dead Artist."

Nick's hand appeared on my shoulder. "Like Dashiell Snowden, dead at 27, last year. Same age as Amy Winehouse and Kurt Cobain."

I responded over my shoulder. "Yeah, but he was an asshole, Nick."

"Respect for the dead, please," he said, trying to keep the peace.

"He was a poser and only moderately talented," I replied. "Known for outrageous pornographic pictures and onanism. He delivered outspoken silver-spoonerisms and rose to view only for a few years. Then left a pretty corpse a la Sid & Nancy, ending up at the Chelsea Hotel."

"That's the story I heard. These New York myths die-hard."

"Too much cocaine," I said.

"Snowden's not included in this show, but he was forlorn, Frank."

"Fuck that guy." We stared at ourselves in the mirror behind the bar. The scene resembled a Baroque painting complete with candlelight.

Nick leaned toward me like Judas. "You are a busy man, Frank. This whole affair is metastasizing."

"Edgar's worth it, don't you think?"

"That's not the issue, not what I mean. I mean that you're playing their game."

"You're one to talk, Nick. You've got a little niche all set up. Nick's niche."

"Not like you, Frank." He smiled and took a swig of his cocktail.

"Let's not argue, Darling." I stood up, glass held high, "Edgar deserves everything we can give and I'm proud to be a part of it. No, it ain't ideal. It's been a bumpy ride. To Edgar."

Sam and Nick chimed in, glasses raised way up. "To Bloom!"

Others at the bar joined in eagerly, half-tanked. "Who's Bloomy. To Bloomy."

We reciprocated, "Bloomy." Sam sucked down the rest of the drink and exited. I put cash on the bar and tried to catch up. The couple stayed arm in arm the whole way to the Museum. I was caboose. Nick looked back at me and grinned with mild distaste and I ignored him as we ascended the steps slowly.

There was a crowd outside already. Buzz-dom had been reached. Can they be here for the guy they once held in contempt? Johnny Bee was on duty in a big way. He greeted us with a Philly flourish and led us inside. He winked at me and squeezed my left arm. "Damn, look at all these folks." I shrugged as if to say, too late to back out now. The place was brimming with benefactors and, to my surprise, there was a very tall cop waiting for me.

45
CHAPTER

Both men were grinning at me. "This is Peter Picard, Mr. Frank. He wanted to meet you. He's Police but he made it big."

I stuck out my cleanest mitt, the right one. "I've met PP a couple of times, Johnny." Pecker reached back.

They laughed, shutting me out. "You guys know each other?"

"We go way back," Picard said. "Mr. Frank and I."

"Small world," I said inaudibly.

"You look a little pale, Frank."

"Ha ha. That's a good one. I'm a little pale this evening."

"Is it because you are the man that made all this possible?"

"Could be." I told him Edgar Bloom was responsible and should get all the credit.

"Of course, he's the talented artist who committed suicide."

"I was never sure he took his own life actually, you know, I mean, on purpose. Neither were you."

"We still have a few questions. Give me a call about that sometime. Maybe we can take it a little further."

"Sure, why not?"

"You've done all right, haven't you, Frank?"

"What does that mean, Pecker?"

He looked around and pointed. "The book came from this, no?"

"They're cousins."

We discussed the show briefly until Johnny spotted Trout approaching. "Time to move, gentlemen." Picard and Johnny withdrew with considerable diplomatic aplomb as if to say good luck, dude. Martha did a subtle slo-mo allowing them time then swept upon me with a grin that made the ice in my veins frost over. She was encased in conservative coutour, a bright blue color with a mermaid scale motif that brought out the inexorable emptiness in her eyes. The crowd was moving like schools of fish; faces a blur, mouths open. Why were so many people seeking pleasure in someone else's pain? Das ist Shadderfreud. The movers and shakers were there in force, most of them well to do benefactors – older couples – accustomed to high class restaurants that I also frequented while employing irony and American Express. Feeding on their young? The couples dressed with confidence, a flash of fur or scarlet here and there, massive diamonds, signifiers of excess wealth. No Timex watches. This was new to me. Who were these Mainliners? Why did they have so much clout? Maybe I'm the naïve one after all.

We gathered around the drinks table. There was a gin and tonic with my name on it. Then Trout led me through the gauntlet. Mr. and Mrs. Warden Sondheim were already negotiating purchases through museum channels. "I like the celebrity text pieces." I said, smiling with teeth.

The Sondheims gushed. "Yeah, we have one of those! It says Cadillac Tax."

"That's a fine picture," I agreed. Trout grinned.

Mrs. Sondheim was giddy. "Our collection is growing as we speak. This is so exiting, Mr. Frank." I told her I wished Edgar could see this himself. "Yes, he'd love it! Wouldn't he?" She turned to the curator. "It's fabulous, Martha. A crowning achievement for the museum, don't you think?"

Martha could not disagree with the Sondheims. "Thank you two for your support." She kept on grinning and we moved on.

The Rochelles and the Blakes stood together, a Protestant Reformation. "We really miss Edgar," they bleated in unison. "We have six paintings now. What a damn shame he is gone."

"I know how you feel." There was a sense of some genuine regret but it was akin to selling a favorite car. "Sorry to see it go, it was beat. We want GPS and an ejector seat." Even their kids were following suit, Preston and Morgan. The Yale kids were interested in investing in art and everything else. It was a Wasp Convention, except half were Jews. Jewish Wasps. Like me, half Jewish. I identify with the Personality Split. You can't win. Martha was having fun. They made the show possible.

I asked Martha's ear, "They are buying Edgar Blooms already!?"

"Like hot cakes," she enthused softly through yellow teeth. I envisioned the auction price index for Bloom's work. "The museum is well pleased, Mr. Frank. We've written a new chapter for the city."

The booze flowed and it all got very jolly. Already tipsy, I stated loudly, "Why shouldn't they sell like cakes? Edgar's a fucking genius!" Trout stopped grinning and applied sharp pressure to my elbow reminding me that this was her turf and I was to behave myself.

"Sorry, Martha. I lost control."

"If critical acclaim turns to green after the years pass by, all the better."

"Remind me to go green, Martha, if I forget."

The patrons laughed even more. Martha added, "Ha ha, Dougie. I'll try and remember. We are at the finish line so enjoy it."

Howard touched my arm. "What's next for you, Mr. Frank? Another book?"

"I haven't finished researching this one yet, Howard." Howard laughed. I had interviewed the Sondheim's about their purchases of Edgar's later work, post death at their home in Ridgemont, a giant estate full of world class art and too much baroque furniture. Their interest in Edgar was new and sprang from their direct connection to the museum director, Forrest Green-Jones. All Yale Men.

Art brings elitists together! Schadenfreud on Steroids! All the sucking up, Boring shit after a while. Can't tell what is good from what is spun. What is mediated from what is authentic. Playing with those issues is for students. We are all bloody students again. Wouldn't wish that on anybody.

Forrest and his white hair joined us. "Look at the speed at which the art was transformed. There's no stopping Edgar Bloom." I liked Forrest. He was jaded in a good way. He could deal shrewdly when needed, but his main preoccupation was with quality and provenance. He was interested in history. He also knew pain in art when he saw it and wasn't fooled by mere craft. Technique. Whether Ancient Greek or Postmodern, the 'making process' in any part of art history. He got it. That has got to be rare. Maybe it's the hyphenated name!

"I wish I'd known him personally," Marsha said.

Dick agreed. "He obviously suffered to pursue this sort of investigation. I'm thinking of Job in the Old Testament. He was Jewish, no?"

I joined back in. "As Jewish as I am. We're both half-breeds. Both conservative and troublemakers in the same bundle." They looked confused so I let it drop. You started it! More like lack of J-O-B. The director grabbed my hand and thanked me for everything. I was speechless and looked at his wavy iceberg hair with envy.

Whiffing perfume and Champagne, Trout led me onto the next bunch. "Come on Mr. Frank and be good," she whispered through her off-white teeth. The face and names began to blur and I was feeling one of those urges to shout obscenities at the top of my lungs. This happens to me once in a while. *Hang on Frank. Don't blow it. Your book says it all for you.* You got it in your rear pocket, so to speak. Edgar was right, as usual. In the bathroom, I popped a Valium for good measure – I think it was a Valium – found a whole bunch leftover in a secret stash in a coffee can at the Bungalow. Was I behaving like a junkie? As the evening proceeded, the bullshit reached seismic proportions so I continued downing the gin and tonics. They left me with less need to regurgitate violently like some strong ales that I love.

Forrest Green-Jones began the formal proceedings and the fish moved toward the small podium. The Director began his speech. The Valium was helping. I was almost positive it was a Valium. My grin felt imagined floating on my face. It occurred suddenly that this wasn't the subtle calmness of a Valium but something more mood arranging. Maybe it was a painkiller? Ecstasy? Oh fuck. *Mr. Frank, your getting stoned at my event!* How transformative! I was positive Edgar was now speaking to me directly. Forrest was now giving his soliloquy. "Thank you all for being here tonight." Trout was beside me, flushed with a deranged glow. She had her own prescriptions.

At one point, she held my arm and nodded her head onto my shoulder. "It's so true. I should have known." Not sure what that meant. Martha was drunk and sighed heavily. I had to nod and wave a few times in recognition of applause. I spotted the mini-critics in the audience but they turned away before noticing my dirty look. Their lawyer husbands kept their heads down. They would rather have been out in the suburbs flossing their shiny teeth. Luckily, Forrest knew what he was doing. He put on quite a show for the tanned and moneyed classes and the few who understood the words. Pecker was also listening intently.

The oratory continued: "What fuels artists to do what they do? Do we really know? Are they rewarded? Oftentimes not." He got that right. Edgar had done them a favor. *Frank, can you hear me? I'm still pretending to be Steve Buscemi. Hey.* Forrest-Green got into serious terrain about commitment of the artists and self-denial in search of proper endorphins. "Mr. Edgar Bloom made a sacrifice, a choice. A tough balance at the best of times." He choked up slightly here. "It was a difficult choice." Trout was crying openly now. Dion, standing next to us, gave her a hug. Deiter, crying like a baby, gave her a hanky. One big happy family. Who are these people? I saw Biggs and Ron with Frank Senior in the back of the crowd. Bizarre! Dad was enjoying himself. He shot me a "Go get 'em, son," double thumbs up. Pecker had vanished. Trout and I were suddenly led up stairs and looked out at all the upturned faces. Everywhere I looked was Mito, networking and Chisel Face. Perhaps, I was seeing non-existent things or they'd brought along clones. I looked up in time to see the Sanchez retinue enter like

218

royalty, a grand Mafia tradition. Sanchez was staring at me with malice. So was her cadre of admirers. She resembled a dragon in a red pants suit and black beret. I rubbed my eyes. What had I done? Exposed them? They should bask in that for a while. *Bask away, creeps.* Sanchez then ignored me and chatted ominously with minions. *Cowardly bitch,* he adds. Edgar's story had implicated them and although they now claimed him as one of their own, they had shown their true evil colors.

Mito was still there mixing it up. Where did this guy get his Mojo? Mito's Mojo? He'd be wheedling a show out of somebody, possibly an assistant curator like Troy. Troy's fussy but he's a pushover. He was young and gawky with a bit of snoot thrown in, always prowling the local gallery scene to sniff out unsuspecting talent. My present fabulations became overwhelming. Chisel Face disappeared. Her star had sputtered out years ago. Though, it was sort of a moon-ish thing to begin with, cold and barren. What had I wrought? A down side was in the air but I couldn't place it in a convenient cubby. It could have been the hallucinations. The gala was becoming hard work and I was suddenly missing my dead friend. Suddenly, two little Edgar's appeared viewing each other under my chin. All I could say was, "Guys, chill out." One Edgar was plenty. *Hey Frank, good job. Yeah, like he said. I knew him first, bitch.* His voice became just another in the crowd.

Missing of course from this event was Sherrie. Understandable. She and what's his name were now living life in the present tense. Not like me lately, in the past or planning for eternity. Had she passed me Edgar's baton. That doesn't sound right. Everything is double-entendre these days. Life is complicated. Beyond her ex-husband's abject plight, Sherrie had made my life bearable lately, meaningful. Now, she was moving on and not paying attention. I couldn't blame her. I admired her for that especially since this sort of fame would have saved her previous husband, Edgar and maybe their marriage.

My few words on the stage were well rehearsed but my mental state wasn't. "Friends, artists and countrymen. If my old friend Edgar Bloom was here now he'd probably have something to say and you might listen. He'd take a big gulp of this delicious Champagne. He loved booze, as you may know." A loud cheer rose up. Then he'd say, 'Let the games begin.'"

The crowd chanted, "Bloom, Bloom." It sounded like booing until it sounded like boom, boom. Was I running for office? We left the stage and merged into the crowd. Warm hands grabbed me from all sides. The spotlights that had been overheating the space, dimmed immediately and colored lights came up. A band came on and started fiddling with instruments and laptops. *Sid Vicious didn't need no fucking laptop.* They were made up of some of the local artists and played a half-ironic, Electro-Goth ala 1982 except with beards. Yes, whiskers. Were they dressed in black? Yes, as a matter of fact. How fitting. How tight? Was it Industrial Punk Funk or Kraut Rock? Germans underlied all house and dub step. Listen for the 'drop' when the beat kicks in after much ambient ado. I didn't want to see Trout doing some sort of awkwardly repressed strut with her colleagues. Lord knows, they deserved to let off steam. I eased towards the Mens' room and found a real Valium in my bag. "Thank you, Lord."

When I returned, Dion was out there with other bodies shaking vigorously. She was with a guy I'd never met and I was jealous. Edgar would have been amused. Sally joined her unabashedly roboting. Next to her was Judy Cheap in full-tilt pogo. Her band mates surrounded her, enjoying the noise. This was unique. Moshing rarely occurs in a Museum! Mito was having no trouble orienting himself on the dance-floor. This was his métier. Go to it, babe. I imagined them dancing the dated, 80's spastic dance (but with no ironic intent) off into the sunset. Nick and Sam were on the edge of the dance floor swaying. Samantha was now scowling. They were deciding whether to stay and celebrate elsewhere. I made my choice. Nick's brother Dwight came to the festivities. He was a cool guy with a pitchfork tattooed on his left forearm. Nick was comforting Sam from one side but Dwight was whispering gleefully in her other ear. He was a local musician and was taking the party in stride. I imagined Nick had a ring in his pocket for Sam. That was silly of me. He's not the type. I liked Dwight or Ike. I liked the name Ike. Nick's brother's name is Dwight English.

2003: Is that incest? I could live with her, no problem. She might kick me out of bed though. I twitch and snore. They should exit also. There really wasn't anything to gain here once you have been passed over. Might as well be cozy and cared for. It is under-rated I think, coziness.

Johnny Bee had his mouth to his cufflink like CIA alerting his team. There must have been some ruffian who needed chucking out by the ear. It was Mickey having too much fun. June was trying to drag him out and he was yelling to no one in particular. "Gotta let loose sometimes and celebrate."

"Don't bullshit me, Mick," yelled June over the din.

"Drink up, dudes." He shouted. "To the venerable Edgar Bloom."

In his earplug Johnny Bee heard, "Family dispute in main hall, go, go." His men were alerted but Johnny was already in control and having a discreet word with the bakers. Mickey nodded with a wide grin and they shook hands vigorously. June and Mickey retreated to the margins.

The Quick-Fix people were basking in vicarious limelights. Denise and Terry stuck tightly together with husbands in tow. Howard Rochelle was among them. He had donated his pictures to the exhibition and was proud of the fact. He knew Martin, Terry's husband, another clean-cut moneyed type with round, tortoise-shell specs. Astoria was dolled up, tall as ever like a glamorous totem pole, her face the hawk-head at the top. If she was on the hunt for a Lawyer, she was in the right place. She stood in a circle with over made-up witches from Shakespeare. They looked at me as if I had two heads. "You are the writer!" They repeated this over and over, pointing long painted nails. Yes. *And you are the bitches that made my life a misery?* Terry asked me if they were all in the book. I said, no. Lying again.

After a time, Edgar and I became oddly calm. Our voices merged. My eyes surveyed the scene and found Peter Stoke. He was left behind again. I figured facing that took real maturity. He was drunk and the guards were keeping us in view. "Mr. Frank is approaching suspect."

"Got him. He's acting erratically. Approaching the old hippie."

I walked up to Stoke and we shook hands. "Condolences, pal."

"Same here, dude," he replied.

"They're watching us for some reason." Perhaps Peter was wishing he were dead like Edgar so he could garner an extra bit of acclaim. A child of the 60's, Peter dressed down, albeit in black. But the color was fading and the knees were ripped. He cut his ponytail in '92 and his chest hairs were white. I noticed (without meaning to pry) the second button of his dress shirt was left meaningfully undone. Within the codes of acceptable arty fashion perhaps, he had an attractive air of authentic weariness.

"Doesn't matter, Mr. Frank." We nodded and shared a moment. "You are quite the celebrity." The aging artist had heard my interview on the radio and seemed to share my view. "The non-profits hold all the cards." He'd had his Goldwater Prize and was now watching with curiosity, perhaps not a little envy. Maybe he was pining for a little more attention as his orbit receded? He had tenure at the University but this ensured a slow disappearing act. The academic door smacks you on the butt as you enter and locks with a big snick. The gig's up. No matter what he did, he remained unknown to anyone outside the place. *Shutter-Froid! C'est froid ici?*

I kept up my rounds. "Enjoy the festivities, Peter."

"Stay outta trouble, man."

I made an effort to steady myself. "As if that was possible."

"Say hi to Edgar for me!"

Johnny Bee was watching and talking into his sleeve, "Stat. I'm on it." No one was going to spoil Trout's evening. *Death, the great Equalizer? A wee bit more, laddie?* Edgar was on my right shoulder again doing a Johnny Depp impression or was it Keith Richards doing Johnny Depp? Was that the evil or good side? Or was it the unknown tablet I digested? I addressed the artist directly: "Make up your mind, Edgar. Are you pleased or not?"

This is where I got to correct history. *Why bother, Mr. Frank? Yeah, it's a lot of work. Other people is hell. Who said that? Not Yogi Berra.*

Edgar was visible. "Hell is where you find it."

I wasn't sure if I spoke out loud or not: "This is more like purgatory, my friend."

Trout approached again, slightly worse for wear. "What a delicious opening." The mob had done it again; expressed their hold over their kingdom. They suppressed reality and kept their sovereign ball rolling forward. I steered clear but they were looking my way. All of them. Shit.

"Congratulations, Martha. It's been fun."

Edgar yelled, invisibly over the noise: *Frank. What a party! I'm shit-faced.*

"You're not even here, stupid. Time for you and me to leave, buddy"

"Who are you talking to, Frank?"

Sam and Nick looked up and motioned me over. "Are you yelling at yourself?"

"I'm communing with the past." We were participating in a grand façade, the fabric!

Then I raised my fist, "Wait till they read my fucking book!"

Nick caught my eye. "Frank, are you stoned?" Sam looked worried. She hugged Nick closer and pulled me into the huddle. Dwight grabbed me and made room. "We've got to stop meeting like this."

Nick had the look of a man planning to go on a bender. "Not enough."

We began goofing around like old times. "You go left. Down, set, seventeen, hut, hut."

I made some bogus football moves. "I'm open, I'm open!" Those not dancing looked on and enjoyed the moment. I nearly fell over thinking myriad thoughts: Maybe, Nick finally got it. He was more like Edgar than he thought. He was more than jealous. It was like he was feeling Edgar's pain finally, first hand. I knew about that. It's akin to finding yourself on the wrong team all of a sudden. You realize you are, in fact, a cruel asshole. Not how your Mother raised you. *Go left, Frank!* Whose voice was which?

As our game ended and the party intensified, I instinctively navigated away from the big stones and searched out the large interpretative panel I'd seen being installed the week before. Dion's ur-text was a blur, lost on me but it sounded good in short bursts. Painfully wordy, it was for an inebriate. It described how *Poet's* was a daring curatorial attempt to capture a fleeting moment in contemporary art where it intersected with several new subcultures and lives of an array of young (multi-generational) artists. Edgar Bloom was one of the artists – not quite the oldest but noticeably the deadest. I suspected he was snuck in late in the process because the show didn't have enough edge without him. In the statement, Dion had not glossed over the reality and wrote of Edgar's sincere adverse reaction to contemporary life: "The late Edgar Bloom sometimes engaged in dangerous pursuits of fancy that led him to the brink of madness. Imbued with the very stress and strain of existence he sought out the edge via the ambiguous nature of art within Debord's "Society of the Spectacle."

"Debord's Spectacle? Give me a break." This wording I'd OK'd but now it read oddly. Plus the letters were vibrating like they had breath. She mentioned the small painting: "Fuck Excessive Toil." These artists aren't war correspondents in the thick of battle! They grew up in a Middle class suburbia or tidy working class homes with garages. Our pain is self-inflicted, inside us. Dion was still dancing, so I thought better of delving further. When I caught up to her later, she'd have it worked out. She would be apologetic and complain that she had Trout breathing down her neck. This was true. I would acquiesce, no biggie. This was a bad time for critically reviewing their work or anything else plus I was suffering effects of substances. They were celebrating and having a group suck-up. I knew I was going to end up very drunk somewhere. One thing at a time. I'd say, "Dion. I know what you mean."

She'd say, "Frank. The book will have more shelf-life than an interpretative panel few people will read." Dion wrapped it up in art-speak and marketing. Perfectly blended. Which was which? Hand in Glove? The panel went on: Bloom continued to shed skins as he embarked on cancelling out his own process…like a chameleon from Mars. His drug addition fueled his mania and his attitude towards the system he despised. Hold on, Dion! I'd advised these people carefully. She stopped just short of admitting the art world killed the guy, which might have been closer to the truth. I'd be happy with that and we could involve inspector Finch and his pal, Pecker. I could hear his gruff voice, "Manslaughter by Neglect?" Are you being altogether serious with me, Mr. Frank? This final copy seemed to diverge from mine distinctly. It may have been heartfelt, but I could sense it wasn't. It was too steeped in self-congratulatory, anti-bourgeois, satiric convention that goes unnamed much of the time. There are losers and winners. There are great people who are profound creeps. I know Mr. Bloom was keenly aware of the odd social entanglements that caused some to rise and others drop from view, but so what? Isn't that par for life? It pissed Edgar off, especially the relationship where those with sway allowed so much failure. They looked away and ignored it deliberately. A Man's Laughter? Justice shall never be done. Never. Then again, the issue was left up in the air. A mystery, Dion thought. Seeds of doubt. OK, I decided; she's better than that. She knew the score and spun it until breaking point. Where the meaning is clear as a bell. *Trash Talk. Truth is overrated. Didn't Picasso say that?*

I ran into Johnny Bee. Maybe we would be going somewhere exciting later. He called me "ghetto brother." So now it was safe to hit the hood, an after hours club of the old school. You know what I mean. Not many skinny white guys are so honored. He winked as I headed for the door and I shot him right between the eyes with my thumb and index finger.

2004: Cowards. The history of the world is full of the shells of the defiant, the failed romantics who couldn't see the state of things or (like me) see it all too clearly. They live cushioned inside lifelong childhoods. If they wake up, the dream stops. They are done. Finito.

I exited thinking about the Dead Sea Scrolls when I converged with Sam and Nick. Together we headed back to the same bar to get some food. They were full of conversation but I was past listening. I focused on

225

the medium-rare burger I was about to order. It immediately settled my stomach. They asked me about the book and the movie shit. I answered with my mouth full and they cheered up a little.

"You're a rascal, aren't you?" Nick was almost congratulatory. Edgar nodded. *Yes! He is!*

"You guys have been most supportive," I said earnestly. This is when I lost track of the festivities.

46
CHAPTER

Artist Edgar Bloom and his work got critical acclaim and monetary value nearly overnight. He also eclipsed Philadelphia after his departure. Trout had nothing to gain in the marketing of the work after the show or with the auction price of her artists but she liked glamour. She was more interested in the critical acclaim. It started modestly with a small purchase by one little officious New York art collector called Snout then grew quickly. Historical acclaim takes longer. It has to snowball into the long-term record. But now the cat was out of the bag now and it meowed. Edgar's death had caused a small outcry among artists he barely knew and even more from those who never gave him the time of day. Ironic, yes? I still can't work it out. This enthusiastic outbreak of cynicism was larger than the recurrent sort that ebbed and flowed as careers rose or languished. A word in your shell like, squire. *Mr. Frank you are such a sly fox! How do you like the show?* Art shouldn't be mixed up with social climbing. *Make all the splash you can while the sun shines.* Strange bedfellows. It was about detachment, critical awareness and brown-nosing in turn. Genius Conventioneers were true to their credo: Crash and Burn. There's no Genius Convention Grant. No survivors and bring as many cretins as possible with you. We were simply meant to make trouble. Someone else could sort it out. Guilty, me? I am thinking I have let no one down. Not yet. The chord *Poet's* struck was a surprise for me, a wide-ranging mournfulness that the general public understood. What a shock. Edgar represented all the undiscovered small fry like Rocky Balboa. They felt the pain close to home, unsettling. But they were still somehow confused by the glow of recognition. They had never seen any themselves. Bow down oh, art messiah, we are not worthy. Stop using ten-dollar words.

It became Sunday. Upon waking I was trying to piece the events of the evening together but it was too dramatic to fit in my head all at one time. I eventually remembered that after the pub we managed to get in a cab and go to First Street Club. We were well drunk by this point. We paid an extra ten bucks to go upstairs. It was Eighties Night. Lucky us. The music sounded great. A man was dressed like Billy Idol or maybe that was his day look. Some wonderful Goths showed up and started moving to the Smiths. What a sweet moment. A rap song followed without effort. An old one, Gangsta's Paradise. The crowd intensified. Getting your bearings is hard. If you never get them that creates an issue. Your digital incarnations are fake.

My eyes opened eventually and I registered the sore head and queasy stomach. I was hoping I was just shy of the vomiting-all-morning stage. J'ai vomi! Is that how you say it? Thank God. I woke up on a couch staring at a strange ceiling. There was a broken-down dog looking at me. It smelled of roadkill. My ears were ringing and I heard some garbage trucks in the distance. "Where am I?" The dog's expression did not change. I turned my head. There were bodies scattered. My voice sounded like a frog with emphysema.

Someone spoke. "Mr. Frank, you know how to party."

"Who is talking?" I replied without turning my head.

"I am a member of the genius convention. Who are you? To your left, buddy." It was Nick.

"No you're not. You're counterfeit genius convention." There was no reply. I was unable to move my limbs or move from a prone position. "Where are we, Nick?"

I heard Sam from under blankets. "Did we get ejected or did I dream that part?"

"Where are you, Sam?"

"To your right. That was quite an opening, part Tom Wolfe and part Caligula."

Nick's voice explained. "Frank took on the bouncer and he threw you in a pile of garbage bags."

"So it was a classy evening then? I remembered Johnny Bee had rescued me and decked the guy with a swift punch.

"These slacker bouncers aren't that hard. Picard took Johnny away quick."

"Picard the cop was there?"

"Pecker you mean. Mickey was with us too."

"Mickey. No shit?"

"Is that punch called a boilermaker or is it a roundhouse?" asked Sam. The hungover men shrugged.

"Do we look like boxers to you?" Silence made us ache more.

"I think Sherrie should have come," said Sam.

I disagreed. "No. She's had enough trouble because of the art world and Dr. Phil wouldn't have felt at home. Did Johnny get home ok?"

"Of course. He's a boxer, born in the hood. All his friends are cops."

"Oh, I forgot."

We all looked at the rug until Sam broke the silence. "My head hurts. Let's do brunch at London Grill. I could use a Willy."

Nick laughed. "I fancy the chorizo egg sandwich and some bitching coffee."

My stomach turned over painfully as I rose slowly to a seated position. Nick encouraged us. "C'mon assholes."

The dog looked up as the door shut knowing we were talking about food.

229

47

CHAPTER

After returning from my first trip west, I was sitting bruised at the bar in The London Grill. The moguls had shot down my attempt at scriptwriting. A week had passed by and there was a lot to mull over in Philadelphia. I had imagined *Work Shy* a small indie film but the book kept growing in popularity. Just check my investment accounts! The producers – the sexist guys with cigars – were banking on this. "Tell the story to as many as possible! Art Through The Ages. For all to witness. No car chase or junkies." Artists, alive and dead, would be sending me thank you telegrams for the rest of my life.

The London Grill was originally the Golden Lager Saloon. It dated from 1843 and the infamous Eastern State Penitentiary loomed nearby. The prison was built eight years earlier (1835) and was the state-of-the-art penury facility of the civilized world. Nick and Sam were late. I was drinking a nice pint of ale named after Bank Robber, Willy Sutton. "Slick Willy" escaped from the prison in 1937 and came straight to this joint for a beer. Two whole blocks! His wanted poster was now taped to a room-length mirror. The original appeared in post offices of yore. Remember where we used to buy stamps? The mugshot didn't do him justice. There was a popular coffee bar across from the prison entrance, Mugshots. Get it? Coffee mug, shot of espresso? Sutton apparently escaped down a ladder made of dental floss. I can't imagine that is correct especially if it was waxed. Eastern State Penitentiary is the most interesting building in Philadelphia if you ask me, including Independence Hall. Much Too Twee for tourists. The architecture of the prison – castle-like from the outside – was groundbreaking at the time and designed to reform criminals through solitude and insanity. It was much copied and the design prefigured Strangeways – another ancient, spoke-wheeled prison in Manchester, UK. "*Strangeways*" is also the title of the Smiths' last album. Serendipity-doo, says Edgar. You can check out Eastern State's website for what movies it served as location. One with Bruce Willis, I think. In *Law Abiding Citizen,* prosecutor, Jamie Foxx gets outwitted by a dangerous, former SAS guy. Lots of explosions in that one. Even the former Mayor showed up, not playing himself, luckily. Stranger than fiction. I always liked Jamie Foxx. He could play the fictional Edgar! "Why can't Edgar be black," you say? Do we really want to open that can of worms? Edgar was a neurotic white guy possibly of a mixed Jewish variety, end of story. Though City Hall, if they had a say – they don't – would make a good case for it. Doctor J. is on a building size mural but is Willy Sutton or Al Capone? Capone was a patron of the prison for one year. Oddly enough, he was picked up on gun possession charges and lived like the Duke of Fairmont Avenue. Come to think of it, if Philadelphia produced a mural celebrating every murderer, there wouldn't be enough room for cars. But, let's be positive!

"Here's your Willy, Mr. Frank," said Katrina.

"That's kinda personal, Katrina." She gave me a look. "The London Grill reminds me of the Jack the Ripper Pub near Liverpool Street in London."

"Does it really? How creepy. Do you know London Pubs?"

"A few. Originally, The Ten Bells. That's where Jack stalked prostitutes named Marie Kelly. Nobody knows why. His name remains a mystery."

"We call them sex workers now, Mr. Frank."

"Of course. I know that. Recently, some writer guy has implied Jack might have been Vincent Van Gogh. Ridiculous! The pub was called The Jack the Ripper for years until they had the sense to re-assign the original name." Katrina's eyes glazed over and she disappeared seeking another patron.

Edgar also wrote about the Grill: *May, '04: Look at all these bicyclists. Let's get cardio, dudes. Where are all the old people? We need old people. They remember what it was like before we were all assholes.*

I sat in a window seat and stared out at people pumping gas. The Museum Area Sunoco station was nicely gentrified with big orange racing stripes. A hideous modern apartment building loomed up behind full of podiatrists. I picked up the City Weekly and skimmed it for art and literature features. A mistake. The ad for *Forgotten Poets* had been in the national and international press for months but this was the first cover story in Philly's leading weekly. Dion had kept a lid on the local buzz until the dam burst and DiStephano got to feather her nest with a controversial article. I'd given her the skinny or what she thought was the skinny. Edgar's mental problems. In her bloated mind, that's what made him worth checking out. I mentioned the rumor of a feature film to her in our second interview. This made her giddy. I looked up and saw my guests had arrived. Sam and Nick were in need of a drink. Sam's eyes looked red from tears.

"Two more Willies, bartender!"

"Right away, Mr. Frank. You know I am a woman, right? And we don't say bartender anymore?"

"Of course, I know, Katrina." She gave me another meaningful look. Sam said quietly, "This is getting interesting, Frank."

"What is?"

"The movie thing and the sales. Paintings, books and price points."

I hated that term. "Yeah, though it is a little late for Edgar to cash in."

Nick responded. "But is it wise to play their game? Isn't that what it is all about these days?"

I countered carefully, "No one makes art outside the system of the Contemporary, do they, Nick? Certainly not you." I wish I hadn't said it but there you are.

He looked thoughtful. "Not sure. Some believe art cannot live along side an overheated capitalist society. There must be some reason the visual world is so precarious." I showed Sam and Nick the article in question.

"What small town shit," he said.

Sam concurred, "Vicarious. How does she know this?"

"My fault completely," I admitted. "There is no such a thing as bad press."

The beer arrived and Katrina asked, "Aren't you friends of Edgar Bloom, late of Germantown?"

"Yes Ma'am. You know him?"

"He watched the Phillies in here on occasion. He didn't make to the '08 World Series. Very sad. We are looking forward to the exhibition."

Word had spread to the masses. "You'd better hurry, Katrina. It closes next week then moves to Atlanta."

"Oh shit," said the bartender lady.

We again considered the news story. "I was supposed to keep things under wraps until the suits were ready but I couldn't resist." I mentioned the trip and the future plans. We were the fan club for an unmade film of a marginally known book.

Biggs told me, "It's a waiting game, Frank. Timing is crucial." I'm sure Edgar would not have cared. Sullied everything.

"I hate Hollywood," Sam admitted.

Nick needed details. "Is it going to be real?"

I finished my pint. "How do you mean?"

"You know, turning the thing into sophomoric tedium. A fake thing."

"Not sure."

"God forbid it be successful, Nick. And popular."

Sam wanted to hear how far the LA connection had gone, "Oscar-Bound Art House film?"

"Let's not count chickens guys. Edgar will certainly have a Philadelphia Foundation named after him so shitty artists can receive grants."

"Oh, hurrah!" Sam said in mock exuberance. I bid farewell to my friends for another week of negotiations in Hollywood. On the way out, they resembled an old couple nearing the end of a relationship. One book opened, another closed.

At the other end of the bar, I thanked Katrina, "Did they name you after the hurricane?" She smiled and discreetly reeled out her middle finger.

CHAPTER

Sherrie sold the Blue House in 2006 and did well thanks to Quick-Fix stagers and a little help from me. I bought the Bungalow. Not a bad investment in the long term; it was nearly free. She bought a big house twenty miles outside the city limits. Kurtz went to better public schools and Dr. Phil could continue to cut up patients after a short commute. What happened to my chances in the romance department? They faded as Dr. Phil Delfonico, future husband came onto the scene. He looked like Bloom but fatter, with a well-trimmed doctor beard. Presto, Sherrie had a new life. Kurtz was making progress in counseling. Unlike his dad, the kid was grounded. I became comfortable as Uncle Frank who sometimes arrived in "Daddy's" car.

Dr. Phil came out to the driveway in over-sized cargo pants and gave me the concerned eyeball. He thought he'd seen the last of me. "What a noisy bug." I gave him my eyeballs back. He'd heard about Edgar's friends. Sorry pal. Am I some sort of snitch?

"I hear you may be making *Work Shy* into a movie. Sherrie's not crazy about that idea."

"I know, Phil, sorry. Can't stop progress. It's out of my hands."

"Sure it is." Sherrie had sent me a big thank you card at the Bungalow. It had furry cats on the front. I'm not sure if it was for helping with the house sale or for promoting her deceased husband. She wrote that I was welcome to visit anytime as long as I gave notice of two weeks! Fair enough. Edgar's residuals had formed on the horizon and it was clear the pay off would be size-able. Her lawyers liked to talk to my lawyers. They spoke lawyer-talk.

I hired Lucy Lawless. She was a hard-nose. The other Attorneys knew I had her watching my back. Mr. Frank has "lawyered up" to the hilt. Another odd verbing. She explained contracts and death duties to me and other earthlings. It paid for her personalized license plate. I was thinking of getting my own, one that said: ART WHORE.

Our coffee meetings went on until Spring 2007, nearly two years after the funeral. *Forgotten Poets* exhibition had moved on to the next museum, Miami. Our last appointment was in mid-March at Café Mystique where we had begun. Sherrie was disappointed in me.

She had finished reading the book and had comments. "*Work Shy* is quite amazing, Mr. Frank, really. You turned Edgar Bloom from a lazy ass, dead-beat dad into a martyr." I sat quietly and let her have her say. "You have made our lives public property, Mr. Frank." I stared at my feet. "Edgar Bloom is one thing, myself and Kurtz another." I stared at my knees. She had me.

I responded with a feeble, "Sorry."

I let the next painful remark sink in. "Plus, you can't continue to be surrogate uncle or father to Kurtz." We sat uncomfortably without sweetness or light and stared at our respective muffins. The butter refused to soften.

She stood abruptly, "I'm not finished, Mr. Frank. No more coffee. No more muffins. Here's the Wedding invitation. Hope you can make it but don't knock yourself out on my account." I watched Sherrie's glistening eyes as she turned. She hurried out and I let her go. Disapproving glances bounced off me. I had wanted to settle down with the woman – or anyone who would have me. Phil saw that. She had other plans, of course. I was a little too much like Edgar in the creative department. Though, I had a steady income, I was tainted. Her long-term plans were to move to the West Coast where her Mom lived in Seattle, far away from the City Art Museum or so she thought. Seattle also has a great art museum designed by Robert Venturi and *Forgotten Poets* would land there in 2009! Edgar's shadow grew post-mortem. Still, my chance of becoming Edgar's belated in-law appealed to me. It wasn't that I was in love, but it was a good match and there was a calm about her that kept the world at bay. Kurtz was a gas; an intelligent, ball of fun. Who'da thunk it? Edgar approved. He was no longer on my shoulder but his past melded with my future.

Saturday Morning: Very Sixties, Sharing Girlfriends. A new year. Hurrah. Same old shit. Mummer's downtown playing banjos dressed as chickens. Misanthrope shit from me. Fucking Head cold. Sam and Nick are coming over for drinkie-winkies at 4. I could use the company. Maybe they can gimme reactions to new stuff, SPOOF! I call it. Found this big picture book in the trash; Joseph Conrad stories. Started with Heart of Darkness. I hope Kurtz never reads it.

When I had fully processed her comments, I wrote Sherrie a letter. It was important to apologize formally on paper through snail mail. Aunt Judith taught me that. Manners. I told Sherrie I was sorry for how it played out. The book wasn't part of her initial plan. I also felt the need to apologize for the future direction it took. I mentioned Cranston and his plans as vaguely as possible. Hollywood was out of my control. A big chapter was ending. In the next one, there was a lot to keep track of. In New York, there were meetings and deals of all sorts. Unfortunately – speaking of bad pennies – Mito pursued me. When I reported back to Biggs and Cranston, he phoned them. He wanted to write his own book. Literary stuff, supposedly. Sounded dreadful to me. Was I meant to give my blessing? Good luck with that. Why did Cranston open the door? Mito got the message slowly. Diary of the Artist as a Young Dude. Get off the stage for god's sake. He'd been out on the periphery for decades teaching aloofly and sitting in bars where he chatted up eager co-eds. Oh, wise one. Fill me with your experience. Some people need a punch in the nose.

The hardcover of *Work Shy* looked good. The design said, "Steam-Punk'd," yet with a mainstream, thriller vibe. I had insisted the cover be clever, no crappy embossed lettering with crimson blood. "That's tacky," I told those publishers, hammering my fist on the table. Who was I kidding? They wanted to change the title to Death of a Genius. In terms of *Work Shy*, I was confident of success.

The book continued to buzz on the NYT bestseller list, inexplicably. It was indeed taking off and the soft cover was planned for the spring. Cranston was busy networking for Albatross, a New York/Hollywood link-up.

Biggs sent me flowers. "Who says the bookshop is dead?" Unfortunately for Cranston, there was now competition. Other companies got word and were keen to battle for the copyright. He had to box clever. I had done my job and was about to move on. Nimbly, I hoped.

"Edgar is going to the movies," I told my Dad on the phone. He didn't get it.

"Let him rest in peace for god's sake, Doug."

"Writing is hard work," I said in my defense.

"I'm glad your Mother's dead."

"She's not dead, Dad. You're divorced and she lives in Mahwah, New Jersey!" I let it drop but the silence was too much. This was our last conversation for a while. Dialogue with Mother was not much better. I was the black sheep for both. Odd, since I remain their only child.

Biggs suggested I leave the East coast, "You don't need to be here now, Mr. Frank."

"There's change a coming. Yeah, I know, Biggs."

"About time too."

Cranston ended the conversation. "Let's do this, Frank."

A real break was needed but LA was as close as I got. The snowball grew and mowed me over. *Forgotten Poets* took on a life of it's own and I wasn't needed. Sally became my personal assistant for both projects. I was inexplicably attached to the woman. She could efficiently co-ordinate things on both coasts at the same time. I wasn't up to that. Too many Red Eyes.

She kidded me when she realized I cared. "Behind every great man is a librarian."

"A great librarian," I replied. She wanted to Skype me and I said no! "It's creepy, Sally."

She agreed. "But I'll miss your ugly face."

"You mean rugged and well-worn visage, don't you?"

49
CHAPTER

My first *Work Shy* trip to LA was disastrous or felt so at the time. I finally met with the big boys at Film Corp and it was agreed that we had a project. I held back my enthusiasm. Their veteran scriptwriter Harris Tweed wanted to milk me first. He'd sized me up and found me wanting.

Out of my depth, the scene got set anyway. Mythical Headlines: Cynical East Coaster No Match For Ruthless Californians. This was new to me: casual meetings where everyone chatted obliquely. "How was the banana colon therapy, Sean?" I shifted in my chair. It helped a lot in LA to be handsome and have sparkly white teeth, but they let me off the plane anyway. I fancied Edgar may have planned this all along, not that it had a shot in hell of actually happening. Not for me. So who came up as suggested for the lead role? I wish I wasn't so ugly and tortured! Lots of young guys, overly handsome. Paul Giambacini could have played the older Edgar, I figured or Woody Harrelson, but most of the diaries dealt with Edgar's youth. Who could portray that over-the-top angst without ruining it? Of course, Scarlett Johannson was going to be Cassandra in full bloom. A nice little Academy Award cameo for Scarlett? I'm not joking though SJ is too old now! And what a Screen hog! How old is she, anyway? The budget grew as the conversation rolled ahead. In the film, Cassandra may not die after all! What?!

Research began immediately as ideas were formulated. Serious film comparisons were opened to discussion. We looked at the *Horse's Mouth,*

(1956) then Kirk Douglas's portrayal (1956) of Vincent van Gogh in *Lust for Life*. Neither seemed to fit the bill as a model for the story of Edgar. *Art School Confidential,* (2006) was closer. It was a very short graphic novel before it was a stupid movie. Nick Nolte did a cool 80's painter in Scorsese's *Life Lessons* segment of the *New York Stories* (2009) trilogy. *Pollock* was an excellent film with dead ringer Ed Harris as doomed Jackson. Don't drink & drive! Critic, Clement Greenberg showed up as villain in that. Going way back to the Baroque period was *Caravaggio* by British director Derek Jarman. Surreal, homo-erotic, art house stuff. "Too Gay!" emailed Cranston nervously. I liked another little-known prospect: *High Art,* an art world based film with formerly, clean cut Ally Sheedy as a drug-addled photographer. "Never heard of it, Frank!" It had a great scene satirizing conniving gallerists. "Too Gay!" emailed Cranston. *I Shot Andy Warhol* was about the crazy woman who tried to kill Warhol or "Drella" – Andy's nickname combining Dracula and Cinderella! "Not keen on that, Frank. Why did she do it?"

"Ask Lou Reed."

Cranston on the phone: "Again, too Gay, Mr. Frank!"

Biggs commented. "Yeah. Check out Indie Band Yo la Tengo as the Velvet Underground, Mr. Frank. True to the seamy NYC underworld, blah, blah. More Lesbians."

"Too Gay!" yelled Cranston in the background. "Put me on speaker-phone."

Art Star Julian Schnabel's film *Basquiat* was much closer to the Bloom-mold, a time capsule instilled with all the right 'artist-genius' shit. It did have some critical distance and a timely brand of cynicism and wit. Edgar loved Bowie's depiction of Warhol. Perfect casting! I mentioned this up in Santa Monica and wished I hadn't. The suits loudly approved. "We love the Spider from Mars." They brought out iPhone clips and shoved them in my face. If I wanted to be nurtured in namedropping, I was in the right place.

Harris and the neo-suits of LA pulled up in Porsches and Beamers with Starbucks and Rolexes. They wore suits with expensive designer tees underneath so they could show off their weight training. "You guys are buff!" They dated aging starlets and read the Wall Street Journal online and off. I was given an introduction to all the classiest escort services.

"When in Rome, Mr. Frank. Nudge, nudge, wink, wink."

"That's how I met my wife, Mr. Frank. She has special skills."

I deferred politely, "Thank you, gentlemen, sincerely. I'm here to work" They laughed the dirtiest laugh I'd ever heard. It bounced off the walls and settled on the carpet. Was I some sort of sacrifice for them to munch on? Paul to Edgar's Christ. Or is it Saul on the road to Damascus?

Unlike the Museum folks who hung on to an Edwardian ideal, these reptiles were on a creepy first name basis. Don Kirsch was American Films' main man. "Welcome to Tinseltown, Frank." He and Harris were in cahoots. Hence, the agro. Harris doodled. Don sported a marvelous fake tan that extended over his shiny baldhead. It was covered in age spots and other deformations of a solar nature. The last wisps of hair were unkempt and stuck out at odd angles from his apricot colored dome. Oddly enough, he was only three years older than I am. When he talked, mountains shook. Underneath the overblown façade, he was a moderately funny and run-of-the-mill narcissist. He was also the biggest asshole I've ever met in a room.

50

CHAPTER

Did Dan Brown have this problem? Movie-making is a minefield and I didn't want my book tainted by some lousy film. I had struggled to give the story both weight and understandability. Unfortunately, I had also relinquished control. Sherrie didn't want a movie at all. The last time we met she told me, "Don't do it. It isn't what I asked you to do!" Phil chewed me out as well, protecting his new wife. *Work Shy* was meant to be a simple, in-between-bigger-things project, the kind where I sorted a friend's chaotic life not a celebrity circus. I almost hated myself.

Only Kurtz stuck by Edgar and me. Who wouldn't want a movie about his Dad? "Blow these guys outta the water, Mr. Frank," he told me on the phone. My dad also knew Edgar had the right stuff. Everyone else was a pipsqueak, taught skills by frustrated hacks. It was not about the art, in other words, no matter how much they stress the art. The medium is the message, bullshit. Covers the bases. Art is about how we live, ipso facto. It is about commodity and what is smugly referred to as consumer culture or theoretically, the Spectacle. Ironically, Edgar knew Spectacle and it didn't do him any favors:

Dec. 25, 1999: Bugger Debord. The French simply turn these ideas into another elitist calling card. Nobody knows real spectacle better that the poor slobs who are stuck with it. They may not know its name but they know it when they see it. The assholes don't get it. They think some impervious bastard at the top is keeping them down. Well, that may be true, but the actual components of their grief is their adherence to the system, abiding the TV and status etc…. Artist learnt nothing if not this. Forsaken Text! Alas, we lose it. Even old-fashioned painters get that part of it. You have to do what you do best not what the progressive automaton society deems. We live by digitized beams, images that aren't really there.

Let's talk guilt. At first, I wasn't in this to re-write the history of art at all, much less at the turn of the multi-layered Twenty-First Century. Every idiot had a CNN-based opinion. Something they knew nothing about.

But then I had a long talk with myself. "How to proceed, Mr. Frank?" Start at the beginning. The crafting of words had become my livelihood and it was nothing like the art game where your damn heart was exposed all the time. With words you can do the impossible. Am I stepping on someone else's footnotes? Of course. I had kept similar teenage journals, now trashed. Maybe that was stupid, but writers have different priorities than artists. We get manic and burn sub-standard stuff in fireplaces after drinking a lot. We carry words upstairs in our noggins and save them for later. Artists simply build on top of all the mistakes and kiss ass selectively. Every wrong mark helps.

Kirsch set all in motion and fast. "Call me Don, Mr. Frank." He understood that Edgar's suffering was a dream set up for some mug like me to scoop up all the credit. Not on his watch! Oddly, they liked the non-narrative style of *Work Shy*, but wanted me to cut it down to a three-act play, simpler for viewers.

Then screenwriter Harris would take over. "The book is far too angular."
I sensed the blade approaching. "What do you mean, angular?"

Biggs wasn't sure. Most writers sank in Santa Monica and lived in their cars. They read Aristotle's *Poetics* yet imagine Bruce Willis in the lead. Well, he could play somebody like his comic bit in *The Player*. Makes sense. 1998: Trailer Parks of the Stars. That would explain it. "I'm a vagrant now. Send money." It became apparent that Kirsch and his guys wanted a narrative to start at the beginning (1982) after the obligatory end point; all would be flashback until the circular denouement. No surprise to me, but I was concerned about when they dumped the writer. Cranston angled for me to get advisor standing. We looked at scriptwriters, large and small. Sure enough, Don and the suits loved the mock-reverence in Edgar's character; anti-hero material. They wanted to twist it into mass consumptiveness for a new millennium. Cranston did his best from New York, with connections between film, script and publishing. I followed his lead, expecting it to fall through gloriously.

Biggs advice, "Act like a big shot. Be unabashedly forward." Bless him. He was worrying about little old me. They didn't know I'd already started the screenplay nicknamed WORKSHYTE. I figured I had just the right connections to segue from "literature" to movies. I didn't consider this while writing the book but Edgar opened a whole new set of doors for me and I was going to pay him back somehow. Maybe even set up that foundation for un-discovered Bloom-ish geniuses.

Sherrie stayed pissed at me and didn't answer my letters from LA. I resembled a money-grubbing opportunist in her eyes. Even if she and Kurtz benefitted. She kept saying I'd gone too far and complained to Phil, "Mr. Frank is out of control. What should we do? Can we sue him? Do you agree with me, Phil? I think he has gone too far."

He stroked his whiskers in agreement thinking I'd gotten away with murder. "I agree, honey. He's a first class schmuck."

51

CHAPTER

All movies should have a scene where the main character gets drunk. Screw the plot. Via an inebriated protagonist, the viewer is given much emotional background. I was waiting for a meeting in the bar downstairs having a discussion with the handsomest barman I ever saw. I mean, I think he was a man. He was Korean and his name was Kenny. I kept looking for his Adam's apple as he filled me in about boy bands. I like talking to normal working people and he was good at his job. He succeeded in selling me six rye-and-gingers. Delicious. We were listening to K-Pop and bouncing around use of music in film. Sweet guy. My accomplice in wine let me have the seventh drink free. I gave him two twenties as a tip. I think it was twenties. That's not particularly generous in LA though I was pretending to be a big shot from Philly. I barely made it back to the office. The elevator opened and I felt the stare of receptionist Belle Tox. She was an infamous ex-model from the 90's whose acting career tanked. She had divorced some famous guy and was vaguely familiar from the front of a vintage Good Housekeepings. I was quickly whisked into one of Kirsch's hideaways and poured into a chair ready to discuss film music.

The suits main concern was now copyright issues! "What issues?" I said, foolishly, "Bands will be lining up to get a bit of a song in this movie, especially washed up punk bands." I had taken up smoking that afternoon and I started to fish out my pipe. "My Korean friend gave this to me. It belonged to his father who's recently passed. Kenny said it made me look distinguished and even lent me some tobacco."

Of course, my liquid lunch made me forget these were not desperate actors but money-hungry, health-nuts. True, actors were given a certain allowance for self-medication but not writers. Writers were treated like dogs. Actors only got fined if they acted up. He he. Bottom Line. Money on the Barrel Head. Bums in seats, luvvy! Bums in seats.

"What is this Frank?" Harris asked. "Are you inebriated?" They were all shocked and resorted to cell phones like I'd insulted someone's mother. I counted seven phones but I am a little blurry on that. Harris glared at me as if I'd pissed in his swimming pool.

I settled in a chair and started to feel around for matches. "Who are you guys calling?" Before I'd lit my tobacco, (Gentleman's Mild) I was being politely but firmly escorted back to my digs by a mountainous man named Hitch. He was somebody's personal assistant and I liked him immediately because I was drunk.

Hitch had a warm soft voice, a muscular build and a bulge in his side. "Here's some coffee, Mr. Frank." He whispered in one of my ears, "from the famous receptionist. Isn't she sweet? Nasty bitch. That's between you and me."

"Bless you, Hitch. Are you a stunt man?"

"Funny you say that. This is to keep you on the straight and narrow." We drove around for a bit and I got a little sleepy. My new coffee regime started and I was ready for my flight. Hitch had re-booked it. I got out at the Wayward Arms and the doorman, Curt saluted us at the entrance. This must have happened all the time. I suddenly blew yellow chow onto Curt's blue walkway. I felt stupid but it was worth it to hear him speechless for once. On the third floor, I prepared to pass out on the Queen Size picturing Christian Bale in the scene struggling with nausea. Hitch caught the flaming pipe as it fell.

"Picture Frank smiling as he drunkenly congratulates himself. Hitch, what do you think about *Work Shy*, 3D?"

"Goodnight, Mr. Frank. Give my regards to Philadelphia." The door shut. Camera shot from above, then a POV shot of blurry ceiling and I was out. In my head, camera pans to TV tennis match, a dream sequence, I think. Close up of handsome tennis pro. There was a massive white swoosh on his red headband. Edgar narrates: *How much does he get for that plug? Dear readers, we hear the door close.* Mr. Frank fades to black.

The next day I woke up a Philadelphian. This transformation confused me. Was I secretly trying to scuttle the whole project? Whatever it was, it felt good. If I was throwing a spanner in the works, it would take a lot more booze. Until the trip to the airport, I took some notes from my memories the day before. What little I remembered.

I put on two pairs of shades, smallish for reading and massive for the damn sunshine. Not another Red Eye. Ciao, Hitch. Bye, Curt.

"See you next week, Mr. Frank," said the doorman.

I spoke out of earshot to spare his feelings. "Missing you already, asshole."

52
CHAPTER

I dozed on the plane and a detective voice-over ran through my brain. This went round my head, so I tried it out a few times out loud, albeit softly. Dialogue is my strong suit. "I am going to fuck you up, man. Fuckin' Galleries!"

This alerted a few of the passengers and somebody summoned the Air Marshall. "There is somebody in business class talking menacingly like Steve Buscemi!"

The Air Marshall was chopping away at his tough chicken with a tiny fork. He repeated. "Steve Buscemi? I like Steve Buscemi! Maybe it is Steve Buscemi complaining about the free Merlot." In a moment he stood over me looking like Magnum PI, a big mustache above his mouth. I looked up at the behemoth. He was disappointed. "You aren't Steve Buscemi."

I responded with a nasty British accent. "You sir, are very bright indeed." He asked me why I was talking to myself? "I'm working on film script about a screwy painter."

He brightened and said, "Cool." I asked him if his name is McLuhan? "No, why?"

"Nevermind." I was planning to shut up at that point and concentrate on the laptop but Magnum made himself at home in the seat next to mine. He's handsome and Mike Farrellini is his name. I liked him too because I was hungover.

"It's about the art world? My daughter is studying painting."

"Good for her. Where?" I asked.

"Bennington. It costs a fortune. Don't get it myself." Common story. Another man who doesn't know the difference between 1960 and 1980, Matisse or Picasso, much less, Pollock or Damien Hirst. Low and Behold. How Low can we Behold? The Marshall who spent most of his time on the cultural plateau of 30,000 feet, was interested in a script about an artist? Everyone likes movies; nobody likes art. "Was he successful, this Edgar Bloom?" Here we go again.

"Of course not." I chuckle. "Go read the book, Mike."

He orders us a couple of Bloody Marys. His legs pushed the seat ahead of us but the occupant knew when to shut up. They settled for tangy gossip. I glanced down at Magnum's Glock, hidden under Mike's jacket and felt safe.

"What's it called, Mr. Frank?"

"*Work Shy!*"

"*Work Shy?*"

"Yes."

All of a sudden, the passenger in front of us turned abruptly and shoved his copy of my book into the lawman's face. Mike was surprised, inspected the cover and handed it back. The passenger quickly withdrew with the novel and recommenced eavesdropping. Perhaps, I would sign it for him later in the flight?

"Nice cover," said Mike, "and the movie?"

"Same title so far, Mike," I said. I sketched out the plot so as not to reveal anything of import to my fan and fellow business class flyer in front.

"So you wrote *Work Shy*. I've heard of it; a how-to-book? How to succeed in art?"

May 11, 2005: C'est la vie, baby. Shitty Books make good movies while you spoil a good book with a crappy cinematic version. My Life Story, no exception! Hey even Joyce and Proust did some self-publishing. Shame on you publishing people making great writer use Vanity Publishing. Musicians do it too these days. It's too easy but, painters can't self publish. It doesn't work. It is unseemly. If they align themselves with the disreputable. There is so much lack of talent out there.

Does Edgar mean me? If everyone knew I cribbed your remarks so directly, Edgar, they'd hire you instead of a ghost-sorta-writer. Get it? A real Ghost Writer? He he. What is the adage about great artists stealing? So very true. The idea of originality is overrated, always was. It helped to be demented though. "Nix the gat, tough guy. We're all friends here." As far as the movie goes, I was thinking the 'detective' story might work transplanted onto an artist's life. Good enough for Ridley Scott and *Blade Runner.* SF blending with Private Detective, the American icon for individuality and non-compliance. Strangely, the Air Marshall understood that combination of tropes.

"A little passé, but I love it, Mr. Frank," said Magnum. This was not everyone's reaction. "Who plays you in the movie? Not Steve Buscemi?" This air cop was not as dumb as he looked. Frank (or whoever plays me) never shows up in the film. Maybe in a mirror like private dick, Dick Powell does in that Noir number *Vengeance is Mine* from 1952 or whatever the title is. It's corny, but they used voice-over really effectively.

"Not sure if the narrator gets into the film but I'd like it to be Hugh Grant."

"That's so cool, man!" In the film *Work Shy*, or whatever title it acquires – fingers crossed – Edgar may wink and give the thumbs up as he heads skyward to the tune of *London Calling.* Cue triumphant choral music. Maybe he is even greeted by great artist heroes in heaven! Basquiat and Warhol! Throughout the movie, my voice or a similar, calm, man of the world – anchors the viewer. This is in comparison to Edgar's monologues, which are manic and raspy, like – guess who – Steve Buscemi. A spaced-out criminal sort?

Mike did his version of the actor in question. "You get the fuckin' picture, Mr. Frank? Fuckin' gallerists. I love Buscemi."

The Air Marshall loved Buscemi? I was impressed. "Not a bad impression, Mike. You've obviously seen *Fargo* a few times." Here's another bromance in development. After downing our drinks, we traded email and I told him I'd catch him on the flip-flop, if he wasn't shooting terrorists in their underwear.

"Not funny, dude. That is serious shit." He waved and disappeared behind the insubstantial curtain to coach. Could this be another fictionalized truth? I pictured him as George Clooney in a small, unpaid cameo. McCluhan would love that! Clooney is the new Bogart and the world really needs a new Bogart.

Back at the Bungalow, I started to rewrite the treatment and behaved. "There are millions of script writers in the world, Mr. Frank," they'd said. Point taken. I barely had any time. I would be on another plane in a few days.

Sally was put to work. "Stay a while this time," she pleaded. I called Judy Cheap. Thought she could help me envision the soundtrack. The unscripted version of the book *Work Shy* was gonna be fun. I figured she might have some down and dirty punk rock history. She had mentioned lost tapes. They would fit in the dissolute soundtrack. Of course, The Trauma Queens could use big break after fifteen years in obscurity. I was looking forward to a burger at the London Grill. Judy was waiting with the four-track mix down and she was way ahead of me with a Sutton or two.

After food and pints, we went outside and listened on her dated Toyota's archaic cassette machine. "That's Edgar on guitar. I'm on vocals. He sings backing too." The tape had a lot of hiss on it but you didn't notice once the band kicked in. We laughed. It was rough in a good way. I looked out the window at the prison's towers up the block. It was good to be home.

Later at the Bungalow, we played the tape on an old ghetto blaster for Sally and Sam. Nick had abandoned us, living the life in NYC. I filled them in on the last two months of scripty-ness. There was comfort in this. "How does it sound to you ladies?"

"Raw. Like a period piece," Sally said.

"I remember one tune. Where have I heard this?" said Sam.

Sally said it was a shame to have to hand it over to film producers. "Is it copyrighted?"

"Yeah, but Hollywood controls everything," Judy admitted. "They fuck things up."

I smelled dope but didn't want to mention it. "Hey, what is that smell?" Sam and Sally giggled. "Have you guys been smoking pot in my Bungalow?"

Sally looked at Sam and giggled more. "Sorry, boss."

I frowned and let it go. "Gee whiz. When the cat's away." They had begun an animated dance like a Mickey Mouse cartoon holding each other's hands. Judy and I went to the kitchen and grabbed more beer. She asked if they always behave like this and I admitted it was a new twist. When Sam and Sally finally settled down, they asked what I'd been up to. We went back to the film topic.

"It's going well, girls. That is the charm, ladies," I said, "like all rough sketched art, it has heart and the film dudes recognize that." They were not convinced. They were not even listening.

"We love Judy's singing. It sounds tortured." Judy blushed. Sam rambled on and asked me about the art scene in LA.

I told her I hadn't seen any of it. "All I see is offices, bars, hotels and the damn highway."

"But you have caught a little sun, Frank."

"That was bound to happen."

"It suits you." Everyone agreed I looked wonderful. We started to go through Edgar's LP's. That led to a party atmosphere. Judy called the other Trauma Queens to join us. We ended up toasting the band and Edgar and his supposed soundtrack.

"What is the song called, Judy?" asked Sally.

"Sweet Betrayal." I wrote it down in my yellow pad.

Back in LA, things came out in the wash. "I've got this, Mr. Frank," said Harris.

"Thank god you're here to help, Mr. Tweed. I don't know what I'd do without you."

"You'll find out soon, Frank. I've decided *Work Shy's* a buddy movie." A fly entered my open mouth. In a script, the book was to be abbreviated and put it into three clear acts for mass consumption. Damn, My daft, half-assed, literary accomplishment was to morph into a silly comic book movie with a few minor celebs looking for a challenging and popular vehicle. Was this going to happen on my watch!? Well, yes, probably. As tempting as the cash was, the opportunity to explain finally an artist's life to the whole bloody world was too good to pass up even if it was marginally off, truthwise. Myth predominates along with complete ignorance. It's something everybody has ass-backwards. Remember William Faulkner working on scripts and Dashiell Hammett? That is ancient history. Maybe David Mamet is available or somebody. The writer of The Great Gatsby? What's his name, the alchie? Dead authors usually aren't available. Get it? Ghost Writers! If a joke works, reuse it oftenly.

Edgar's theories gathered weight out West, though Hollywood had long since stolen the painter's stage. The film screen was bigger and better than canvas. Painting was eclipsed but movies have never replaced the intimate, cosmic gesture, that powerful single signature, hand-made mark. I sound like Fred Nietzsche. This occurred historically in the early Twentieth Century changing what a painter did up close with a brush and sweat. As the impartial storyteller, I took this as sign that the world was mad, having gone for the facsimile rather than the real item.

Rock musicians always ask, "What is reality, man?" Something on paper made by hand? Something with soul what theorists refer to as aura. Aura this, aura that. Which is which? Unlike the art world, movies are made to be directly popular even so called Indie productions. Hollywood has less pretense to eclecticism, only vague nods. Critics be damned. There is deep shit when you immerse yourself in film theory, much less feminist and leftist politics. Edgar believed art should be popular.

Meanwhile, I needed another bungalow. Didn't matter as long as it was cheap and clean. I checked the local Craiglist and wrote an ad. "Struggling Screenwriter from East Coast needs tacky room." There were hundreds of responses from the land of the almost famous. One mohawked tenderfoot contacted me about a small room above a skateboard factory called Big Silver Bird In Sky. I passed. Speaking of mail, a postcard from Kurtz arrived from Washington State. It was addressed to Mr. Hollywood Frank, Hotel Kasbah, Santa Monica, USA. The *Forgotten Poets* exhibition card from the Seattle Art Museum featured his dad's painting on the front. The image said BEGGARS ARE CHOOSERS in bold caps! They were looking for houses. I stuck the card on my temporary fridge with the Andy Warhol magnet of a cow and stood looking at it for hours. It was signed, "To my creative pal, Uncle Frank, Love, Kurtz Bloom." Was it too late to procreate?

CHAPTER

Magenta Rice was Hollywood royalty. Her father Maxwell was a renowned director from the Sixties. I'll spare you the details. The suits were used to her.

"Even lesbians will want to read this book," the men boasted. Like a good Bro, I agreed and they grinned. "We're on to something here, Frank."

Rice was used to the misogyny and homophobia. "Whatever."

"That's what we want," said Miles, second suit from the left, "Controversy."

"Controversy? That's not controversy."

"How's Papa, Magenta?" Kirsch inquired.

"You saw him at his funeral, Don. Don't you remember?"

"Of course, I do. I loved his movies." Don continued, "He hated fairies too." Don was referring to *Lord of the Rings* kinda creatures.

"You mean elves, Boss," Harris corrected.

"And those Hobbit things. They're ugly."

"What about the Orcs? Wow, ugly!!"

"I hate the Orcs," continued Kirsch.

"They look like vampires to me," Harris chimed in.

Magenta tried to corral them. "Guys, please. What does this have to do with *Work Shy*? I'm here specifically to talk to Frank about *Work Shy*. So can you contain yourselves for a moment?"

In LA, book sales translated to movie audiences and that meant big money. Finger on the pulse, eh? "The widest demographic possible, Frank."

The deals piled up and my money problems went to the back of my mental list. To the top of the list was a car to match my new "LA" writer image. I bought a cool green, Audi, 1972, 2000 series. This was my vintage head-turner with removable top. Original miles, 89,000! Every detective must have the distinctive motor. Like Columbo! What a piece of shit motor that was! Japanese. "You can do better than Peter Falk, Mr. Frank." My journal this time was that of Mr. Douglas Frank, novelist. Celebrity News Headline, page 12: Novelist Frank's car collection grows! This I read in a gossip column. I was impressed by the intensity of journalistic prying, much inventiveness to stretch spectacle. Frank is seen lap dancing in tuxedo. Excuse me?!

The final payment for the book arrived so I bought Edgar's bug for five hundred dollars. I also got new antique vanity plates saying, "Work Shy!" Sherrie threw in two spare tires and a pair of old window dice. What a sweetie. That made two vintage cars and one leftover. I eventually let the Miata go because the brakes were shot. The new Philly car (where real people continued to live) was nice clean Subaru, metallic brown in color. Subaru loves you back and they hug the road in rainstorms beautifully.

The suits seemed to like my aged Audi. For them it was oddball. "Do you really like the look of that car, Mr. Frank?"

"Yeah, it says middle-aged guy in showbiz."

"That was your reasoning?"

"Yeah."

Much laughing. "You kidding, right?"

"Kidding about what?"

"Nobody cares about your vintage car."

I made a little boy sad face. "You guys are really cruel."

Magenta backed me up. "Leave him alone, assholes."

On a good day, Harris and the suits were interested in how the "Genius Convention" thing worked. "Why so much ego among young painters?" Funny question. These guys knew a thing or two about ego. "What informs the creative spirit, Mr. Frank? What's the essence?" I again tried to explain that Art was not "the Arts." The Popular Arts were associated too closely with singing and dancing for me. Every singer-songwriter is an "artist." Every actor. Every celebrity dick. Washed up or no. Back in the day, Art was profound. But this was the wrong place for that discussion. Maybe up the road at Cal Arts where John Baldassari taught conceptual art. He poked fun at the establishment and museum culture. Not art for "art's sake" but art for the brain.

We got down to business at last. "High School leads to Art School but doesn't prepare you for eminent disregard. Let's revisit the noir-ish early 80's. Way back in college, (the screen goes blurry) we were mugs."

"What's a mug when it's at home, Mr. Frank?" asked an impolite Harris.

"British colloquial for a dope, a patsy."

"A loser, you mean?. Patsy is an oldie term?"

"Not exactly. It refers to "schlub" also."

"That's Hebrew. No, Yiddish, right?"

"Also, people without a clue."

"There's a lot of them around," added Miles.

Magenta spoke up. "You mean experimenting latch-key kids, Frank? I remember doing that. My parents were fucked up hippies. They named me Magenta for Christ's sake. They had bad trips all the time. Dad was in a sanitarium in San Diego near the end. He was totally sedated."

Don interrupted, "Too much info, Mag."

Miles disagreed. "Wait Don. This is interesting."

"Because you have the hots for Magenta."

Miles blushed just a little. "Maybe a little."

Magenta pleaded. "I'm sitting right here, guys! Let's move on."

My mind wandered. It could have been the six-pack I had for lunch. Sally appeared. "Must you, Mr. Frank? This is about that painful experience, yes?"

"Yes, Sally, it is."

She put a calm hand on my shoulder. "Which one, Edgar's loss or the art school dilemma?"

"Never sure how to describe the dilemma. And I miss Edgar."

"As long as it helps us to ultimate victory."

"What would I do without you?" She disappeared into her small sanctuary in my head. For the benefit of the suits, I went way back to imagining Art History class taught by Dr. Oscar Konitz at RISD. His voice boomed. I can describe the back of Edgar's head for you: his hair a clump of frizzed waves never finding a natural parting. In rapt attention, he took notes in a spiral bound notebook with illustrations:

Sept. 1982: Mr. Konitz spoke at length about Picasso's painting from that year, Madames des Marmalades, whatever it is called. The big year for Modernism was 1906. Pictured are cubist Prostitutes with African masks welcoming you to their brothel. Nice place you have here Cherie. This is, I am told, a great turning point. I recognized the painting, of course, but I had no idea you could discuss it for 90 minutes! How do flat angular forms relate to primitive prostitutes? I am wondering how many of these artists had the clap.

The Hollywood guys related to this facto-loid. Suit number three summed it up for the group, scoffing, "Venereal Disease ain't sexy now." Their hands were a blur, high-fiving and fist-bumping. "Thank goodness for penicillin." They still didn't get it; not even the silent expressionist films where art and film so directly intersected like never before. How stupid is this?

"Have you guys seen Metropolis?"

Magenta showed recognition. "Of course, Frank."

Harris said. "Sure. That's the science fiction with Tom Cruise in the future."

Magenta caught my eye across the table. "Sorry, Frank. These guys are all Gen-X or younger. They don't look beyond *Pulp Fiction*."

Don corrected him. "You're wrong Harris. It was Keanu Reeves."

I threw up my hands. "With all due respect. That was *The Matrix*."

Magenta was there waiting. "Frank, you can sleep with me anytime."

October Fifth, 82. Afternoonish: Nice out. Half way through Modern Art of the Twentieth Century, Jacoby passed me his class notes, a whole page where he'd written

257

ART WHORE three thousand times. I guess he was bored. Not sure if he was referring to the lecture or sex performance in the hallway. I guess it is more relevant than drawing strangely nude people all day long. What are we little daVinci's?

Jacoby may have been mildly stoned, as was his fashion. Had he only known that this fastidious doodle could be presented as art a few years hence. Was he reviewing Marta's live burlesque in the hallway? On top of the refrigerator box, a crude sign said Sugar Shack. She sat suggestively inside with a small Sony camera aimed at her crotch. Way ahead of the curve. No social media then, blah blah blah.

The bros wanted more. "Yeah, Marta. She's not a character in the book, is she Frank?" I regretted my frankness and suggested she was from a movie of John Waters.

"Lots of wanton women in art?"

"But not "gratuitous" nudity," I said holding up "quotes" fingers.

"The drugs drove her to it!" They cheered, over the moon.

Kirsch asked hopefully if Edgar dallied with Marta, "Did they have sex, Mr. Frank?"

"Don't think so. She looked like Sean Penn."

Kirsch looked worried and raised hairy hands to his face. The yes men did likewise. Were they for real? Perhaps he imagined Marta in a scene, all set to start on the ground level of the porn industry. What a lech. In 1981, blue movies still had some shock value but not in the 21 Century when the term porn is used euphemistically to mean day-to-day internet "eye candy" aka "Teddy Bear" porn.

"Yeah. Click-bait. That is another solid kernel of narrative," Kirsch said, "but it ensures an R rating, something to consider. We want wide release."

"Forget whether it's classy or not. Marta's activities were hers. She has talent," said Miles, fiddling with his pencil. One-track minds.

I said, "This is getting gross, gentlemen."

Suit number three loved coining titles. "Ivy League Lies."

"I like it," agreed Kirsch, cracking his knuckles. "Nice one."

They looked up, catching a whiff of conspiracy theory in our story. Perrier glasses clinked. "Seminal, yeah." I wrote "Ivy League Lies" on a legal pad. Phones appeared from nowhere. Back to the original story: "What about his family? What leads to his demise, Frank?" Someone was frothing a cappuccino. Smelled good. Can I get one of those darling? Hello, I'd like one of those too if you don't mind.

Tox gave me a look that grew on me slowly. "Make your own fucking cappuccino, Mr. Frank."

54
CHAPTER

At lunchtime, I called my sweet Watson and gave her an update on my negotiations. "Is there any mention of a Marta woman in the journals. Back in Art School?"

There was a long buzz while I waited. "No. No Marta, Mr. Frank. Who was she?"

"Nevermind, Sally. Talk soon." There was none of this salacious shit in the book *Work Shy* because I must have edited out. But it wasn't in the journals. Not sure how it turned up. I would have to find another nugget of vice suitable for parental guidance for the West Coasters. The next week in La La Town we again perused the earliest diaries for juicy stuff. Some notebooks were in tatters covered in ink and torn up. I had color copies. The museum minions were gone but Sally remained on call.

"What now, Mr. Frank.?"

"We need to tighten this narrative and lose the crappy grammar and typos."

"Yes, sir, no problem. It's nice to be appreciated."

"You know how I feel, kiddo. Do you ever remove your spectacles, Sally?"

"No, I'm blind without them. Watch out for those California bimbos."

"I don't need no stinking bimbos, Sally!"

Some of Edgar's adolescent musings painted a vivid picture of the deranged illusions that formed in first year of art school. It wasn't like high school. There were no parents, no line in the sand. No curfew. Egos were set free to expand beyond a decent level. We aren't just talking binge drinking. This was wholesale condemnation of existence, not just bourgeois things. Our snotty disapproval of the whole rest of the world was intriguing to a degree, possibly timely. The LA suits were into it. It's Providence, RI further spurred on by punk nihilism! They liked envisioning prequels. While the first single narrative worked itself to completion, they developed another parallel storyline. I found that distracting. Herman Melville worked on *Moby Dick* before *Moby Dick*. *The Awakening*, it was called. It sank by the way.

Nov, 09, 1998: Nobody is named Herman anymore. There are a lot of Brandies and Candies and hippie names like Asha, Santana and Rainbow. Not in my Fantasy Dystopia! I am going to change the world as it changes me. I am going to add to the past and prove the future is a fake image. God will return with fire and brimstone. They are called Russians! This weeks love interest is May Richards. I sent her a lovelorn note. She doesn't yet know my name so I signed it Love, John. It's a "Love, John" Letter!

My has-been detective persona was wearing thin and his reflexes slowed. The twist on an overused familiar trope, macho avenger. He could have sorted out both the art world and Hollywoodtown. I liked him but he wasn't real. Perhaps the violence and desire in the movie could be culled from memories of art history itself. Imagine Adolph Hitler fighting along side the painter, Otto Dix in the trenches of World War I in 1915. Otto asks, "What is this preoccupation with the Jews, Adolf? What did they ever do to you?" Adolph tells Otto he doesn't understand and Otto replies, "It seems to me the Fatherland is currently fighting the Englander and the French. You'll be lucky to get out of here with your stupid head attached. The chances are you will end up Belgium compost."

Adolf looked serious and said softly, "Fuck off, Otto." He wanted to paint little Austrian barn scenes and was busy envisioning himself with a small mustache like Charlie Chaplin. Oliver Hardy was doing the same thing somewhere in the USA. Funny how Edgar's preoccupation remained warfare for a long time because he saw it as Man's natural state. He dug the gritty work of Otto Dix. Otto shrugs as a new artillery barrage begins. Both Germans hit the muck, face down and are showered with limbs and feces.

Nov. 11, 1998: Oh, the humanity! Weimar, Berlin was sin city! That was when all the cool expressionists were working before their legs got blown off. They liked prostitutes also. Legs optional. Look at the work of George Grosz. With enemies like that who needs friends?

Please don't quote Edgar Bloom. He has few enough friends. I feared he would have it even worse after he comes out. I mean in movie form. In his case, these Expressionists guys don't take stuff lightly and would probably throttle an MFA critique-squad single handedly. "Das ist harm-chair intellectuals!" Bohemia is a real place, dude. Yes, it really existed. Somewhere in Europe I'm told. The Ivy League schooling of the post-Vietnam era didn't connect with the zeitgeist. Neither did Vietnam connect with consciousness raising represented by minimalist art. See the disconnect? Edgar's toy tank work was proto in that sense, before its time. It was an age designed for thousands of kids born in the 50s who lived in great comfort under a grand illusion. So did their parents. A static bubble; it got looser and more insular as the decade degraded capped by the Sex Pistols. Teachers should know that, shouldn't they?

Nov. 12, 1998: Art school staff, always outdated. It would be unseemly if they weren't, like your 70's Dad in purple bell-bottoms and very wide lapels. Yuk. Colleges always insist your major leads to a career. Why? Staying up working all-nighters don't make you a talented architect. That's out-an-out fiction. They want the tuition. Once you've graduated, it's goodbye for life. There are no sports teams to cheer.

Jacoby had a career as a drug addict before teaching High School. Are children ever safe? Marta had a big heart to match her sexuality. She became a male nurse after the sex change. Makes sense and is definitely the stuff of art. *More gas masks. More penicillin.*

"Speed it up, Adolf." Otto looks up just in time to see a red Fokker Tri-Plane driven by an aristocrat clad in leather and metal.

The Germans retreat. "God Bless the Fatherland!" Rumor has it he was shot down by a bullet up the wazoo. Fitting end for an ace?

55
CHAPTER

The movie gelled slowly. My buddy, Biggs was in a twist because he was already planning that *Work Shy* return to Broadway as a musical called "BLOOM." Usually Broadway hits become lousy films, not the other way around. There is a *South Pacific* in every record collection and one *Fiddler on the Roof*. But who now writes songs that are good enough? U2? I think not. I'm thinking, Re-assemble a retro Joy Division. That would work on a big stage. Really dark stuff like an opera. Normally, I hate opera especially rock operas. *See Me, Feel Me, Touch Me, Heal Me.*

"That's pretentious and out-dated stuff," said Miles across the table."

My pitch started to work. "Now you're getting it, boyo!"

I envisioned the last act. Something in Edgar's confused youth led directly to the ending and credits of *Work Shy*. Genius/suicide is a trope for the suits. The last dying words on the screen after the theme song starts, cue for the audience to leave. I like reading the credits as they file by sadly, slowly. Sometimes as long as *War and Peace*. "Was the crowd scene in Vienna all CG or was it some other city? Where was the village where the bomb went off, Corfu?"

My view was that Edgar was like any other art student. It was clearly a story of the survival of the fittest and even the fittest have to be coached. Need mentors. In Edgar's case, it was fate. He would've taken an easier path if one had turned up. *Work Shy* (book or film) didn't explain that so much as raise the question. I was supposed to give it a name. How do these artists pull it off? Set the record straight using Fairy Dust? The meetings picked up steam after this point. They were looking for Edgar's "Rosebud" moment.

Once your work was established as commodity, no matter how abstract, it is then down to Three Marketeers. People who, once given the ok, plan the attack via search results and demographic precision. It's all-important where you end up on the priority list. Near the classifieds will not do. Art historians supply the content, staking their names on their words. How does documenting this help me script? I know where it leads. Edgar always figured he was always going to be marginal. That was his point. 'Marginal' has value. Glance at a fifty year old art magazine. Regard the staid, forgotten leftist-types who used Picasso as a model. So many forgotten practitioners. "Been there..." said Andy Warhol. "It's so boring."

Day after New Years, 1983: How did Cezanne (a Frenchman) remove all sexuality from his nudes? Answer me Mr. Greenberg? If the world is going to end, I might as well illustrate it, whether it is simply in my head or outward reality. I mean, what is real, man? Painting is a dead form but I love it. It has a great fecal quality and smell. I mean turps and oil. We are addicts. It is a shame it is so out of step with the computer world, pop bands, jets and microwaves. Drugs and Reality, Gender. Geesh. What is what? We are so post-counter-culture.

Oddly enough, it also came out in the diaries that Edgar had views on who would play him in a movie. No spoilers. It's not Brad Pitt. Executives didn't agree wholly with Edgar's assessment; all in keeping with the purpose of art; screwing with fiction, reality, and illusion. This befitted Edgar's certain daft bias on cinematic nexus of art and reality. Edgar had an imagined view of a fictional success story.

The ladies worked feminism, which was cool, then the post feminism back-lash/ continuation, freeing women to be more objectified and sex-objected than ever! It opens this Pandora's Box, if you'll pardon the double entendre. Hard to avoid, like trains in tunnels. There I go again.

Enough stereotyping the decades, Mr. Frank. Vetting vats of arcane non-fiction to get a fix on Edgar's position relative to common held cultural norms.

"There's no sentence here, or noun, Mr. Frank, sorry." Sally offered, shyly. "But I know what you mean." She's trying to spare my genius.

"You should wear sun screen when you are out there. Your neck is burned."

Camille Paglia states there are no great women artists; basically because they had to withdraw to have babies. My theory is that many great artists are gay because they never had to support families or get married. They never got pregnant! This is very serious stuff said the LA suits.

Oct 12, 2003: It could be that Homosexuals have always been outsiders; that gives them a step in the right direction towards being tortured souls. Hence, creatives. Here I am sunken in a trashed hovel with music blaring waiting for Frank and dinner. If you're not gay, you will require a serious drug problem or domineering insider parents to rebel against. They ruin you in a good way!

I hope you will pardon Edgar's brusk notions. He has a way of putting things for added affect and they aren't as wacky as they read. This one goes way back to art school…

Dec. 12, 1981: Creative geniuses, I dunno. Auto-eroticism as art, Marta? It's been done. There are a lot of incredibly talented women around these days and they are into men. Terrifying! Speaking of Marta, doing her thing again. They didn't call the police this time because it was school property. The camera outward. She videoed the reaction of stunned men. Looks of embarrassment, astonishment and muffled glee. Is this her way of getting a date?

Beat That Camille! Later on, Edgar was a big Paglia fan. Not sure why. The Philly connection? She took not the standard feminist line. He wasn't sure what line it was. Where had feminism lead? He was all for it, especially considering the lost ground. In Philadelphia, there were large pornographic graphics on vans advertising Gentleman's Clubs in Atlantic City. They paraded slowly down Broad Street. "There is children here for god's sake." What are we thinking? Signs of the times? Literally. The last disturbing dystopian development Edgar saw first hand was glaring digital billboards on 95. "How am I supposed to keep my eyes on the road?" He never get as far as an iPod, thank god. He would not have approved. Progress needs limits, I hear him say.

56
CHAPTER

My creepy doorman was waiting with a dead cigar in his face. "You look good, Mr. Frank." Aren't all doormen creepy? He had the teeth of a meth user and the eyes of a pedophile. In movie terms, Buscemi-lite. That was what the casting call said. He was right though, my skin had changed color.

"Nice of you to notice, Curt."

"Fuckin' A, Mr. Frank." Tempted by the praise of others. "Are you getting coffee at Castro's this morning?"

"Yeah, unless you have another suggestion."

"Nope. They have the best coffee in Santa Monica."

"That'll suffice, I'm sure."

"Where've you been, working?"

"I guess. I've been a bit cooped up. Work, you know?"

"You wanna try your elevator speech on me?"

"Not today. I need some fresh air now."

"You East Coast people gotta take advantage of the sunny weather. It may rain tomorrow. It hardly ever rains in Tinseltown."

"I'll bear your advice in mind."

"I finished your book last night."

"No, really. You surprise me, Curt. I didn't know you could read."

"Sure I can read, Mr. Frank. It was pretty good. I like the cops the best. Very true to form."

I moved on slowly maintaining eye contact for much too long. "I appreciate the comments."

"Don't forget the SPF 50!"

I pointed. "Thanks, it's on my neck right now."

"Fuckin' A, Mr. Frank."

I spent more time in my room looking over the treatment and making comparisons with what was in *Work Shy* the book and what should stay in *Work Shy* the movie. In the grips of negotiations, burning issues were never settled. Such are scripts. "How plot driven do you want?" I wanted to tell the story in reverse and they didn't. The classic flashback treatment. On my deathbed in 2058, I will retell my life story surrounded by hopeful recipients of my estate, the *Citizen Kane* scenario. Imagine linking that classic to this project? The Chutzpah! Some of the suits didn't like this idea – Orson Welles was not on their radar – but they were paid to lick Kirsch's ass. It was well tanned. Eek. T.M.I. Mr. Frank. What is TMI? Is that like a URL? Oh Christ, he really is out of the loop. Trouble arose. My name was not "domained." I was used to being a ghost man writer. Albatross was old fashioned too. Of course, for the book, they bought the URL and Cranston and Dion combined to formulate a business plan, a decisive conduit of website links with the cloud and god. All leading to the "Singularity," as writer William Gibson hinted. Are you following this? Not sure what the singularity is but it sounds like the secular term for The Rapture.

October 18, 2003: Don't get me started. The End of Days was last year! Sticking chips in our bodies. How Philip Dick! It never works out. Look at SF. Goodbye, Humanity. What hubris. Let's shirk the future. Union of Man and Machine! Future Rot. I'll be back.

Planned for Thursday was the meeting where all sorts of contractual complexities were signed. They also wanted some suggestions for soundtrack. No problem there. "Our content farming leads trending in a direction, beneficial to us, Mr. Frank. A grabber?" A wide demographic combining cultural seas, linking "sub-cultures" as Edgar might say.

I remembered what Biggs told me previously on the phone: "The failed artist has been overlooked. It is a huge demographic! Are they idiots? Some of them can afford to visit the movies but they still use the local library. They prefer tactility."

The new hipster in massive yellow-framed spectacles said, "We measure the buzz, Mr. Frank." As if I didn't know! A whole period piece needed making. The 80's or 90's, whichever. The past is never past, to quote Faulkner. Google *Work Shy* music. It is taken by an 80's band. I had to keep the music lobbyists at bay. I never liked them. They were bought, sold and quartered. *When I hear the word democracy, I reach for my shotgun.* Funny, eh? Who said that? There will be lots of the music for the movie, and it'll be used at length not just as mood material. You know what I mean. Then there is the possible film score, CD sales, iTunes. Connected stuff. Cloud-sourced. Compressed for compressed people. I am merely interested in the content. Most of the musicians were dead. Dramatic intervals in the film will be peppered with doomy modern era, classical stuff like Dimitri Shostakovich and Bartok; adds weight. There will be some good jazz obviously, bebop for some creative studio scenes with quick cutting. Bang Bang. I suggested, the Roots have to appear as well for topical proximity. And probably the Sun Ra Arkestra for some crazy hood scenes, if there is anyone left alive. Sun Ra lived right down the road from the Bungalow. Edgar was not aware. Edgar loved the AB-EX period. Splashy Pollock. But the real meat would come from the early 80's, a lovely transitional moment for us and many others. Besides, Gary Numan needs a comeback! I luv Gary Numan! Perhaps Blondie should switch their name to Blue Rinse!

57

CHAPTER

Work Shy opened as a minor summer blockbuster not an art film. Odd, eh? That was the whole point. Exploding elites and providing education. Opening it up for view. Take it to the cleaners. Around the block and back. I went see it at an anonymous suburban maxi-plex in Edgar's VW. Sentimental Fool. I stopped by a cash machine but I had forgotten the password. 1984? Close, but not right. What is going on? Am I stupid? Cannot see the screen anymore. Better see an optometrist. Outside Cinema Randolph, the sign held titles of twelve movies crammed together, not one spelled correctly. Ours was WORQ CH3Y. There were several other oddly worded anomalies. Was the grounds man named James Joyce? Was he drunk? Or had the cinema been unable to afford new letters? The economy was still aching as the empire strained but it's a bad sign when a reversed number three stands in for a capital E.

The theatre was packed with rowdy teenagers laughing and yelling and there was a whiff of ganja in the air. Some things never change. The kids, mostly guys, seemed to identify with the excellent portrayal of Edgar, the consummate underachiever, a hero for a new age of diminished men. Maybe he represented their itinerant fathers? I was astonished and that takes a lot. I wasn't worried so much that the "me" in the movie was up-staged by Johnny Depp's Edgar but that Mr. Frank was portrayed a money-grubbing cheat who steps on anyone in his way. I'm not that person, just so you know.

The movie differed from the book in many ways, but was true to the main precept: the art world is a nasty place. As the book developed, it went where I had no control. Fate of the Work Shy? The script was another story, no pun intended. I had to fight in Edgar's corner; otherwise, a serious dilution was gonna take place. In fact, before ejection – I was squeezed out – Mr. Frank got involved everywhere he was not supposed to, casting, art direction. Even wardrobe. They banned me from the set. It wasn't as if I were always drunk, though that was tempting. So easy to follow Hollywood lushes whose footsteps remain eternally in cement. It was too late by then. I had befriended the director, David Lynch. He's more conservative than you'd imagine but was committed to a real artist's story. Not a bullshit Hollywood movie. Don't get me wrong, I like bullshit Hollywood movies.

So what did the unwashed make of the film? Was it Box Office Poison or Champagne? Didn't take long to find out. The book-spin worked and matched the script-spin for once. Perfect Sturm und Drang. Now was time for Mr. Frank to avoid spotlight. What's another bloody red carpet. I already had Steve Buscemi's phone number. His and Charles Satchi, the Brit-art star maker of the nineties. Damien Hirst and I have been shark fishing together. A good lot that will do Edgar or me. The premiere was for the actors. I could let the film people relish those unremarkable moments.

This caused agro. "Mr. Frank remains anonymous, Don and he doesn't return our calls," said Belle Tox.

"Fuck him," said Kirsch – and he liked me.

"What an ingrate," said Belle.

"He can fuck off back to the East Coast"

"Maybe, if I won an Oscar for the adapted screenplay, he'll hold me in higher esteem?" I said to myself. Well, technically, I was intern to the assistant screenwriter, Cassie Boneweather. She was a real ballbuster.

"Don't let the bastards get you down, Mr. Frank. You should get all the credit." said Sally.

May 6, 2006: No speck of insignificance is below their radar. Significance is virtually unimportant. It puts people off. Some days, everything and anything seems possible. I am connected to a long narrative arc like Romeo and Juliet. Balcony stuff. Who was this Shakespeare and who painted that crappy painting that we think is Shakespeare way before bald dudes had the sense to shave their heads? Maybe I mean Marlowe, that is, Sam Spade. Either way, spells skullduggery. Daggers in the Eye!

It seems, not surprisingly, Edgar got overly caught up despising the people who could have directed him and didn't. Not a pretty picture, and yes, as for the story, it was sold and sold again. Whether that was Edgar's way of getting his own back, I'll never know.

Back in the East Coast Bungalow, it was a beautiful September day. Sally was at Trader Joe's with the bug getting us coffee, sweets and a big wedge of Gorgonzola. I could sense all the new art students venturing out to classes with their oversize backpacks festooned with punk rock buttons new and old. What awaited them? They will meet friends and teachers whose words they will keep forever. They will sleep with people whose names they will forget. The students are churned out, but better for it. At least, they will never be suits. And they will be seeing me soon, selling my wares, my portion of Spectacle. It's called intellectual property, you know, or so my lawyer Lucy tells me. It is protected in the Constitution along with our right to bitch about our lawns.

I sat back in Edgar's chair, working on the syllabus while I listened to Faces for Radio, a new alternative band. It was an old straw. I become dour and switched to Shostakovich. He did his thing and my mood adjusted, comfortably. I heard recently he composed music for an opera called, *The Nose*. Can't remember the date. It was about a man whose nose disappears. Wasn't that Kafka? I started combing record stores. "I am looking for *The Nose*?" I asked sheepishly. Weird looks. "You kidding? It's right there, man," said one witty, overweight clerk, drooling slightly. Was he mocking me? The provenance for *"The Nose,"* is complicated but includes writer Laurence Stern (1713-1768). He stuck a novel in a novel: *Tristram Shandy*, where a man lost his nose. Nobody has ever read this fascinating book as far as I can tell, but it is renowned in literary circles. Cervantes and Gogol also went there, but don't quote me. Literary traditions are hard to break once deeply engraved. Deep footnotes, dude.

Sally handed me a piece of the smelly cheese and I finished my wine to wash it down. The only question unanswered was this: why had Sherrie armed me with the journals in the first place – Where was her grudge? Did she know the contents of Edgar's maniacal scribbling that had been kept hidden away for 25 years? Was she out to cover something or gain anything or was it merely for closure? I will never tell. After this moment, his entire life and medical records are opened, for the whole multi-cultural universe to see. Not just his actions, which are not normal, but his daftest ideas and manias. "Does anyone care?" Another question I asked myself is there something Edgar himself leaves out? Something critical for some reason, some thread that I have been exposed to but cannot recognize? A hidden message? I have claimed that I am no Dan Brown – a good thing – but puzzles are interesting. That is another story. Alas, too late for those queries. Spectacle calls. The optometrists call. I can't see the pictures on my studio walls!

Bloom's legacy is now secure. *Work Shy* became a must read on every MFA course for its portrayal of contemporary art people. It even turned up in the syllabi of some cutting-edge undergrad departments. Edgar was getting known as someone who struggled through the adversity and managed to make his mark despite terrific obstacles. How'd he do it? I don't know. Was it through help from me? If so, it was only after the fact. The book had sway, but those were things to set straight, to be made known. Pushing that wee tipping point past the point of recognition. I, myself am apparently sought after thanks to Edgar. Claire Craig-Martin, a curator at MOMA in New York called and worked out a meeting through my agent. She had bought several of Bloom's works for their contemporary collection and thought a comprehensive retrospective was in order. I imagined another well-attended reading and book signing on Fifty-Third Street. She also wanted to discuss more populist writing about art and museums. I agreed, of course. See you soon, Claire.

Considering the fact he'd been sunk by the Philly mob, Edgar's ship continued coming in big-time. Guten Tag. Das ist mein schnellboot. There were calls from Biggs and Cranston about the next step, my new book, and a brief, secondary career as a thespian or whatever, just in case it was needed. The only acting I'd done was reading this book aloud to adoring middle-aged hipsters. Cranston envisioned more than one Hollywood version of *Work Shy*. Edgar foretold the past:

Any day this week, 2005: Jesus was born and died almost 2000 year ago to the day! Or not! But history is misleading. Look at a 40-year-old art magazine. Nearly all forgot. The internet changed nothing. It only expands human nature exponentially or doubles it or whatever. Loadsa paradigm shifts are found (after the fact out in the trash cans). It is dirty work.

I was happy with these results but not resting on my laurels. My bursting ego was helpful in this department. Raves for *Work Shy* poured in. New York Times: "*Work Shy* is Pure Genius Convention! A fabulous behind the scenes tale of the art world." Wall Street Journal: "Just when you thought the cultural waters' safe, writer Douglas Frank skewers the scene; Unusual Debut!! Two Stars." London Review of Books: "Conservative Rubbish!" "Cosmic Crap from American Author." Do I care? My next thriller, *Killer Instinct* was also underway. It was an authentic cold-case based in Philadelphia and I used Vidocq to help with research. Village Voice: "Acclaimed *Work Shy* author, Douglas Frank has returned to Germantown with striking results." Other teachers of Edgar appeared, meta-fictionalized, of course. Museum people too. In the first chapter, someone akin to Trout is found face up in the Schuylkill River staring at God through bulging eyes. The body was floating behind the Art Museum near the neo-classical, Nineteenth-Century waterworks. Didn't take much imagination! Freddie French investigated in a trench coat. The book interwove more people from the shaded past.

275

Mito and I conferred over this by phone. He was invaluable as a low-grade sociopath. Hopefully, I shall knock him off also, literally. My pal, Gibson could do it with a baseball bat and make it look like another suicide. Edgar would like that. Kamikaze, get it? In the book, the mayor calls for action!

I imagined Pecker and Finch discussing the case: "Wow, Pecker."

"Seppuku. That's serious stuff."

"How can someone bludgeon themselves to death?"

"It is difficult to digest, Captain. Maybe a ball player could do it? Perhaps, if one were bipolar in the extreme?"

"Interesting Pecker. Do we know anyone like that?

"I'll make some calls, Captain."

I am now teaching scriptwriting at a Philly art school. *One point for our side, Anarchy!* Hopefully, it will appeal to the rebellious youth that don't seem to exist anymore. I know they want me to help destroy the rest of the Master Narrative and lose all connections to Hollywood. Why? Not sure. I made the point of doing the opposite or so it seemed. At the moment, the film students model themselves after Ben Affleck. Imagine that; art subsumed by the Spectacle. No one liked me in the media department but I got a call from Camille Paglia in October. She had a new book out, *Toxic Women* and wanted to network. They used to call it dating, but I am way past that point. In her case, I made an exception; the bar at the Ritz Carlton at seven. It looks just like the Pantheon, shape-wise, except it's full of Lawyers. In the top of the dome, the oculus keeps the rain out via heavy weight plexiglass. Before I left, Sally told me to behave.

"Keep your pants on Toy Boy."

"You're embarrassing me." We made evil grins with our noses nearly touching.

Commodity Edgar Bloom was prodded and sold like all such efforts. Pundits needed something to laud or loathe until they decided it was a new-ish idea. The book began with a certain cult following and built from there. The buzz around the movie, of course, built even wider interest. Talk shows and such. There were Stuckist, high-end detractors who thought books should stay books. Such are Academia and high-minded peeps. I am that way to a degree. But the movie was another sort of fish. It was going to be much bigger than the book while making the book more popular; a curve ball! A bigger delivery. Symbiotic? Is that synchronicity? Movies are most people's only port of call, except for clever elites who compare texts with moving images carefully. How old-fashioned and POMO of them. They get miffed when a book or other cultural phenomenon sinks into popularity. Let's face it, most things of wide appeal suck. I knew the drill. Hardback to remaindered pile in Walmart for $3.99. I was ahead of the game, detached enough because the figure of Edgar took the attention away from me. Unfortunately, as Edgar's star rose, the research ended and his light dimmed. I missed him. Another mystery involving another oddball? It had been done before. Remember Cold Cases? Edgar stood by his conviction: careering was the worst crime. In retrospect, it was devious of him to let me handle that part so I got the credit and the shame! Cheers, mate! Clever for a right-brained guy.

Sherrie and Kurtz finally saw sizeable cash flow. I felt happy about that. Edgar Bloom would have been thrilled to have finally made good as conventional breadwinner. In my head, he told me, "Frank, I'm absolutely thrilled. Forget Phil and his stuffed shirt." I did well without any guilt what so ever. The other people, the ones who deserved to be kicked in the teeth, didn't know the difference. They got off scot-free and have indestructible rationales. For the In-Crowd there is always mileage to be made. Just another day at the art office hiding behind the image reflected in those peculiar shaped-glasses they prefer. They have all the more reason to drop Edgar's name at appropriate functions. "I knew him when he ran naked through City Hall." Milk it, baby, like Edgar says. Same for me, now I was a player. It was as if I joined their club via a secret passage or back door. Still not sure how that happened.

My one and only Cold Case did me a world of good. Now, I'm the pretty detective who catches a glimpse of Bloom's vindicated spirit loitering the streets of Philadelphia. I bid him farewell solemnly through a linked fence. Next to me Sally sheds tears. She squeezes my hand and we walk towards Chestnut Hill. Into the sunset, you could say. Now that I am a two Bungalow man, I split my time between coasts. I love it. When I get sick of one, I head off to the other. The only difference is I bring my Watson. If only I had sixteen kids. Children are a blessing. For this life, I am eternally grateful. I decided against a flight to Seattle. Sherrie needed space and Phil would never forgive me. He didn't need the emotional agro or the money. Kurtz Bloom and I corresponded faithfully via the United States Post Office.

Edgar's last diary didn't get anywhere near *Work Shy*. My little secret. I kept this one locked away in a Safety Deposit Box in case the "topic" ever got reopened.

"Never thaw anything twice," Mom used to say. This composition notebook is decorated with sticky playroom letters. It may have belonged to Kurtz for a week or two given the crayon drawings in the front. The contents are a complex mix of ramblings melding Poe, Walter Benjamin and Iggy Pop. Gothic or "Emo" not to be confused with Elmo. Never trust a muppet. They have dark sides. The last pages of the final journal held a few veiled threats against persons vaguely familiar. At first, I overlooked it and didn't alert Captain Finch or Sgt. Pecker. Nothing evidential. A paranoid Edgar was not a surprise. Witty and sharp, to the last lines – *Farewell, Cassandra* – he signed out, literally: *See you soon. EB.* The last sections possessed an un-hinged, negative outlook like lead overshoes. What was he really capable of? Homicide? He not only focused on the central target, the damage done by the art world but a few other key individuals. I'm thinking Sanchez in particular. On this, I am compelled to remain schtum and you'll have to retrieve it from my cold dead fingers.

Edgar loaded, aimed carefully and waited. It was Mr. Frank who obligingly pulled the trigger. The target imploded and immediately disappeared after it came into a view swallowed by the next spectacular disaster. The vision became fixed in space and distracted you like a sincere and awkward poem by a minor poet you find in a faded compendium, coverless and naked in the trash in front of your local train station. Not the way to treat literature – I'm old fashioned. Some oldie must have died and the grown-up children downsized all the detritus from the attic. All previous possessions ended up in a heap on the curb. Looking left then right, you pick it out of the bin before sticking it discreetly under your arm. You board the train as per usual; find a deserted aisle seat so you can flip through the faded pages. You read a bit as you travel through the gutted outer city heading for your job. For the rest of the day, you can't get it out of your mind.

Printed in the United States
by Baker & Taylor Publisher Services